HEARTS
on
FIRE

TO THE PEOPLE, THEY WERE GODS—
TO EACH OTHER, MERELY DIVINE

King Ameni had won the hand and the heart of lovely Nefrytaten and together they vowed to bring peace and prosperity to the kingdom of the Two Lands.

Warring tribes, court intrigues, and their own headstrong wills brought troubles that threatened to destroy not only all Egypt, but the blazing love they had found.

Against a glowing backdrop of incomparable splendor, their story unfolds—a tale of treachery, consuming passion, and fierce rival desires—the lush, romantic sequel to DAWN OF DESIRE!

Other Avon books by
Joyce Verrette

DAWN OF DESIRE   27375 $1.95

DESERT FIRES

JOYCE VERRETTE

AVON
PUBLISHERS OF BARD, CAMELOT AND DISCUS BOOKS

DESERT FIRES is an original publication of Avon Books.
This work has never before appeared in book form.

AVON BOOKS
A division of
The Hearst Corporation
959 Eighth Avenue
New York, New York 10019

First Avon Printing, February, 1978

AVON TRADEMARK REG. U.S. PAT. OFF. AND IN
OTHER COUNTRIES, MARCA REGISTRADA,
HECHO EN U.S.A.

Printed in the U.S.A.

DESERT FIRES

☲☲☲☲☲☲☲☲☲☲☲☲☲

CHAPTER 1

☲☲☲☲☲☲☲☲☲☲☲☲☲

THE MID-AFTERNOON SUN glared like white fire against the plastered shop walls in the marketplace, heating the dry air to shimmering waves over the pavement. The Nile was no longer a slim, green ribbon against the golden earth. It had become a swollen brown lake. This was the season of the annual flooding. Black soil came to Tamera to enrich the next planting. The people of the land believed this was a personal gift bestowed on them by the river god.

The usually steady north wind had become unreliable and sluggish, and the people of Ithtawe wore only light, loose-fitting cotton garments over their well-oiled bronze skin.

Nessumontu, Tamera's military commander, paused beneath the shade of an olive tree. Moving aside to let others pass, he took off his headpiece and ran a hand through his flattened black hair. "It's unusually hot for this season," Nessumontu remarked.

Rahmzi followed his friend's example and removed his headpiece. He sighed with relief. "The heat does not wither the enthusiasm of the marketplace," he observed.

Nessumontu glanced up at the green lace of the tree against the bright blue sky and said, "With the

1

river now in full flood, the farmers who would otherwise be idle have come to join the work gangs beginning the king's pyramid." Nessumontu smiled faintly. "Their families fill the city and almost make a festival of it."

"Why not?" Rahmzi asked, his black eyes narrowed against the sun-bright streets outside the circle of shade sheltering them. "They earn instead of sitting idle, and many of these people seldom get to come to Ithtawe otherwise."

"It makes the census takers in this area happy not to have to travel from one remote farm to another to accomplish their task," Nessumontu said. His voice trailed off as he noted the flow of the crowd. "They seem to go in one direction," he commented slowly. "I wonder why."

Rahmzi watched the crowds thoughtfully. Everyone did walk in one direction.

"There must be some attraction," Rahmzi decided. "Even the brewers of beer across the street have put aside their work to follow the others."

Nessumontu's slanted eyes narrowed. "I'm curious. Let us join them and see where they go."

As Nessumontu and Rahmzi followed the crowd, the sun became even more like a heavy hand weighing on their heads, but they quickly put aside thoughts of discomfort as they mingled with the traffic. The mood of happy anticipation soon penetrated Nessumontu's usually stoic expression, and he found himself smiling.

"Why are you walking so fast?" Rahmzi finally asked. "Although my legs are longer than yours, I'm getting weary of keeping pace with you."

Nessumontu's widened smile was for himself. He

2

slowed his steps. "I don't know why," he admitted. "The mood of the crowd is contagious."

The crowd became denser, and soon Nessumontu and Rahmzi found themselves standing shoulder to shoulder in the throng before the temple of Hat-Hor. Everyone was intent on getting into the temple.

Nessumontu found himself looking into the dark, almond-shaped eyes of a girl. She smiled self-consciously at his gaze. So engrossed was he that Rahmzi's voice startled him.

"Do all these people come for the service?" Rahmzi asked, incredulous. "I know the people of Ithtawe are faithful—but in such great numbers, and in this heat?"

Nessumontu scanned the crowd hastily. "If these were all men, I'd think the priestess Kuwait had returned from the dead to entertain us. But women and children are here as well. What new attraction does the temple hold?"

Rahmzi chuckled. "I wouldn't mind seeing Kuwait dance again. But you're right, my friend. If she were here, no women would be waiting calmly in this place. They'd be doing their best to drag their men home."

Nessumontu laughed softly. He remembered the scenes that had occurred when Kuwait had been priestess, as well as the scandals she had caused. She had even pursued the king!

Nessumontu and Rahmzi entered the temple. It was less crowded. They moved through the groups of noblemen and ladies, almost to the foot of the Platform of Offerings, where the statue of Hat-Hor stood. Although there were many more chambers to pass through before one came to the innermost sacred chamber, Nessumontu assumed this was the room in

3

which they wished to be. The rituals held in the inner rooms of the temple were attended only by priests. Whatever it was the crowds had come for would take place in this more accessible chamber.

When the last trickles from the water clock had dwindled to nothing, the small temple bells rang, signaling the beginning of the ceremony. Through the great doors came a company of temple novitiates, dressed in white robes. They walked to the Platform of Offerings. Several priests and one priestess followed them. These were dressed in robes of red and palest green.

On the far side of the platform stood a group of singers. As the holy company entered, the chorus began a song to welcome Hat-Hor, goddess of love, music, and dancing, and protector of infants.

Nessumontu wondered again what it was about this service that had attracted such unusual crowds. The ceremony was proceeding as it always did. His silent question was answered almost immediately.

From among the singers there came a voice that no quantity of voices could have vanquished.

Nessumontu studied each of the singers in turn. Among them he saw the girl he had noticed in the crowd outside the temple. He knew at once that it was from her throat the silver song came. Unlike the others, who merely opened their mouths to sing, this girl gave her soul to the hymn.

Her eyes were closed, her long thick lashes like black fans against her golden cheeks. Her breasts rose and fell with joy, and her expression was rapturous. Suddenly her dark eyes opened, and Nessumontu could see, even from his distance, the gleam of ecstasy they held. The volume of the voices grew, in prepara-

4

tion for the triumphant ending of the song, and Nessumontu saw the girl stand straighter, her soul pouring out from her throat. He was reminded of the song of the meadow bird, delirious with joy at giving out this beauty.

Although the other singers were numerous and their voices were strong and growing louder with the hymn, the girl's sweet, clear voice rose over them, like the voice of a goddess. Nessumontu's heart was so moved by the sound that his flesh rose in bumps along his arms.

Through the remainder of the ceremony, Nessumontu waited only for the next song. Each time the music ceased, he listened to its echoes in his mind until another song began.

By the time the ritual was over and the crowd was leaving the temple, Nessumontu had determined he would meet this girl. He was sure she possessed not merely a beautiful singing voice, but the depth of spirit that made a voice divine. She had eyes to penetrate his soul, and the form he had glimpsed beneath her sheer garments had been lovely.

"That girl's voice," Rahmzi sighed as they stepped into the sun, "is surely a gift from the golden goddess herself."

"I would meet her," Nessumontu said firmly.

Rahmzi glanced at his commander, surprised at his tone. "How do you plan this?" he asked.

Nessumontu looked at Rahmzi, his face alight with anticipation. "I'm unsure as yet, but I'll do it," he answered. He suddenly turned to an ancient man who was walking near them. "Father," he said politely, "do you know the name of that girl who sang with Hat-Hor's own throat?"

The man's myriad wrinkles rearranged themselves into a warm smile. "She isn't a girl who mingles with strange men," he warned.

"That merely adds to her allure," Nessumontu said. "I have it in mind to mention her name to the king," he added, silently congratulating himself on this inspiration. "Her voice is worthy of royal ears, and I think King Amenemhet and Queen Nefrytatanen would enjoy her."

The old man's face lit with pleasure. A royal audience would be a great honor to the girl, whom he knew. "Her name is Djanah," he said slowly, trying to conceal his eagerness. He knew what Nessumontu and Rahmzi's insignia meant. "She lives in that house farther down the street whose enclosing wall is the color of Ra's early light. It's the only wall that color and will be easy for you to find."

"Thank you, father," Nessumontu said, his heart leaping in anticipation. He noted the man's humble garments and impulsively removed from his finger a gold ring set with an amber-colored stone. He placed the ring in the man's hand and closed the gnarled fingers around it.

To the man's look of growing protest, Nessumontu said quickly, "The king would wish you to take this. The pleasure Djanah will give them will be worth it."

"But this is your ring, not the king's," the man said weakly, staring at the treasure he held.

"Making my king and queen happy makes the ring a small thing indeed by comparison," Nessumontu replied. He smiled and nodded to the man, then turned and walked away.

Rahmzi chuckled softly. "You go through quite an expense to meet that girl."

Nessumontu replied, "I'll mention Djanah to the king. Also, I'll have flowers sent to her as a tribute from myself," Nessumontu smiled faintly. "When Djanah comes to the palace, she'll seek me out to acknowledge the bouquet."

"And if Djanah doesn't seek you out?" Rahmzi asked.

Nessumontu considered this a moment. "Then I'll approach her myself," he said firmly. His smile widened. "But I think she'll wish to thank me for the opportunity to sing in the palace—if not for my bouquet."

"And you'll make sure she knows it was you who put her name into the king's ears?" Rahmzi ventured.

Nessumontu's smile grew even larger. "Of course," he replied.

Prince Senwadjet and Princess Maeti came down the hall followed by their guardian-servant, Senet.

"Is the king in that room?" Senet asked the guard. He nodded. "The children would bid him good night," she explained. "The queen?"

"She has not yet returned," the guard answered. "The king awaits her." He saw a stealthy look pass between Senwadjet and Maeti, and he knew what their first words to their father would be. The sentry had his own children, no doubt pestering their mother to wait for *his* homecoming, thereby delaying their hour of sleeping. He smiled faintly, thinking of them. Their mother would give in to their pleading, he knew, and he was gladdened by the thought.

Senet tapped lightly on the door and, at Amenemhet's muffled command, she opened it. Before the door closed behind them, the guard heard the prince ask, in a voice filled with innocent concern, "Mother hasn't come back yet?"

Amenemhet smiled. He knew what was coming. "May we wait with you, father?" Maeti asked, her blue eyes round with hope.

"She'll come to you," Amenemhet replied.

"Perhaps we'll fall asleep too fast," Maeti said sadly. "Then we won't know when she comes."

"Why don't you begin bathing?" Amenemhet suggested tolerantly. "Before you go to bed, she'll be here."

Senwadjet thought it might be possible to delay a little longer. He decided to change the subject.

"Maeti and I have been wondering how old you were when you had your prince's lock cut." Senwadjet, having just thought of this, found himself fingering his own prince's lock. "We're also curious why a prince must wear his hair all pulled over to one side, plaited and bound this way."

Amenemhet hadn't missed Maeti's startled look and knew Senwadjet's motive. "It's an old custom," he answered patiently, "and probably the best answer to keeping the prince looking at least somewhat presentable despite his activities." Amenemhet smiled faintly, remembering his own yearning to have his hair cut like adult men. His father had been occupied with raids from Kenset and Djemeh and had been away from the palace so much of the time that he hadn't seemed to note his son's height until Amenemhet had reminded him. "I was two years older than you are," Amenemhet answered.

Senwadjet's face fell. "Must every prince be that old?" he asked.

8

Amenemhet's eyebrows lifted in mock reproach. "It wasn't that I was slow!" he declared. "My father had many things on his mind and didn't think of it."

"How long do you think I'll have to keep this thing?" Senwadjet asked. "I consider it unsafe," he added solemnly. "When I run through the forest, I find it often catches on a twig and nearly pulls my hair from its roots."

Amenemhet controlled his increasing urge to laugh aloud and said quietly, "Your mother and I will discuss it. Now go upstairs and begin preparations for sleeping. We'll come up together to wish you fair dreams."

Senwadjet was prepared to protest, but Maeti sensed that her father was distracted by Nefrytatanen's delay. She gave Senwadjet a look, a message he understood, and he shrugged and surrendered without further argument.

When the children had left, Amenemhet turned to the window openings overlooking the garden, wondering if it were too soon to cut Senwadjet's hair. He was still smiling at the request when his thoughts were interrupted by another tapping on the door. He turned to face Nessumontu and Rahmzi.

"Do you have a free moment, or is it too late?" Nessumontu asked, coming in slowly.

"It seems I have spare time I don't need," Amenemhet answered. "I'm waiting for Nefrytatanen, who has been delayed for some reason. The time crawls by like a lazy caterpillar. Come and distract me," he invited.

Amenemhet sank into a couch, and seeing his servant standing nearby, he said, "Yazid, bring us a goblet of wine so we may pass the time more pleasantly." Yazid disappeared. "Sit down," Amenemhet urged.

"Rahmzi brought news from Uto Province," Nessumontu said, sitting down.

Amenemhet looked up, his face immediately filled with concern. "It isn't good news, I perceive."

"My patrol saw signs of Hyksos soldiers inside our border," Rahmzi replied. "They were in small groups, but that they traveled inside the border makes me most uneasy."

Amenemhet sighed, his gold eyes darkening to topaz shadows. "The Hyksos never cease plotting," he said. "Dispatch another patrol to the area to supplement Semerkhet's guards," he directed.

Nessumontu nodded. "I anticipated that decision and have already given the order." He took the goblet of wine Yazid offered and sipped it slowly. "Also, reports have come to me from the nearby farms that a lion has been terrorizing the people."

"Has anyone been hurt?" Amenemhet asked in concern.

"Three have been killed," Nessumontu answered. "The latest victim was a man who sacrificed himself to distract the lion from his small daughter. The child ran home screaming and crying, covered with her father's blood. Two of the man's farm helpers came with spears, but it was too late for them to help the man. They did get a look at the beast, and they report that it's a lioness—very big, though not heavy in years. She has a crippled foot."

"She's not fast enough to hunt her normal prey, so she stalks an easier meal—people," Amenemhet said slowly. He shuddered. "We'll have to lay traps for her."

10

"Nessumontu has a more pleasant subject to discuss," Rahmzi said, wishing to turn the conversation to something less grim.

"Which is?" Amenemhet asked, looking expectantly at Nessumontu.

Nessumontu, glancing at Rahmzi and seeing the gleam of his dark eyes, knew Rahmzi meant to tease him. For a moment he said nothing, gathering his thoughts, until he began in a casual tone, "When Rahmzi and I were on the street this afternoon, we noted crowds of people going to the temple of Hat-Hor. We followed them in curiosity."

Amenemhet sat a little straighter, wondering where Nessumontu was leading, hoping they didn't have to contend with another ambitious priestess.

Nessumontu smiled in understanding. "It's not what you're thinking," he said. "There's a girl among the temple singers whose voice is so unusual that she's attracting great throngs of people. I was wondering if you and the queen would enjoy hearing her. I could arrange for her to come to the palace."

Amenemhet was relieved. Nessumontu spoke of nothing more serious than an entertainer. But the orange gleam in Nessumontu's eyes didn't escape his notice. "You would like to attend this audience?" he asked slowly.

Nessumontu smiled faintly. "It would be a great pleasure to hear her sing again," he replied.

Amenemhet asked, "Is it also a pleasure to look upon her person?"

"It gives no pain," Nessumontu answered.

Amenemhet turned to Rahzmi. "She sings well?"

Rahmzi nodded. "In addition to her other attractions, she has a voice that sounds as if she came from Tuat," he replied seriously.

Amenemhet looked at Nessumontu. "You know her name, I'm sure, and where she lives," he said, smiling faintly. Nessumontu nodded. "Then tell Meri of her tomorrow. He'll make the arrangements."

Amenemhet was ready to ask Nessumontu about another matter, but just then he heard the great door in the entrance hall close. He stood up, his eyes shining.

The door opened and Nefrytatanen came in quickly, followed by her maid, Dedjet, who struggled to unfasten her mistress's cloak while Nefrytatanen walked.

Nessumontu and Rahmzi leaped to their feet. Amenemhet took no notice of them. His attention was all on Nefrytatanen.

"I'm sorry I kept you so long," Nefrytatanen said, going to Amenemhet and taking his hands in hers. "I had a strange experience in the temple, and I spent some time thinking about it before I left."

"As long as there hasn't been any trouble," Amenemhet said. Her sapphire eyes looked up into his, and he saw a darkness in their shadowy depths. "What happened?" he asked.

Nefrytatanen glanced at Nessumontu and Rahmzi meaningfully, and they turned toward the door.

"We bid you fair dreams," Nessumontu said quickly. They left immediately, and Dedjet followed.

In the hall Dedjet paused, wondering whether to prepare Nefrytatanen's bath or to stay in case she wanted something else.

Yazid came through the hall and, seeing Dedjet's confusion, stopped. "Stay, if you wish. I'll prepare their bath myself," he offered.

Dedjet smiled in appreciation, but her smile was distracted. She whispered, "A very peculiar thing happened in the temple tonight. I'll tell you later over a cup of tea."

Yazid asked nothing more, but turned and climbed the stairs to the royal bedchamber.

Nessumontu and Rahmzi had just reached the entrance doors when they overheard Dedjet's words and turned back to look at her.

"There's no secret to what happened," Dedjet said slowly. "My lady only wished to discuss it with the king in privacy and without interruption, for I'm sure she had more to tell him than I know."

As Dedjet related the incident in the temple, she found herself choosing words hesitantly. Looking up into Rahmzi's eyes made her wish to prolong the telling of the story. She had never seen this officer before, but she knew he must have been in the army for some time to have attained so high a rank. She was certain he was from a noble family.

Rahmzi's dark eyes remained steadily on Dedjet as he listened. He did not interrupt her to ask questions.

When Dedjet had finished telling them of Nefrytatanen's experience and they had thanked her, she watched them walk toward the door. She noted Rahmzi's posture, which was very straight, and the way he walked, which resembled Amenemhet's light, catlike step. She wandered if Rahmzi had a wife.

When Rahmzi reached the door, he turned to glance at Dedjet over his shoulder, and she didn't mind that he had caught her looking at him. For a moment their eyes met, and a strange feeling ran through her. She smiled faintly. She didn't drop her eyes, but continued looking at him until the door closed. She found herself having to resist an impulse to open the door and watch him walk through the courtyard.

"That is too much," Dedjet chided herself aloud.

The sentry gave her a sideways glance, but said nothing.

Dedjet took no notice of the guard. She turned and sat on a bench against the wall and waited for Nefrytatanen. She passed her time thinking about Rahmzi and reminding herself she was merely a servant. "Don't be silly," she muttered. "You're only a maid."

"You're the queen's personal attendant!"

Dedjet looked up in surprise. The sentry was smiling at her. She flushed. "I'd forgotten your presence," she said.

"I'm not the commander of a garrison," said the guard, "but my place isn't too humble. My wife did no more than mend garments—and not the queen's either. I married her without a thought for her rank."

Dedjet's face became deep crimson. She didn't know how to answer the sentry, who seemed genuinely friendly and not insolent.

"I know," he said softly. "It's none of my affair. But standing guard can be a tiresome business, requiring little thought. I see so much of what happens in the palace I feel as if I'm personally acquainted with everyone, though I seldom speak to anyone. Forgive me if I seemed to pry. I'll tell this to no one."

Dedjet nodded and said no more. The guard had put an idea in her head that she couldn't dislodge. She wondered if Rahmzi would consider her status too far below his.

"What does that woman do in the palace?" Rahmzi asked Nessumontu as they walked through the courtyard.

"Dedjet?" Nessumontu looked at Rahmzi and smiled. "Yes, you do mean Dedjet," he said. "She's Queen Nefrytatanen's personal maid."

"Is she married?" Rahmzi inquired.

"No," Nessumontu replied, "nor has she ever been. You're attracted to her?"

"I'm curious about her," Rahmzi answered cautiously. "How well do you know her?"

Nessumontu stopped walking and faced Rahmzi. "I haven't thought about her very much before this," he said slowly. "I do know her quite well."

"What is she like?" Rahmzi asked.

"She is an attractive woman, isn't she?" Nessumontu said. "I've never really thought of her as a woman. She's always so serious and intent on her own business." His eyes lifted to meet Rahmzi's. "I like her very much as a person," he said suddenly. "She had a bad time of it, I remember, with some officer long ago. I don't think she has been seriously involved with anyone since then."

"Is she bitter?" Rahmzi persisted.

Nessumontu considered this a moment. "No," he said slowly. "I think she's always been too occupied with her work."

"What is she like personally?"

Nessumontu glanced at Rahmzi in surprise. Rahmzi was more than merely curious. He thought a moment before answering. "She's a woman to be at ease with, because she's not a woman a man feels will try to pick his bones clean. I think she would neither harass nor manipulate a man." Nessumontu paused. "She's

15

honest," he continued. "From her you may expect justice."

He looked at Rahmzi and added, "Let that be your warning, Rahmzi. I think that if you do wrong Dedjet will sentence you to exile from her without blinking an eye. But if you deserve reward, Dedjet will be generous."

Rahmzi began to walk again, asking no more questions. Nessumontu gave him much upon which to reflect.

Amenemhet remained standing, watching Nefrytatanen.

"What happened caused me no injury," she said quietly. Her blue eyes shifted beyond him a moment while she reflected on her experience.

"Then why are you pale?" he asked.

She lifted her head, and a gleam from the lamp sent a myriad of sparks from the golden ornament in her hair. "Because what happened may mean nothing, or it may mean great sorrow to come," she whispered.

Amenemhet took a step closer and laid his hands on Nefrytatanen's shoulders. "Tell me," he urged. "Perhaps we can find the answer together."

Nefrytatanen suddenly put her arms around Amenemhet's waist and drew closer to him, laying her head on his chest. He held her tightly to him but said nothing.

Finally she began to speak. "When I entered the temple, it was deserted. Ankhneferu had known I would come, but he wasn't there. He had left several lamps lit for me. Dedjet stayed behind and was so quiet I forgot her presence. When I approached Aset's statue, I saw that light from the lamp caught her golden face. It seemed a radiance came from

her eyes, meant for me. It was so peaceful. I stood
there and gazed at her. A serenity had taken such
hold on me that I took off my cloak without thinking
about what I was doing and dropped it on the floor.
I knelt before I lit the incense, allowing the peace to
saturate my being. When I lit the incense, I spent
some time staring into the flame I'd used. I felt en-
tranced. I went to the offering table and knelt before
it, touching my forehead to the stone at Aset's feet.
Then I straightened and looked again into her face,
feeling very light in my body. It was a sensation not
unlike that of my testing.

"I know I wasn't dreaming, though it felt much like
dreaming," she murmured. "The sensation of the cold
stone under my knees was vivid, and I was aware all
the while of this headpiece I wear." She shook her
head slightly as if to confirm its reality. The golden
beads of the ornament sparkled. "I wasn't sleeping,"
she said firmly. "Yet I saw such things as can only
come from an evil dream—or a vision.

"I saw a city with high walls being most success-
fully stormed. I couldn't see what city because there
were dense billows of smoke. I caught the glimpse of
a flag," she whispered. "I fear the city was Ithtawe
because the emblem on the banner was that of Zahi.
I am afraid I saw a Hyksos attack on Ithtawe!" Nefrytatanen glanced down and whispered, "I saw the
shattered face of a man in the dust. The sight of him
made me weep." She looked up at Amenemhet. "I
couldn't tell you who he was, for he was ruined beyond recognition. But he wore a crimson tunic—like
Nessumontu's."

"All the palace guards wear crimson," Amenemhet
soothed.

"His death made me weep," Nefrytatanen insisted.

She paused to swallow her tears and take a deep breath before continuing. "Senwadjet was there, also," she whispered. "I tried to hold him close to me, but he stepped away and walked into the smoke billows. I saw the red glow of the fires reflecting on his back before he disappeared. I was terrified for him. After a time, he came back. But, oh, beloved! He was different! It was as if he'd been gone a very long time, for he returned as a man. You were with me all through this and, although I never saw you, the strength of your invisible presence sustained me." She dropped her eyes, and he saw the glitter of moisture on her lashes.

"When I awakened, I was lying on the floor. Dedjet and the guards were anxiously trying to awaken me. They said I had fallen like a stone. I felt well, but at their urging, I remained for a time, resting while I thought about what I had seen." She lifted her eyes. "I hadn't tried to receive a prophecy, and such things require certain efforts. I don't know what happened to me. I think Aset gave me a vision to warn us."

Amenemhet struggled to control his rising panic. He wasn't thinking of visions. He was thinking of his brother, who had been afflicted with the falling sickness, and he remembered vividly how his parents had described the seizures. The boy had been taken very suddenly by a seizure at about Senwadjet's age and had fallen before the wheels of a racing chariot and been crushed.

Very quietly and carefully Amenemhet said, "Perhaps Horemheb should examine you."

Knowing Amenemhet's fear and the root of it, Nefrytatanen replied, "I'll go to him to ease your mind, beloved. But it was, I think, a foreseeing of things to come." She shivered. "I'd rather have the physician tell me I have the sickness."

"I would not!" Amenemhet declared. "I would rather Ithtawe be laid siege upon."

"But it seemed that the city I saw was ready to fall!" Nefrytatanen exclaimed, looking up at him. "Ithtawe must never fall into the hands of the Hyksos.

"Some evils are greater than others," Amenemhet whispered. "Ithtawe could be won back—you could not."

Djanah sat on the little colonnaded walkway looking out onto her garden. She liked to admire it while she ate her morning meal. She enjoyed the feeling of triumph it gave her to know it was her garden, her house, and her walls surrounding the place. Djanah was, by nature, one of those people who grasped tightly to what was hers—or what she believed to be hers. Having been born to a humble family, Djanah's strong inclination to possessiveness had been amplified. All she owned carried her name, even to her ivory comb, whereon her name was deeply carved. No one saw her comb other than her maid and herself, but that Djanah saw her name on her comb was sufficient reason to have placed it there.

Djanah finished the fruit she was eating and stretched luxuriously. The flower beds made the morning air smell sweet and fresh. Djanah inhaled the scented air and enjoyed this hour before the garden began to gather heat from the sun. Slowly getting to her feet, she turned toward the little chapel she had had built separately from her house, as was the custom among nobility. The pale light turned the stone to rosy gold, a color Djanah admired greatly, and she gazed at it in pleasure.

Suddenly she heard the sound of voices from the street outside her gate. The voices subsided, the gates opened and closed, and Djanah saw her servant Absee hurrying toward her carrying a bouquet.

"Mistress," Absee panted, holding out the bouquet, "a messenger brought this." Shrewdly Absee added, "He was dressed in the crimson of the royal guards, and he said he was aide to the commander of the royal army."

With satisfaction Absee noted the rise of Djanah's winged eyebrows. He had known she would be pleased.

Wonderingly, Djanah took the bouquet. It combined fragile, orange, cup-shaped flowers with golden blossoms. The arrangement was held together with golden wires worked in the motif of Montu, the god of war. Scarlet ribbon loops streamed from beneath the bouquet. To one of the ribbons was attached a small roll of papyrus.

Absee saw the gleam of excitement in Djanah's dark eyes and smiled with anticipation, but his mistress turned away and walked slowly toward her chapel, leaving Absee staring after her, burning with curiosity.

Djanah deliberately moved from Absee. She didn't wish him to observe her trembling hands. She recognized the seal on the papyrus as coming from the royal house itself. Taking a deep breath, Djanah sat on a bench under a tree and carefully broke the seal so as not to spoil its design. She unrolled the papyrus. Upon reading Nessumontu's complimentary note, her smile grew and her heart swelled in joy.

Djanah read the papyrus again and again until she noticed the flowers beginning to wilt around their edges. Gathering what dignity she could manage, so the servants wouldn't think her foolish, Djanah stood. But before she began to walk toward the house, she pulled one of each of the flowers from the bouquet to press and save in memory. As she walked, she reminded herself to save the golden wires and scarlet ribbons when the flowers died.

Djanah was near the wall gates when she heard hoofbeats pause outside; holding her breath, she stood as if paralyzed. Seldom did chariots stop at her gate. Did the commander come to see how she had received his gift? Her temples pounded, and she felt her knees lose their strength.

When Absee stepped through the gateway, Djanah saw that his eyes were so rounded the whites glowed. He was followed by a palace soldier.

"You will not faint," she chided herself and stood a little straighter.

Were all palace soldiers so tall? Djanah wondered, as the crimson-uniformed figure approached her. Did all of them walk so proudly? In spite of her wish to appear sophisticated, Djanah felt like prostrating herself at his feet. He stopped in front of her, and she dropped her eyes, afraid to lift them.

"You are the lady Djanah?"

The quiet voice seemed to come from the height of a tower, and she dragged her gaze up to look into the bronze face before her. The soldier's black, slanted eyes looked at her with admiration. There was a slight smile on his lips.

"I'm Djanah," she said softly.

"You sing in the temple of Hat-Hor?"

Djanah nodded. She was certain that the voice that served her so well in the temple had temporarily disappeared.

"I have brought a request from King Amenemhet and Queen Nefrytatanen for you to sing for them," the soldier said quietly, holding out a scroll bearing many golden seals and scarlet cords.

"The king! The queen!" Djanah managed. "They want me to sing for them?" She stared at him openly now. Then her eyes dropped to the scroll. She could say no more. She took it and almost dropped the flowers in her confusion.

"The day and the time you will come to the palace are in the message," the soldier said softly. "Perhaps you would like to look at it and see if you find the appointment convenient."

Djanah stared at him. "I'll come whenever it is!" she exclaimed. Then, still intoxicated with her good fortune, she blurted, "Are you Commander Nessumontu?"

The soldier's smile grew. "I wish I were," he said. "I'm merely one of the palace guards acting as messenger. I think you'll find the commander's name mentioned in the scroll." He paused, watching Djanah carefully a moment, then said, "You're certain that you can come? The date is a request, not a command. Other arrangements can be made."

"Oh yes, yes!" Djanah burst out. "I'll surely come."

"Then I bid you a day of joy," the soldier said and turned to the gate. His smile grew wider. He was thinking she would have a day of panic, not joy. The date of the audience was today, and the time was after the evening meal.

Djanah again almost dropped the flowers in her

struggle to open the royal seal without destroying its beauty. She was grateful she could read and wouldn't need someone else to decipher the elegant formal writing. Before she unrolled the papyrus, she paused to imagine the king himself dictating this message to his scribe, the king himself setting his seal. She shook her head in wonder. It was too much to grasp.

Djanah's wide eyes got even wider as she read: "The commander of the Royal Army, Nessumontu, visited the temple of Hat-Hor several days ago and returned with so glowing an account of your singing that King Amenemhet and Queen Nefrytatanen wish to hear your wondrous voice and request . . ."

Djanah gasped at her sudden remembrance of the two soldiers who had stood beside her a moment as she had hurried through the crowd. They had been from the palace! The one with the slanted eyes had stared at her so intently she had grown uneasy.

"Oh, Hat-Hor," Djanah whispered, "was that the commander?" She remembered the black hair ruffled by the vagrant breeze and the slight smile on his lips. In her rush she had thought of him merely as a soldier, but now she remembered the red tunic of the palace guards, and she remembered his noble bearing.

She looked again at the scroll and read the day and hour she was to appear at the palace and grew pale. Tonight? This very evening? Her mouth fell open. What would she wear? In the splendor of the palace any of her garments would seem to be rags. Perhaps the robes she wore when she sang for special high services. Perhaps . . .

Before Absee's amazed eyes, his mistress turned and ran full speed into the house, flower petals flying behind her.

CHAPTER 2

"You MAY NOT HAVE WINE," whispered Nefrytatanen. "The juice of the grape before fermenting is sufficient for you."

"Grape juice is grape juice," Senwadjet muttered, playing with the foot of his goblet.

Nefrytatanen silently prayed he wouldn't upset the goblet, but she said nothing. Instead, she observed, "There's considerable difference."

Senwadjet's face was sulky. Nefrytatanen knew that beneath the long, black lashes, the golden eyes staring at the table were filled with disappointment. His other hand played absently with his prince's lock, which had lately become an annoying symbol of childhood. Nefrytatanen smiled faintly. Senwadjet wished to be a man too soon. She raised a hand to the servant standing behind them, and the girl stepped forward with her wine jar.

"Pour a little into the prince's and princess's goblets," Nefrytatanen ordered.

Senwadjet and Maeti looked up in surprise. They didn't mind that their mother's fingers now indicated how little wine would go into their cups of grape juice. That is was there was enough.

On Nefrytatanen's right, Amenemhet leaned closer

to whisper, "Are you spoiling them?" His golden eyes held amusement.

Nefrytatanen pushed aside a tendril of hair that brushed her ear and murmured, "It's only a few drops and it means so much to them." She looked with satisfaction at Senwadjet's and Maeti's bright eyes. "See how they sit a little straighter?" she whispered. "They think they've taken a large step forward, and I doubt they can even taste the difference."

"Their imaginations supply the taste," Amenemhet murmured, laying his hand on hers.

A servant entered the dining room and walked to the royal table. "The singer is ready whenever you wish her to perform."

"We wish it now," Amenemhet replied. "I'm told she's extraordinary." He turned toward the door and signaled the guard to admit Djanah.

Amenemhet glanced at Nessumontu, who stood by the private entrance to the royal apartments, intently watching the doorway on the opposite end of the room, which was where Djanah would enter.

"I hope no one tries to attack us at this moment," Amenemhet murmured humorously to Nefrytatanen, "because Nessumontu wouldn't know it." Then he turned his eyes to the doorway.

On the threshold stood a girl in a simple white robe. She wore no jewelry, but around her forehead was tied a crimson ribbon whose streamers fell to the side, mingling with her long black hair. Tucked in the ribbon was an orange flower. Slowly she walked toward the royal table. When she reached the dais on which it was placed, she dropped to her knees in a deep, graceful bow.

"Rise, Djanah," Amenemhet directed. As her eyes

met his, he smiled in a friendly manner. He could see how nervous the girl was. "Share with us this marvelous voice I've heard so much about," he added.

"May it be worthy of your hearing," Djanah whispered. She stepped back a few paces and looked at the musicians awaiting her signal.

Djanah's heart was a turmoil of conflicting emotions. She had meant to glance around the room as she entered so that she might take another look at Nessumontu. But she had been so nervous she had forgotten.

For a moment Djanah was terrified that her voice would fail her or that she would forget the words to the song. As the music began, she frantically searched her memory for the first phrase. She was grateful the song had a musical introduction of some length. As she waited to begin singing, she felt the music taking possession of her being, and she knew the spell it wove for her would render her unaware of everything but singing.

Amenemhet and Nefrytatanen saw the expression in Djanah's eyes change. She no longer seemed conscious of them. As she began to sing, the look on her face confirmed this. They glanced at each other and smiled. As Nessumontu had described, her voice was like radiant light.

When the last faint echoes of the song had trailed off, Amenemhet took a deep breath and said, "Djanah, your song casts a spell over us."

Djanah smiled faintly.

Amenemhet added, "You sang a temple song, which was beautiful. But will you sing another, perhaps less formal, song?"

Djanah bowed and looked again to the musicians,

this time indicating that only the girl playing the lyre accompany her. Djanah began a song that spoke of love, not the kind of love enjoyed by those only beginning to love, but the richly burnished love born of knowledge. Her voice became lower and a little husky, adding a note of subtle seduction. Her manner held the allure of one who needed no hasty answers, but who waited in confidence. Her voice was like a quietly burning flame.

Amenemhet and Nefrytatanen joined hands. They knew the song was their own. When Djanah finished, Amenemhet urged her to sing another.

As Nessumontu listened, he felt again his flesh rise in small bumps along his spine. He wondered how he could manage to speak to Djanah later, in privacy. Each time she sang of love, he was certain she looked at him, and he knew the flower she wore in her hair was from his bouquet. She finished her last song, and he felt his heart on fire, but he did nothing to hint of his wish to approach her. He waited, planning his way with careful determination.

Amenemhet and Nefrytatanen gave Djanah many generous compliments, and even Senwadjet and Maeti stared at her wide-eyed. Then Amenemhet looked across the room at Nessumontu, and Nessumontu saw Djanah's eyes turn toward him, also.

"Commander Nessumontu," Amenemhet said clearly, "will you escort this lady to her litter?" Amenemhet saw the orange gleam flash in Nessumontu's eyes, but Nessumontu never smiled as he approached.

"It will be a pleasure," Nessumontu said quietly. He waited for the moment it took Djanah to complete another deep bow before Amenemhet and Nefrytatanen. Then Nessumontu took Djanah's hand and, placing it lightly on his arm, escorted her from the room.

Amenemhet looked at Senwadjet and Maeti meaningfully, and they got up to leave without argument. Their spirits were caught in the music's spell, and their bodies cared little about what they did.

Nessumontu walked through the corridors, sharply aware of Djanah's hand on his arm, yet unsure of what to say to her. At the same time, Djanah hesitated to speak first to him.

Finally Djanah ventured, "The flowers you sent were most beautiful." She was silent for a moment, wondering what to say next. Then, realizing they were quickly coming to the outer doors, she added, "It's not only flowers I must thank you for, but your kindness in mentioning me to the king."

As they walked through the courtyard's fragrant shadows, Nessumontu finally paused to look down at her. "A small bouquet is nothing compared to the pleasure I received from hearing you sing in the temple. That your songs would give joy to the king and queen was sufficient reason to bring you here. You aren't in my debt, but I am in yours."

"Your words are as pleasing as your offering of flowers," Djanah murmured. She dropped her eyes. She didn't want to resume walking and leave the courtyard now, but she didn't know what more she dared say.

Nessumontu began again to walk, and Djanah's heart fell in disappointment. What could she expect, she silently scolded herself. She was merely a temple singer. And Nessumontu wasn't only the commander of the king's army, but he was of noble birth as well.

The courtyard's gates opened before them, and she looked regretfully at her waiting litter.

"The king and queen will send you a gift in thanks for your music," Nessumontu suddenly said.

Djanah looked up at him in surprise. "I came only for the reward of pleasing them," she said.

"They were most pleased," he replied. He smiled at last. "Would it please you if I delivered their gift?" he asked. "If not, I will have another bring it." His narrowed eyes watched her carefully.

Djanah dropped her gaze and got into her litter, wondering how to agree without sounding too anxious. After an embarrassingly long silence, she raised her eyes and said, "If you brought nothing, I would welcome your visit."

Nessumontu nodded and stepped away from the litter. As he watched it move down the street, he smiled.

Senwadjet made sure Yazid had left him for the night, then got out of bed and went out on the terrace. The night air was cool and fragrant after the day's heat, and he sat on the low wall and gazed down at the garden. The trees were black silhouettes against the sky, and their crowns moved gently with the north wind.

Senwadjet felt restless and knew sleep would be long in coming. He wondered again about his hair. It hadn't been a thing he had given much thought to before he had mentioned it to Amenemhet. Now Senwadjet found the idea in his mind often.

Senwadjet went back into his room. Carefully, so he wouldn't send something noisily tumbling, he picked up the polished gold mirror on his table and took it onto the terrace where he could see by moonlight. He held his long hair tightly together at the nape of his neck, trying to imagine how he would look with it shortened. He found the results most satisfying.

"Are you preening like a dancing girl?" Maeti's whisper came from the terrace doorway.

Senwadjet hastily put the mirror down. He turned to her, embarrassed.

"I was teasing you," she added softly. "I know what you were doing." Senwadjet came into the room and sat on a chair. Maeti lay across his bed and said thoughtfully, "It means much to you to have it cut, doesn't it?" Senwadjet nodded. "You've never mentioned it before," she commented.

"I hadn't thought of it before," Senwadjet admitted. He looked at her. She was laying on her back with her head dangling off the bed, gazing at him upside down. "Don't you realize we're growing up?" he asked suddenly. Maeti nodded, undisturbed. "I don't feel the same as I used to feel," he said. Maeti nodded again. "Don't you feel different?" he asked.

"I'm beginning to at times," Maeti replied, "but I'm in no rush to grow up. Though I know changes are happening to me, I would enjoy what I am before I've changed too much."

"What changes do you feel?" Senwadjet asked curiously.

Maeti's face flushed. She was glad the room was dark. "Some physical changes," she answered slowly.

Senwadjet tilted his head to look at her upsidedown face and asked again, "What changes?"

"I don't wish to discuss them," Maeti replied coolly.

"They aren't visible to me," he observed.

Maeti rolled over and lay on her stomach. She was

insulted. Had he not noticed the new curving of her hips? Was the beginning roundness on her chest that small?

Senwadjet smiled at her expression. "I was teasing you," he said, "but I wanted to look at you right side up." He was silent a moment, reflecting on his own body. "Sometimes," he began slowly, "I also wonder about growing up. Sometimes, " he said faintly, "I'm very confused about it—and everything. Sometimes I feel very sad. I often tease you for reasons I don't even know. Sometimes I'm afraid I'll make you hate me," he admitted.

"There have been moments when I've been unsure," she sighed, "but they pass, and I know I love you." She swung her feet over and sat up. "Growing up seems a thing I look forward to and fear at one time," she confessed. A look of mischief came over her face, and she smiled. "I do often think with longing of the day when I can give orders the servants will obey without going first to mother or father.

Senwadjet smiled wryly. "It seems useless to be a prince if my own servants ignore most of my orders," he said.

"I remember when you threw the oil jar at Yazid," Maeti teased.

"You did a few things I could mention," he reminded.

"Yes," she sighed. "Before this it was easier. You could do such things, and everyone would think you're a child and scold you and dismiss the matter. Now, they expect us to behave with restraint."

"It is tiresome," Senwadjet agreed. A crafty look came into his eyes. "I've found, though, the more I practice it, the more freedom they give me."

"You are clever," Maeti laughed, "but I've done the same. If we become sufficiently restrained, perhaps your lock will be shorn." She lay again on the bed with her head hanging off to the side, her feet up in the air as she contemplated her toes.

"I think I heard talking coming from here." Yazid's voice came from the hall. The door opened, and he stepped into the room. Dedjet followed him, carrying a lamp.

"Maeti!" Dedjet exclaimed in exaggerated horror. "Is that the proper posture for a princess?" Maeti shot Dedjet a look of anger and lowered her feet. "What are you two plotting?" Dedjet asked. Neither Maeti nor Senwadjet offered a hint, and Dedjet added, "Enough of it, in any event. Maeti, you must go to your room."

Maeti gave Dedjet another cold stare and got to her feet. "Growing up looks most attractive to me at the moment," she muttered as she stalked past Senwadjet.

"What is she talking about?" Yazid asked, puzzled.

"Nothing," Senwadjet replied coldly and got into bed. He closed his eyes and said no more, commanding with his deliberate silence the servants' dismissal.

Yazid rubbed the back of his neck, turned to Dedjet, and shrugged. She turned to the door. When they were in the hall, Dedjet remarked, "At least he no longer hurls missiles at us."

Yazid smiled. "For that I give thanks," he said. "His arm is strong and his eye too steady now."

"Maeti will eagerly learn the queen's skills. She has her mother's powers in her very blood and knows it," Dedjet observed. "Did you see the look in her eyes when I told her to go to bed?"

"Yes," Yazid muttered. "If she had known how to

do it, she would have caused your nose to grow a wart."

"It's always been the same when she's been given orders, but now she makes no threats as she did when she was small," Dedjet said. She smiled faintly.

"All the princess needs is her mother's teaching," Yazid agreed. "I'm glad the queen waits before beginning that."

Dedjet nodded solemnly. "My lady knows Maeti is yet too impulsive and stubborn for the power such knowledge will give her."

"The queen is wise," Yazid agreed. "We'd all be wearing warts—or worse!"

Dedjet stopped by the door that opened onto the garden. "I think I'll shorten my trip by going through the garden," she said, her fingers resting on the door handle. "Fair dreams, Yazid."

"Fair dreams," Yazid replied, continuing down the hall.

Dedjet stood quietly a moment, watching Yazid's receding back, reflecting on his devotion to the royal family and absence of a personal life. The royal family had become Yazid's family. He thought of no other. Dedjet loved them, too, but there were times she wished for her own child and for a husband's body sleeping warmly close to her. She sighed, opened the door, and stepped outside.

Dedjet closed her eyes. From the fragrance on the wind she could tell which flowers were blooming, and she saw them in her mind's eye, savoring their beauty for a moment. Through visions of swaying multi-colored flowers came the low trembling of a bird's song, and Dedjet tried to guess what kind of bird it was. It was unfamiliar. Bewildered, she tried to listen more closely, and finally she understood. Her mysterious bird was someone playing a flute. She listened for a moment, then began to trace its direction.

As Dedjet reached the lotus pool and the silver veil of the fountain's mist drifted over her, the flute stopped.

She stood in uncertainty until a quiet voice said, "I'm here—in the pavilion."

Dedjet looked toward the pavilion. The dark figure on its threshold stepped forward, allowing the moonlight to shine on him.

"Captain Rahmzi!" Dedjet exclaimed. "I thought you were a bird."

Rahmzi smiled. "I've been called worse." He walked closer.

"I like solitude from time to time," Rahmzi explained. He saw Dedjet shiver in the cool breeze and suggested, "Let us go into the pavilion. You're wet from the fountain. You have some spare time, haven't you? Or will I keep you from a necessary task?"

"No—I mean, yes, I have time," Dedjet replied through suddenly chattering teeth.

"Do you mind?" Rahmzi asked, as he carefully arranged his cape around her shoulders.

She shook her head. "I'm grateful for the warmth," she replied. "But what of you?"

"I've known far colder nights in the mountains across the Narrow Sea," Rahmzi said.

The pavilion was filled with shadows, but its latticed walls effectively shut out the wind. Dedjet sat on a bench, her shivering slightly lessened. A streak of moonlight warmed Rahmzi's dark eyes as he watched her.

"Perhaps," he said, "you should go back to the palace. You've really gotten chilled, it seems."

"Your cape helps," she said quickly. "I'll be all right in another moment." Now that she had him alone, she had no intention of leaving Rahmzi so fast.

Although Rahmzi sensed Dedjet's purpose, his expression revealed nothing. Instead, he said, "Nessumontu told me you're yet unmarried." She looked up at him, too surprised to answer. He smiled faintly. "I asked Nessumontu many questions about you—and he answered them."

"What questions?" Dedjet managed to ask. "Why did you ask him?"

"I asked what you do in the palace, what you're like. I asked Nessumontu because I can believe his answers." Rahmzi paused, then slowly added, "I asked because I'm interested in you."

"Why?" Dedjet was amazed by his candor.

"Do you never look in a mirror?" Rahmzi's voice was warm.

Dedjet said nothing. She was remembering a man who had noticed her some years ago. Her face reflected unhappy memories.

Rahmzi put his fingers under her chin and tilted her face to his. Almost roughly, Dedjet pulled away.

"Don't fear me, Dedjet." His hand dropped, and he looked away. "When I first saw you, I confess I briefly considered your potential in the very fashion you would avoid. But when I inquired about you, Nessumontu's answers reflected his respect for you." To Dedjet's startled glance, Rahmzi added, "That impressed me. Nessumontu's respect isn't easily won. I thought more seriously about that and decided you were to be considered in a different way."

"And what way is that?" she asked.

Rahmzi's eyes met Dedjet's in a steady gaze. "A man must love you," he said simply.

"But I cannot love you!" she exclaimed.

"Why?"

"You're not mine to love."

"I might be won over," Rahmzi said softly, "but for you to try to do that, you'd also have to love me. Why does loving someone terrify you?"

Dedjet was silent a moment. Rahmzi's frankness startled her and made her uneasy. She wondered what to say, then decided she wouldn't look at him as she said, "Were I to allow myself the luxury of giving in to that emotion, I would endanger us both."

"Endanger us—how?" Rahmzi leaned forward, curiosity overcoming his caution.

Dedjet was embarrassed, but she didn't know how to stop her words. "Love comes to me," she whispered, "as a mighty river flooding my being. It isn't a trickling stream that can be stopped up at my command." She paused and took a deep breath, then plunged on, "I'm not an easy loser either. I would fight with all my strength until there could be no question that I'd lost or won—everything." She paused again and then her words came so faintly he could barely hear them. "And when I hurt, every part of my being knows pain."

"You speak from experience," Rahmzi observed quietly.

Dedjet nodded. "Now you know more about me than anyone," she admitted. She looked up at him, perplexed. "Why did I tell you what my innermost heart contains?"

Rahmzi stood up, drawing Dedjet up by her hand. His lips brushed her forehead, and he said, "Perhaps I'm the one man you should tell."

Still holding her hand, he began walking toward the palace. Beside the fountain, he again stopped and faced her. "Do not fear me," he whispered. "I have no need to hurt you."

He bent and, without touching her in any other way, kissed her lips gently, then stepped back.

"Your mouth is warm and soft and very pleasant to kiss," he murmured. "I would kiss you with more enthusiasm, but I won't hurry you." He smiled. "Besides, this fountain's spray chills me, and if we stand under it much longer, I'll need warming—a problem you're not yet ready to help me solve."

Senwadjet's chamber was flooded with moonlight, which sent the night's shadows hurrying into the far corners. Amenemhet could see Senwadjet's face clearly as he stood over him. Amenemhet looked at his sleeping son who, though far from manhood, was no longer truly a child.

Amenemhet reflected on Senwadjet's progress, which seemed faster than many other children's. He had a wisdom beyond his years, but he was free, as yet, of adult worries. Amenemhet smiled, remembering his own frustration at this crossroads of life, a time of conflicting emotions and physical changes.

He studied his son, as if to engrave on his mind Senwadjet's childhood likeness, which soon would pass. Senwadjet's nose held no more of the delicacy of childhood, but it was finely drawn. His jaw already had begun to show hints of coming strength. Though his mouth was sensitive, Amenemhet could read its promise of future sensuality. He made a mental note to watch this aspect carefully in the next few years. Amenemhet's smile returned as he considered this. He knew that girls would pursue his son even if the inheritor of the crown were plain faced. But Senwadjet would not be plain.

He touched a wisp of Senwadjet's hair lightly, so as not to awaken him, took a deep breath, and left the room.

Gobryas's black eyes glittered in the wavering firelight. He glared angrily at Manuzah. "I considered most carefully what would wring her heart the most," he said clearly. His words struck the crumbling stone columns and echoed. "I found how I could rid myself of an enemy at the same time. You'd deny me the joy of watching all this set into motion?" Gobryas took a step closer to Manuzah.

Manuzah was not intimidated. "I'm the best worker of magic in Zahi," Manuzah said calmly. "I do such things only of my will. If you threaten me, you'll have to look for someone else to do your work."

Gobryas heard the sound of crumbling stones sliding down some hard surface, and he reconsidered. He continued to glare at Manuzah, however, as he said, "I have no desire to anger you, Wise One, but I wish to share in the excitement of my coming triumph."

The firelight flickered across Manuzah's face. His eyes were set so far into his skull that they seemed like pits. His yellow skin looked like old papyrus. He was thinking that it might be good for Gobryas to watch him set the curse. Not only would Gobryas's hatred add to the power of the curse, but the arrogant prime minister might learn more respect for him.

"Have you brought the article I requested?" Manuzah asked.

"It's a piece of his jewelry." Gobryas held out a pendant on a chain. "I know it wasn't quite what you wanted, but getting a piece of clothing from a king is a task even beyond Adadni. There may be something here which will make you happier," Gobryas added slyly. "A strand of his hair is caught in the clasp."

Manuzah said nothing. He lifted the chain, turning the pendant in the faint light. Finally he murmured, "A hair from Amenemhet's head will be excellent for my purpose—even better than clothing." He looked at Gobryas. "Can we be sure it is his hair?"

"Who would wear a king's jewelry but the king?" Gobryas reasoned. "Adadni took this from Amenemhet's own bedchamber."

"Amenemhet wears his hair this long?" Manuzah asked looking at the black strand.

"I suppose so," Gobryas said sharply. "I haven't laid eyes on him for some time."

"Yes, I know. As I heard the story, King Amenemhet ordered you to leave and made sure you did so by sending his own palace guards to escort you to the border," Manuzah observed. His chuckle was a soft rasping sound. It held no humor.

"Save your passion for when I begin the curse," he advised. "I want only to be sure this is his pendant and his hair. I don't care to curse the wrong person. But as you said, who else would touch the king's jewelry, much less wear it?" Manuzah continued to examine the pendant, a disc representing the sun, with a hawk on it. He calculated the cost of the article, which was worked in solid gold. "It's a handsome piece," he remarked.

"Stop weighing it!" Gobryas snapped impatiently. His dark eyes narrowed. "If your spell works, you will have many times that trinket's value. And if it doesn't work, you'll have no need for gold."

"Have no fear." Manuzah's thin lips spread in a smile. "What I'll do will be successful. You'll see." Manuzah turned the pendant over. "Something is written here," he mumbled, "but I cannot read their hieroglyphs. Do you know what it says?"

"Adadni told me it's Amenemhet's name. He showed me what each figure says. It means 'house of Amen.'" Gobryas answered eagerly, knowing a name added to the power of the spell.

"It doesn't have a signet loop around the characters," Manuzah observed. "Is that not unusual for a king's name? Are you sure it's not merely a title?"

"Adadni assured me Amenemhet means 'house of Amen.'" Gobryas felt the last of his meager supply of patience rapidly diminishing. He wanted to leave this ancient ruin that Manuzah had chosen as the place to set the curse. The area made him uneasy. He could hear the flight of bats nearby. "What does it matter if a loop doesn't surround the characters?" he asked quickly. "Adadni said it's Amenemhet's name, and I believe him." He glared at Manuzah. "We're wasting time."

Manuzah wrapped the pendant in a square of red cloth. "You're correct," he admitted.

Gobryas looked uneasily at the shadows. "I don't know why we had to travel all that distance to this miserable place," he mumbled.

Manuzah smiled. "In this ancient ruin, deserted by all but the spirits, I will call Lamashtu from her dark domain. She will inhabit the house of Amenemhet and slowly kill him. There's no better place than this," he said. He looked appraisingly at Gobryas. "I told you not to come. If you lack the strength of purpose to see this through, leave me now—for you can't leave once I've begun, and I cannot be distracted by your hysterics."

"I won't be hysterical, and I will stay—if only to assure your not cheating me," Gobryas replied contemptuously.

"The results will be my proof," Manuzah answered calmly. "But consider this well, Gobryas. In the presence of Lamashtu, I must keep my full attention on what I do, or the she-demon may kill both of us."

Gobryas sat on a broken block of stone. "I'll stay," he said firmly, his voice echoing in the stillness.

"Then be silent," Manuzah snapped and knelt on the square of cloth he had spread over the dry leaves.

By the light of the fire, he began to arrange a square of stones on the soil. When the square was complete, he put a second layer on the first, then a third layer and a fourth, until he had built a structure like that of a small, roofless house. With great care, Manuzah dug a hole in the soil within the little house's enclosing walls. Then he placed the bones of a small serpent in the hole and covered it with soil. Manuzah took the red cloth containing the pendant and re-wrapped it a particular way.

Then, through the silent night, came Manuzah's murmuring voice speaking words Gobryas couldn't understand, though he flinched at the sound. In his loose, black, long-sleeved robe, Manuzah looked like a great vulture. Gobryas began to wish he hadn't come.

Manuzah turned his head once to glance at Gobryas over his shoulder. Seeing the growing fear on Gobryas's face, Manuzah's eyes glittered.

Manuzah put the pendant in the little house exactly on top of the bones. He took a container from the bundle he had brought with him and uncapped it. Gobryas got to his feet to see more clearly, and he shuddered as Manuzah poured a crimson liquid over the cloth containing the pendant. Gobryas knew it was blood, the substance so loved by demons. Its scent would surely attract Lamashtu. Manuzah next emptied a container of yellow powder on the bloody cloth, and its acrid smell confirmed Gobryas's suspicions. It was sulphur, another substance favored by demons. Gobryas fervently wished he could flee.

Manuzah laid a flat rock over the little house, making a roof for it. He began to plead with Lamashtu to come to this house and dwell therein.

Gobryas wondered if all those who did magic must always beg the demon they evoked in so humiliating a manner. He remembered how Nefrytatanen had threatened to send Lamashtu or Pazuzu to him. He smiled faintly. Now Lamashtu, the most dreaded of all demons, would reside at Ithtawe. And she would attack Amenemhet, slowly withering away his life. Gobryas's smile faded slightly as he remembered more clearly what Nefrytatanen had said—that she would command the demon. He looked at Manuzah, who was on his knees groveling in the dust. Why did Manuzah have to beg, while Nefrytatanen had said she would order the demon? Gobryas shook his head. She had said it to frighten him, he decided. His thoughts were interrupted by Manuzah.

Still on his knees before the little house, Manuzah opened another container. While he continued speaking, he poured blood over the little house.

"Oh, Lamashtu," Manuzah chanted, "maker of

hatred and prolonger of enmity, I conjure you to complete this work."

Gobryas felt as if every hair on his body stood on end while he watched Manuzah gather up his bundle and put out the fire so slowly that Gobryas thought he would never be finished. Gobryas offered to help him—hoping to speed their departure—but Manuzah insisted no one could touch these things but himself.

Gobryas stood helplessly aside, first on one foot, then the other foot, wishing to be out of this place where the crumbling columns loomed over him as if ready to fall on his head, where the bats wheeled through the darkness as if choosing which of the men to attack, and where the spirits of the priests and priestesses of this ancient temple still walked near the old fire pits searching for a new victim to use as a sacrifice. By the time Manuzah was ready to leave, Gobryas was sure his nerves were shattered and that his very sanity hung on a fraying thread.

They rode away from the ancient ruins. Gobryas neither reflected smugly on what they had done, nor did he dwell happily on the certainty of Amenemhet's coming death. His whole being was filled with the desire to escape, and he never glanced back.

Nefrytatanen hurried through the sun-filled corridor with Maeti at her heels. The child was talking rapidly. Finally Nefrytatanen stopped her swift stride and, brushing back her hair, looked down at Maeti.

"Maeti—" Nefrytatanen began in exasperation, then stopped. Her daughter's sapphire eyes stared up at her imploringly, and Nefrytatanen's annoyance faded.

"Why can I not begin to learn now?" Maeti asked

quietly. "Must I be completely grown before I can know anything?"

Nefrytatanen shifted the garments she was carrying from one arm to the other. "I'll teach you what I know, as my mother taught me, as you'll someday teach your own child," Nefrytatanen said calmly. "It won't be long before I begin this teaching, but prior to your learning anything regarding the casting of spells, you'll need to learn patience and control of your emotions. Wouldn't it be terrible if you did a thing on impulse and caused harm by it?"

Maeti thought about this and nodded reluctantly.

"This is why I wait. Your temper is too volatile," Nefrytatanen explained. "Restraining it is essential."

"I've seen you angry," Maeti reminded.

"But you've never seen me lose control," Nefrytatanen replied. "Anger is a powerful emotion, to be used as a tool when it's just. But it can be destructive if you haven't learned to leash it. So it is with all emotions," she said firmly.

Maeti knew her mother was right and silently resolved to remember this. "Will you one day teach me all you know?" she asked quietly.

Nefrytatanen smiled. "I've learned more than my mother knew, just as she learned more than her mother taught her. I'll teach you everything I've learned, and you'll learn more than that. So is our knowledge expanded and passed on through generations." Nefrytatanen paused to let this be absorbed and to observe Maeti's reaction. Maeti looked awed and solemn. Satisfied, Nefrytatanen promised, "The time your lessons will commence is soon."

Nefrytatanen saw Maeti's eyes glance past her, and she turned to see Amenemhet and Nessumontu coming toward them down the hall. She turned again to Maeti. "Do you understand, my daughter?" she asked. "I've given you my promise, and I don't break promises."

"I understand," Maeti said quietly. "You're right about me. I am too impulsive yet. I'll learn discipline while I wait for the time when you decide I'm ready." Her pink lips curved in a smile. "Does not my calm willingness to admit my fault speak in my favor?" she asked.

Nefrytatanen smiled. "It does," she agreed.

"You'll see how I'll control my temper and practice restraint," Maeti promised.

"Don't restrain yourself so much you forget to be happy," Nefrytatanen advised. "Learning the work of Aset doesn't mean an end to the joy in your life."

"Then you'll be my example," Maeti said slowly. "What you know hasn't caused an end to your laughter."

"There would be only one thing that could do that," Nefrytatanen murmured as if to herself as she watched Amenemhet nearing them. "That would be when he no longer walks through these corridors to me."

Maeti pressed Nefrytatanen's hand and whispered, "I'm old enough to understand at least some of your meaning and to anticipate with joy the day when I'll understand all of it for myself." Maeti released Nefrytatanen's hand and, with a wave to Amenemhet, ran down the bright corridor toward the garden.

Nefrytatanen stood quietly looking at Maeti until Amenemhet was at her side. Then she turned to him and said softly, "It won't be very long, beloved, before she's ready."

Amenemhet's golden eyes lifted to watch Maeti disappear into the garden, and he smiled faintly. "They grow quickly," he said.

Nessumontu came closer and took the garments from Nefrytatanen's arm. "Why don't you have a servant carry this for you?" he asked. "I see you always burdened with something," he said smiling. "Other queens, I think, don't carry laundry."

Nefrytatanen took back the garments and laughed softly. "I have only a few more steps to go with this," she said. "Other queens have ten servants for every task, and it's easy for them to find one who's idle." She looked up and down the hall pointedly. No one but sentries were in sight. "I'd have to spend half my day searching for a servant, and I have more important things to do than go through the effort necessary to be waited on. It's easier to carry this small burden myself."

She looked at Amenemhet's face more closely. He had a worried expression. "What's wrong?" she asked.

"The lame lioness has made off with a woman on a farm not far from here," Amenemhet said. "She was gathering honey from her hives only a short distance from her house. That lioness is getting much too bold. Something must be done quickly. I was thinking of riding to the area."

"Why don't you send someone?" Nefrytatanen asked.

Amenemhet smiled. "Everyone is occupied. Besides, I'd like to take a ride away from the palace and thereby avoid going through the latest pile of census reports awaiting my seal."

Nefrytatanen considered a ride in the open meadows and said quickly, "I'll go with you, beloved. I'll have Dedjet instruct the cook to pack a basket for us to take for our midday meal."

"Do you think it's safe to go?" Nessumontu asked. "What if the lioness attacks you?"

"She's just carried off a grown woman," Amenemhet said grimly. "You said the body hasn't been found, though you've searched. I can only think the lioness has dragged her away to finish her off leisurely." He shuddered at the vision this brought to mind and added, "I should think that would be enough for one lioness. She must be hidden somewhere, sleeping. We must trap her," he said firmly.

Amenemhet looked at Nefrytatanen. "Are you sure you want to come?" he asked.

"If there's a chance of your meeting the lioness, I want to be with you to help if I can," she said quickly.

"No doubt it will only amount to a pleasant ride in the meadows and a midday meal among the flowers," Amenemhet replied, taking her arm. "If I thought we were that likely to see the lioness, I'd rather not go at all than take you with me."

"I would go for sure in that event," Nefrytatanen said firmly.

An area filled with tall grass revealed many tracks. Amenemhet carefully studied the place to plan a strategy for a hunt. He didn't like the idea of settling anywhere in this area for their midday meal. He could not relax, although he was sure the lioness was sleeping, so he suggested they go to the royal reserve for their picnic. Nefrytatanen made no protest.

Sipping cool spiced wine, they strolled beneath the trees. Then they exchanged their leafy roof for the blue arch of sky and walked in golden grasses reaching almost to their waists. The grass was crowned with tiny flowers, and each time the wind coaxed the stalks into movement, Amenemhet and Nefrytatanen were showered with spicy-scented petals.

They paused to look back toward the river and gazed at a large hawk circling low over the edge of the water. The feathers of its wing tips cupped downward, then spread flat like fingers, finally arching up. The hawk swooped, glided, and soared lazily. Amenemhet and Nefrytatanen clasped hands, and the forgotten reins fell to trail behind them. The horses continued to follow from affectionate habit.

Nefrytatanen turned into a hollow between two folds of earth that sheltered a row of golden orange lilies, and Amenemhet followed her, smiling at her delight in them. She bent to put her nose in one of the orange cups and closed her eyes. She knew the lilies had no perfume, but she couldn't resist the silken smooth sensation of their petals against her face. Amenemhet stood with legs apart and tilted his face to the sky, looking from horizon to horizon, breathing the scent of the warm air in great slow breaths, feeling the sun on his forehead.

A movement caught Nefrytatanen's eye. She lifted a face smeared with golden pollen to stare in sudden horror at the lioness. The animal raced silently among the rocks, heading directly for them. She seemed not to see Nefrytatanen. Her eyes were fixed on Amenemhet, but he was still unaware of it.

Nefrytatanen could think of only one thing she had time to do. She ran into the path of the oncoming lioness. In her rush, she stepped into a hole and tripped. Her sudden movement caught Amenemhet's attention, and he turned quickly to see Nefrytatanen fall almost under the lioness's jaws.

Surprised by this aggressive move from the kind of

creature that usually fled at her appearance, the lioness stopped her charge and stood half crouched, looking warily at Nefrytatanen, who slowly got to her feet, then stood unmoving.

"You will not have him," Nefrytatanen said softly, staring into the beast's yellow eyes.

Unblinking, the lioness watched her, her black lips drawing back to bare long ivory fangs.

Nefrytatanen was sure her life was over, but she didn't move. She knew Amenemhet's lances and bow were tied to his horse, and she had heard the horses leap away at the appearance of the lioness.

"You will not have him," Nefrytatanen said again while she stared at the ivory fangs. She hoped the divine beings would be merciful and her death swift.

"Do not cast me down," Nefrytatanen began her funeral prayer, "not have I done evil—"

Then, Nefrytatanen was being brushed aside as easily as a willow's supple branch, and Amenemhet stood between her and the lioness.

"No, beloved!" Nefrytatanen screamed. Through the tears filling her eyes, she saw a flash of metal in the sun.

Amenemhet held his short sword. He had worn it with the intention of using it to hack away branches. He held the sword low, its gleaming tip pointed up toward the lioness. His eyes were triangles of golden fire as he motioned Nefrytatanen back with his free hand.

She couldn't move. She watched the lioness take a few slow steps sideways, as if to examine this new victim from another angle. Amenemhet's sword seemed so small and fragile, and Nefrytatanen knew he would have to get too close to the lioness to use it. She wondered if she could get to the horses. She ached to put the long shaft of a lance into his hands.

The lioness's hindquarters began to sink as she gathered her muscles for a leap. Nefrytatanen took one backward step toward the horses. Unable to tear her eyes from Amenemhet and the beast, she took another slow step back.

Seeing one of her adversaries retreat, the lioness bared her fangs and leaped. Amenemhet was ready. He stepped swiftly to one side, hoping to stab the beast, but he managed only to slash her in passing. The lioness roared in pain and sprang away, the scent of her own blood a surprising thing to her.

Nefrytatanen ran to Amenemhet's horse. Tightly grasping a handful of its mane to hold it, she tore a spear from its case and ran to Amenemhet with her prize.

Glancing gratefully at Nefrytatanen as he took the lance, Amenemhet ordered, "Get back."

Nefrytatanen withdrew reluctantly, wiping away the tears that blurred her vision.

"Come, beast," Amenemhet said softly. "You've had enough of the flesh of my people."

Seeing the sun flash on the weapon that had wounded her, the lioness again prepared to spring. A low rumble sounded in her throat. Amenemhet dropped the sword and lifted the lance.

Not knowing how Amenemhet could get past that huge head to spear the lioness in a vital part, Nefrytatanen lifted the silver pendant from her breast and turned it slowly so it caught the sun's fire. The lioness turned her head to glance at Nefrytatanen.

In that moment, Amenemhet ran forward and added the momentum of his running to the strength of his arm. He drove the lance deep into the lioness's tawny chest. She collapsed in mid-leap, tumbling forward from her own momentum, and landed on her back, tongue lolling from her mouth.

Nefrytatanen's legs surrendered, and she sat weakly in the grass. Amenemhet looked incredulously at the animal's extraordinary size. Then he turned and came to Nefrytatanen and sat beside her. His face was moist and pale under his tan.

Amenemhet whispered, "I want to get no nearer Tuat for a very long time."

Nefrytatanen took his hands and held them silently. She trembled too much to speak.

After a moment, Amenemhet said softly, "You deliberately got between the lioness and me. You offered yourself to her to save me."

Nefrytatanen's eyes lifted to meet Amenemhet's. She did not reply. There was nothing to say.

CHAPTER 3

YAZID STOOD BESIDE Nefrytatanen, his thin face wrinkled with concern. "My lady," he said softly, "the prince doesn't wish to have his morning meal." He glanced at Amenemhet. "I've offered to bring it to him, but he said firmly he won't eat it, and I don't know what to do."

"How does he seem?" Nefrytatanen asked, looking up at the servant.

"Weary, I thought," Yazid replied. "When I asked him how the night had passed, he said sleep had been long in coming and capricious about staying."

Nefrytatanen put down her cup and turned to Amenemhet. "When Senwadjet doesn't sleep and isn't interested in food, something's wrong."

"Perhaps he's overtired," Amenemhet said in a soothing tone, but his eyes were clouded with worry. "He is a sensitive boy, however robust his health."

"His sensitivity has never extended to missing meals," Nefrytatanen observed. She stood up. "I'll see for myself what this problem is," she said. "Go on with your meal, beloved. I'll tell you what this is about when I return."

Amenemhet stood up quickly. "If Senwadjet is unwell, I would see to it, also."

Senwadjet was sitting on the edge of his bed. When

Amenemhet and Nefrytatanen entered the room, he glanced up at them. Approaching him, Nefrytatanen noted the dull look in his eyes. She put her hand on his forehead.

"Your brow is cool," she observed. She sat beside him. "Do you have pain somewhere?" she asked.

Amenemhet had remained standing, watching Senwadjet closely. When Senwadjet shook his head in answer, Amenemhet observed his slow and listless movement.

"Would you sleep longer?" Nefrytatanen asked.

Again Senwadjet shook his head in reply, but he didn't seem eager to get up. Nefrytatanen turned to look at Amenemhet, and he saw the message in her eyes.

Amenemhet turned to Yazid, who stood in the doorway. "Get Horemheb," he directed.

"I don't need Horemheb," Senwadjet said in a disgusted tone. "Nothing hurts. I have no fever. I don't know why all this commotion must be made over my not sleeping well one night and having no taste for the morning meal."

"If my horse behaved in this fashion, I would seek help for him," Amenemhet replied. "Are you less than my horse?"

Senwadjet stared at the floor. "I'm a person, not a horse," he mumbled, "and I can answer your questions."

"You're my son," Amenemhet said firmly. He came a step closer. "I want you to have vigor and spirit. This dullness and sluggishness is unlike you."

Senwadjet glanced up, then looked at the floor again. "I'm not a baby," he said, his hand unconsciously going to his long hair. "It's only a passing mood."

"We will examine this unusual mood of yours," Amenemhet said sternly. "You're my child and heir to my throne. Before you can sit upon it or even have your hair shorn, you must learn the wisdom of preventing small problems from growing into large ones." Then he added more gently, "If you're ill and too stubborn to care for yourself, you'll make a very foolish king."

Senwadjet sighed. "Send for Horemheb, then," he said in resignation.

When the physician came, Amenemhet and Nefrytatanen discreetly walked out onto the terrace to afford Senwadjet privacy. They stood silently waiting, looking down at the garden. At Horemheb's call, they quickly went back into the room.

"I think the prince has overexerted himself these last few days," Horemheb said carefully. "I find nothing wrong with his body."

He turned to Senwadjet. "Lie back," he directed, "and rest even if sleep passes by without touching you." At Senwadjet's disgusted look he added, "If you won't do that, I'll mix a potion to put you to sleep. It will taste very unpleasant, I promise."

"All your medicines taste like the inside of a horse harness," Senwadjet muttered, but he obeyed the physician and lay down.

"Later I'll have some broth sent to you," Horemheb said, "and you will drink it."

At the door, Nefrytatanen turned back to Senwadjet. "If you want anything, call for it."

"He will—have no fear," Yazid muttered.

Nefrytatanen smiled. But as she closed the door, she

54

wondered at Senwadjet's dull eyes and forced smile. She felt as if something ominous hung over him.

Nefrytatanen turned from the window opening to face Amenemhet, who was seated at his writing table behind a pile of scrolls. "Beloved, since you're engaged with all those census reports, I think I'll take a walk in the garden," she said.

Amenemhet looked up at her. "I wish I could go with you," he said wistfully, "but I must examine these before a fresh pile comes." He smiled, and his eyes lit with warmth. "Have a care which path you take," he warned. "I've noticed Dedjet often walks through the garden, and lately Captain Rahmzi accompanies her."

"I heaven't heard his flute tonight," Nefrytatanen said, again glancing out the window opening.

"It would be safer if you did," Amenemhet replied.

Smiling at his comment, Nefrytatanen stepped outside. The night was warmer than usual at this time of year, and she decided not to bother getting a cloak. She went down the stairs and chose a secluded path to follow.

A slight breeze from the north caused the palm fronds to whisper, and the air was fragrant with flowers. Nefrytatanen found a little bench and sat down to tilt her face to the sky, which was scattered with stars. She thought about Dedjet and Rahmzi. She hoped her maid had at least found love.

A deep affection had grown between Nefrytatanen and Dedjet, and Nefrytatanen had come to regard her servant almost as a sister. Although Nefrytatanen was inclined to like Rahmzi—and his friendship with Nessumontu spoke well of him—she was concerned that some unforeseen situation might cause Dedjet further unhappiness and turn her forever from all thoughts of love.

Nefrytatanen's mind turned to Senwadjet. He had spent another night in sleepless turning, and she knew he was very tired. Each time food was brought him he played with it until it cooled, eating very little. She reflected on his lack of appetite, which was a thing she had never seen in him before. Not only was this peculiar, but the food he did eat seemed to give him no strength.

Certain theories had begun to rise in her mind like formless shadows, but she found these difficult to believe. She couldn't think of any reason why someone would do such a horror to the boy, but she found herself considering the making of an amulet to help Senwadjet.

"Kheti just rode in as if a demon pursued him." Nessumontu's voice came from behind Nefrytatanen, and she turned quickly. Nessumontu added, "I'm sorry I startled you."

"I was deep in thought," Nefrytatanen said, dismissing the matter.

Nessumontu sat beside her. "You're worrying about Senwadjet?" Nefrytatanen nodded. "He's going through many physical and emotional changes now," Nessumontu said sympathetically. "Often boys his age become restless and lose their appetites."

Nefrytatanen stared at her lap. Tears had come to her eyes, and she didn't wish Nessumontu to see them. He took her hands in his.

"Don't make more of this than it is," he said softly. "I wouldn't like to see you go through anguish of your own making."

Nefrytatanen looked up at Nessumontu, and a tear clinging precariously to her eyelash released its hold and fell. He wiped it away with a finger tip.

"I cannot help it," she whispered. "I have an ominous feeling about this I can't ignore."

"If my mother were alive today, she could tell you I was the same at one time," Nessumontu murmured. He smiled faintly. "My loss of appetite and sleeplessness was due to a certain girl I liked very much. I didn't know why or what to do about it." He shook his head slowly. "Even if I'd known what bothered me, I'd have been too shy to speak of it. I watched her walk through the sunlight, then tossed in my bed at night, and my mother worried about my increasing thinness."

"Why did you not tell me how you felt about her?" Nefrytatanen asked. "I was like your sister, and we confided in many other things. If I could have done nothing more, I could have listened and perhaps given you comfort."

Nessumontu's eyes narrowed slightly. Then his face brightened. "I was too shy to speak of it even to you," he said. He paused a moment, as if remembering, then suddenly exclaimed, "I almost forgot about Kheti! He has something of importance to report, and Amenemhet would like you to hear it." He stood up and waited for her.

"I wonder what it is now," Nefrytatanen said wearily. She took Nessumontu's hand and stood up to face him. "I'd best not delay going inside," she murmured. Her eyes lifted to meet his. "Thank you for trying to comfort me," she whispered.

"I hope your heart heard my words, for I think my

reasoning is accurate," Nessumontu replied, starting to walk toward the palace doors.

"You're probably right," Nefrytatanen replied. She smiled and took Nessumontu's hand as they walked. "I wonder what girl it is who attracts him."

Nessumontu smiled faintly. "You'll probably never know," he said softly. "My mother didn't."

From the pavilion's shadows, Djanah stood watching Nefrytatanen and Nessumontu. She had again come to sing for Amenemhet and Nefrytatanen after the evening meal, and instead of going home, she had lingered in the royal garden hoping Nessumontu would follow her.

Djanah had waited a long time. Just when she had thought about giving up and leaving, she had seen Nefrytatanen slip out of the doors and follow the path to the bench. Djanah had wondered why Nefrytatanen chose so lonely a place to sit, but after seeing Nessumontu join Nefrytatanen, Djanah concluded she knew the reason.

When Nessumontu and Nefrytatanen disappeared through the doors, Djanah briefly considered staying longer, then decided to leave. She crept out of the garden, feeling like a thief.

As Djanah rode home in her litter, she remembered how Nessumontu had touched Nefrytatanen's cheek. Nessumontu had taken the queen's hand without first asking permission to touch her—as if he had done it often and was used to making such impetuous gestures. Djanah's eyes narrowed. When she had gotten up to leave, Nefrytatanen had taken Nessumontu's hand and had continued holding it all the way to the doors.

"Does she not have enough to satisfy her?" Djanah

muttered as she alighted. Unaware of Absee's startled look, or even of his presence, Djanah marched past him into her house and slammed the door after her.

Nessumontu stood before Djanah's house in indecision. Djanah expected him. He had sent a message he was coming. Where was everyone, then? His patience was rapidly diminishing and his eyes glittered. He knocked on the doors, then took out his dagger and pounded on the gates, making a clamor. He didn't stop when he heard sandals hurrying across the courtyard pavement. He only stopped when the gate opened.

"Does the lady lock me out?" Nessumontu demanded. "If so, I will know why before I leave here."

"No! Oh no, commander," Absee said quickly. "There was a venomous serpent in the garden, and we were hunting for it," he lied.

"Did you capture it?" Nessumontu said stepping into the courtyard. He glanced around, his hand on his sword.

"Yes, commander," Absee replied. "It's dead. You need not fear it."

Nessumontu gave him a hard look. "I was going to offer my help," he said coldly.

"Of course, of course. Thank you," Absee muttered, nodding rapidly. "We are grateful." He turned as if to lead Nessumontu to the house.

"I know the way," Nessumontu said and stalked past Absee. When he was in the best of moods, Nessumontu didn't like the servant. Absee reminded him of a certain treacherous burrowing animal that lived off the unhatched eggs of birds. He wondered how Djanah endured him.

Nessumontu found the house doors tightly closed. He turned to see Absee hurrying up the path.

"I feel less than welcome," Nessumontu snapped.

Absee opened the door, puffing, "The snake—we were afraid it would get in."

"That serpent must travel at a marvelous speed, that you feared its entrance at the front while you pursued him in the back garden." Nessumontu's tone dripped sarcasm.

"We weren't sure where it was—" Absee began, but Nessumontu had entered the house and closed the door with a crash.

In the hall, Nessumontu stopped. The place seemed deserted. He was considering going home when Djanah's maid came quietly and asked him to follow her. She led him to a sitting room where Djanah waited. Nessumontu paused in the doorway and studied Djanah's expression, which still contained a hint of anger.

"Am I welcome here?" Nessumontu asked coolly.

"You are most welcome," Djanah answered in the low, inviting tone he had become so familiar with.

Nessumontu wanted to ask why she hadn't ordered him admitted immediately, but he said, "You look very alluring tonight, Djanah."

She murmured her thanks. She stepped away to pour a cup of wine for him. Putting the goblet in his hand, she asked, "It is spiced to your liking?"

Nessumontu tasted the wine and smiled with approval. Then he sank into a couch piled with multicolored cushions and looked up at her. "Come and sit close to me," he suggested.

Djanah did as he had asked, and he kissed her lightly.

"Is that the extent of your enthusiasm?" she asked, tilting her face toward him in further invitation.

Nessumontu sipped his wine and leaned back on the cushions, closing his eyes. "No," he whispered, "but I would relax first. My head aches with thoughts of all I'll have to do tomorrow."

Djanah leaned over and rested her cheek on his chest. "Tomorrow will arrive soon enough," she murmured. "Let us not think of it now." After a moment, she lifted her head to look at him. Then she kissed his chin, wondering why he didn't move. "Are you that weary?" she asked.

Nessumontu didn't open his eyes. "I wait for the wine to send my headache into exile," he murmured.

Djanah said nothing for a time, but she began to wonder if his delay in coming was Nefrytatanen's work. "Are you worried about something?" she asked. Could she gain some clue about what passed between him and the queen? "Tell me what's on your mind that so heavily weighs upon you," she urged.

Nessumontu opened his eyes. He said vaguely, "I have many things to accomplish tomorrow."

"And these tasks so occupy your thoughts that you have no room left for passion?" Djanah's voice had become tight with tension.

Nessumontu sat up. "I'm trying to drive away my worries," he said quietly. "I had accomplished this on my way here, but with the strange mood I feel hanging over you and this house, my worries have returned."

"Nothing hangs over this house," Djanah declared. She looked at him from the corner of her eye, wondering if he put her off while he regained the energy he had used with Nefrytatanen. "I begin to suspect you think of another woman."

Nessumontu smiled without humor. "I think of no one else."

"I am unsure of that," Djanah persisted.

"Are you jealous?" he asked in surprise. He was silent a moment, then said slowly, "I have no other woman now, but. . . ." He looked at her meaningfully.

"Then you have dreams of one, don't you?" Djanah demanded.

Nessumontu stood up. "I don't understand what you're talking about," he said.

"Yes, you do!" Djanah got to her feet and stared accusingly into his eyes.

Nessumontu was confused. His previous irritation had returned and began to grow into anger, but he controlled it and said, "I think you should explain your meaning."

Djanah's smile was filled with poison as she asked, "Haven't you dreamed of someone even since your boyhood?"

"Of course," he answered, very confused. "Doesn't everyone remember their first adolescent love?"

"But thoughts of her yet fill your heart," Djanah prompted.

"I yet have great affection for the lady," he said slowly, then added quickly, "but that affection isn't the kind you seem to think—"

Djanah interrupted, "She's beautiful, this woman who yet haunts your soul?"

Nessumontu stared at Djanah. "No one haunts my soul," he said coldly. "If someone did, what do you have to say about it? You don't own me. You take too much for granted, Djanah."

She looked as if he had slapped her. "Don't deny your feelings for her," she said in a deceptively soft tone. "I know such a denial would be a lie."

Nessumontu shook his head. "I don't lie," he said firmly.

"Tell me nothing of what you have fooled yourself into believing," she murmured. "I am a woman, and, as women have always known these things without being told, I know the truth."

Nessumontu stared incredulously at Djanah. "What are you talking about?" he asked. "Have you believed some rumor you've heard?"

"I know what I know," she whispered. She dropped her eyes. "How can I hope to compete with her?"

"Compete with who?" he asked a little loudly. He was becoming alarmed.

"This woman has the form of Aset herself, and the skin covering her body is the texture and hue of the golden lily. Her hair is silk, of a blackness deeper than onyx, yet lustrous as moonlight on the sea."

Nessumontu's eyes narrowed. Djanah was taunting him with careful deliberation, and he didn't like it. "Cease your foolish words," he ordered. "Whatever your purpose, you anger me."

Djanah ignored his warning. "Her mouth is the sweetness of honey gathered from lotuses," she said. "The voice issuing from her lips is the music of the north wind in the papyrus rushes, but it has the strength of a withheld storm. Her very fingers are tipped with precious gold. Your enchantress holds her head very high and rightly so—"

"Stop this nonsense," Nessumontu said sharply. He

was beginning to realize who Djanah had in mind, and he was furious now. He took her shoulders in a tight grip. "Cease talking of such things," he demanded.

"You will hear it all," Djanah whispered, looking directly into his eyes. "This woman you love, Nessumontu, wears a perfume like no other. No scent I can devise or have a chemist mix can compete with her fragrance. Your remembrance of its magic makes her perfume seem divine, and my own scent has no effect on you."

Nessumontu was holding Djanah's shoulders so tightly he could see his fingers making purple marks, but he was becoming terrified that she would dare speak the name she had in mind.

"But of all her wonders," Djanah murmured raising her brows, "the greatest marvel is her éyes—"

Now Nessumontu knew for a certainty what Djanah was saying. He released her shoulders and stepped back, his hand resting on his sword. "Speak carefully, Djanah," he said quietly. "Say any name but the one I think you have in mind. It is the one name that cannot be soiled. If you dare even begin to utter it, you are a traitor, and I would be a traitor to let you say it. I am not a traitor. I would have to silence your lips before that name has left them."

Djanah stared at Nessumontu, her lips parted, ready to say aloud the name of the queen. But it would not come out. Nessumontu's eyes had narrowed, and they gleamed with a terrifying light. She looked at his hand resting on the sword at his hip, knowing he would do as he said. She shivered.

Djanah was silent a long time, thinking of how far she had gone. Finally she whispered, "Well are you named after Montu, god of war." Again Djanah shivered. Then she turned and ran out of the room.

Nessumontu's hand fell to his side. He looked at the doorway Djanah had disappeared through. He couldn't believe such an accusation. His temples throbbed, and when he brushed his forehead, his hand came away shining with moisture.

"Wadjet," he whispered, "forgive Djanah this foolishness."

Then Nessumontu left the house. When he walked toward Absee, the servant looked at his face and stepped quickly aside. Nessumontu heard the gates close behind him, and he knew he would never go through them again.

CHAPTER 4

THE GOLDEN LIGHT OF DAY slanting into the throne room seemed to offer no warmth, and the blue lapis walls looked chill and lifeless. The great chamber was filled with ominous silence broken only by the prime minister's soft breath as he leaned close to Amenemhet.

"Ambassador Mulai has come with an urgent message from Retenu," Meri whispered. "He begs a private audience." Meri straightened and waited for Amenemhet's answer.

Amenemhet's golden eyes were filled with shadows. He could guess Mulai's purpose, and he was in no mood to hear of more trouble. All through the morning, petitioners had come asking favors, and Amenemhet had listened to them dutifully, though with only half an ear. His mind dwelled with his son.

Although Senwadjet had never before asked for medication of any kind, he had called Horemheb just before dawn and asked for a sleeping potion. Horemheb had examined the prince again and still could find no physical malfunction. With fear in his eyes, he had turned away from Senwadjet's bed.

Horemheb, mixing a sleeping potion, had called for Amenemhet and Nefrytatanen so they could see with their own eyes what he gave their son. Later, in the hall outside Senwadjet's room, Horemheb had told them frankly of his fear. Horemheb admitted that something very serious was wrong with the boy but that he had no idea what it was.

Amenemhet had known Senwadjet was very ill. One look at Senwadjet's pale face and dull eyes was enough. Those eyes, usually alert as a bird's, were empty. Senwadjet's movements were slow and hesitant, and his lips had a bluish tint. Senwadjet's body—always slender, but strong and bronzed from hours in the sun—had become as white as the underbelly of a fish. The flesh seemed to melt from him. Now he was so thin his hip bones were clearly outlined when he lay on his back.

Nefrytatanen had listened to Horemheb and walked out with her eyes blank. She had tried to disguise the terror that lay behind them so Amenemhet wouldn't see it. But he, who knew her mind as well as he knew his own, had recognized it and understood.

Today Amenemhet sat on his golden throne without Nefrytatanen at his side. She had gone to the temple to consult with the high priest, Ankhneferu, about the disease that had struck Senwadjet. It seemed to be a malady of his soul rather than his body.

Amenemhet took a deep breath, trying to focus his mind. He regarded Meri. "Have the room cleared," Amenemhet ordered. "Then bring Ambassador Mulai to me."

Amenemhet settled back in his chair. While he waited, he struggled with his whole spirit to turn his thoughts from his stricken son and concentrate on this political matter. All the tears that would have fallen from his eyes were filling his heart, and their pressure made an aching that invaded every part of his being.

After the last of the crowd had filed out the room, Mulai came through the great golden doors. He looked grim. Nessumontu closed the doors and posted himself as sentry to assure them privacy.

Mulai walked slowly toward the dais. Although he held his head high, his eyes were downcast. Amenemhet could see dejection in his every step.

Mulai bowed humbly, and when Amenemhet instructed him to rise, Mulai lifted dread-filled eyes.

"If King Ami-enshi were able to be here, he would bring you this news himself," Mulai said quietly, "but he cannot cross his own borders." Mulai paused to swallow, then continued, "The soldiers of Zahi now stand at the line dividing Zahi from Retenu. They're making plans to invade my land."

Nessumontu left his post and walked swiftly across the room, stopping to listen a few paces behind Mulai.

"King Ami-enshi sends you this news so you will send no trade caravans or visitors to Retenu until the impending conflict is over." Mulai paused again and took a deep breath. "My king also urges that you build up your forces. If Retenu falls, he's convinced that King Shalmanesser will send Sargon and his army to conquer Tamera."

Amenemhet stood up and stepped off the dais to face Mulai. He laid his hand on Mulai's shoulder. "My heart is filled with grief for Retenu's plight," he said quietly.

"There's more to the message," Mulai murmured, looking embarrassed. "King Ami-enshi asked that you send help if you can—if you would be so generous." Mulai met Amenemhet's gaze. "He's aware that the treaty between Tamera and Retenu says nothing regarding military matters. But my king is desperate."

68

"What are King Ami-enshi's immediate plans?" Nessumontu asked softly.

"We will fight, of course," Mulai replied raising his head a little higher. "My king has called for reinforcements for the army, and the peasants have dropped their plows and gone to the governors of their cities to offer themselves for training. The women are helping collect weapons and making preparations to treat the wounded. Many noble families have urged their daughters to flee, but the girls are refusing to do so." Pride flashed in Mulai's eyes as he added, "The girls had a public meeting in the Place of Appearances before the palace in Yenoam. They pledged to remain in Retenu and share the fate of their families. In case of defeat, they vowed to end their own lives rather than give themselves over to Hyksos soldiers."

"When Queen Nefrytatanen ruled the North Kingdom and there were numerous raids from the Hyksos, many young women of Tamera did the same rather than allow the Hyksos to carry them off," Nessumontu said quietly. "My own sister was one of them."

Mulai glanced at Nessumontu and shook his head slowly. "It's a better fate than to be thrown into Zahi's fire pits as sacrifice to evil gods—and even that is preferable to living in a Hyksos house as a slave," he said sadly.

"Where are Sargon's forces most numerous?" Amenemhet asked.

Mulai turned to look at him. "They're all over," he replied. Anger flashed in his eyes. "They're worst at the pass through the mountains on the way to the royal city."

"Before they reach Yenoam, they must march through many other towns," Amenemhet observed.

"That's true," Mulai agreed," but these towns are small. They have little defense. The only thing in Retenu's favor is the mountains. We can hold them back for a time and reduce their numbers in our mountains. No one knows this part of our country as we do."

"I can give you no answer now," Amenemhet said.

"I know that," Mulai replied. "King Ami-enshi doesn't expect an answer. I've already sent the courier back just to say that I've relayed this message to you." Mulai stepped back a pace. "King Ami-enshi expresses his deepest gratitude for anything you may decide to do and his understanding for whatever you may decide not to do."

Mulai inclined his head, turned, and walked across the throne room toward the doors. Amenemhet watched him go, then looked at Nessumontu.

"Tell Meri to cancel the rest of the day's audience," Amenemhet directed. "Between this and Senwadjet's illness, I can hear no more petitioners."

Nessumontu nodded and followed Mulai, closing the doors behind him.

Amenemhet felt like a prisoner in his own throne room. He stood for a moment gazing at the empty chamber. Then he stepped upon the dais and again sat on his throne.

"Heru, what can I do now?" he said softly.

He looked at the sun slanting through the narrow window openings high above him. He looked at the shadows between the lotus bundle columns. He could think of no solution. He wished his father could sit beside him and give him advice. He longed to speak with someone who had wisdom to share with him.

Amenemhet took off his crown and placed it on

Nefrytatanen's throne, then laid his scepters beside it. He peeled off his ceremonial beard and threw it beside the scepters. Standing, he unfastened the elaborate ties of his long overrobe and slipped out of it, dropping the long robe on the dais. Its weight dragged it over the dais's step to flow smoothly and soundlessly to the floor below. Amenemhet watched it with a disinterested eye, then sank again to his throne to rest his elbows on his knees and his chin in his hands and stare sightlessly at the great empty room. He stilled his heart and listened to the air currents in the room. Once, he had thought they seemed like the whispers of long-dead kings.

"Where are you now?" Amenemhet demanded aloud. He stood up. "I need you!" he cried.

The whispers were incomprehensible to him. There were no benevolent spirits present, wishing to share their wisdom with him. The sounds were only the movements of the air.

"Damn those Hyksos!" Amenemhet said fervently. "Damn Shalmanesser, Sargon, and especially," he added in a low and savage tone, "damn Gobryas." Amenemhet stepped off the dais, kicked his robe aside, and stalked out of the throne room.

As he turned to the corridor leading to his private quarters, he slowed his steps. Nefrytatanen was standing in the hall outside Senwadjet's bedchamber. When Amenemhet reached her, he stopped and regarded her with dread.

"Why are you standing out here, beloved?" Amenemhet asked.

"Ankhneferu came back with me," Nefrytatanen said quietly. "He wished to see Senwadjet, and asked me to wait here." She looked down and added,

"Ankhneferu thought my presence might influence Senwadjet into minimizing his feelings. He also suggested that my will could, without my knowing it, give Senwadjet a temporary strength he may not really possess." She sighed. "If only I *could* give him strength! I would sit at his side day and night pouring it out to him until he was well."

"How long has Ankhneferu been with him?" Amenemhet asked quietly.

Nefrytatanen looked up at Amenemhet. "I cannot say exactly. It has been some time. To me, it seems forever." She smiled faintly. "I've never been patient about waiting."

Amenemhet put his arm around Nefrytatanen's waist. "Perhaps we should walk in the garden while we wait," he suggested.

Nefrytatanen shook her head. "I want to stay," she replied. She looked at Amenemhet intently for a moment, then remarked, "Let Ami-enshi send that viper Zaroya to negotiate with the Hyksos for him. She should confound them sufficiently to send them away."

"How has the news traveled so swiftly?" Amenemhet asked. "My meeting with Mulai was private, with only Nessumontu present."

"Don't be angry with Nessumontu," Nefrytatanen said quickly. "He said nothing to me, though I passed him in the hall." She paused a moment, then whispered, "Forgive me, beloved."

"Why?" Amenemhet was confused.

"I have never allowed myself to explore your inner mind, but your vexation over the problem with Ami-enshi caused your private thoughts to scream out to me. I read them too easily," Nefrytatanen answered.

Amenemhet smiled. "My mind is always open to

you," he said softly. "You may explore it freely." He sighed. "Princess Zaroya would seal Retenu's fate at her first word," he said. "We almost went to battle with Retenu ourselves because of her."

Nefrytatanen managed to summon a smile, but it quickly changed to a look of anxiety. Senwadjet's door opened and Ankhneferu came out. He closed the door carefully behind him. Looking meaningfully at them so they wouldn't speak, he started walking down the hall.

"Where may we discuss this matter?" Ankhneferu finally asked.

Amenemhet paused at the door to the room where he set his seal. "We'll have privacy wherever I demand it," he said firmly. He looked at the guard. "You will not allow anyone to come near this door," he ordered.

The sentry tipped his lance in acknowledgment. Amenemhet led them into the room, closing the door behind them. He walked to the window openings and looked out.

"No one is in the garden except some gardeners far to the other side," he advised, turning to face Ankhneferu and Nefrytatanen. He sat in a chair, and after they had followed his example, he asked, "What have you found, if anything?"

"I've found absolutely nothing wrong with him," Ankhneferu said slowly. "As Horemheb already told you, Senwadjet has no physical ailment. I, myself, can promise you that his mind is healthy and his emotional state unblemished—aside from the strain he's under trying to understand what's happening to him." Ankhneferu paused and looked at the sun coming through the window openings to splash on the floor.

73

"I must say," he remarked, raising his eyes to meet Amenemhet's, "the prince is quite a young man, even for his lack of years." Ankhneferu sighed. "I can promise you that whatever is causing this change in him hasn't affected his inner spirit. He seems listless and dull, but behind those shadowed eyes is a mind ceaselessly trying to put the pieces of this puzzle in order."

"It's a relief to hear you say he yet has his spirit," Amenemhet said, "but it's a thing I would have expected of him."

"You found nothing," Nefrytatanen said softly, as if she were speaking to herself.

"Nothing," Ankhneferu replied. "But that, in itself, can point to the cause of this mysterious illness."

"Which is?" Amenemhet asked quickly.

Ankhneferu looked first at Nefrytatanen, then at Amenemhet. "There's only one malady that has no physical, or emotional source. Forgive me for bringing such news," the priest said sadly. "It wrings my heart to have to tell you this."

"Tell me what?" Amenemhet's voice was heavy with dread.

"Why this has been done to him I cannot imagine," Ankhneferu said slowly. Anger was in his voice. "To do such a thing to an adult is evil enough, but to do it to a child is unbelievably wicked."

"Do what?" Amenemhet shouted, rising from his chair.

"I fear," Ankhneferu said slowly, "that someone has caused a curse to be placed upon the prince."

Amenemhet stared at Ankhneferu speechlessly, then turned to look out the window opening. How could Ra shine on such a day, he wondered. Over his shoulder he whispered, "I cannot believe this. I cannot accept that this would be done to him."

Ankhneferu looked at Nefrytatanen. Although her face had paled, she looked unsurprised.

"I knew it," she said. "I knew it."

"What can be done?" Amenemhet asked in a hoarse voice, not turning to look at them.

"Very little can be done to stop so vicious a thing without knowing what was done to begin it," Ankhneferu replied helplessly.

Abruptly Amenemhet turned to face the high priest. His eyes were filled with fire. "We'll sit and watch Senwadjet, our son, the next king, waste away a little each day until he dies?" Amenemhet's voice was tight with fury. "We will do something more than that!"

"I'll make an amulet," Ankhneferu said quietly. "I'll make one more powerful than I have ever before made and place it on the prince's breast with my own hands. I'll prostrate myself full-length on the floor of the sanctuary and beg every divine being for guidance." He looked down at his lap. "Without knowing how this thing began, I'm helpless to do more."

Nefrytatanen had sat still all through this discussion. Finally, she raised her head and stood. She looked at Amenemhet, her eyes glowing like sapphires, but she said nothing.

"Are you also helpless?" Amenemhet asked.

"I'll do something," she said quietly. "I'll stop this thing somehow." She took Amenemhet's hand in hers, and her skin was like ice. "Senwadjet will not die from this. I'll find a way. I promise." She turned to Ankhneferu. "I don't care how it was done or who did it. However powerful the spell, however effective the one who cast it, I will stop it somehow." She turned again to look into Amenemhet's eyes. "I'll stop it, belovĕd. I promise."

Amenemhet and Nefrytatanen told no one else about the cause of Senwadjet's illness, and during the rest of the day, they didn't even speak of it between themselves. After the evening meal, Nefrytatanen dismissed Yazid and Dedjet for the night. The servants, confused by the queen's unusual order, left hesitantly.

Amenemhet asked no questions. He thought Nefrytatanen planned to do something about Senwadjet that very night. When they went to their chamber, he sat on a couch and silently watched the fading daylight. Nefrytatanen sat on a pillow on the floor at his feet, her cheek resting against his legs.

Together they marked the appearance of one pale star. With the deepening of the skies, others joined it. They grew brighter until the blackness was scattered with points of white fire. The full moon rising above the dark shapes of the trees spread its light over the land, and by the time the moon had risen entirely, the land was washed with translucent silver.

Nefrytatanen rose from her place at Amenemhet's feet, and his eyes followed her movements. She pulled the window hangings down. Putting a silver dish on the floor, she filled it with oil. Earlier she had ordered a new jar of wine brought to their chamber, and now she took it from its place and put it next to the silver dish along with a goblet and several other small containers. Amenemhet broke open the seal on the wine jar, while Nefrytatanen removed her robe and loosened her hair.

When Nefrytatanen was ready, she poured a little of the wine into the goblet and tasted it to be sure it was good wine. Then she lit a fire in the silver dish and tossed powder on the flames. Sparks—the same color as her glowing eyes—rose from the small fire and released the scent of her perfume.

Nefrytatanen called upon Anpu, patron of physicians, to enter the wine and drive out any elements unfavorable to her purpose. She crumbled white frankincense and myrrh into the wine jar and added shavings from a shiny black stone. Then she poured more wine into the goblet and held it near the fire. The flames made deep red lights in the wine as she consecrated the mixture to Anpu and Ra.

Nefrytatanen spoke many words Amenemhet didn't understand. He knew they were words of power, secret words. Finally she chanted, "Great fire, my defender and protector, son of Ra who is the source of all healing fire, equal of Ra who cleanses the earth of foulness, deliver Senwadjet from the foulness that torments him night and day."

The next morning Nefrytatanen brought a cup of the wine to Senwadjet and asked him to drink it. Seeming to know the wine had special significance, Senwadjet swallowed it without comment or question.

The same day, when the sun was at its high point, Ankhneferu made his way through the heat of the streets to the palace and asked to see Senwadjet. Amenemhet and Nefrytatanen met the priest outside Senwadjet's door.

"I have spent the whole morning in the temple," Ankhneferu said wearily, "as I will do until the prince is restored to health."

"You look as if you also spent the night there," Amenemhet observed.

Ankhneferu said nothing. He had been in the sanctuary most of the night, alternately praying and sitting in quiet meditation, fruitlessly waiting for some revelation that might help Senwadjet.

Ankhneferu reached into his robe and drew from its folds an amulet of the Wadjet eye. It was usually worn for health and good fortune, but because it bore the name of the goddess who guarded the royal crown and whom Senwadjet was named for, the amulet was particularly suitable to the prince.

"It was carved from lapis lazuli," Ankhneferu said, "and covered with purest gold. At the solstice it was consecrated before the lights of the Twelve Altars, and this morning I consecrated it to Prince Senwadjet. I know of nothing more powerful that I can give him without knowing the curse."

Once they had entered Senwadjet's room, none of them spoke of the amulet's purpose, for it was possible that if Senwadjet learned he was under an evil spell, his emotions would affect him adversely.

Ankhneferu showed Senwadjet the amulet. He said it was a gift to help Senwadjet fight off his weariness. Senwadjet smiled weakly, expressed his gratitude, then teased the priest about the kind of prayer that went with the gift, saying that priests did nothing unaccompanied by lengthy prayers. Ankhneferu smiled and answered tartly that prayers harmed no one and that lengthy prayers taught the virtue of patience.

Ankhneferu put the chain around Senwadjet's neck and placed the amulet carefully over the boy's heart. Ankhneferu's smile faded. Standing over Senwadjet, Ankhneferu raised his arms and said, "I am sound, and it is sound. I am sound, and it is sound. And Senwadjet, prince of the Two Lands, is sound."

Senwadjet's golden eyes watched Ankhneferu carefully. Though he asked the priest nothing about the amulet or the strange prayers, his thoughts were confirmed. Senwadjet knew there were few ailments Horemheb couldn't heal, and he had already decided either they knew what he was stricken with and were afraid to tell him—it was that dread a thing—or it was an illness whose origin was evil magic. The thought of magic used against him had made Senwadjet shudder at first, but he had slowly accustomed himself to the idea and gave no outward sign of his suspicions to the others.

For the next nine mornings, as prescribed by the laws of the temple, Nefrytatanen brought Senwadjet a cup of the wine. On the last morning she left Senwadjet's room, forcing herself to close the door calmly. Then she raced through the halls, eyes blinded with tears, to the royal bedchamber where she slammed the door shut, threw herself across the bed, and wept violently.

When Amenemhet came in, he put his arms around Nefrytatanen and held her close to him.

"It made no change in him," Nefrytatanen whispered. "Neither Ankhneferu's amulet nor my wine has helped him." She leaned away from Amenemhet and looked at him in despair. "It was not enough—not enough," she murmured.

Amenemhet pulled her close and held her tightly. He stroked her hair, wishing to comfort her, but he could think of nothing to say.

"You! Sand dweller!"

Kheti knew the call was for him, but he continued stroking his horse as if he hadn't heard. His face was expressionless. The lord of Orynx Province, he had been asked by Amenembet to spy on the Hyksos.

Disguised, he was behaving as he knew a sand dweller would.

"You! Desert man!"

The voice was directly behind Kheti, who now spoke softly to his horse in the language of the sand dwellers.

"Have you no ears? Or would you like to have no ears?"

Kheti felt a hand on his shoulder. He turned swiftly, his own fingers curving ominously around the handle of his sword. "Keep your hands from my person, thing who crawls under the rocks by day," Kheti said softly.

The Hyksos understood the threat in Kheti's tone, if not his words, and he stepped back. "Do you speak my language?" asked the Hyksos.

Kheti stared unwaveringly at him with eyes like grey stones and nodded unenthusiastically.

"My master wishes to see your merchandise."

Kheti looked at the sun. It was high, and the time for the noon meal was approaching. "I'm busy," he replied, again turning to his horse.

"My master is Prime Minister Gobryas," the Hyskos said threateningly.

Kheti turned his head and spat, narrowly missing the feet of the Hyksos.

The Hyksos turned crimson. "You came to Zahi to sell your merchandise, did you not?" he said loudly.

In the sand dweller's tongue, Kheti made a highly uncomplimentary remark about the Hyksos' ancestry.

The Hyksos glared at him, not knowing what Kheti had said, but very suspicious. "If you don't come to my lord's house, you won't leave Avaris alive," he said.

Kheti turned slowly to look at the Hyksos. He muttered something unintelligible to the Hyksos, then shouted orders to his group. The rest of his "tribesmen" promptly gathered the little merchandise they had managed to unload, replaced it on the camels and horses, and prepared to follow him.

The house of Gobryas was luxurious by the standards of Zahi, but Kheti shuddered at the colors as he followed the guard through a long corridor to the main hall. Kheti passed a number of slaves in the corridor, and his heart contracted with pity for them. They were people from many lands who had been dragged from caravans and ships—if not their own burning houses—and Kheti could recognize that some of them were from Tamera.

In the main hall, Gobryas sat on a couch facing the doorway. Kheti was reminded of an insect waiting for a fly to enter its trap.

Gobryas was berating a slave girl, who was serving him wine, and as Kheti stopped in front of Gobryas, the girl lifted her bowed head. Kheti looked into a golden, heart-shaped face with the almond eyes of his land. His gaze lingered on her for only a moment. Then he quickly looked at Gobryas. He couldn't endure looking too long into the eyes of a woman of Tamera who was being humiliated. The girl stepped away from Gobryas and stood off to the side.

"What is your name, and what do you have to sell?" Gobryas asked, quietly looking up at Kheti.

"I am Ashad of Almansur," Kheti answered. "I have a whole caravan of goods." Amenemhet had been generous in outfitting his caravan with tempting merchandise from Tamera that was seldom available in Zahi.

"From where does your merchandise come?" Gobryas asked.

"Mostly from Tamera, although some came from Kenset and other lands to the south," Kheti answered, while he thought again of the slave.

"Look not so harshly upon me," Gobryas said. "I'm interested in your merchandise, not your neck."

Kheti allowed his expression to soften somewhat, reminding himself that a sand dweller who was a trader was certainly interested in making a profit.

Gobryas looked at the slave. "Pour Ashad some wine," he directed. He turned to Kheti. "Sit down, Ashad. We will converse awhile."

Kheti sat on a nearby couch, wondering at this invitation. What could Gobryas want to discuss with him? He accepted the goblet the girl offered him, looking again into her dark eyes that were filled with a hatred she did not reveal when she looked at Gobryas. Before she turned from Kheti, her face again became expressionless, and he realized the girl had deliberately revealed her true feelings for Gobryas to him. Kheti wondered if she recognized him from somewhere. A cold stab of fear ran through him, then faded. If she knew Kheti and intended to betray him, she would have done so already.

"You're from Tamera, Ashad?" Gobryas asked. "Look not too much at my Nassurti," he warned. "She's a favorite I won't trade—though she's often a trial to me." Gobryas glanced at the slave girl, and Kheti saw an expression that sickened him. He knew, then, that Gobryas kept this girl for the pleasure he got from tormenting her.

"I was born in Tamera," Kheti answered.

"Are you ever at Ithtawe?" Gobryas inquired.

"From time to time," Kheti replied. His eyes narrowed. "You want some sort of information?" he asked slowly.

"How loyal are you, sand dweller?" Gobryas smiled.

"I'm loyal to those of my tribe," Kheti replied. "But gold interests me very much."

"I have considerable gold," Gobryas said. "The information I seek has a high value and is, therefore, difficult to learn."

"I know many things," Kheti murmured. He sipped his wine. "What I haven't seen with my own eyes, one of my friends may have seen and told me." He was aware of the slave girl's close attention to what they said, and he was very curious about what Gobryas wanted to know. "Is it military movements that concern you?"

"I have my own spies for that," Gobryas hissed. "I wish to learn of a matter in the palace itself. Do you know anything about the inner palace?"

Kheti allowed his face to appear greedy. "There are sand dwellers who work in the palace, and I have a friend or two among them," he replied. "What do you wish to know?"

Gobryas said slowly. "I would pay much for the truth, if you know it. Is the king well?"

Kheti was confused. "My source is close to the king and would see for his own eyes if there were illness," he said quickly. "Amenemhet is very healthy. His vigor is such that he practices with the sword almost daily."

"You're certain of this?" Gobryas looked incredulous.

"Recently he killed a lioness. He did it alone, with a lance," Kheti said noting Gobryas's growing anger. "I think this should attest to his health."

"When was this?" Gobryas demanded.

"Not long ago," Kheti replied. "As I passed through Ithtawe's gates on my way here, I saw the king walking with Commander Nessumontu, inspecting the palace guards. He seemed very fit."

"He was not thin? He was not pale?" Gobryas pressed.

"He seemed to have his normal weight, and his steps were sure and steady. He was deeply bronzed from the sun," Kheti replied. He looked curiously at Gobryas. "If you've heard some rumor that Amenemhet is unwell, the rumor is false," he said firmly. "In the face of your obvious disappointment, I will demonstrate my sympathy by asking no payment for this news."

Gobryas glanced distractedly at Kheti. He said nothing, but abruptly got up and walked to the door. Although Kheti didn't turn his head, he heard Gobryas speak to a guard and the name Manuzah mentioned in a tone portending evil for the man. Kheti decided to try to discover Manuzah's identity.

When Gobryas returned, he threw himself on the couch and said nothing for a time. He looked grim. Finally remembering he wasn't alone, he looked at Kheti. "Does your caravan include slaves?" he asked.

"I don't deal in slaves," Kheti answered.

"You have women in your caravan, though," Gobryas pressed.

"They're our own women," Kheti answered coldly.

Gobryas frowned. "I'm no longer in a mood to look at your merchandise," he said and stood up. But then he thought of the rare articles the caravan had been reported to carry. He didn't like to think of someone else buying something before he had seen the goods. He smiled at Kheti.

"I have room in my courtyard for your animals," he said slowly. "I have space where your people can raise their tents in more comfort and security than outside my walls. I would have you stay as my guests this night. Tomorrow we can trade."

Kheti stared in surprise at Gobryas. This was a great honor in the eyes of the Hyksos and one he couldn't readily refuse. "Is it our women who interest you?" Kheti asked cautiously.

Gobryas's smile faded. "I've asked you about slaves and accepted your answer," he said. "Your women are safe, as is your whole caravan." Gobryas wanted no woman of the desert people. Slaves would be well cared for. They were merchandise meant to bring a profit. But the women of the sand dwellers were hard working and dried out by the sun at too early an age.

Kheti forced himself to smile. He got to his feet. "We accept your invitation," he said. "It's an honor for us."

When Kheti rejoined his group outside, he quietly explained the new plans for the night. He used only the language of the sand dwellers. He instructed the women to keep hidden. He knew any close examination would arouse suspicion because the women of this caravan were the wives and sisters of Tamera's army officers. Although they were darkly tanned, their skin was the texture of flower petals, and their bodies were supple and most pleasant to look upon. Gobryas would know they were not really sand dwellers.

As evening approached, the women, carefully swathed in voluminous burnooses, lit small fires and cooked the meal.

After Kheti had eaten, he rose to inspect the encampment as a good leader of a nomadic tribe would do. He strolled between the tents, thinking over his situation.

Gobryas's house wasn't the place for his purpose. Whatever Gobryas knew about King Shalmanesser's intentions would surely never be spoken anywhere in Kheti's vicinity. Kheti had hoped to carry on a good bargaining session in the marketplace and, in the confusion, listen to the conversations of the nobles and soldiers. He had also hoped this very evening to have some of the women dance and to pass wine freely among those who were drawn by the entertainment, thereby encouraging a drunken Hyksos to speak of matters he would not discuss if he were sober.

Kheti found himself standing before a wall at the edge of the tented area. He leaped up and caught a glimpse of Gobryas's extensive garden. No Hyksos guards seemed to watch Kheti, and he considered the possibility of getting nearer Gobryas's house by way of the garden.

Gobryas clearly had accepted Kheti as a sand dweller. Kheti decided there was no particular reason for Gobryas to suspect otherwise.

"You're supposed to be a spy," Kheti muttered to himself, "so get about your business." He leaped to catch the edge of the wall and pulled himself to the top. For a moment, he lay flat on the surface, scanning the garden for occupants.

Kheti crawled along the top of the wall, sought a place where there were trees to shield him, and dropped soundlessly off the wall.

For a moment he crouched near the ground among the shadows, again cautiously looking over the area. Nothing moved. There was no sound but the slight wind in the trees. He straightened slowly and picked his way carefully between the shrubs, following the line of trees. He reached an open space and stood motionless, testing the air, listening, staring into the shadows for danger. He ran silently across the open space to another patch of trees.

Kheti heard voices coming, and he fell on his face among the ferns, hardly daring to breathe lest the passing guards note the sound. But they paid no attention and walked on, complaining among themselves that Gobryas drank wine until he was drunk while they must remain parched as the desert. In spite of his position, Kheti smiled. If Gobryas were drunk, Kheti's way might be easier. As the guards passed around a corner, Kheti heard one of them say that Gobryas's little slave would have an easier night if he were unconscious from wine. Kheti's smile faded. He wondered if they spoke of the girl he had seen in the main hall. Kheti rose carefully and crept nearer the house.

In the shadows of a large, thick bush growing against the house, Kheti paused to consider which window opened into Gobryas's writing room.

"Are you mad?"

The whisper came from above and behind Kheti, and he whirled around quickly. He looked up at the face of the slave girl, who was leaning out a window opening He didn't know what to say. She had spoken in the words of Tamera's language.

"The garden is filled with guards," she whispered. "He doesn't trust strangers camping in his courtyard and has added more guards than usual." Kheti stared blankly at her, afraid to let her know he understood her words. "Wait," she whispered and turned to look at something in the room, then turned again to Kheti.

"I'll come out," she said. "He won't awaken before tomorrow morning."

Kheti remained motionless, not knowing whether to stay or go. If the girl betrayed him—but the look on her face made him think she wouldn't. He waited.

Nassurti came like a shadow. She wore a dark cloak, its hood pulled over her head, hiding the glimmer of her golden skin. "Come," she whispered, "we must get away from here to speak safely."

"Where do you want to go?" Kheti asked in the Hyskos language.

"Speak not that tongue to me," she hissed. "I hear enough of it and more. Let us converse in the words of Tamera for they are a beauty I seldom know— except in dreams." She looked closely at Kheti's wary face. "I know you aren't a desert man. Your disguise, however, is excellent. You've fooled them all. You cannot fool me because I am what you are." She shook her head. "No, you cannot fool me with those grey eyes, though you know enough about sand dwellers to fool a Hyksos. As well as you speak the desert language, your tongue yet reveals the slightest hint of Tamera's own sweet sound." Her eyes gleamed with pride as she said, "I would never betray you, though I may yet pay for this with my life." She sighed. "Life with Gobryas is not so valuable at that, and its ending would be small penalty."

"If you hate him so much, why don't you do something to make him end your existence?" Kheti couldn't help asking.

"Because nothing I can do would induce him to have me killed. He would punish me, instead," she whispered. "But if I thought I'd spend all the rest of my life with him, I would open my own veins to end it." She looked up at him. "I long to go home, and if I can someday accomplish that, it will be worth what I suffer until then. I have no wish to be buried in Zahi's soil if there is a chance I can see Tamera." She took Kheti's arm and tugged at him. "Come," she urged, "for I have much to tell you."

Kheti followed her along the paths until she stopped where there was a small building, now fallen into ruin. She picked her way among the scattered rocks, then abruptly bent and struggled to move a heavy slab of wood. Kheti came closer.

"It's a door," the girl whispered over her shoulder. She had moved the wood to reveal a dark hole. "Get in," she directed.

Kheti leaped into the darkness and the girl lowered herself in after him. Then he replaced the slab.

"I have a small lamp here," she said, groping past him. In a moment the small chamber was filled with wavering light.

"I can offer only a seat on the floor. This is the lower chamber of an old chapel ruin," she explained. "No one knows of this room but me. They all think this is merely a pile of rocks." Her smile faded. "I had reason my first day in this house to find a place where I could weep unobserved." Her eyes met Kheti's. "My tears make him very happy, and I give him no happiness if I can avoid it."

"Who are you?" Kheti asked.

She took a deep breath. "My name is Nassurti," she answered. "I was born in the north kingdom of Tamera when King Tefibi-Siut ruled."

"He was Queen Nefrytatanen's father," Kheti whispered.

Nassurti smiled wistfully. "I saw her once when she

was a princess. She was barely older than I and I was then a small girl. My family had gone to Noph for a festival—" Nassurti stopped. Her eyes were glazed with tears. "Forgive me," she whispered. "Such small happinesses—memories—are all I have. I was not yet ten years when the Hyksos raided our province. My family was killed, and I was carried off." She looked intently at Kheti. "I had a brother, an older half brother. You remind me of him."

"I have no brothers or sisters," Kheti replied. "I never even knew my father."

"I've often wondered if any of my family is still living," Nassurti said quietly. "To know one of them is alive would be a great comfort to me." She sighed. "No doubt it was my desire to find one of them that led me to hope. But you do look much like him. What was your father's name?"

Kheti looked away. "I don't know," he replied. "He was of a noble family, I think, but he never bothered to marry my mother."

Nassurti's mouth fell open. She recovered herself, then cautiously asked, "Do you know anything about him?"

"No," Kheti replied shortly, "and I don't care to talk about this. My memories are bitter. My mother and I had a hard life when he stopped sending her help. She died sooner than she should have—of overwork and loneliness."

Nassurti grasped Kheti's hand, and her eyes took on a strangely eager look. "During the years I've been a slave, I've begged the One Alone that I might learn if anyone of my blood is yet alive. Perhaps I was heard after all."

"What do you mean?" Kheti asked sharply.

"Some things stay in a child's memory even when he or she grows into an adult. I remember overhearing a conversation between my mother and father, which greatly impressed me," she said quickly. "My father told her he had met a woman who he loved in the south. He had seen this woman often on his journeys to Wast, and the result of their love was a son. He asked my mother's forgiveness because he also loved her. He begged he might acknowledge this son and give the child his name, for he and my mother had only daughters." Nassurti's eyes dropped. "I knew there was love between my parents, and I knew he must also love this woman in Wast from the way he spoke of her. My mother realized it, too. They spoke of it at some length, and she finally agreed that my father should take this woman as a second wife. I was most happy. I would have had a brother, and I would have welcomed his coming."

Nassurti lifted her eyes to Kheti's. "I never saw my half brother or his mother. Before Ra rose the next morning, the Hyksos attacked while all the household was yet sleeping." Her eyes dropped again, and she murmured, "I saw them kill my father. I saw them start after my mother, who plunged a sword in her breast rather than let them take her. I ran, but they caught me. They either killed my other sisters or carried them off somewhere else, for I saw nothing of them again."

She took a deep breath and looked at Kheti. "This brother I described was the half brother I just told you about. Earlier my father had a small figure carved of him, and it was this figure he showed to my mother when he told her of his illegitimate son. The statue looked much as I think you might have looked as a child." She sighed. "This was the resemblance I spoke of. Perhaps my memory of it has faded too much. Perhaps I hope too much. Do you think it's possible?"

"I don't know," Kheti said slowly. He privately thought the chance very slight, but he didn't want to take this hope from her. "I never knew the name of my father," he said slowly, feeling the old bitterness rising. He put it down. "She truly loved him—that I know. I hated him for abandoning us."

"Don't hate him," Nassurti whispered. "He may not have been my father, although I would like to think so—but that your mother loved him should be proof he was a worthy man. Perhaps death prevented him from coming back to her, just as my father never returned to Wast."

Kheti took a deep breath. "I suppose that's possible," he admitted. He considered the idea, then said, "It's strange to look upon a girl who might be my sister and never know for certain whether she is or not."

Nassurti smiled. "That I'm of the Two Lands makes me your sister in a way," she said. Her smile faded. "I have to tell you something of great importance."

"What is it?" Kheti asked, anxious at the look on her face. "My reason for being here is to learn what I can."

"Then you're speaking to the one person who can tell you what you wish," Nassurti said urgently. "I know everything Gobryas plots, for he brags to me about it. He wishes me to suffer at the thought of Zahi conquering Tamera. But before I tell you about military matters, I must mention something else. Gobryas asked about our king for a good reason. Is King Amenemhet healthy, as you said?"

"Yes, he's very healthy," Kheti answered firmly.

Nassurti sighed with relief. "Then the curse failed. Queen Nefrytatanen is stronger in her power than Manuzah."

"What do you mean? Who is Manuzah?" Kheti felt a shiver go down his spine.

"Manuzah is a worker of magic," Nassurti answered. "Some time ago, Gobryas had Adadni steal a pendant from King Amenemhet's room. He even showed it to me. He bragged because it had one of the king's hairs caught in it. I saw the hair. It was long and black. He offered Manuzah much gold to cast a spell on King Amenemhet. They went to a place near Zurim, the ruins of an ancient temple that had been used for worship of Lamashtu, a demon goddess of theirs—" Nassurti stopped talking when she saw the look on Kheti's face. "What is it?" she asked.

"Prince Senwadjet is suffering from a mysterious ailment Horemheb doesn't seem to know how to heal," Kheti said softly.

Nassurti stared at him. "Who is Horemheb?"

"The royal physician," he answered. He put his face in his hands. "It was Senwadjet's hair," he murmured. "Senwadjet often played with Amenemhet's jewelry. The prince yet wears his child's lock, and his hair is long, but the king's hair is the same length as mine."

"The hair on the pendant was much longer than yours," Nassurti whispered. "That must be how the curse was distracted from its intended victim." She was aghast. "The inheritor of the crown instead of the king," she murmured. She looked at Kheti, horrified. "You must return to Ithtawe immediately," she urged. "You must tell the queen what I've said so she may help the prince. I can't tell any more about the spell than what I've already done. I know only that the spell was meant to end in the king's death. No time can be lost, or the prince will die."

"There are other things I must also know," Kheti whispered.

"I will tell you these things quickly, for I must hurry back to the house."

"But what of you?" Kheti asked softly. "You can't stay here. I've seen how he treats you. . . ." His voice trailed off. He couldn't say what he was thinking.

Nassurti's face was growing brighter with rising hope. "Can you take me back?"

"Tomorrow I must trade with Gobryas," Kheti said, thinking quickly. "I will, no doubt, have a cup or two of wine with him."

"Oh, yes. He'll serve wine hoping to dull your brain and secure a better bargain," she agreed.

Kheti reached into the folds of his burnoose. "Here's a packet of powder Horemheb gave me," he said handing it to Nassurti. "He did this in case I needed to have someone sleep soundly and long. Can you put it into Gobryas's wine so he'll get drowsy and end the bargaining? Perhaps while he sleeps, you can slip away and join our caravan. You're so small I could put you in an oil jar on my camel's pack. No one would look for you there, even if they searched the caravan."

Nassurti's eyes shone. "I would more happily put poison in his cup," she said, "but if I can escape, I'll gladly settle for temporary slumber." She tucked the packet in her sandal. "When we reach Ithtawe, I'll be more happy than I can say," she whispered, "but I must ask one favor yet."

"Name it," Kheti said.

"I beg you to let me go my own way," she said

94

imploringly. "As much as I would like to learn if we're related, I don't wish to have it known that I was Gobryas's slave. Will you promise, if we meet again, never to recognize me?"

"But this way of life wasn't your choice!" Kheti declared.

Nassurti dropped her eyes. "Once I've left this place, I wish never to speak of it. I've been forced into much evil, and I want no stories to follow me." She looked up, pleading. "No man of Tamera would look at me if I allowed my past to be known. I would never be able to seek love. And what else, Kheti, would I seek, but love? I have had none of it all these years. I am like a well, emptied of water. I am parched."

Kheti nodded. "I understand," he said. "I promise I won't recognize you."

Nassurti took a deep breath in relief, then told Kheti in great detail all the military plans she had heard. She remembered everything Gobryas had told her, everything she had overheard during his meetings with Commander Sargon. When she finished, Kheti was speechless. He had learned all he needed to know.

"I must go back now," Nassurti whispered. "Tomorrow I'll give Gobryas the powder."

Kheti moved the wooden slab that covered the chamber and climbed up through the opening. Then he helped Nassurti out and moved the wood again into place.

Before Nassurti turned to leave Kheti, she put her hand on his arm and whispered, "I've put my life in your hands, told you everything I know, shared personal matters with you I haven't spoken aloud about in years. And I don't know your real name." She smiled. "You aren't Ashad of Almansur."

Kheti smiled. "My name is Kheti," he said. "Also
Khnumhotep, lord of Ornyx Province, count of Menet
Khufu."

Nassurti's eyes widened, and she squeezed his arm.
"Not only count over a city, but lord of a province
as well." She smiled. "You have risen far. If you are
my half brother, I know our father would have been
very proud of you," she said. She turned away and
ran into the shadows.

Kheti was called to the main hall very late in the
morning. He was alarmed when he saw that another
slave tended Gobryas while he inspected the caravan's goods and made his choices. When the prices
had been decided and the slave poured fresh wine
for them, Kheti could no longer endure the suspense.

"Where is that pretty little slave who served us
yesterday?" he asked casually.

A thundercloud came over Gobryas's face as he
answered, "The little cow was seen sneaking into the
house late last night." He patted the girl who served
him. "Asha told me. I suspect Nassurti met a lover,
though she remained silent despite some persuasion
to answer my questions."

Kheti felt sick, but he could say nothing. He was
helpless to protest, but he was so filled with anger
that it took all his control to hide it. He couldn't even
look at Gobryas for a moment, but stared instead at
his wine. He wished to kill the Hyksos.

"She will be, shall we say, indisposed for a day or
two?" Gobryas hissed.

As he got to his feet, Kheti glanced up at Gobryas,
who looked disgustingly smug. "It seems you can
trust no one," Kheti managed to remark, then put his

goblet down. "I must go now," he said quietly, "for we have goods we can yet sell in the marketplace." Kheti tried to smile, but he couldn't. He remembered Nassurti's dark eyes filled with the hope of going home.

"It has been pleasant doing business with you," Kheti said in the Hyksos tongue. In the language of the sand dwellers, he added a prayer for Gobryas's prompt and painful demise. At Gobryas's confused look, Kheti said in the Hyksos language, "I wished you a happy future." When Gobryas smiled, Kheti could endure it no longer. He turned and walked stiffly out of the house.

Kheti directed the caravan's preparations, but he had only a small part of his mind on the work. He looked into the eyes of each woman among them, and he glanced into every oil jar, hoping Nassurti might yet have found some way to join the group.

But he could not find her.

CHAPTER 5

NEFRYTATANEN QUIETLY OPENED Senwadjet's door. He
seemed to be sleeping. She walked soundlessly to the
bed to look for a moment at his thin face. His eyelashes were black against his white cheeks. They
seemed to be painted lines on a wax figure.

Nefrytatanen couldn't endure for long the sight of
Senwadjet's helplessness, and she turned away to walk
to the window openings and look out at the garden.
So short a time ago had Senwadjet run there with
Maeti, his bronzed body smoothly moving, his eyes
filled with golden lights. Nefrytatanen swallowed, trying not to weep.

No longer did Senwadjet make demands and give
the servants orders. Nefrytatanen wished his eyes
would flash again with the fire of his old temper.

Nefrytatanen turned from the window opening, and
taking a chair to Senwadjet's bedside, she sat and
looked at him, becoming newly angered. Who, she
wondered, could be so evil as to call a curse upon
this boy. Many were those who might think of sending
such a thing to Amenemhet or herself, but why to
the child?

Whenever Nefrytatanen entered this room, she felt
a presence. It was so darkly evil that chills came over
her. Ankhneferu had said he had also felt the pres-

ence. Beside Amenemhet and herself, only the high priest, Horemheb, Yazid and Dedjet entered this room. When Maeti begged to come to her brother, Nefrytatanen refused. She feared for Maeti's safety. Nefrytatanen knew Maeti sent Senwadjet notes and small gifts to cheer him.

Nefrytatanen gazed down at the face of her son, and her anger grew in proportion to her grief. Would this child be taken from them, this young Heru, prince and inheritor of the double crown? Would Ithtawe be enveloped with fire? She shuddered. Perhaps this marked the beginning of the fall of Tamera.

One of Nefrytatanen's tears fell on Senwadjet's face, and his eyes opened. They were no longer the eyes of a child. They held a new wisdom.

"I don't want to die," Senwadjet said softly, "but if I must die from this thing, your tears can't change it. I don't like to see you weep."

Nefrytatanen couldn't speak. As quickly as she wiped away her tears, new ones formed.

"When Ankhneferu came to place the amulet on me," Senwadjet whispered, "it only confirmed my suspicions. I, too, am aware of this evil presence hovering near me."

"I don't like to hear you speak so," Nefrytatanen said angrily. "It's as if you've surrendered. You must fight with all the strength of your will. That is all we can do to keep the evil from winning you."

"I'm fighting it as well as I can," Senwadjet said. He smiled faintly, and Nefrytatanen's heart was torn at the sight. "Mother," he said calmly, "I have thought of what will happen if we can find no way to stop it." Nefrytatanen opened her mouth to protest, but he went on quickly, giving her no chance to speak. "I must think of it, although I wish to live more than anything I've ever wanted. Merely to look at your face, to speak to father when he comes, fills me with renewed spirit so strong I almost ache with it. But if we cannot find a way to stop this thing, I know my will cannot hold it off forever, and I must ask a favor of you."

Nefrytatanen stared at Senwadjet, marveling at his courage. Would this shining spirit be taken from them before he had had a chance to fulfill his destiny? His fate was being altered by the hand of evil, by a person who went against all the forces of good and the intentions of the divine beings.

"I have promised your father I would stop this thing," she said quietly. "I make the same promise to you. Have I ever broken a promise?"

"Never," Senwadjet agreed, "but sometimes promises are beyond your power to keep. And if this is so, I yet must ask my favor."

Nefrytatanen realized his request was of great importance to him. "Tell me what it is, and I'll grant it—though I think the need will not arise."

"If I must meet Asar because of this curse on me, will you—before my spirit leaves this body—cut off my child's lock?" he begged.

"That is so small a thing to ask," she said softly.

"I would meet Asar with dignity," Senwadjet added, "instead of going to him merely as a child." His eyes on Nefrytatanen's face held an echo of their old fire. "Will you do this?"

"Yes," she answered, unable to see him for her tears.

Senwadjet took a deep breath, then added, "After all, I would have been king, mother, wouldn't I?"

"You will be king," she said firmly. "I think one day you'll be as good a king as your father."

Senwadjet smiled faintly and whispered, "I would try."

Dedjet had passed through her day like a traveler rushing to a destination. Her destination was nightfall, when Rahmzi would meet her in the garden. Her emotions were a confused mixture of excitement and apprehension, and she had had no head for her tasks.

During the last few days, Yazid had been exceedingly gentle with her, she had noted, making her way a little easier and even doing some of the tasks himself, particularly those requiring physical exertion. Yazid had asked no question and made no comment, but Dedjet knew he had guessed her secret.

Rahmzi hadn't yet arrived in the shadowy pavilion, and she sat on a bench near the pavilion where she could watch for him. Surely Rahmzi's happiness would equal her own, she reassured herself. But she couldn't drive away the shadow lingering in her heart. He might not welcome the news. Dedjet sighed. Whether Rahmzi smiled or frowned, the situation couldn't be changed now.

Dedjet's head came up. Rahmzi was coming down the path. As she watched him walk, she felt even more acutely the longing that he be as happy as she was. Surely he would be pleased. He was not a man to flutter like a bee from flower to flower. He was like the birds that sang at her window in the morning, who found mates and built nests and stayed together all their lives.

When Rahmzi approached the pavilion and looked

up to see Dedjet waiting, he smiled warmly. His smile made Dedjet feel more secure.

"I'm sorry I made you wait," Rahmzi said quietly as he kissed Dedjet. "Nessumontu wished to consult with me, and I found it difficult to escape." His smile faded, and his dark eyes took on a distracted look. He sighed. "With the preparations for war, I find I have little opportunity to relax, after all. I might as well have delayed taking my free time until this was over. I'm sure it's more peaceful at my garrison."

"Had you delayed, you might have decided to go somewhere else," Dedjet said slowly, her apprehension rising suddenly. "We might never have met."

Rahmzi held her closer. "I'm sure the paths of our lives would have joined," he whispered into her hair.

Reassured by Rahmzi's words and by his arms warmly enclosing her, Dedjet resolved to tell him immediately. "Rahmzi—" she began.

As if he hadn't heard her, he stepped away, saying, "I don't know how Nessumontu can expect his new recruits to be trained in the short time he has scheduled for this. The men are farmers, weavers, quarry workers, shepherds. Although they're fired with enthusiasm, some have never even held a sword before!"

Dedjet took a deep breath. "Nessumontu always seems to accomplish things no one else thinks he can," she said patiently.

"A sword can be placed in a man's hand, but if he's unfamiliar with its weight, it takes time to strengthen his muscles so he can wield it with control," Rahmzi said shaking his head. "And to teach a man to be an archer requires lengthy practice." He looked at Dedjet. "An effective army consists of men who are so used to taking orders they obey without question or thought. That kind of discipline takes time to build."

"If there's anything Nessumontu can inspire, it is obedience," Dedjet soothed, anxious to get to her own news.

"A good fighting man must be used to fighting. He must react through an impulse instilled in his mind by repeated practice." Rahmzi sighed. "His life depends on this reaction."

"If my life depended on my reacting when someone came rushing at me with a weapon, I'd react immediately—without training," Dedjet declared.

She frowned. Her patience was diminishing. She opened her mouth to speak, but Rahmzi had turned away, pacing as he worried.

"Controlling a chariot during a charge with arrows flying around you is considerably different from driving a cart filled with produce on your way to the market," he muttered. "A good war chariot is so light in weight it will move if you lean against it, and a high-spirited horse trained for battle is a far different creature from a docile farm horse—"

"Enough of this talk of horses, chariots, and war!" Dedjet exclaimed.

Rahmzi turned quickly, surprised at her tone. Dedjet stood with her hands on her hips, determination in every line of her body. He smiled faintly. "I'm sorry," he apologized. "My head is so full of schedules and plans I've forgotten myself."

Dedjet softened a little, letting her hands drop to her sides. She looked at her feet, feeling shy once again.

"What is it?" Rahmzi asked, becoming apprehensive.

Dedjet lifted her head and came closer, holding out her hands. Rahmzi took her hands in his, and she looked up into his eyes. "It isn't that your troubles don't concern me," she said softly. "I like you to tell me everything you do. It makes me doubly proud of your ability."

Rahmzi smiled faintly. "But you're right," he admitted. "Enough is enough. Let us go from this place and speak of other things." He began to turn as if to lead her out of the pavilion.

Dedjet didn't move. "I would discuss something here," she said firmly. "This is the place our love began."

Rahmzi looked curiously at Dedjet. "If you wish," he said quietly. He followed her to the bench, then sat beside her, still holding her hand. "What is it you want to discuss, Dedjet?"

Looking into his eyes, Dedjet knew his mind was yet half occupied with Nessumontu's schedules, but she took a deep breath and said quietly, "It has been some months since our first meeting here." She stopped, not knowing how to tell him.

"These months have been most happy for me," Rahmzi murmured.

"I look not for polite comments," Dedjet said a little sharply. "What I have to tell you is most serious." She frowned. "Have you not noticed that I've gained some weight?" she asked.

Rahmzi shrugged. "Be at ease. You're more beautiful than ever."

"That is not my concern!" Dedjet exclaimed. She looked down at her lap. "I don't know what words to use," she murmured. "I think I'm not very good with words." She looked up at him and took a deep

104

breath. "I must tell you plainly. I'm going to have a child," she said.

Rahmzi stared at her. "My child?" he blurted.

"Do you think I go from one man to another?" Dedjet exclaimed. "The child is certainly yours!"

Rahmzi's dark eyes slid slowly over her body, taking note of the increased curve of her breasts, the rounding of her abdomen. She saw the look in his eyes when they had finished their examination, and she felt a chill run through her.

"Do you believe me?" Her voice was low.

"I believe you," he replied and said no more.

Dedjet's eyes looked at Rahmzi without wavering, but they were black with the shadows they had gathered from her fear. "You say nothing," she whispered. "Did you never consider the possibility that our love would bear fruit?"

Rahmzi shook his head slowly. "It has never happened before," he said quietly, "and I had ceased to think of it, concluding I was unable to give any woman a child."

"Did you love those others?" Dedjet asked.

Again Rahmzi shook his head. "I realize now I didn't, though I'd thought so then."

"Perhaps that was the difference," she murmured looking down at herself. "I think the child doesn't please you." She waited for his denial, but he was silent. She sighed. "Still, it pleases me." Her eyes lifted to his, and she saw that confusion dwelt in them. Her gaze remained fixed on him. "You had no thought of ever standing before a priest with me," she whispered. "It was a lie."

"No!" Rahmzi said loudly. "I never lied to you."

"The truth is invincible and may be spoken softly,"

Dedjet said, her lips trembling. "Lies are fragile and must be announced in a larger voice."

Rahmzi stared at her. "I do not lie," he said more quietly. "It's that this news astonishes me."

Dedjet longed to go to Rahmzi and be taken to his breast, encircled with his arms. She dared not. If she did at this moment, she was certain he would push her away. Rahmzi was afraid to follow his heart.

"I had hoped," she whispered, "you had the same courage in love you possess in battle."

Rahmzi came one step toward Dedjet, still looking steadily at her, but too uncertain of his feelings to take another step.

"You are ready to promise nothing." She felt bitterness rising in her. "My disappointment is apparent in my face." Her hand touched her abdomen. "Perhaps you are not deserving of this son I carry. I will consider this matter, while you reflect upon your own decision."

Holding her head stiffly high, Dedjet walked past Rahmzi in a drift of perfume, her robe whispering with her steps. She took care not to touch or even brush him as she passed. She walked slowly and with dignity out of the pavilion and down the path. As she passed the lotus pool's fountain, the drifting veil of its spray mingled with her silent tears.

By the time Dedjet reached the palace doors, she could no longer contain the fire of her emotions. She tore open the door with such force that Rahmzi could see it from the pavilion. He hung his head in shame.

Rahmzi knew he loved Dedjet. This child awed him. He stood for some time in the pavilion, thinking. He wished he possessed the courage to follow her and beg forgiveness. He didn't understand his hesitancy. It was as if a door had closed in his mind. He left the pavilion, baffled by his feelings.

Dedjet walked swiftly through the palace corridor, tears streaming down her face.

"What's wrong, Dedjet?" Nessumontu met her and, putting his hands on her shoulders, stopped her.

"I cannot speak of it," she whispered.

"Are you ill?" he asked in concern. He'd never seen her weep. She shook her head, still unable to speak. He stepped back a little and looked at her closely. Noting the roundness of her body, his eyes widened. "Is there something I can do about this matter? Who is it that has done this?" he asked softly, though he was sure he knew.

Dedjet looked up at Nessumontu. "There's nothing I wish you to do," she whispered. "It is he who began this who must decide what will be done." Tears again filled her eyes, and she looked down. "Release me and let me go my way," she whispered.

"You really love him," Nessumontu murmured, letting his hands drop.

"Not for as long as I can remember have I been so miserable," Dedjet said. Then she turned and walked quickly away.

Eyes narrowed, Nessumontu watched her go wondering if he should speak to Rahmzi about this matter. He was amazed. Rahmzi had never seemed the kind of man who could deny his own child. Nessumontu considered this. Perhaps Rahmzi hadn't. It may be they had merely had an argument, a misunderstanding. Nessumontu decided to say nothing unless Rahmzi spoke of it first.

Amenemhet lay on his stomach across the bed, eyes closed, smiling contentedly. Nefrytatanen knelt beside him, vigorously rubbing his back. After several minutes she stopped rubbing and straightened, preparing to end the session.

"Are you quitting already?" he mumbled. "It has been a long and tiring day, and I need considerable rubbing to relax me," he added.

She took a deep breath and bent to resume her work. "I've had a less than peaceful day myself," she muttered. "I could also use some relaxing." She rubbed his head rapidly, turning his hair into a frenzy of whorls.

"You're pulling all my hair out," he said, opening his eyes. "At this point I know I'll get no more gentle treatment." He turned over to look up at her. "Lie down, beloved," he invited. "I'll take my turn."

Nefrytatanen needed no further urging and did as Amenemhet suggested. She closed her eyes while his gentle hands smoothed the stiffness of her shoulders. She felt her muscles softening, lengthening, growing limp.

"Beloved?" Amenemhet's voice seemed to come from a distant place. "Beloved?" he called again. Nefrytatanen opened her eyes with a start.

"You fell asleep," Amenemhet whispered, leaning closer. He smiled. "I don't think you need massaging any more."

Nefrytatanen turned over on her back and looked up at him. "See how good you are?" she said smiling.

"Or how tired you are." His smile faded.

"It isn't a weariness of the body," she said, "but a weariness of my mind."

"You worry about Senwadjet." Amenemhet lay beside Nefrytatanen and stared at the ceiling. "I also worry," he said.

108

"I think and I think," she whispered, "but I don't know what I can do."

Amenemhet turned his head to look at Nefrytatanen and saw that she wept. He pulled her gently until her head rested on his shoulder. He held her close, saying nothing more for a time, feeling the moisture of her tears on his skin. Finally he whispered, "We have seen many moments of helplessness, but we've come through them. You were lost to me and returned. I was poisoned and survived. We'll find an answer to Senwadjet's sickness. I cannot believe he'll die."

"He can believe it," Nefrytatanen whispered. "He asked that we cut his hair—" She paused to swallow and continued brokenly, "He wishes to meet Asar with dignity—that was his word—not as a child. He said he would have been king—" She pressed her face against Amenemhet's chest, unable to say more.

When she finally looked up at him, she saw that his face was grim, and, although his eyes were closed, a tear clung to his eyelashes.

"He asked that?" Amenemhet whispered. He was silent a moment, then added, "I cannot say I'm surprised. Though he has many boyish ways, he is not really childlike in most respects. What was your answer?"

"I promised we would do it, if needed, but said it wouldn't be needed. I again promised to find a way to help him."

"What did he say?" he asked softly.

"He reminded me that promises are sometimes beyond keeping," she murmured.

Amenemhet's arm tightened around Nefrytatanen's shoulders. "That's sometimes true," he admitted, "but

I think there will be a way. I cannot endure thinking anything else."

A light tapping sounded on the door. Amenemhet sighed and drew a cover over them. With a corner of it, he wiped the tear streaks from Nefrytatanen's face.

"What is it?" Amenemhet called.

The door opened, and Yazid entered the room. "Lord Kheti has returned," he announced. Noting their expressions, he added, "Shall I tell him to wait his report until morning?"

Amenemhet looked at Nefrytatanen and read the message in her eyes. It would be a long time before either of them would be able to sleep. Turning to glance at Yazid, he answered, "We'll dress and see him shortly."

When Amenemhet and Nefrytatanen came down the stairs, they found Kheti waiting, still wearing his burnoose. He turned to face them.

Amenemhet commented, "That little beard and mustache doesn't look bad on you."

Kheti grinned and slipped off the hood of his burnoose. "Perhaps so," he said, running his fingers through his hair, "but I wouldn't want to keep it. The sand blowing in my face clings to the hairs and makes my skin itch."

The outer door opened, and Nessumontu came in with Rahmzi following him. Nessumontu's face was carefully expressionless, but Rahmzi seemed disturbed.

"I thought Rahmzi should hear Kheti's report," Nessumontu explained.

Amenemhet nodded in agreement. "It can be retold one less time, then." He turned. "Let us go into the room by the garden and sit down. Whatever you have to tell us can be related in comfort."

He looked at Yazid, who had followed them. "The night air is chill," he said, "and I think Kheti should have some tea to warm him."

"I would warm faster with a cup of beer," Kheti commented.

Amenemhet smiled faintly and directed, "Bring us beer, then."

"I would have tea," Nefrytatanen said.

When the group was comfortably settled with their cups, Kheti recounted the military information Nassurti had given him. As he spoke, Nessumontu's face was expressionless, though his slanted eyes glittered ominously. Rahmzi's forehead contracted in a frown.

Amenemhet stood up and began to pace the room. "So the Hyksos intend to take Retenu and place themselves more advantageously to later invade Tamera," he finally said in an angry tone. "Although it is as I anticipated, it disturbs me no less."

"It's what Gobryas bragged to the slave girl," Kheti replied. "He's now their prime minister and should know Shalmanesser's plans." He took a sip from his cup and sighed. "Gobryas is insufferable," he remarked. "He was born under the sign of Ra and he thinks the same radiance emanates from him."

"He would more suitably have been born under the sign of the Sabau, if there were such a sign!" Nefrytatanen declared. "You couldn't rescue the girl who told you this?"

Kheti frowned. "I could do nothing," he answered grimly.

"I wish I could have met her," Nefrytatanen remarked. "She has great courage."

"She wouldn't want to meet you," Kheti answered. "She was ashamed. She asked I leave her on Ithtawe's streets, never speak to her, and never mention her name. She wanted all she had suffered to remain behind her. She wanted no stories to follow her and, perhaps, ruin her future."

"No tales would be told of her if she served me," Nefrytatanen said firmly.

"I saved the best news until last," Kheti said, smiling. They looked up at him curiously. He took another sip of beer and put down the empty cup. "I don't know how much help it will be, but I think I have a clue to Senwadjet's mysterious sickness."

Amenemhet and Nefrytatanen stared at Kheti, frozen.

Kheti looked at Amenemhet and said, "Gobryas very pointedly asked me about your health and was very upset when I told him you were well. Later, the girl told me Gobryas had somehow obtained a pendant of yours—a gold one with a hawk on a sun disk."

Nefrytatanen turned pale. "That was the one Senwadjet wore until it disappeared one day."

"Now you know where it went," Kheti said quietly. "The girl said Gobryas got a worker in magic—whose failure has probably brought him death—and went to a place near Zurim. The place is the ruin of an ancient temple dedicated to their demon goddess Lamashtu, a place where human sacrifices were once made. She didn't know exactly what was done, but she was sure it was intended to bring you sickness and eventual death."

Amenemhet sat down. "Instead of me, Senwadjet wastes away," he said softly, "because he wore my pendant."

"I would go to that place," Nefrytatanen said angrily. "I would start right away."

"No," Amenemhet said. "You'll go with us when we march toward Zurim with the royal army."

"You'll attack Zurim?" Nessumontu asked. He had often urged Amenemhet to lauch an invasion on Zahi, but Amenemhet had never wanted to cross another's borders.

"No," Amenemhet replied. "We will go to the old temple to heal Senwadjet. Our presence should pose a threat that will force Sargon's forces in Retenu to return to Zahi and protect Zurim."

"They'll only come after us another day," Nessumontu said, disappointed.

"In my visions, I saw a city in flames," Nefrytatanen reminded. "I don't know what city it was, but I know there will be a battle."

"That may well be," Amenemhet conceded, "but I don't intend to start it. The army will accompany us on a mission of peace. If we're attacked, then we must defend ourselves, of course." Amenemhet cast a knowing look at Nessumontu. "I think it's very possible this will happen."

"Then we'll fight," Nessumontu said. "Only it won't be written that we invaded Zahi as conquerors."

Amenemhet got to his feet, and the others did also. "You will prepare to leave Ithtawe as soon as possible," he directed. "Tell me tomorrow when we'll be ready to march."

Nessumontu turned toward the door. "It won't take long to get ready," he said.

"Senwadjet's condition won't allow much time," Amenemhet said grimly. His tilted eyes glowed with fire. He had every intention of making the Hyskos pay for Senwadjet's pain.

Senwadjet lay awake wondering if he would ever again sleep through a night without Horemheb's mixtures. He longed for the warm peace of sliding easily into normal sleep like a traveler on the desert longs for cold water.

Senwadjet's attention was drawn to the sound of voices downstairs. At night when the palace was quiet, noises seemed to carry through the stone-paneled halls for impossible distances.

A soft sound came from the window opening, and Senwadjet turned his head. The window hanging rustled, and a shadow crept into his room.

"Are you awake?" came a whisper. The shadow glided to Senwadjet's bedside. "Greetings, my brother," Maeti said softly.

Senwadjet smiled. "Greetings, my sister," he answered in their special affectionate way. "Should you be here?" he asked.

"We have been too long without speaking, and I think I should be here," she whispered. She bent and kissed his forehead, then gently hugged his shoulders, trying to ignore his thinness. When she drew away, she glanced around the shadowy room in defiance. "Whatever is here," she said firmly, "will not harm me."

She turned to Senwadjet, her eyes glowing in the darkness. Maeti managed to smile at him. "I knew I'd never coax my way past the sentry at your door, and if I went down the terrace steps, I was sure to be seen. So I climbed down the tree by my bedroom and climbed up the tree by yours."

Senwadjet's smile widened. "Dedjet wouldn't approve. She would say princesses don't climb trees."

Maeti's smile grew warmer. "Princesses do what they must in an emergency," she said. "Who else would tell you what happens in the palace? No one would bring you the news I do." She took his hand in hers. "If mother and father weren't so occupied with Kheti at this moment, I wouldn't have been able to come."

"What of Dedjet and Yazid? What about Senet?" Senwadjet asked.

Maeti made a face. "You know Senet sleeps like one made of stone. Yazid is downstairs listening to the news. When he tells Dedjet about it, I'll make sure I hear. Then I'll tell you. Dedjet won't come out of her room if she can avoid it. Her eyes are red from weeping."

"Why?" Senwadjet asked in surprise.

"She's going to have a child," Maeti replied. She sat on the edge of the bed, noting, with satisfaction, Senwadjet's widened eyes. "You see? I told you I had news no one else would bring you. It is said Captain Rahmzi is the father, which I believe. Dedjet was seeing no one else, I'm sure. No one knows why she was crying, but they think it's because she wants to stand before a priest, and Captain Rahmzi won't. I disagree with this. His eyes don't contain such a soul as that."

The door rattled, and Maeti leaped off the bed. But before she could hide, Amenemhet and Nefrytatanen opened the door and saw her. They stared at her in surprise for a moment. Instead of scolding her, however, Nefrytatanen said, "Sit on the bed, Maeti. We have good news to share with you both."

115

Maeti sat down wonderingly, and Nefrytatanen followed Amenemhet into the room. Amenemhet remained standing beside the bed, and Nefrytatanen sat next to Maeti. Senwadjet noticed they were smiling widely, and he wondered at this. He had seen few smiles these last weeks.

"Kheti has just returned with the military information I need," Amenemhet said, "but he also learned that the Hyksos prime minister, Gobryas, paid a worker in magic to put a curse on me using that pendant I gave you, Senwadjet. They thought it was mine. You suffered the curse instead of me."

Maeti's eyes narrowed with anger. "What will we do?" she asked in a sharp tone.

"The army is being prepared to escort us to the place where it was done," Amenemhet answered, noting the blue glow of her eyes. "When your mother sees what was done, she'll perform her magic against it."

"What if they left nothing to see?" Maeti demanded. "What will we do then?"

"I think they chose the abandoned temple ruin as the place to cast the curse because they wanted what they left there to be unseen and untouched," Nefrytatanen replied.

Senwadjet had been absorbing this news with rising joy, but he was curious to know more. "How can such a thing be done?" he asked eagerly. "I don't understand this."

Amenemhet turned to Nefrytatanen. "If you can explain it to those of us who know nothing of magic, please do. I would also like to know."

"I'll try," she said. She considered this a moment, then began. "You've been taught that our souls hold the capacity for both good and evil. We call he who personifies the goodness in man Asar, and we name the evil part Sutekh. When magic is used for good, it's the force of goodness within the magic worker that is sent forth. When it's used for wicked means, the magic worker releases the evil in his own spirit."

Maeti stared at Nefrytatanen. "I cannot believe you have a demon in you. You've never done evil magic."

Amenemhet looked at Nefrytatanen and smiled faintly. "Your mother has sometimes been strongly tempted," he said.

"Yes," Nefrytatanen sighed. "I surely have—which proves the truth of what I say. One must choose which path to follow. What I do, I think most carefully about before doing it." She looked at Amenemhet. "Sometimes I've needed your father's help to choose the right path."

She paused to reflect a moment, then continued, "You've heard of a certain game young men and women sometimes play to amuse themselves by frightening themselves? Sometimes it becomes more than a game. They darken a room and stand before a mirror holding one lamp to see by. If they stay there long enough, sometimes they see what they think is a demon behind their left shoulder. It isn't a thing apart from them. It's their own evil nature they see."

Maeti shivered. "I would not wish to see it," she said.

"I've never been inclined to look," Nefrytatanen admitted. "To know it's there is enough." She took a breath and went on, "The choice is truly ours. Magic only sets free what we are. Gobryas and his magic worker released their own evil thoughts. In Zahi, they

often beg the help of a demon they call Lamashtu.
They don't know the force is their own."

Senwadjet stared at Nefrytatanen. "Then what can
you do to stop what is theirs?" he asked.

"I will take apart the material thing they made," she
replied. "Then I'll unleash my own forces to drive
theirs away."

"How do you know your spirit is stronger?" Amenemhet asked. He had no doubt about this, but he
wanted to know more.

"It is as Ankhneferu taught me," Nefrytatanen answered. "Evil is darkness in the spirit. Goodness is
illumination. When Ra rises in the East, does not the
night withdraw? That's what the priests really celebrate at dawn—the symbolic driving back of evil. If
the good force is resolute, the evil must depart, just as
the shadows of the night flee from the morning sun."

"That's why you have not yet begun to teach me,"
Maeti said softly. "I have not yet learned to control
my own demon."

Nefrytatanen smiled. "You're learning," she said.
"While your demon is yet a small one, even a small
demon is powerful."

"Will you teach me magic, too?" Senwadjet asked.

Nefrytatanen shook her head. "We'll teach you how
to control yourself and choose the right path, but your
father will teach you to be king. That's job enough
for one person. You have noticed that, although I'm
queen, it's your father who rules? Both tasks would
be too much for me. I have given him the scepter
gladly." Her eyes met Amenemhet's gaze a moment
before she again turned to Senwadjet. "Maeti will
learn what I know," she said. "One day Maeti will
help you with her powers when you have need of

them. You will hold the scepter of Heru. Maeti will hold the scepter of Aset." Nefrytatanen stood up. "We must rest ourselves as much as possible for the journey," she said. "It will be rigorous."

Amenemhet took her hand. "Perhaps you'll be able to sleep tonight," he said to Senwadjet. He smiled. "I think you can relieve some of your worry knowing this evil is but a shadow that has fallen on you—and that you are a being of light."

Senwadjet looked at Amenemhet and Nefrytatanen with some of his old fire. "I will also be strengthened by knowing it's your spirits that will conquer my darkness," he said.

CHAPTER 6

SUNLIGHT POURED GENEROUSLY into the palace courtyard, making golden fire dance on the standards bearing the banners of the royal regiments. The flags of
each province fluttered brightly on the north wind,
their gay colors more appropriate to a celebration than
a march.

The officers, wearing scarlet uniforms, rapidly super-
vised the formation of their companies. Most of the
foot soldiers were already in neat lines, and they had
sat down in the dust, resting their legs while they
could. Though many men would ride horses or chariots, the slingers, archers, axmen, and spear throwers
walked.

Officers who had proven themselves outstanding in
previous combat wore scarlet feathers attached to
their headpieces. These symbols of their courage
fluttered brightly in the breeze.

Nessumontu turned from inspecting the bridle of his
horse to observe Djanah on the palace steps accepting a gold box from Nefrytatanen. Watching from his
distance, he wondered how Djanah could look into
the eyes of her queen and take her gift without feeling shame. He watched Djanah bow. Dismissed, she
turned to make her way through the crowd to the
gates.

When Djanah saw Nessumontu, she paused and looked at him, waiting for some sign. Nessumontu raised a hand in greeting but didn't smile. His narrowed eyes moved past Djanah. Djanah walked on, head drooping, the golden box less precious to her now.

Nearby, Dedjet picked her way through the throng carrying a large basket. She approached Nessumontu and, seeing his expression, paused. "Don't be so angry with yourself," she whispered. "Everyone can be foolish in such matters."

Nessumontu looked at Dedjet. "When a man is young and inexperienced, he may be called foolish and be excused," he said bitterly. "When a man is more than three tens of years, he is no longer foolish. He is a fool."

Dedjet squeezed Nessumontu's shoulder in sympathy. "Look at me," she said softly. "I cannot serve my lady on this journey for my condition, and I am so foolish I wonder if this child I carry will ever know his father, much less his inheritance."

Nessumontu's eyes softened. He wished he could reassure her, but Rahmzi had said nothing to him, and Nessumontu didn't know what he could tell her. Understanding his embarrassment, Dedjet gave his shoulder one more squeeze and turned to go to Nefrytatanen.

In the shadow of the palace, Nefrytatanen watched Senwadjet and Maeti. They were talking quietly, their faces solemn, and she wished again that Maeti could accompany them.

As if Maeti had read Nefrytatanen's thoughts, she turned from Senwadjet's litter and went to Amenemhet. Nefrytatanen knew from Maeti's face what she would say.

"Father, I want to go with you more than anything I've ever wanted," Maeti said looking up at Amenemhet.

Amenemhet sat on his heels to face her. "You cannot," he replied patiently. "I've explained this several times to you."

Maeti's eyes filled with tears. "Oh, father, if there's a battle and you and mother and Senwadjet die, what will I do with this crown? I know nothing of ruling the land. I would be too stricken with grief to learn."

Amenemhet put his arms around Maeti and drew her close. "You would learn," he whispered. "Meri, Ankhneferu, and others would help you." He put her a little away from him and looked into her eyes. "Maeti," he said quietly, "this is part of the meaning of our place. Being rulers gives us much more than comfort and power. It gives us more responsibility than other people have. You are the daughter of a long line of kings and queens and should know that, though many of them were saddened by personal matters, they continued to rule the land. Responsibility must come first in the heart of a queen."

"I think I have not the strength," Maeti murmured, looking away from him, "though others lend me their wisdom."

Amenemhet very gently pinched her cheek and smiled. "That sounds like the influence of your demon," he teased.

Nefrytatanen had come nearer. Hoping to distract Maeti, she observed, "I've been looking at our soldiers and admiring their courage." Nefrytatanen's eyes warned Maeti to beg Amenemhet no more. She knew it was painful for him to refuse.

Amenemhet stood up. His golden eyes moved to a nearby squad of archers. "It's the sharpness of their eyes, the quickness of their feet, and their excellence of skill that make our soldiers effective. They've been trained to advance and fight—not to hide under armor or flee."

"It isn't merely training and equipment," Nessumontu said as he approached them. "It's their love for the Two Lands and their loyalty to their rulers." His slanted eyes gleamed amber in the sun. "The men are ready," he added.

"Those on foot will go first," Amenemhet directed, "for they'll raise little dust and their spirits will be higher if they don't have to breathe dust all the way to Zahi. We'll follow, and those with animals will come last."

Maeti, knowing the moment had arrived, embraced Nefrytatanen, then went to Amenemhet.

When Amenemhet clasped Maeti, he murmured, "You would be a good queen."

Maeti looked into his eyes without faltering and asked no more questions. Instead, she whispered, "I will beg Montu and Sekhmet to bring you victory and Wadjet to protect you." Then she turned to hurry and say goodbye to Senwadjet.

A phalanx of archers marched past, then the lines of spear throwers. Watching them, Nefrytatanen wondered about each one. Is this one with round, dark eyes a career soldier? Those eyes are so gentle, like a deer's. Is that one with the broad shoulders a farmer? Perhaps he has a son who has known playful rides on those shoulders. That one with the long, tapering fingers might be a weaver. I wonder if even those who are professional soldiers are soldiers in their secret hearts. They march toward possible death. Surely many of these men will not pass our gates again. Many will return with missing limbs, their white tunics stained with blood. And many will be carried home in their shrouds.

Nefrytatanen looked past the marching men, above Ithtawe's walls to the golden mountains in the south. She whispered, "Anpu, spare as many as you can. Those who must fly to Tuat, make their journey easy. Oh, Asar, why must we always fight?" She felt Amenemhet's hand on her arm, and she turned to look into eyes streaked with sun fire.

"We fight," he said softly, "to survive."

"And will we?" she whispered.

Amenemhet drew his reins to one side. "We will," he said firmly. His knees urged the horse forward.

Maeti's sapphire eyes followed Amenemhet and Nefrytatanen. As they approached the outside gates, Maeti could see the people alongside the road kneel in homage to their king and queen. Her heart swelled with pride.

"You'd think they'd ride in a covered litter and avoid the sun and dust like other kings and queens," Dedjet said beside her.

Maeti looked at Amenemhet and Nefrytatanen's straight backs and high heads as they raised their hands in greeting to their people. "In many ways they are unlike other kings and queens," she said softly. The horses paced through the gates, and Maeti lifted her hand and whispered, "If it becomes necessary, father, I promise to summon the strength somehow."

Dedjet sighed. "They'll return," she assured Maeti. "I think they're invincible—like divine beings."

Maeti smiled. "They are mortals," she said watching Amenemhet and Nefrytatanen disappear beyond the gates. "They only behave like gods."

The news of the royal army's coming spread quickly through the land. As they marched through Tamera, crowds of peasants gathered on the roadside to watch their king and queen pass. Amenemhet knew that among them were spies from Zahi. When they approached Tamera's northeast border, tension descended upon them all.

At last, they arrived at the ruins, near Zurim. After the evening meal, while Nefrytatanen was preparing herself and Senwadjet to go to the ruins, Captain Rahmzi sought out Nessumontu.

"I've been thinking over a personal matter," Rahmzi said, facing Nessumontu, "and I have made my decision." He stopped talking as a soldier approached and waited for him to pass.

"I've wanted to speak to you about this decision, but I didn't want to bring the matter up first," Nessumontu said softly.

Rahmzi's dark eyes lifted to meet Nessumontu's. "It wasn't really a decision," Rahmzi said quietly. "It was a gathering of courage I required." He smiled wryly. "Getting used to the idea of love is enough shock for a man who has been free so long, but to also have to accustom oneself to a child at the same time is doubly difficult."

"I won't ask your decision," Nessumontu said. "If you would please me, you'll tell the lady concerned."

Rahmzi held out a small roll of papyrus. "I've done

that in writing," he said. "I haven't sealed it, and you may read it if you wish." His eyes traveled to the west where there was now only a faint light in the sky to mark the sun's setting. "You have assigned me to accompany the queen, and I don't know what will happen in that ruin," he said, not looking at Nessumontu. "I've never dealt with demons before. I've also considered the possibility of my death in case of a battle." He turned to Nessumontu. "I want you, then, to deliver this message to Dedjet."

"How do you know I won't fall in battle myself?" Nessumontu asked.

"You'll never fall in battle," Rahmzi said quietly, "but if you truly fear that, give my message to Ineni to assure its safety."

"I don't like to hear you speak of dying," Nessumontu murmured.

"I don't like to think of it. You know I have never liked to think of it," Rahmzi replied. "Because of Dedjet, life seems even sweeter than it ever did. But I must think of her and the child's future. I must be sure they're taken care of."

"Why don't you keep the scroll and let its contents further inspire you to survive?" Nessumontu suggested.

"I don't need inspiration," Rahmzi said quietly. He was silent a moment, then added, "It's not that I've had a premonition. I just want to be certain Dedjet will know how I feel, that there's no misunderstanding." He looked at Nessumontu and said calmly, "I'm a man with a simple spirit, who keeps away from tombs and magic. To be candid, I'm not enthusiastic about going with the queen tonight. The idea of facing the Hyksos demon, whatever its name, makes me shudder."

"You don't have to worry about that," Nessumontu assured. "The queen will control the thing."

Rahmzi's smile was embarrassed. "I may sound like an easily frightened child," he said, "but such matters terrify me."

Nessumontu took the scroll and tucked it in the belt that held his sword case. He put a hand on Rahmzi's shoulder. "I've seen you in battle many times, and I know you're fearless regarding mortals. I think you neither foolish nor cowardly to fear demons." He smiled and began to walk toward the royal tent. "I haven't heard any of the men murmuring that they're jealous of your assignment tonight—although it's a high honor to be chosen for such a mission."

Rahmzi looked at Nessumontu, a glint of humor lighting his eyes. "I haven't heard one murmur either," he admitted.

Rahmzi followed Nefrytatanen's white-robed figure. He rode with one hand holding the reins and his other arm clasped around Senwadjet, who was seated in front of him. Senwadjet's body was so weak that he had to lean against Rahmzi's chest, but his mind was fully alert.

The woods they rode through were soggy enough to resemble a swamp and the clammy gloom of the atmosphere made Rahmzi's flesh rise in bumps on his arms. The clouds were so dense they completely blotted out the moon, and this darkness didn't lessen Rahmzi's uneasiness. Although Nefrytatanen rode only one horse's length ahead of Rahmzi, he could see her only as a ghostly white figure. Even the sparkle of the gold trim of her robe was swallowed by the darkness.

"This is the place." Nefrytatanen's voice came like a shadow through the gloom.

Rahmzi stopped his horse, wondering how she could see where they were. He heard Nefrytatanen dismount, but he stayed in the saddle, continuing to hold Senwadjet, while she moved around the area. Suddenly she bent, and Rahmzi realized she had been looking for a place to spread the blankets on which Senwadjet would recline.

Rahmzi dismounted and helped Senwadjet off the horse. Then Rahmzi lifted Senwadjet in his arms and waited, watching until Nefrytatanen straightened and he could carry Senwadjet to the blanket and put him down.

"Don't you need a light?" Rahmzi whispered.

"We'll build a fire," Nefrytatanen replied clearly. She turned and walked several paces away, then stopped. "Here's the place for the fire," she said. "Will you gather some wood?"

Rahmzi glanced around, straining his eyes in the darkness, wondering how he could find firewood in this place. He walked slowly and carefully, feeling his way with his feet, until he felt against his knees the scratchiness of a fallen branch. He bent to break it into smaller pieces. It was a large dead limb, and it was very dry.

Nefrytatanen watched Rahmzi's dark figure moving cautiously through the shadows. Satisfied with his progress, she stooped to open her bundle.

"What will you do, mother?" Senwadjet asked in a soft voice.

"I'm not yet sure," she replied. "When the fire has been lit, I'll be better able to see what Gobryas's spell caster did here."

"You've found something?" he asked in an awed tone.

"Yes," she answered. She heard Senwadjet make a sound, and she quickly said, "Don't try to move anywhere!"

"I would like to see what you've found," Senwadjet said. "I'm not so weak that I couldn't get that little distance."

Nefrytatanen took a deep breath. "I don't want you coming any closer to this thing," she said firmly. "After Rahmzi has gathered the wood, I'll direct him where to put it, then have him join you on the blanket. I don't want him approaching this evil thing either."

By the time Nefrytatanen had finished arranging what she had brought with her, Rahmzi had returned. She directed him to walk nowhere but to the place where she wanted the fire begun. Rahmzi asked no questions and made no protest. She watched him meticulously following her orders, and smiled ruefully, knowing he was afraid.

The small circle of light cast by the fire gave Rahmzi little comfort. He could see their surroundings now. They stood in the middle of cracked and broken pavement, surrounded by tumbled walls and crumbling columns. Over the ruins hung the smell of decay. Rahmzi shivered.

He could see why it had been so easy to find dead branches. All the trees ringing the paved area seemed lifeless, their dry and barren branches lifting to the sky like fingers beseeching the divine beings to end their misery and let them fall. Rahmzi turned his head to examine what he could see of the ruins, but he knew there was nobody present he could protect the queen and prince from. Even the weeds looked dead. He turned to watch Nefrytatanen and was a little encouraged by her lack of fear. She walked around the area with confidence. She stooped to examine something on the ground. Curious, he came a little closer.

"Stay where you are," Nefrytatanen warned. "This is the thing I've sought."

Rahmzi stopped instantly. "It looks like a little pile of rocks," he whispered. "Are you sure that's what you search for?"

Nefrytatanen straightened and turned to face him. "Those stones didn't fall neatly into a square by accident," she answered. "They were deliberately placed in that pattern."

Rahmzi shuddered. "Is there some way I can help you?" he offered.

Nefrytatanen smiled faintly. "You would help me best by going back to that blanket and sitting beside Senwadjet and remaining there," she answered. "From this point on, I must do everything. I command that you not move from that place until I'm finished."

"What if someone else comes?" Rahmzi asked slowly.

"Once I've begun what I must do, no one will intrude upon us," Nefrytatanen replied grimly.

Rahmzi asked nothing more. He didn't care to know the details of what might happen to a possible intruder. His imagination brought him visions grim enough to satisfy his curiosity.

"Put away your fear," Nefrytatanen said. She approached Rahmzi and Senwadjet and instructed, "Put these around your necks." She handed each of them a silver ankh on a chain. "I'll do something more to keep that demon from you."

She turned from the blanket and sat on the ground

before the fire, saying nothing for a long time. Finally she stood up, and opening a silver container, she threw a handful of its contents on the fire.

A cloud of blue sparks burst from the flames, and Rahmzi recognized the scent of Nefrytatanen's perfume spreading over the area like a blanket. The sparks floated up into the darkness, rising in spirals. The fire made no smoke now.

Nefrytatanen held her hands over another container and said, "Homage to thee, O Anpu, he who rules minerals and their uses. Enter this salt and gypsum so wherever they are sprinkled, all evil will depart. All unclean things will be cast out by the might of the One Alone."

Nefrytatanen approached the little pile of rocks. Over her shoulder she explained, "This may not look like the palace, but that's what it represents. It's from the palace and, therefore, from this little house the evil must be driven."

Nefrytatanen poured some of the water on the stones, and Rahmzi saw dark stains run from their surface. He wondered what the stains were, but he didn't ask. She smeared bitumen on the stones and scattered gypsum crystals over them. Rahmzi leaned forward anxiously. Nefrytatanen removed from the cord around her waist a white lotus, and she tucked it in the diadem on her head. She bent toward the little house, the silver ankh she wore on a chain around her neck sparkling in the firelight, and picked up the slab of stone that served as the roof of the house. She threw the stone to her left, and it smashed on the pavement making a strange hollow sound.

One by one she lifted the stones forming the little walls and smashed them, chanting, "One Alone, who knows neither death nor diminishment, who through Asar's eternal soul and Aset's devotion taught us to destroy death and diminishment, vanquish this evil without delay."

Rahmzi stared incredulously. From the place where the house had been, there rose a murky yellow vapor. It hung in the air over Nefrytatanen like a living thing, threatening her. Rahmzi watched as Nefrytatanen dug her fingers into the loose earth and lifted out a sticky-looking piece of cloth. Carefully picking apart the folds of material, she revealed the gold pendant, which she quickly rinsed with water.

Nefrytatanen stood motionlessly staring at the pendant. After a moment, she tilted her head to look up at the yellow vapor hanging over the clearing. Although her lips moved, no sound came from them. She was speaking silently from the bitterness of her heart. "It would give me so sweet a satisfaction to redirect this curse and send you, Yellow One, to the house of Gobryas. No one would know what I did. No one would understand it—not even Rahmzi and Senwadjet would know."

Nefrytatanen considered this idea, which filled her with almost overwhelming desire. She enjoyed the thought of knowing Gobryas would weaken, turn pale, and waste away as Senwadjet had done. Only Gobryas would be aware that she had done it.

Nefrytatanen wanted passionately to do it. Again her silent lips moved. "Aset would know I use the powers she lent me for evil," she said soundlessly. She lifted her face to the vapor and sighed.

Nefrytatanen sprinkled water and a handful of salt and gypsum crystals on the ruined house and said aloud, "I command, ancient serpent, by Asar—judge of the living and the dead—by the creator of the universe, who has the power to send you to darkness—that you depart forthwith from this house!"

The yellow vapor moved away from the place, and Nefrytatanen walked three paces toward Senwadjet and Rahmzi. There, she stopped and sprinkled more water and crystals saying, "I command you, cursed demon, by He who ordered the winds and the sea and the tempests—harm no one!"

The yellow vapor withdrew again. Nefrytatanen walked three more paces, following the vapor, and sprinkled water and crystals again chanting, "I command you by He who ordered you to be plunged from Tuat to the dark regions, to depart to the place appointed you!"

The yellow vapor moved a little farther, and she followed it. Rahmzi noted it moved in a circle around the ruined house, as if loathe to leave the place.

Nefrytatanen sprinkled more water and crystals and said, "I command you by He who ordered you, to go back—there to remain forever!"

This continued, the dirty yellow vapor moving away, and Nefrytatanen following it, until only three more steps remained to complete the circle. Nefrytatanen took the steps and sprinkled the water and crystals. The yellow vapor hovered directly above her head.

Unafraid, Nefrytatanen tilted her head to glare up at it and said clearly, "Listen, Lamashtu, and be afraid. Obey me and withdraw, subdued and prostrate!"

The vapor ascended a little. Nefrytatanen threw another handful of powder on the fire, and fresh blue sparks shot from the flames, mingling with the yellow vapor. Nefrytatanen cried out, "Obey me, Lamashtu! Depart forthwith!"

The vapor remained. Rahmzi held his breath.

Nefrytatanen stared unwaveringly at the vapor and said firmly but more quietly, "I command you, Lamashtu, depart now!"

The vapor retreated only a little.

Nefrytatanen lifted her silver pendant and held it up toward the vapor. The light from the fire struck the metal, making the pendant seem like a star in her hand. Again she commanded, "Lamashtu, withdraw!"

The vapor disappeared into the blackness of the night.

Nefrytatanen stood quietly a moment, looking up at the clean darkness, silently grateful to Aset that she had resisted the temptation to redirect the curse. Then she took a deep breath, straightened her shoulders, and turned to Rahmzi and Senwadjet. She smiled as she approached them.

"It is done?" Rahmzi whispered, not quite able to believe the thing was finished at last.

Nefrytatanen gestured toward Senwadjet. He was curled up on the blanket, his eyes closed and his face peaceful. Rahmzi looked questioningly at Nefrytatanen.

Her face shone with happiness, and she said softly, "He has much sleep to catch up on. You'll have to hold him very tightly on the way back to camp."

Rahmzi smiled widely. He got off the blanket and knelt on the broken pavement to wrap Senwadjet in the cloth. Then he lifted the prince in his arms.

Nefrytatanen gathered together her bundle, attached it to her saddle, and returned to Rahmzi. She managed to arouse Senwadjet only enough to enable him to stand leaning against her while Rahmzi mounted his horse. Rahmzi held out both hands and helped Senwadjet up to sit in front of him. Senwadjet yawned hugely, rested his back against Rahmzi's chest, and again closed his eyes. Rahmzi put both arms securely around Senwadjet and laced his fingers together, assuring Senwadjet's safety.

"You'll have to lead my horse," Rahmzi whispered. "I cannot guide it."

Nefrytatanen took the reins and led the horse to her own animal. She mounted, then turned to look once more at the place where she had cast out the demon.

A new peace had entered the shadows. She was satisfied. She took a deep breath, smiled, and turned the horse to guide them back to camp at a leisurely pace.

CHAPTER 7

THE ROUND SILHOUETTES of the roofs of Zurim looked like the black bellies of bloated spiders, and Amenemhet turned from them with an expression of distaste.

The hard line of his mouth softened into a faint smile. His eyes had fallen on Senwadjet, who was seated on a pile of pillows before the royal tent and eating a small roasted duck.

There could be no doubt in anyone's mind that Nefrytatanen had succeeded in removing the curse. Since they had returned from the ruins of the Hyksos temple, Senwadjet had spent a great deal of his waking hours eating. And he slept for long spaces of time, as if to compensate for the slumber he had missed. He awakened with a smile on his lips and the old brightness in his eyes.

Amenemhet's smile grew. Between bites of the duck, Senwadjet was teasing Yazid. Although Yazid replied sarcastically, his dark eyes glowed with happiness. Amenemhet listened until he realized Senwadjet was aware of his audience and was beginning to show off. Then Amenemhet took a sip of his wine and turned away, pretending to meditate on Zurim.

"One of the observers I sent to watch Zurim's walls has reported some activity," came a voice behind him.

Amenemhet turned to face Nessumontu. "What does it appear to be?" Amenemhet asked.

"It would seem there are military maneuvers," Nessumontu replied. "The observer heard orders being called, the sound of marching feet, the stamping of hoofs, heavy wheels creaking."

Amenemhet looked perplexed as he considered this a moment. "Do they try to frighten us?" he asked incredulously. "Could they contemplate attacking us? We overwhelm them."

Nessumontu turned to gaze at the city, which was becoming obscured by the gathering darkness. "I've been wondering if they're that foolish," he said.

Amenemhet rested his foot on a rock and contemplated Zurim. He was confused. "Surely they cannot consider launching an attack," he muttered. "If I were their leader, I would hope the battle could be delayed until Sargon comes. But I wonder if he's certain Sargon will come. . . ."

"Would Shalmanesser allow Zahi to be invaded and one of his cities taken, rather than delay his conquest of Retenu?" Nessumontu asked. "I think if I were Shalmanesser, I'd feel less secure in Avaris knowing Tamera's army sharpened their weapons in Zurim."

"A point well made," Amenemhet said softly. "What would you do if you governed Zurim?"

Nessumontu took a deep breath. "With the few forces Zurim has available compared to those they face, I'd try to delay combat. I think I'd send emissaries to talk with you. I think I'd try to get a few spies closer to this camp." He shook his head. "I think I'd try to make you believe I have more soldiers behind those walls than there are. I'd do my best to confuse you."

Amenemhet smiled faintly. "You'd try to make me think you're stronger than you are? How?"

Nessumontu again looked at Zurim. "I'd begin by making a lot of noise—as they are. I'd send out a few patrols and instruct them to behave with confidence if they're seen."

"You'd risk much," Amenemhet observed. "I'm not sure the Hyksos commander would act with such imagination—or boldness."

"You asked what I would do." Nessumontu shrugged. Then his body stiffened, and he stared at Zurim in surprise. "Now what are they doing?" he exclaimed.

Amenemhet looked at the city. Above the black outline of Zurim's walls, a faint orange glow was rising. The light grew brighter until it became orange flames crowned with yellow tips.

While Amenemhet and Nessumontu stared at the city, others of the camp had noticed the light. Many put down what they had been doing to come closer to watch. The camp suddenly grew quiet, and in the silence, the sounds Nessumontu had described carried clearly across the distance.

Amenemhet and Nessumontu exchanged looks of confusion mixed with alarm, but they said nothing. Noticing the gathering crowd, Nessumontu turned to face it.

"Go back to your business!" Nessumontu called sharply. He stepped in front of an officer. "Send word to the sentries to be even more alert. It may be that the Hyksos wish to distract us," Nessumontu warned.

Nessumontu watched the officer hurry to his task. Then, with a calculating look in his eyes, he turned to Amenemhet. "That may be just what the Hyksos are doing," he said. "While they draw our attention to their main gates, they may be sneaking out another exit."

Amenemhet studied the orange light over Zurim for a moment. When he looked at Nessumontu, the flames reflected gold in his eyes. "Send a patrol to investigate," he ordered. "Make it a small patrol to move quietly," he added grimly.

"They make such a blaze it almost looks as if they burn their city," Nessumontu commented.

"They don't," Amenemhet replied in a tight voice.

"If our patrol discovers a Hyksos patrol, should they fight or withdraw?" Nessumontu asked.

"Choose someone whose judgment you trust to lead this patrol," Amenemhet answered. "I don't want to begin open conflict yet, but the patrol's commander will have to decide what the situation warrants."

"If you approve, I'll have Captain Rahmzi do it," Nessumontu said.

"He's satisfactory to me, if you recommend him," replied Amenemhet. "Make sure they wear dark cloaks."

"They'll leave as quickly as possible," Nessumontu promised and turned to look for Rahmzi.

Rahmzi had been standing nearby, looking at the light over Zurim. He was turning to leave when Nessumontu called. Rahmzi raised a hand in acknowledgment and waited for Nessumontu.

"Are the Hyksos burning their city to save us the chore?" Rahmzi asked drily, looking at Nessumontu from the corner of his eye.

"I doubt that," Nessumontu answered, falling into step with his friend. "I want you to take five men and find out what they're doing."

"You suspect some of them slipped out of Zurim by another way while our eyes were on the fire?"

Nessumontu nodded. "The king directs you to use your judgment regarding what you discover. He also ordered that your men wear dark cloaks."

Rahmzi sighed audibly. "I left mine at Ithtawe. Sitah mentioned it only this morning."

"You can use mine," Nessumontu said. He put his hand on Rahmzi's shoulder and turned to go. "Just bring it back without bloodstains on it."

Rahmzi smiled. "Even Hyksos blood?"

Nessumontu answered, "As long as it isn't yours. Go now, Rahmzi. The king is anxious to learn what they're doing."

Rahmzi nodded in understanding and walked quickly toward his tent.

Dedjet plodded slowly through the garden. All morning she had felt as tired as if she hadn't slept during the night. In the sluggish air of the warm afternoon, her weariness had increased.

Pausing by the lotus pool, she put down the basket she carried and straightened her back. The basket, which contained only a piece of linen, seemed as heavy as if it held quarry stones. She regretted having taken it.

Dedjet sat on a bench. The sun-warmed stone felt pleasantly soothing against her spine. She couldn't understand why her back had ached all day. She wasn't prone to such disorders, and minor pains annoyed her. She arched her back to stretch, but the sharp pang this movement brought made her flatten her spine against the stone for relief. While she waited for the ache to subside, she turned her thoughts to Rahmzi. When her mind rested on him, she could ignore the pains of her body.

Although Dedjet was anxious for Rahmzi's safety, she wasn't terribly worried about it. She didn't believe there would be actual combat—and certainly not hand-to-hand fighting. Her thoughts were more pleasantly occupied with memories of their happiness together.

When Dedjet's disappointment had had time to lessen and she had been able to think with a calmer, more ordered mind, she had acknowledged that Rahmzi had been shocked at her news. She had realized Rahmzi would need time to accustom himself to the idea of marriage. A child he had never expected to have had been too much of a shock.

Dedjet's lips curved in a faint smile. Now she again realized Rahmzi loved her and she was convinced he would come back eagerly to her welcoming arms. Although there were yet two months before the child would be born, Dedjet was unsure how long the expedition to Zurim would last. She brought offerings of flowers and fruit to the temple of Hat-Hor each day, and she asked the goddess that Rahmzi return in time.

The ache in Dedjet's back hadn't lessened. It had grown into a pain that was becoming sharper with every breath she drew. Slowly she got to her feet. The pain became stronger, and her legs felt strangely weak. She turned toward the palace, and her robe caught on the basket handle, overturning it and spilling its contents on the stones. She gazed at it a moment, then decided she couldn't bend to pick it up. The pain was too great.

She started walking in wavering steps down the path, and when she felt the coolness of moisture gathering on her forehead, she increased her pace. Fear held her hand.

"Dedjet! Are you unwell?" Maeti stood just inside the doorway. "You're so pale."

Dedjet looked down at Maeti through a blur. "I don't know," she whispered. "There's a pain—"

Maeti put her arm around Dedjet's waist. "Come with me to my room," she invited. "You can lie on my bed. It's too far to your quarters."

"Your room, princess?" Dedjet asked in surprise. "I cannot use your room."

Maeti looked up at her. "Have I not just asked you to?" she said. "You can't go all the way to your quarters. Lean on me," she ordered imperiously.

Dedjet smiled weakly. "You're too small to hold me up," she replied.

"I'm not too small to hold a baby," Maeti retorted. "I will, at least, bear the burden of his weight while we walk."

Maeti's warm arm felt comforting to Dedjet, and she argued no more, but walked slowly beside Maeti, trying not to lean on the girl too much and at the same time leaning enough so Maeti was satisfied that she was helping Dedjet.

On the stairs, Maeti felt Dedjet stiffen, and she stopped to wait a moment. "Perhaps the child comes early," Maeti finally said. At Dedjet's fearful look, she quickly added, "Senwadjet and I came early, and we were healthy."

Dedjet took a deep breath. "If this is what's happening, I cannot go to your room."

Maeti looked up at Dedjet, smiling happily. "But why not?" she asked. "Evil has never entered my chambers so no residue of its spirit lingers there to harm you. Your child's birth would bring Hat-Hor in seven forms to guard you, and Bes would come to make you smile and ease your pain. Their presence would bring my sleeping place good fortune even after they had left."

Dedjet gazed at Maeti's eager face. "I don't know what to say," she murmured.

"What is there to say?" Maeti said coolly. "Father and mother are both away. And although I realize my age limits my authority, I'm yet the highest-ranking person here," Maeti reminded. "It is, after all, my room. I would have you stay there." Maeti paused, then added, "Unless you find the idea distasteful."

Dedjet smiled faintly through her pain. "My lady, I need no royal order to accept your invitation," she whispered. "I will be honored." Dedjet stiffened in renewed pain and leaned her shoulder against the wall until it had passed.

"We'd best hurry," Maeti urged. "When you're settled, I'll send for Horemheb."

Dedjet gave no answer, but continued slowly up the stairs, wondering that she might give birth to the child in the princess's chamber, attended by the royal physician. She had expected to have the child in her own quarters, attended by a midwife.

When they entered Maeti's room, Dedjet paused just insider the doorway and looked regretfully at the fine embroidered covers on Maeti's bed.

Maeti left Dedjet to cross the room and throw back the sheer drapery surrounding the bed. When she had taken away the headrest and arranged pillows in its place, she turned to Dedjet and smiled.

"Come on, Dedjet," Maeti invited. "Lie down and rest while I search for Horemheb." When Dedjet hesitated, Maeti came to her and took her hands. "If my bed becomes the place you'll have the child, these linens can be laundered," she declared, then added gently, "Get in without delay."

For a moment longer Dedjet stared in awe at the bed of a princess. Then she took a ragged breath and obeyed.

Rahmzi glanced up at the full moon and frowned as he rode slowly beneath the trees. His men had spread out to form an uneven line, reminding him of a flock of migrating birds. Rahmzi was apprehensive. The forest was flooded with the moon's silver. Although his men were careful to ride only in the protection of shadows, the branches swayed with the capricious breeze, causing shafts of light to glint on them. Rahmzi flinched each time he noted this, thinking the flame of a torch could be no more revealing.

A small animal moved in the shrubs to Rahmzi's right, and the hairs on the top of his head lifted with a prickly feeling that spread to the nape of his neck and crept down the length of his spine. Rahmzi turned his head slowly to scan the forest shadows carefully. He saw nothing disturbing. Still, the flesh of his arms rose in small bumps. He found himself making an effort not to shiver visibly.

Chiding himself for such useless fear, Rahmzi decided to turn his mind to more pleasant thoughts. He knew imagined fears left uncontrolled could paralyze him when reality dictated action.

Dedjet's image stood as clearly in his mind as if her body in its flesh walked beside him. His finger tips recalled the soft sensation of her skin. He saw her great, dark eyes looking at him from the shadows of the forest; and he was sure, in that moment, that Dedjet knew he loved her. He was certain she understood, even without his saying it, why he had behaved as he had. He smiled faintly, thinking of the fullness of her figure. He wondered what kind of soul would choose to inhabit the body she was forming within her.

From the depths of the forest came a fragrance, and Rahmzi closed his eyes to enjoy it fully. Reason told him it was not possible for Dedjet's perfume to come to him, and it was only his imaginings that were so vivid. Her perfume was the clean scent of a summer day, of grass and herbs warmed by the sun.

Rahmzi could see Dedjet's face on his closed eyelids, and with her perfume still saturating his senses, he was convinced that in this one moment, Dedjet must be thinking of him, also. Their spirits must be reaching out to each other through the distance separating them. . . .

The arrow that struck Rahmzi was a clean shot. It had been propelled at high speed from a strong bow by a sure hand, and it went much deeper into his body than had been needed. The sweet aching in his heart for Dedjet was not marred by the pain of death. The arrow ended Rahmzi's life without his knowing it. He fell against his horse's neck without a sound.

The other soldiers of Rahmzi's patrol weren't so fortunate. Rahmzi was spared hearing their moans and cries. Neither did he suffer the sight of them falling one by one.

The ambush was over in a minute. Six lives ended as quickly as it took to snuff out the flames of six lamps.

A grinning Hyksos soldier led Rahmzi's horse to his leader. Pahzen turned to inspect his catch. When he saw the insignia, now smeared with blood, he was filled with elation. His eager fingers ripped the insignia from the cloth to bring back to Captain Tilgath. Then Pahzen took a handful of Rahmzi's black hair and, grasping it tightly, lifted Rahmzi's head to look at the face of his defeated enemy.

Rahmzi's eyes had opened, and their dark depths looked sightlessly at the face of his murderer. The final sensation his body had experienced, that of his heart longing for his love, was frozen in his eyes. Pahzen stared at the expression and was shocked at his own grief.

To conceal this incongruous sorrow, Pahzen roughly pushed Rahmzi's face back into the horse's mane.

"What does the great Nessumontu look like?" asked a curious soldier standing beside Pahzen. He reached out as if to touch Rahmzi.

"Bring me some rope," Pahzen commanded. The soldier looked at Pahzen in surprise, his hand still outstretched. "Now!" Pahzen snapped.

The soldier lowered his hand and turned to obey. Pahzen watched the man go into the shadows. By the time the soldier emerged with a coil of rope, Pahzen felt better about what he planned to do. He thought of how joyful Captain Tilgath would be when he received Nessumontu's bloody insignia. He contemplated his subsequent reward from Lord Sharuhen.

Taking the rope, he tied Rahmzi's foot to the stirrup. Pahzen kept his eyes firmly focused on Rahmzi's boot and the rope he knotted. When he stepped forward to take the horse's bridle, he was careful not to glance at Rahmzi's sagging shoulder, his limply hanging arm, or his rumpled hair. Pahzen needed to regard the body, not as that of a man, but as that of an enemy. He couldn't allow himself to feel regret.

"Sir?" inquired a soldier. "What would you have us do with these bodies?"

Pahzen turned to the man. "The people of Tamera, I understand, are very particular about how their dead are handled," he said quietly. "Let the others lay where they fell as a sign of our contempt for them."

"And this one on the horse?" the soldier asked.

Pahzen turned the horse to face the direction of the enemy camp. He took his hand from the bridle and, stepping back, slapped the horse's rump sharply. The animal leaped once in protest, then raced forward. As he had anticipated, Rahmzi's body slipped from the saddle and dragged along the ground. Rahmzi's boot, bound to the stirrup, gleamed once in the moonlight before the horse disappeared into the shadows.

Dedjet screamed at last with her final pain. Feeling the body of her child at last separated from her own, she held her breath and waited. When she heard the fragile sound of the infant's first sustained cry, she breathed again.

"You have a son," Horemheb said clearly, raising his voice over the baby's wail. "He's a fine, healthy-looking child." There was a smile in Horemheb's voice as he added, "Senet will give him to you as soon as he's presentable."

Dedjet smiled widely, thinking of Rahmzi's joy when he would first look at his son. "Whatever his condition," she whispered, "he's presentable to me."

Horemheb laughed softly. "You can endure one moment of waiting after all these months," he said, "though, perhaps, his early arrival is a sign of your impatience."

From a corner of the room Senet said, "Do you have a name yet?"

Dedjet's eyes widened. "Are you using Princess Maeti's dressing table to cleanse my baby?" she asked.

Senet chuckled. "It seemed best," she answered. "I think the princess won't complain. After all, she was most insistent on your staying here, and she must know we'll use what's necessary." Her voice had become clearer, and Dedjet knew Senet had turned toward her.

Dedjet's heart leaped in anticipation as she heard Senet approaching. When Senet came into view, Dedjet could see only the linen-wrapped bundle in Senet's arms.

"Do you have a name yet?" Senet asked, placing the bundle beside Dedjet.

Dedjet's hand shook so violently that Senet folded the linen from the infant's face for her. Dedjet gazed wordlessly at the black curls of hair and slanted, almond-shaped eyes like polished black onyx.

"They're *his* eyes," Dedjet finally whispered.

"And the name?" Senet asked again. "Or will this handsome boy have no name?"

Dedjet laughed softly, not taking her eyes from the small face, and answered, "His name will be Rahmzi."

"Captain Rahmzi won't have a chance to see his son," Senet said laughing. "You will use him up with your own eyes before the captain returns."

Dedjet tore her gaze from the baby and looked at Senet. "He's such a fine baby that *you* want him in your own arms," she chided in good humor. "All the looking I do, all the touching, all the kissing will only

148

prepare Rahmzi for what he'll receive when his father
sees him." Her eyes went again to the child. "Little
Rahmzi," she whispered, "your father will be filled
with joy when he returns."

Senwadjet was carrying on a spirited debate with
Nefrytatanen, who insisted he now prepare for slumber. Overhearing the argument, Amenemhet stayed
out of the way. He didn't want Senwadjet to glimpse
his expression and further delay sleeping. He was
glad to hear Senwadjet's lively words.

Finally Nefrytatanen drew herself to her full height.
Looking sternly at the prince, she said, "I do not request your going to bed. I command it."

"Yes, mother," Senwadjet said in a disgusted tone.
"I go now."

"I rejoice," Nefrytatanen replied and turned from
Senwadjet to walk slowly to Amenemhet. "You heard
it all," she murmured, smiling now that her back was
to Senwadjet and he couldn't see her expression. "It
now takes a royal command to make him obey me."

Amenemhet looked at her from the corner of his
eye. He said nothing because his voice would reveal
laughter.

"You applaud the renewal of his spirit," she whispered. Amenemhet nodded. "As do I," she admitted.

The sudden sound of clattering hoofs startled them,
and they looked at each other in surprise. They turned
quickly to see Senwadjet tugging at a horse's reins,
his slight form almost lifted off the ground in his
struggle. The animal's dark coat was white with
foam, its nostrils were distended, and its eyes were
bulging with fear.

"What is this?" Amenemhet called and started walking forward. Abruptly he stopped. Senwadjet was kneeling beside something on the ground. Now Amenemhet ran. He had begun to get some idea of the nature of the thing on the ground. He was too late to stop Senwadjet. When Amenemhet reached the prince, Senwadjet looked up at him with horror in his eyes.

"It's Captain Rahmzi—I think," Senwadjet whispered, his face pale. "It's Captain Rahmzi," he murmured again, as if he couldn't believe it.

Amenemhet put his hands on Senwadjet's shoulders and, with his touch, encouraged Senwadjet to rise. Senwadjet stood up slowly, still looking horrified, but said nothing more.

"Nessumontu!" Amenemhet shouted.

Nefrytatanen stepped forward, glanced down, and turned away quickly.

"Don't look at him, beloved," Amenemhet warned, too late. "He has been dragged through the forest."

Nefrytatanen stared toward the fire, only half aware of others running toward them, and whispered, "May Asar receive his soul with gentle hands." She wiped away a tear and swallowed. She could say no more.

Nessumontu raced up to them and, seeing the body, glanced fearfully at Amenemhet. When Amenemhet nodded, Nessumontu dropped to his knees. "Someone cut that rope!" he snarled.

Senwadjet, who was closest, took out his dagger and, stepping around the body, carefully sawed the rope binding Rahmzi's foot to the stirrup. He caught the foot in his hand and lowered it gently to the ground. He looked at Amenemhet, not wanting to look at Nessumontu, who knelt beside the body, head bowed.

Finally Nessumontu reached into Rahmzi's tunic and took out the flute Rahmzi had always carried. Covering Rahmzi's ruined face with a strip of cloth torn from his cloak, Nessumontu got to his feet and faced Amenemhet with cold eyes.

"They must have been ambushed," Amenemhet said quietly. "The others must lay where they fell."

"Why did they do that to Rahmzi?" Senwadjet asked. "Why did they not let him lie with the others?"

"Because he wore my cloak," Nessumontu said tightly. "They thought Rahmzi was me, and they tore my insignia from the cloak to bring back as a prize."

"They sent him to us in this fashion to humiliate what they thought was Nessumontu's body," Nefryta-tanen whispered.

Amenemhet nodded.

"I took his flute," Nessumontu murmured. "I would give it to Dedjet when we return." He shook his head slowly. "Rahmzi gave me a letter to hand her in case he wasn't able to return."

Senwadjet took a deep breath and opened his mouth. No sound came out. He closed his mouth.

"We must find the bodies of the others," Amenemhet said. At his words, several soldiers came forward and volunteered to go.

"I'll take them myself," Nessumontu said, his slanted eyes gleaming with orange fire in the light of the wavering flames. "I would also look for those who did this, though I think they must be safe behind Zurim's walls by now."

Amenemhet looked at Nessumontu. "I need not tell you what to do with any you may find," he said coldly.

151

Startled, Senwadjet looked at his father. He had never heard such a tone of voice from him.

"You needn't issue instructions for that," Nessumontu said in a strangely soft voice. He turned and went to his tent calling for Sitah, his aide.

"Is Nessumontu not angry?" Senwadjet asked. "He speaks so quietly. When others are angry, their voices grow louder."

Amenemhet looked down at Senwadjet and replied, "He is beyond anger." Amenemhet paused, then added, "I wouldn't care to meet him in the woods."

Senwadjet turned to watch two soldiers lift Rahmzi and carry him away. He looked at Amenemhet. "Will we attack Zurim?" he asked.

Amenemhet waited a moment to calm himself, but his eyes were no softer when he answered, "That decision would be better made in the morning, not when I feel this way."

Senwadjet stared at Amenemhet, wondering how he felt. "If I were a Hyksos, I would not wish to have you come upon me in that forest," Senwadjet whispered.

Amenemhet put his hand on Senwadjet's shoulder and smiled faintly. But Senwadjet saw no humor in the smile and no lessening of the golden fire in his eyes when Amenemhet said, "You'd best go to bed and sleep if you can. Try not to let your thoughts dwell on what you saw."

"It won't be easy to avoid that," Senwadjet replied and turned away.

Amenemhet watched Senwadjet go into the tent. He was impressed with the young prince's composure. "Senwadjet took it well," he commented.

"Senwadjet is more advanced in his mind in some

ways than many who are older in years," Nefrytatanen replied, "but I wish he hadn't seen Rahmzi."

"Yes," Amenemhet agreed, "but if the Hyksos continue in their greed, he'll likely see blood all his life. We won't be able to protect him from it always."

"That is true," Nefrytatanen murmured. She started to walk slowly toward the tent. She paused and looked up at the dark arch of the sky and sighed. "Yet, I wish the experience might have been delayed."

"When did you first see violent death?" Amenemhet asked grimly.

Nefrytatanen looked at him. "I was just a little older than Senwadjet when I witnessed an execution," she answered. "It was violent in that it was messy." She thought about it a moment, then said, "A Hyksos soldier had been captured in a raid on a farm near Noph, and I was present when my father sentenced him. I was so enthusiastic about the death sentence that my father decided I should see the execution carried out."

"How was it done?"

"He was beheaded," she replied, looking at the tent ahead of them. "He didn't die well," she added. She shivered, then turned to Amenemhet. "Beloved, what of Dedjet? What of the child? Rahmzi never got the chance to marry her."

Amenemhet's eyes were sad as he considered this. "Though they never stood before a priest, I think they were as closely bound as if they had," he said slowly. "I'll have the records show the child as Rahmzi's legal heir. Then Dedjet won't have to live in shame, and the child will have his birthright. This will never be spoken of again."

It seemed to Amenemhet that eternity came and

passed three times while he waited for sleep to enter his troubled spirit. Behind closed eyes he saw Senwadjet kneeling beside Rahmzi's battered body. Although Nefrytatanen lay still, not turning and twisting impatiently as he did, he was aware she also didn't sleep. He knew her mind dwelt on the identical things his did.

Nefrytatanen sighed, and he felt her breath on his shoulder.

"Thinking of tomorrow doesn't encourage my sleeping," she murmured. "It strikes terror in my heart, just as tonight's events filled me with anger."

"My being contains as much discord as yours," he replied, "but we must sleep anyway."

Nefrytatanen said nothing for a time. Finally she asked, "What will we do, beloved?" Amenemhet said nothing, and she whispered, "We sent them a message that we came on an errand of mercy. Whatever else they think, we made no aggressive move toward Zurim."

"They're afraid," he replied simply.

"And in their fear, they killed Nessumontu's friend and desecrated his body, which was exactly what they should not have done," she murmured. "Nessumontu isn't sleeping tonight. I know, if he had his way, he would attack Zurim right now. I saw it in his eyes."

"I know—" Amenemhet began, but he stopped when he heard racing hoofs, then the heavy noise of a horse being hurriedly stopped in front of the tent. "One of our couriers, I think," Amenemhet muttered and sat up, swinging his legs from the low bed.

Nefrytatanen quickly got up, and from the far side of the tent came the sound of Senwadjet leaping from his bed. As soon as Amenemhet had pulled on a robe, he lit a lamp. The light revealed Nefrytatanen, hair askew, fastening her robe. Senwadjet came to them, a cloth wrapped around his hips, his unbraided hair standing out from his head like a wreath of black feathers. Glancing at him, Amenemhet smiled faintly, then nodded to Yazid to pull aside the door hanging.

A tall, broad-shouldered courier stood in the opening. At Yazid's nod, he came inside. The messenger handed his cloak to Yazid, who accepted it carefully so as not to spread the dust from its folds on the tent floor. The courier's tunic was dark with moisture.

When the messenger started to kneel, Amenemhet said, "Never mind that. Tell us the news. Does Sargon come?"

"Yes, Your Majesty," the courier replied. "He left Retenu, and the whole army of Zahi is right on my heels."

"When will they arrive?" Amenemhet asked, thinking his own army could be caught between Sargon's forces and those of Zurim.

The messenger made mental calculations. "I think in another two days," he answered. "I rode hard from Retenu, but they were traveling fast."

"What will we do?" Senwadjet asked.

The courier's dark eyes watched his king intently. He didn't know if his presence was wanted, but he dared not leave without dismissal.

Amenemhet looked at Nefrytatanen. "It wasn't my intention to fight a full-scale war," he said softly.

"But can we run?" she murmured.

"What of Rahmzi?" Senwadjet asked.

"What of the curse?" Nefrytatanen reminded in a sharp tone. "Shall they do such things?"

"Perhaps they'll next send an assassin to Ithtawe for you, father!" Senwadjet said suddenly.

Amenemhet's golden eyes shifted to the courier, and he said, "Tell Commander Nessumontu to prepare the men for battle."

"Will we fight Sargon, when he comes, or lay siege to Zurim?" the messenger inquired, knowing Nessumontu would ask.

"It seems we must capture Zurim before Sargon arrives to avoid fighting both at the same time," Amenemhet snapped. "We can't run!"

"No, sire," the messenger replied.

"Go now," Amenemhet ordered. "Commander Nessumontu isn't sleeping. Tell him to have everything ready before dawn."

"Yes, sire," the courier said and, taking his cloak from Yazid, disappeared into the night.

The operation was quietly prepared so that when the first light of dawn spread across the plain, the sentries on Zurim's walls would see the full might of the army of the Two Lands spread out before them. Nessumontu intended to wring from the citizens and soldiers of Zurim every morsel of terror he could in the hope that fear would demoralize them and weaken their defenses.

Amenemhet and Nefrytatanen made no further attempt to sleep nor did they try to persuade Senwadjet to do so. Instead, they dressed. When Nefrytatanen told Amenemhet she wouldn't go back to where the supply caravan had been moved for safety, he didn't argue with her. She wouldn't go near the battle, she promised, but would sit on her horse close enough to watch.

While Amenemhet struggled to examine his chariot's condition by the light of a lamp, Senwadjet gave orders for his own horse to be readied. Amenemhet knew this but said nothing. He thought Senwadjet did so out of wishful thinking.

"Tighten this wheel more," Amenemhet ordered. "I won't have it fall off when I need it most." He studied the horse's harness and, finding some fault with that also, quickly pointed it out. He wasn't in the best of temper when he saw, from the corner of his eye, that Senwadjet had mounted his horse and was directing it to repeatedly rear up.

Amenemhet turned to Senwadjet and snapped, "Senwadjet! Horses were made to stand on four legs. Don't try to improve upon Ptah's design!"

Senwadjet stared at Amenemhet in surprise. His father was never so impatient. He steadied the horse and then slid from the saddle quietly. Amenemhet had again turned to his chariot, this time criticizing the placement of his lance case. When he had finished, Senwadjet waited a moment, then approached him.

"Father, is the hour upon us?" Senwadjet asked.

"Soon, my son, very soon," Amenemhet answered. He looked down into Senwadjet's eyes, which regarded him with an expression of gravity. "What more would you ask?"

Senwadjet swallowed. "Will you send me back with the supplies?"

Amenemhet considered this. "What else did you have in mind?" he asked.

Senwadjet lifted his head a little higher and straightened his shoulders. "It seems an unsuitable place for the prince," he said.

Amenemhet was silent.

"I know I can't go into battle," Senwadjet added quickly. "I'm too small, and there's no room in the ranks for someone who can't fight." He looked at Amenemhet with steady eyes. "Mother isn't going back. She will sit on a horse to the side so that she can watch how the battle goes."

Amenemhet nodded.

"I would stay with her," Senwadjet said firmly. "I also wish to see how it goes." His golden eyes regarded Amenemhet solemnly. "I could help guard her. I have learned much in my lessons with Nessumontu." He took a deep breath.

Amenemhet put his hands on Senwadjet's shoulders, studying him thoughtfully for a moment. Finally he said, "Then you'll stay where you ask."

Senwadjet smiled with relief and turned to go for his sword.

"Wait," Amenemhet said. "Stay here. Something more will be done before we begin."

Senwadjet stood still, watching curiously as Amenemhet went into the royal tent. He heard Amenemhet and Nefrytatanen talking, and he wondered what they spoke about. Senwadjet watched as the tent flap drew away. Yazid hurried out, giving Senwadjet a wide smile as he passed. Senwadjet was puzzled. Yazid seldom smiled so openly even when he was happy to the point of ecstasy.

When Yazid returned to the tent, the priest Senbi came with him. Senbi, too, smiled at Senwadjet as he passed but said nothing.

A number of men had noticed Yazid and Senbi, and they followed curiously. At Nessumontu's arrival, a small crowd began to gather. All of them waited with Senwadjet outside the royal tent, not speaking to Senwadjet or each other, the firelight glancing sparks off their shining weapons.

Senwadjet looked imploringly at Nessumontu. He knew Nessumontu knew what was happening, but the commander's eyes revealed nothing, and neither joy nor sorrow touched his lips.

Finally Amenemhet, Nefrytatanen, and Senbi came out of the tent with Yazid and Ineni on their heels. Senwadjet stared until his eyes began to sting. He tried to penetrate their thoughts, for their faces were solemn.

Amenemhet and Nefrytatanen came closer to Senwadjet. Senwadjet continued to stare at his father, wondering what was in his mind. Senwadjet didn't look from Amenemhet's face, even when he glimpsed the flash of Amenemhet's dagger in Nefrytatanen's hand.

When Amenemhet touched Senwadjet's braided and bound hair, Senwadjet's heart stopped, then resumed at a highly accelerated rate. A smile broke upon his lips, and gladness filled his eyes.

Gently Amenemhet pulled the clasp from Senwadjet's prince's lock. He ran his fingers through the twisted strands of hair and loosened them.

Amenemhet straightened to look at the eastern sky, which was becoming orange above the hills. He waited quietly while Senbi lit the incense. The smoky scent of burning myrrh drifted on the morning air. Senbi came closer to Senwadjet, and taking from his robe an amulet of the Golden Eye of Ra, he gave it to the prince.

"Homage to thee, O Amen-Ra. We await your shining face," Senbi prayed. "I address thee, O Lord of Life, for the sake of Prince Senwadjet Ra Kheper Kha, who has gained the mastery of many of his duties. Thy beauties shine from his eyes. He will be strong upon the land." Senbi looked down into Senwadjet's face and said, "Embraced art thou by Maeti of the double truth. Thou hearest the One Alone with thy two ears. Let none stand up against thee in evidence, none make opposition against thee among the leaders of men."

At this pronouncement, all those watching knelt. Senwadjet also knelt, but Senbi quickly whispered, "Rise up, my prince, stand up!" Senwadjet got up hastily, realizing the soldiers had knelt in homage to him. He could see a faint smile on Senbi's lips.

"Pure art thou, Royal Son, and pure is thy soul. Pure is thy power on earth. Pure is thy soul among the divine beings." Senbi looked at the horizon, which was bright gold. "I speak for Prince Senwadjet Ra Kheper Kha," he said clearly. "He is devoted in his heart without feigning. He is pure. He is strong. Ra makes his soul like the gods." Senbi stepped back quickly because the sun was ready to adorn the sky.

Nefrytatanen came closer and paused to look into Senwadjet's face. Her eyes were as deep a blue as the sky in the west, and they were as shining as a lotus pond. She handed the dagger to Amenemhet.

As the first golden curve of Ra rose over the hills, Amenemhet took Senwadjet's hair in his hand, recalling the words his father had spoken to him and the fathers of his family had spoken to their sons since the first king.

"His heart will not falter nor will his feet take one step back from fear, for this prince of the Two Lands is today a man and so will he remain until his soul ascends to unite with the sun, his divine body merging with its maker."

Amenemhet cut Senwadjet free of his child's lock.

The light in the east became a golden column that lifted the ceiling of darkness from the earth and filled the sky with light. New sentries climbed to the top of Zurim's walls. They looked confidently out over Zurim's plain, and then they paled. They turned and shouted into the space below.

Captain Pahzen ran out of his house with long strides and leaped up the stairs, taking three of them as one. His face was pale and tight with fear as he looked out over the wall. He had expected to see the place empty, to view the confusion of Tamera's retreating army.

Instead, halfway across the plain stood a horse, its rider holding a standard pole that glittered like gold in the new light. From the standard flew the banner of the Royal House—the hawk and the sun disk. Behind this man were two more men on horses, one rider holding the scarlet flag of the lower kingdom and the other rider the white flag of the upper kingdom. Behind them stood a long line of horsemen bearing the banners of every province of Tamera. In their other hands they carried torches, whose flames were like ragged orange veils blowing in the wind.

Behind the banner carriers stood a line of mounted officers. Each of them had a red feather affixed to his headpiece, and the feathers waved brightly in the wind.

Captain Pahzen involuntarily put his hand over his mouth. Rows of archers waited behind the officers. There were ranks of soldiers carrying spears, axes, and maces, soldiers in chariot after gleaming chariot, soldiers on horses. There was a ramming device. Above the men rose the hated specter of catapults, and next to the catapults smoke billowed from pots of burning pitch.

It seemed to Pahzen that the sun reflected from the copper points of endless weapons. He stepped back a pace.

At his side Tilgath cursed and then snapped, "I thought you said you killed Commander Nessumontu."

"Yes! Did I not bring you his insignia?" Pahzen asked.

"Then who is that?" Tilgath demanded, pointing his finger.

Pahzen looked. A man on a horse had come around the side of the ranks. The horse paced slowly toward the center of the first line. The man wore a scarlet tunic and headpiece emblazoned with a gold insignia that matched the one Pahzen had torn from the cloak. The rider's bearing was such that his identity couldn't be denied. As he passed, the soldiers tipped their weapons in salute. When he reached his place at the front, he stopped and turned to face the way he had come.

"Who is that?" Pahzen whispered.

Now the soldiers not only tilted their weapons, but bowed their heads, and from around them came a chariot drawn by a great black horse. The chariot seemed to be made of gold. Even the horse's harness seemed encased in gold. The vehicle flashed like fire in the sun as it drew to stand beside Nessumontu's horse.

"That," said Tilgath, "is King Amenemhet."

"Their king would lead the battle?" Pahzen said, incredulous.

"Some kings do that," Tilgath answered grimly.

CHAPTER 8

SENWADJET LOOKED AT Nefrytatanen from the corner of his eye and realized the extent of the pain she tried to hide. He had never seen fear in his mother before. That it was possible for even her to know fear surprised him. In this moment, she wasn't a queen or a priestess, she was a woman—and her fear confirmed Amenemhet's mortality.

Senwadjet reflected on this discovery and saw his parents with new perspective. He had always thought them indomitable, more divine than human. Suddenly, he realized his mother was very vulnerable, and Senwadjet felt emotion rush through him. He sat down and straightened his shoulders.

"He won't fall," he said gently.

Nefrytatanen looked curiously at Senwadjet. He had a tone in his voice she hadn't heard before. His face seemed that of an adult. Was it his shorn hair? Pride welled up in her as she realized what it was. It was his eyes. They were Amenemhet's eyes. Today they held the look of the hawk's eyes. Today he was Heru. She smiled faintly but said nothing. She could not.

Senwadjet moved his horse closer and put his hand over Nefrytatanen's to give her comfort.

"Are you ready?" Nessumontu asked at last.

Amenemhet turned to look one more time at Nefrytatanen and Senwadjet. Their horses stood very close together. Senwadjet lifted a hand, as if in salute. Amenemhet did the same, then turned to Nessumontu.

"I'm ready," Amenemhet said.

Nessumontu raised his arm and held it high a moment, giving his captains time to prepare themselves. The line of captains signaled their own officers, and, abruptly, Nessumontu dropped his arm. The trumpeters lifted their horns and blew the signal. Amenemhet and Nessumontu began moving forward slowly.

Behind Zurim's walls, there was a rush of activity. Men ran across the space behind the wall carrying armloads of weapons. Others rushed up ladders and stairways to the top of the wall. Officers shouted orders and cursed at slowness.

Wheels creaked, and animals snorted in fear as they were led to sheltered places. Slaves raced in crisscross paths carrying baskets of weapons and waterskins for the soldiers. Women stared anxiously at the figures on the wall, trying to follow the movements of loved ones. A crowd of children seemed mesmerized by the scene, until a passing officer noticed their exposed position and ordered them to safety. They turned and ran silently away.

Great wooden beams were dropped with heavy crashes against the gates, further reinforcing them. Smoke from fires heating pots of oil rose in black spirals against the blue sky. The sun sparkled on drawn weapons.

Captain Tilgath turned from the activities below to gaze over the plain at the advancing army. He wondered at the ease with which they paced, almost leisurely, as if they moved through a pleasant forest on a lazy afternoon.

"Archers!" called a nearby voice.

Tilgath turned to watch the row of men beside him raise their bows menacingly.

"Fire!"

Arrows, shining like needles in the sun, burst from the top of the wall with a slithering whir. On the plain, Tamera's foot soldiers lifted their shields expectantly, continuing to walk forward while the arrows rained down on them. Others raised their own long bows and, at their leader's signal, returned their missiles.

Amenemhet handed his reins to the officer riding with him and held his shield high while he watched the arrows' flight. They traveled close together in a shimmering arc that seemed to hesitate, poise over the walls a moment, then fall in a deadly swarm. Another silvery shower of needles rose from the wall's top in answer, and Amenemhet turned to look at his own men, who replied to the Hyksos arrows with more missiles of their own.

Nessumontu shouted orders to an officer, then sent his aide to relay a message to the crew struggling with the ramming device.

The wind shifted and pungent oily smoke from the catapults' fires assailed Amenemhet's nostrils. He coughed and turned his face away in time to see the officer driving his chariot sink slowly to the webbed flooring, the feathered shaft of a Hyksos arrow protruding from his head. Amenemhet took the reins and stepped aside regretfully, and the dead officer fell out of the chariot.

The catapult crews now had their mechanisms in place. As they loaded the machines, their naked backs and chests shone with moisture, looking like wet bronze in the hot sun. Quickly they stepped aside, simultaneously releasing the ropes. The catapults' long arms snapped up, sending flaming missiles through the air. After a moment, several puffs of brown smoke spouted from behind the wall.

Another shower of arrows fell on the plain. Near Amenemhet's chariot, a horse screamed in pain and collapsed heavily. A man went to his knees moaning. Another man pitched backwards without a sound and moved no more. Others fell, arms and legs flailing. Officers shouted orders. The catapults released another line of fiery missiles. The ramming device struck Zurim's gates with a crash.

The smell of burning oil and pitch mixed with those of sweating men and horses. The familiar smell of battle and death made Amenemhet shudder. He glanced down and saw the body of a soldier lying next to the chariot, dead eyes imploring mercy.

Over Zurim, smoke was rising in a curving column, and the wind caught its crest, turning it in upon itself, forming a small circle at its top.

A trickle of moisture ran down Amenemhet's cheek. Its path traced to the corner of his mouth, and he tasted salt. He wiped away blood from a cut on his brow, briefly wondering what had caused it, and lifted his water container to wash the taste of blood from his mouth. The water was tepid and tasted like the goat-skin container holding it.

The sun rose higher. Arrows flying regularly in both directions sparkled in the light. Flames set up an ominous crackle. Over the firepots, the air shimmered in the heat. Bow strings snapped and whirred softly. The thump of the catapults became a rhythmic sound as their crews loaded and reloaded the weapons.

Officers shouted orders, and a replacement crew went to the ramming device, accompanied by archers and some unlucky foot soldiers carrying shields. No one wanted to handle the ramming device because, being directly below Zurim's walls, it was the target of many arrows and spears. Again and again the ramming device pounded the gates. The gates protested loudly, and a shout went up from the crew. A small crack had been made.

Nessumontu glanced Amenemhet's way for the next order and Amenemhet gestured to proceed.

Nessumontu turned away and called, "Close ranks!"

The trumpets reinforced his command, and the foot soldiers obeyed, moving together so they stood almost shoulder to shoulder. The first line held shields of almost a man's height. The men following lifted their shields slightly above their heads, forming a roof and a wall of shields to protect them as they advanced.

The catapults continued their fire. More rooftops in Zurim exploded into crowns of flame. The archers increased their hail of arrows, and the crew at the ramming device, now encouraged by their progress, smashed at Zurim's battered gates with great enthusiasm.

Nefrytatanen wiped the perspiration from her forehead and opened her waterskin. Taking a sip of the warm liquid, she swirled it around in her mouth, hoping to dislodge the gritty sand in her teeth. Leaning away from Senwadjet she spat it on the ground, then took a long drink. Her teeth still felt sandy. The sun was hot on her head, as if Ra meant to roast her brains, and she realized the battle had been going on for hours. It hadn't seemed like hours, she thought, then changed her mind. It had been an eternity.

"Shall I get something for you to eat, mother?" Senwadjet asked.

Nefrytatanen shook her head. Senwadjet asked nothing more, but turned to resume watching the battle. Nefrytatanen wondered if he should be allowed to view all this. How could he think of eating while he watched men die? She hoped he didn't think it entertaining. She studied his profile, considering this. His golden eyes were narrowed against the glare of the sun as he watched the scene intently. Noting the grim set of his mouth, she decided he wasn't entertained.

When she heard a shout from the ramming crew, she anticipated the next move. She watched the shielded foot soldiers advancing toward the wall. The cape she had worn in the early morning chill had become stiffling, and she unfastened it without looking and let it drop from her shoulders. It slipped to the ground unnoticed. Now her attention was on the ladders being placed against Zurim's walls.

Soldiers leaped upon the ladders even before they were steadied—the men had to get up the ladders before they were pushed away. Few of them succeeded at first, but as Nessumontu's archers increased their hail, fewer ladders fell back to crush the men who fell beneath them. Nefrytatanen shuddered as she saw hot oil being poured on some of the climbers.

"Mother!" Senwadjet suddenly exclaimed. She turned to him. "Is this all being done because of me? Surely, all this is not being done for Rahmzi!" His eyes were wide with horror.

"It's being done for the prince who will inherit the crown," Nefrytatanen said carefully. Senwadjet opened his mouth as if to protest, but Nefrytatanen gave him no chance. "The curse on you was meant for your father and, therefore, for all Tamera." She frowned. "We cannot allow such a thing to go unanswered. Yet, your father planned to make no move against Zurim until they ambushed Rahmzi and his patrol. Did we not send them a message that we were on a peaceful mission?" Senwadjet nodded slowly. "We cannot let them think they may attack us without answering for it," Nefrytatanen said firmly. "With Sargon's forces coming, a decision had to be made either to fight or flee. We cannot run, Senwadjet. If the Hyksos saw us do that, they would be at Ithtawe's walls."

"Then this thing has no end," Senwadjet said slowly, looking at the fires over Zurim.

"Your father and I have discussed this sadness on many occasions," Nefrytatanen replied. "As long as the Hyksos think to fatten their storehouses with what they steal from others, we must remain alert." Her eyes moved to Zurim's walls. "This is part of what you will inherit," she said regretfully. "It's what I fought when I ruled the lower kingdom—what your father and I have struggled against all these years."

Senwadjet reflected grimly on this as he looked at the city. He could see the tops of flames reaching greedily above the walls all over Zurim. The banner of Zahi, which had seemed so menacing to Senwadjet at the beginning of the battle, was now only shredded ribbons fluttering in the wind. A crumbling noise attracted his attention, and his eyes followed its direction. Zurim's gates were giving way.

No triumphant shout rose from the crew at the battering ram. They continued silently with their struggle.

Although other soldiers on the plain looked at this event with joy, those at the ramming device had no happiness in their expressions. With their task nearing completion, the rain of arrows and spears increased, and many of them were suffering wounds. The thick wood of the gates seemed to moan in protest, the sound rising in pitch as the damage continued. The great bolts and hinges strained in their places in the stone wall.

It seemed as if all of Tamera's army held its breath waiting for the door to fall. Those nearest the ramming crew ran to help protect the men with their own shields. The wood finally shrieked in anguish, and the stone of the walls cracked ominously one more time. The doors fell in a crash of splinters, and the stones around the entrance collapsed. The ramming crew and those helping them leaped back, and the stones fell with a roar like an avalanche.

With great relief, Amenemhet watched the destruction of the gates. Nessumontu reined his horse next to Amenemhet's chariot and regarded Amenemhet with satisfaction.

"Shall we take the city now?" Nessumontu asked. "Or is laying open the wall enough lesson for them?" He watched Amenemhet carefully. Amenemhet was silent. "It would be easy to take them," Nessumontu added.

"You're the military commander," Amenemhet finally said. "Do what you must."

Nessumontu turned his horse from Amenemhet and waved to a signal horn bearer, who promptly blew the call to attack.

Through the distance Nefrytatanen heard the first horn, and she sat up, stiffly alert.

170

Senwadjet knew the meaning of the sound, and he again stood up in his stirrups to see better.

When Tamera's soldiers heard the signal to attack, they shouted in triumph. At the same time, a thunderous crash from Zurim announced the collapse of a burning building, and the separate sounds merged into a mighty roar that stunned Nefrytatanen's ears.

The foot soldiers on the plain quickly massed themselves for the charge, while the archers and the catapult and ramming crews dropped back. Their job was done. It was time for the men who carried spears, axes, slings, and maces.

Amenemhet exchanged his chariot for the horse of a fallen officer and waited at Nessumontu's side for the rush to begin. "I don't wish to hold this city," he said as he drew his sword. "I wish only to take it from them to demonstrate our strength."

"You're saying you want the destruction kept to a minimum?" asked Nessumontu.

Amenemhet nodded. "Also the casualties," he added. "I have no wish to return to Ithtawe with our numbers too diminished. Also, we must remember we have yet to subdue Sargon."

"We will subdue Sargon," Nessumontu muttered. "If I had the choice, as I've said before many times, I would march all the way to Avaris. I would like to settle with Shalmanesser for good."

"It is a pleasant thought," Amenemhet agreed, "but as I have said before, also many times, I have no wish to govern the Hyksos. It would bring us nothing but trouble to keep those people under control, and I would have to acquire food tasters and double my guards against assassins."

"I would make sure there were none left in Zahi

with the inclination to assassinate you," Nessumontu said grimly.

"To assure that, you'd have to blot out half the population, and, although they may seem like a plague on the earth, I wouldn't have their blood written in the records under my name." Amenemhet sighed. "The next generation would make that much more trouble for Senwadjet."

"He'll have it yet," Nessumontu persisted.

Amenemhet opened his mouth to answer, but seeing the officers look to him for his signal, he raised his arm and waved them to advance.

There was no longer a chance to debate. The soldiers sent up a fierce cry and rushed toward the gap in Zurim's wall. A new shower of arrows fell on their uplifted shields, and as they approached the entrance, spears were added to the barrage.

Amenemhet was attacked as soon as he rode through the entrance, and his sword swiftly added its ring to the other clashing weapons. All around him men cursed and moaned, while officers continued shouting orders.

From out of the billowing smoke a javelin came, passing so close to Amenemhet's ear that he could hear the whirring sound of its flight. He looked up to see who had thrown it and saw the Zahi captain standing at the wall's top lifting another lance. There was no question in Amenemhet's mind that this shaft was also meant for him because the captain stared directly at him. Amenemhet watched him carefully as he drew back his arm and let the lance fly.

Amenemhet suddenly turned the horse. Through the crackle of flames, the horse screamed and fell, the missile in its neck. As the horse went down, Amenemhet leaped away, narrowly missing being trapped under it. He looked up again and saw the captain raising another lance. Amenemhet ran to the wall and flattened himself against it, using for shelter the platform on which the captain stood.

Amenmhet stood quietly, wondering why the captain chose him for such intense attack. Although Amenemhet was the king, he thought this wasn't the reason for the man's determination. The man's eyes revealed a deeper reason. They were filled with hatred —or fear. Amenemhet knew he couldn't let this pass. The Hyskos wouldn't give up.

He glanced at the platform above him and at the ladders and steps leading to the platform. If the captain had so great a determination to kill him, he would probably not have the patience to wait for him to expose himself. Amenemhet smiled faintly. He would do nothing at all. He would wait.

Amenemhet's sword felt strangely cold in his hand, though his skin was hot and moist from tension. It also felt sticky, and when his eyes moved down to investigate, he saw that the dried blood on it had become wet and smeared from his perspiration. He looked away.

The nearby flames crackled. A horse screamed in pain. A discarded cape blew past Amenemhet's feet, its color indistinguishable under a coating of filth. A few paces in front of him, two men were struggling with a mace. Amenemhet couldn't tell which of them was his—they were both covered with soot. They were enveloped by the crowd of battling men, and their struggle carried them from his view.

Again, Amenemhet's eyes lifted to the platform. Between the planks of its floor, he could glimpse the captain, who stood as motionless as he did. He wondered how long the man could endure the wait.

A knot of battling men detached themselves from the others, and in their struggle they backed into one of the posts that supported the platform on which the Hyksos captain stood. The post moved. Again they bumped the post, and that section of the structure vibrated. Amenemhet saw the danger of remaining under the platform, but the only alternative was moving into the open. He glanced up. The sparkle he saw was from the copper point of the captain's spear. Amenemhet didn't move.

One of the men in the nearby group lost his fight. He staggered a few steps from the others, a surprised look on his face, the shaft of a lance piercing his abdomen. He fell against the unsteady post. There was a crackling noise, which grew into a tearing sound, and the platform section began to collapse.

Amenemhet saw it falling, and he hurried out from under it, but a passing fragment struck his shoulder and tore the sword from his hand. Pain shot through his arm. He grasped his shoulder, feeling dizzy. The platform collapsed with a roar, almost smothering him in a cloud of dust. Amenemhet backed away, coughing. When he managed to focus his eyes, he saw that the Hyksos captain faced him, still holding the spear.

Amenemhet stepped away, testing his arm, flexing his muscles, moving his wrist. It seemed unbroken, though pain yet wrenched him. The captain stared at him, eyes glittering.

A fiery wall from the building collapsed, and fragments of flaming wood fell around them. Amenemhet saw one sizable piece a few steps away. The Hyksos captain saw it at the same time. He raised his spear and darted forward. Amenemhet dove under the spear, rolled, and leaped to his feet holding the burning wood in his uninjured hand.

Amenemhet carefully moved toward Tilgath, who felt less confident when he looked directly into Amenemhet's eyes.

"How did you manage to keep your spear?" Amenemhet asked in the Hyksos tongue. "How were you not injured in the fall?"

Tilgath noted the grace of Amenemhet's movements and decided to test it. "I need my lance and strength to kill you," he said and made a sudden thrust with the spear. Amenemhet leaped back lightly.

"Why do you seek my death so passionately?" Amenemhet asked. His accent softened the Hyksos words, but not the threat behind them.

"Because you're the enemy king," Tilgath answered, again looking into Amenemhet's eyes. Their golden fires chilled him and he added, "Because I fear you, and a soldier must not be afraid."

"We don't murder prisoners. If you surrender, fear is unnecessary," Amenemhet suggested.

"I am under orders not to surrender," Tilgath replied, secretly wishing he could.

Amenemhet was surprised. "But you're lost! Would you not surrender to save those left? Would you fight to the last?"

Tilgath shook his head. "My orders are not to surrender Zurim."

Amenemhet straightened, yet remained alert. "Shalmanesser wishes to sacrifice this city for some reason," he said slowly. "If his purpose is accomplished, Zurim's populace won't thank you. They'll be dead," Amenemhet reasoned.

"Perhaps that's why I must face you," Tilgath said quietly. "If I die, the city will be able to surrender."

The fire in Amenemhet's eyes faded. "Then the reason you come after me so determinedly is so the city can live," he said. "I have no wish to murder, and I think you have no desire to die. Surrender quietly to me, and I'll have it told I vanquished you."

"I cannot," Tilgath said. "I have no wounds."

Amenemhet smiled faintly. "Drop your spear, and I'll knock you senseless. Then you'll have nothing to say about surrender."

Tilgath looked at Amenemhet carefully, wondering if Amenemhet intended to kill him once he was weaponless. His only alternative was to continue fighting. If he killed Amenemhet, another would kill him—another must. He knew Zurim could be slaughtered by Tamera's army. He wondered why King Shalmanesser was willing to make a sacrifice of the city.

"If you hesitate from fear that I'll break my word, I will not," Amenemhet said quietly. "If you hesitate from honor, I ask what honor would it bring you to see the whole populace die?"

Tilgath studied Amenemhet's expression for a moment, deciding whether Amenemhet was worthy of trust. He shrugged. It didn't really matter. He was doomed anyway.

"Put down that fiery club," Tilgath said.

"Let us first make some show of fighting," Amenemhet said softly. "Let us move into the shadow of that rubble. I will capture you there."

Tilgath took a deep breath and raised the spear threateningly. He took a step forward, and Amenemhet moved back. Tilgath made another thrust with the spear, and Amenemhet swung the fiery club at him.

They threatened each other in this way until they were out of sight of the others. Then Amenemhet dropped the wood.

Tilgath looked at him a moment, as if deciding whether to keep his promise. Then he smiled grimly and gave Amenemhet the spear.

"Zurim is yours," Tilgath said.

"I have no intention of keeping it," Amenemhet replied softly. "I never did." He grasped the spear in the middle of its shaft and raised it. "One thing more, before the others are in hearing," he said. "One of our officers was killed in the forest, having been mistaken for my commander. Who did it? Commander Nessumontu has the right to learn this because the officer was his friend."

"There's no need for me to hide his identity," Tilgath answered. "Pahzen is beyond your punishment. Tell your commander it was Captain Pahzen, who was killed when the gates came down."

Amenemhet nodded. "Turn around," he said.

Tilgath looked at him suspiciously, but slowly obeyed, wondering if it would be the spear's shaft over his head or the point of it in his back.

"You will awaken later," Amenemhet muttered and struck him sharply. Amenemhet caught Tilgath by the shoulders as he fell and dragged him out of the rubble into the open. He lowered Tilgath to the ground and waved to Nessumontu, who was nearby.

"The battle is over!" Amenemhet called. "Their commanding officer lies at my feet."

All through the night, torches dotted the plain before Zurim's broken walls. Physicians and their helpers searched for the wounded among Tamera's dead.

Amenemhet and Senwadjet stood just outside the entrance of the royal tent watching the lights moving in the darkness. Amenemhet had left soldiers in the city to make sure the peace was kept, but he was sure Zurim's people were too occupied with attending their wounded and mourning their dead to think of rebellion.

"Victory seems less sweet when I see those lights and know their purpose," Senwadjet murmured.

"Preserve this moment in your memory," Amenemhet said softly. "There will come times when you'll give the order to fight only because you must, but there will also be times when your blood rises hotly, begging to do violence. Remembering this moment will cool your head and give you time to think."

Senwadjet nodded. "I found no joy in watching that battle."

"I will not suggest you view the wounded to increase your dislike of war," Nefrytatanen said coming out of the tent. "You've seen enough as it is."

"I wouldn't care to do that anyway," Senwadjet replied. "Getting a close look at Rahmzi was enough for me and—" He stopped abruptly at the sound of a rapidly approaching horse.

The horse's heaving sides were white with lather and the rider stopped the animal so abruptly it almost went down on its hindquarters. The man flung himself from the saddle and ran to Amenemhet, bowing hastily.

"Sire," the soldier panted, "Sargon's army has changed direction. They go now toward Avaris!"

Amenemhet stared at him. "When did they do this?" he asked.

Nessumontu came running. "What's the news about Sargon?" he demanded.

The soldier turned to him. "Sir, only an hour's ride from Zurim, Sargon received a messenger who came from the north. Immediately afterwards, they turned to march toward the north," he said quickly. He looked again at Amenemhet. "Sire, it seems to me they go to Avaris!"

Nessumontu frowned. "Is Shalmanesser afraid we'll defeat Sargon, I wonder?" He looked up at Amenemhet. "I don't think so," he added.

"I don't think so, either," Amenemhet agreed.

"The messenger must have had alarming news," the soldier said quickly. "They almost trampled themselves in the dust in their haste to go."

Nessumontu smiled faintly. "When Shalmanesser gives orders, he allows no extra time for them to be obeyed," he said. "Sargon has no desire to be parted from his head."

Amenemhet was silent a moment, gazing at the winking torch lights on the plain. Finally he looked at Nessumontu. "I don't know what their reason is," he said firmly, "but I will find out. I want you to go after them and learn what they're plotting now. Take the mounted men and the chariot forces with you in the event of a clash."

Nessumontu didn't move. "What if it's a trick?" he asked anxiously. "What if they wait for us to split our forces and double back to attack you?"

"That is possible," Amenemhet agreed, "but enough men will be left here to at least hold them off until you return. Go now and learn their purpose. If they seem to circle in this direction, come back fast. We'll wait for your return."

"I'll waste no time—have no fear on that account," Nessumontu promised. He walked away quickly.

Not even one more hour of the night had passed before Nessumontu swung himself onto his horse and raised his arm in signal.

Some of Zurim's people who came out from behind their broken walls, and those of Tamera's soldiers staying behind gathered to watch the lines of mounted men and charioteers go past. Nessumontu had promised to waste no time, and he set a fast pace for the soldiers. The earth shook in their passing, as if its very core trembled from their might.

Amenemhet ordered several patrols to go farther from the encampment to watch for any hint of surprise attack. Both the camp and the city went about their tasks of cleaning up, and all of them felt uneasy. Neither side was eager to do more fighting now.

Early in the evening on the third day, when the sun was low on the horizon and the smoke from the cooking fires hung low in the golden air, a great rumble like the sound of distant thunder was noticed in the camp. Everyone stopped to reach for weapons. They turned in the direction of the sound, hoping it was Nessumontu returning but alert for trouble if it was not.

Amenemhet stepped out of the royal tent with Nefrytatanen and Senwadjet on his heels. Amenemhet drew his sword and stood in front of them, knowing it was possible for Sargon's men to slip past the guards he had posted. His face was a mixture of hope and fear as he waited.

Many riders appeared in the distance, their figures black and impossible to recognize. The men in the camp took positions for defense. A gleam of golden

light from the sinking sun touched the banner the approaching riders carried, and Amenemhet drew a deep
breath and relaxed. It was his own insignia they bore.

Nessumontu and his men rode into a camp filled
with curious faces. When he stopped by Amenemhet's
tent, he dismounted unhurriedly, a faint smile touching his lips.

"I think, from your expression, that the news is
favorable," Amenemhet remarked.

"I was somewhat disappointed I had no chance to
draw Hyksos blood, especially Sargon's," Nessumontu
replied, brushing the dust from his garments, "but I'm
glad to report we may go home whenever you wish."

Amenemhet put his sword away and stepped to the
side so Nefrytatanen and Senwadjet could move out
from behind him. "What happened?" he asked.

Nessumontu gazed at Zurim's walls a moment, then
said softly, "We traded one city of Zahi for Rahmzi's
life, which is all we'll get from them now. In my
opinion, we lost in this trade."

"Many lives were lost here," Nefrytatanen observed.
"Dedjet won't be alone in her grief."

Nessumontu nodded, then sighed. "We never caught
up with Sargon's men," he said slowly. "They really
were in a rush. But we did find Retenu's army in hot
pursuit of them. It was difficult to persuade their
commander to give it up."

"I wasn't aware that Retenu's people were so war-
like," Nefrytatanen remarked.

Nessumontu smiled. "Nor was I," he said, "but they
were much shaken by the idea of being invaded. Their
commander spoke frankly to me. He said the people
were fearful at first. But later, their ire was greatly
aroused. When Sargon left to come after you, they

were angry enough to give chase. They hoped we would join them in a combined invasion of Zahi."

"That was what Shalmanesser feared," Amenemhet breathed. "He thought we'd all come after him. That was his reason for ordering Tilgath not to surrender. He hoped Tilgath would delay us or so diminish our numbers as to make it easier to defend Avaris."

Nessumontu nodded. "That's what I thought, too."

"What did you tell Retenu's commander?" Senwad-jet suddenly asked.

Nessumontu smiled again. "Many things, my prince. Among them, I emphasized the fact that I couldn't go to Avaris with them until I had those orders and I doubted I would get such orders." Nessumontu looked at Amenemhet. "I was correct, was I not?"

"You were," Amenemhet answered.

"You would have been proud of me," Nessumontu said lightly. "I put down my own longing to fight and explained, in the words you have so often used, why Tamera isn't interested in taking Zahi. I said you would surely let King Ami-enshi know if you wanted his help."

"You did well," Amenemhet said, smiling faintly.

"My men and I are hungry," Nessumontu said. "We rode fast to come back with this news, and we haven't stopped for a meal since early this morning."

Amenemhet turned to Yazid. "Have the fires stirred up," he directed. "These men deserve a good meal in celebration." Amenemhet looked at Nessumontu. "Send a messenger to bring this news to Ithtawe as soon as he can."

Nessumontu smiled. "A warm welcome will then await us," he said. His smile grew wider. "It will be pleasant." He turned and walked away.

Amenemhet looked at Nefrytatanen. "I would take a walk and think on these things," he said softly. "When you're able, catch up with me, if you wish."

" I will," she promised.

"Can I come?" Senwadjet asked. At the look he received from Amenemhet, he changed his mind. "On second thought, I think I'll join Nessumontu," he said. "He can tell me tales of what happened on their trip." At Amenemhet's smile, Senwadjet grinned and turned to follow Nessumontu.

CHAPTER 9

NESSUMONTU'S SLANTED EYES gleamed with satisfaction as he watched the well-calculated moves of Senwadjet, who was engaged in a spontaneous wrestling match with his friend, Ameni. Several years ago, when Amenemhet had cut off the prince's child's lock, Amenemhet had instructed Nessumontu to teach Senwadjet all he knew. The military commander knew a great deal, and Senwadjet was a willing and excellent pupil.

Senwadjet stood lightly away from Ameni, smiling faintly, but alert for Ameni's next move. Senwadjet was sure he knew what Ameni would do, but he was ready for anything. Having been thrown to the grass several times, Ameni got up slowly, his face set with determination. As Senwadjet anticipated, Ameni pounced too soon and was a little off balance when he struck. Senwadjet threw him easily back to the grass, laughing aloud in triumph as he lay across Ameni and pressed him helplessly down.

"Do you concede?" Senwadjet asked. Ameni struggled silently, panting a little while he considered alternatives. There were none. Finally, Senwadjet got up. Dusting himself off and frowning at the grass stains on his new tunic, he said, "You had to concede, whether you admit it or not. I had you. Didn't I have him, father?"

Amenemhet had stood silently with Kheti, watching their sons' playful match. Amenemhet had seemed impassive while he watched Senwadjet's swift, graceful moves, but his golden eyes were filled with pride.

Kheti ran a hand through his black hair and remarked with a smile, "Ameni, you need more practice."

Ameni smiled wryly as he got to his feet. "Yes, yes, yes. I concede. I'll have to learn more tricks from Rakkor before we meet again." He sighed. "I am tired of looking up at Senwadjet from the grass."

"You moved too soon," Kheti said. "What you need is more patience."

"You both have much to learn," Amenemhet commented as they turned toward the door, "and much time to learn it in." He noticed Senwadjet's eyes following the path of a pretty young housemaid as she crossed the courtyard. Amenemhet leaned closer to Senwadjet and remarked in a low tone, "I would not look too much at servants. They can become difficult when they speak among themselves and compare such matters." Senwadjet grinned at his father but made no reply. Amenemhet added, "Besides, you're a little young for such activities."

Senwadjet looked at Amenemhet, humor lighting his eyes. He teased, "Father, how old were you when you looked at maids with more than casual interest?" Amenemhet gave no answer and suppressed his smile. "And when was the first time you did more than merely look?" Senwadjet persisted.

The others overheard these remarks and waited with some interest for Amenemhet's answer. But he was spared a confession by the approach of Nefrytatanen.

"You'd best keep to your wrestling matches with Ameni for a time yet," she advised, "for women are by far more complicated to wrestle with."

Senwadjet looked quickly at his mother, wondering how she knew what they had been saying. He was embarrassed, but she laughed at his expression.

"Surely," Nefrytatanen said, "you don't think I'm ignorant on such matters." She slid her arm around Amenemhet's waist as they walked, her sapphire eyes looking into Amenemhet's as she continued addressing Senwadjet. "It would be wise to follow your father's advice on love—he knows the subject well."

Amenemhet smiled down at Nefrytatanen and put his arm around her shoulders. Then he looked at Senwadjet. "You might also learn from your mother— especially when she gives advice on the complicated workings of the female mind."

"I've learned something of that already both from mother and Maeti," Senwadjet observed. "I'd still like to know how mother seems to have keener ears and sharper eyes than anyone I know."

Nefrytatanen laughed lightly. "I don't intend to give away my secrets," she said.

"Mothers and sisters are wells of information," Ameni said, "but it's far better to observe them closely than ask them questions. I still think experience outside the family teaches best," Ameni added loftily.

"And what do you know of this?" Kheti addressed his son. "You're two years younger than Senwadjet!"

"But Senwadjet is a prince and more closely observed." Ameni's green eyes sparkled mischievously.

More than a little surprised, Kheti gave Ameni a long look. He said firmly, "Perhaps you and I should speak of this in greater detail later."

Nessumontu, who had listened to all of this, chuckled softly.

Nefrytatanen's eyes turned to him. "I think you've influenced them with your casual habits," she commented.

Nessumontu smiled. "I've given them neither encouragement nor discouragement. If they observe my activities, I can't help it."

"You might consider marriage," Nefrytatanen observed, looking over his slender figure speculatively. "I think you could find some suitable lady who would end your restlessness."

Nessumontu's eyes narrowed slightly, looking wolfish. "I haven't remained unmarried because I'm afraid to ask," he said.

"Or because of the scarcity of willing women," Nefrytatanen remarked. She was smiling slightly, enjoying teasing him.

"There's the problem," Kheti said. "They're too willing for Nessumontu to be inclined to marry."

Nessumontu continued looking straight, making no comment for a long moment. Then he said thoughtfully, "There is some truth in that. But if I were inclined to choose a wife, my profession must be considered. I have no wish to leave a grieving wife and children if I'm killed in battle."

"That's a poor excuse," Kheti chided in good humor. "Tamera has been at peace for several years."

"You can never tell when something will happen to change that." Nessumontu grinned. "Besides, my life is peaceful now. Shall I deliberately look for conflict by getting married?"

"All marriages don't have conflict," Amenemhet said softly, pressing Nefrytatanen closer as they entered

187

the palace. "And sometimes," he added, "a man need not have many women for variety. Some women have as many moods as the facets of a jewel and are, in themselves, more fascinating than a hundred others."

"You speak as if you're still newly married," Kheti said.

"We are." Amenemhet smiled and looked at Nefrytatanen. He noted that the sun caused a certain transparency in her robe, and his gaze lingered a moment.

Seeing this, Ameni smiled triumphantly. "See, Senwadjet?" he whispered. "I told you one can learn from observation."

Senwadjet smiled happily. "If you mean the look father just gave mother, I'm far ahead of you," he mumbled. "I've seen them exchange many such looks, and more than looks, all my life."

"What are you two whispering about?" Kheti asked.

"Nothing much," Senwadjet replied in a casual tone. "It's pleasantly cool in the palace, isn't it?"

Kheti frowned. "It seems that coolness is what's needed."

"I hope you're ready to leave now," Nefrytatanen said. "I was coming to tell you that everything is ready for us to inspect the pyramid." She stopped abruptly, looking at Senwadjet's tunic in dismay. "Go and change," she directed. "We can't have you looking like one of the workers." She shook her head. "Call Ahmes to help you."

Senwadjet sighed and started upstairs to his chamber. He had known she would see the stains. "Ahmes!" he called loudly. "Get another tunic out for me!"

"You'd better hurry," Maeti said, glancing critically at Senwadjet's tunic as she passed him on the stairs. He made a face at her in answer.

"If the princess were a little older, or I a little younger, there would be the lady I'd court." Nessumontu was watching Maeti.

Maeti smiled. "And if such a thing were possible," she said softly, "I'd make sure you didn't escape me."

"How do you charm them all, Nessumontu?" Kheti exclaimed in mock dismay.

Nessumontu said nothing for a moment. He wondered how surprised they would be if truth were separated from rumor and they learned how much time he spent alone. He turned to Maeti and said softly, "I don't know what you're talking about, Kheti. Maeti alone has won my heart."

Senwadjet ran lightly down the stairs and, reaching the bottom, unconsciously straightened his posture. Amenemhet had noticed it was Senwadjet's habit to assume an air of dignity when he was about to make a public appearance, and Amenemhet was pleased with this. Whether or not he looked at maids, Senwadjet was aware of his position. And unless he became indiscreet, Amenemhet would say little about such matters. He clearly remembered his own interests at that age.

Amenemhet asked, "Will there be more delays or is everyone ready?" He deliberately gave them each an approving glance. "Let us be on our way," he said. He was anxious for them to see the progress on his pyramid. He had forbidden them to visit it until the complex of buildings had taken on a recognizable shape.

The pyramid complex was only a short ride from Ithtawe. There had been no prior announcement of the visit, and as the royal party approached the construction area, the workers put down their tools in surprise to stare, then bow, as the group came closer.

"What do you think of it, beloved?" Amenemhet asked, stopping his horse.

With obvious delight Nefrytatanen studied the rising shapes of the pyramid and its adjacent structures. "It's beautiful!" she exclaimed. "I had no idea it was so nearly finished."

"It has some way to go," he said softly, "but it will be completed before long."

When they had dismounted, Senwadjet said eagerly, "I'd like to go to the top as soon as it's ready and have Senbi teach me about stars."

"There will be many things for all of us to learn from these structures," Amenemhet said, narrowing his eyes to the bright sun as he looked at the top of his pyramid. "We'll all have the opportunity to do this as soon as it's finished." He turned to the supervisor of the workers. "You're making excellent progress, Antefaker," he said. "I am satisfied."

Antefaker's round face showed his pleasure. "I'm pleased to hear this, sire. Do you wish to walk around and inspect more closely? Would you honor me by sharing a cooling drink in my tent?"

"It's our intention to inspect the whole place," Amenemhet answered, "and a cool drink afterwards will be most welcome. Proceed, Antefaker, and we'll follow you." Antefaker bobbed his head excitedly and began to hurry forward. "Don't rush," Amenemhet said, "because we want to look at everything carefully." Antefaker immediately slowed his steps, resolving to keep this in mind.

"We haven't begun work on the enclosing walls," Antefaker explained. "They'll be one of the last things to do, but you can see the markers where they'll be built. Here's where the outer temple is taking shape."

"The columns of the portico will be of simple design," Amenemhet told Nefrytatanen, "and the inner wall will be granite with our emblem in relief at appropriate intervals. When the limestone casings are in place, the open areas will be planted with grass and shrubs."

"And flowers?" Maeti asked hopefully.

"Yes, flowers," Amenemhet answered. He smiled at Nefrytatanen. "What would you choose, beloved?" he asked.

"A small pond?" she suggested. "I would like some lotuses somewhere and a place where ibises might wade."

"Yes, there can be a pond," Amenemhet replied, "as well as a fountain."

"Perhaps some roses and jasmine?" Maeti begged. "They are so fragrant."

"All those things, yes," Amenemhet agreed. He turned to Senwadjet. "Do you have a suggestion?"

"I hesitate to mention anything, father." Senwadjet paused. "Someday I'll plan my own pyramid. I think it will be much like yours, for when yours is complete, it will be truly beautiful." He looked at the structure's top. "My only suggestion is the pyramid be capped with gold."

"That was already my intention." Amenemhet smiled. He turned to Nefrytatanen and added softly, "It was built here, beloved, for a reason. The engineers and those who know such things have calculated the placement of the pyramid. At the proper time, the waters of the Nile will be allowed to seep into the lower chamber. This should not only be a sufficient deterrent to thieves, but also confusing to curiosity seekers in the future."

Nefrytatanen nodded but said nothing, not wishing to think of that day. Amenemhet turned to watch one of the workers measuring a block of granite. When the worker realized who was looking over his shoulder, he leaped, startled.

"Go about your business," Amenemhet said. "You know what you're doing. Perhaps I may learn something if I watch you a moment or two."

Disconcerted by his king's friendliness, the worker obeyed and hesitantly resumed measuring the stone. Amenemhet became engrossed with the work and soon asked the man several questions. At first the worker's answers were self-conscious. He glanced at each of them to see who was listening, and found the royal family alternately watching him and looking curiously at the other workers nearby. Senwadjet came closer and, stopping beside Amenemhet, also began asking questions in a friendly manner. Soon the worker was enthusiastically explaining the details of his job.

Maeti, standing first on one foot and then the other, finally said, "If we stay this long at each place, we'll never see all of it."

Amenemhet smiled at her reminder and thanked the worker for his explanations. The royal family moved away, leaving the man and those near enough to have heard the conversation staring after them in pleased surprise.

They stopped to watch a finished column being raised slowly by ropes. The workers struggled with its weight, carefully balancing it so it wouldn't topple. They were terrified when they realized who watched them, afraid that the column might fall and its smooth surface be marred. Their sun-bronzed skin was shining with their efforts when the column finally stood straight and graceful.

"It's beautiful," Nefrytatanen breathed, "beautiful!"

"There will be a whole line of the same columns along here," the crew's leader said impulsively. Remembering he spoke to the queen, he added quickly, "If it pleases Your Radiance."

Seeming to take no notice of his uneasiness, Nefrytatanen replied, "The king is designer here, so he must answer that."

"Do you like the idea?" Amenemhet asked.

"It will be most beautiful to see a line of such gracefully worked columns," she answered eagerly. She turned to the leader of the crew, who was smiling widely with pride. "What will the roof be like?" she asked.

The man looked at Amenemhet, who nodded permission to answer. He turned to Nefrytatanen. "Divine lady," he said slowly, "if you can imagine it, the roof will be flat and carved all along its edge with a lotus and papyrus design, like that on the side of the thrones—although I, of course, have never seen the thrones."

"That would be very appropriate," she said softly. "I can imagine it clearly. Thank you." She turned to move on, then stopped and turned back to the worker. "Perhaps you should visit the throne room sometime before the roof is begun. Then you'll see how the design looks and will be better able to work it into the roof's edge here."

"Oh, my lady!" he exclaimed. "May I be so honored? It would greatly help me in this work."

"You must come when you're ready to begin that task," she answered warmly.

When they walked on, the workers stared after them.

When they approached the pyramid, even Amenemhet felt small. Its apex soared sixty-six cubits from the stone pavement.

Senwadjet tilted his head back and gazed at the top. "With polished limestone sides and a capstone of gold, it will be brilliant in the sunlight and will surely rival the old ones."

"It's not nearly as large," Amenemhet said, "but I believe it's large enough. And its proportions are perfect."

"You've used all the same proportions on a smaller scale?" Senwadjet was thoughtful a moment. He looked up with a curious expression on his face. "Will you use it in all the ways the old kings did?"

"Yes, I plan on it," Amenemhet answered softly. "How much do you know about this?"

"I've had long conversations with Ankhneferu and Senbi," replied Senwadjet, smiling. "You see, I haven't only been looking at girls."

"I hadn't thought so." Amenemhet smiled. He was about to say more when he noticed Maeti climbing the side of a precariously balanced pile of rocks. "Maeti!" he called. "Come down from there. You may fall and have the whole thing tumble after you."

At the tone of her father's voice, Maeti realized there was no point in arguing or trying to coax him into letting her continue. She began down slowly. As she stepped lightly from place to place, she put her foot on a stone that rolled, and she began a wild descent, skipping and hopping ungracefully to keep her balance, falling into Nessumontu's arms.

"Thank you, Nessumontu," she panted. "If you hadn't caught me, I would have landed on my face."

Nessumontu released her and turned to Amenemhet. "The escort guards are having a difficult time keeping watch over all of you climbing over rocks and scattering this way, then that way. They're sliding in the sand, and their equipment encumbers them. The guards would be more effective if you'd keep together."

"You're right," Amenemhet agreed. "Everyone is as excited as I am, and we haven't been careful." He waved to Nefrytatanen, who was standing some feet away examining a large block of red granite, wondering how the workers would manage to move it. Seeing Amenemhet's gesture, she came to him.

"And do you think," Nessumontu went on, "that it's wise to move so closely among the workers? What if one of them isn't friendly? Standing shoulder to shoulder among them makes it impossible to guard you."

Senwadjet looked at his father, then at his mother, then at Maeti. They were all as dusty and disheveled as he was. He smiled, remembering his last minute change because of a few grass stains. He commented, "I'm not sure they'd be able to recognize us now."

The work crew standing nearby, looked at the royal family and saw that the prince was right. The workers began to smile.

"Look at their faces," Amenemhet said. "Nessumontu, I think this closeness poses no threat. It is, rather, most wise."

Glancing at the open and friendly faces, Nessumontu couldn't argue this point. The workers seemed delighted with their ruler's attitude, his friendliness.

Antefaker, not wanting to chance any mishap where

he was in charge, said tactfully, "The sun is very hot. Perhaps you might now enjoy that cool drink in my shady tent?"

Nefrytatanen understood his motive. She smiled and said, "You're right, Antefaker. A cooling drink in a shady tent would be most welcome. Come, beloved, let's rest there a moment."

Amenemhet was a little disappointed, but he knew she was right. He mumbled something unintelligible under his breath and took Nefrytatanen's arm. They turned to Antefaker.

"Yes, lead on," Amenemhet said. Noticing Maeti's pink face, he realized it was best to get her out of the sun. He took her hand. "Maeti, didn't you have Senet oil your skin?" he asked. "You will burn and peel tonight if you stay in the sun much longer and that is not only a most painful experience but also an ugly sight."

"I wouldn't mind getting darker from the sun," she said, "but I don't want to burn and peel and be ugly."

Senwadjet laughed. "You're naturally ugly," he teased. "Perhaps some peeling will improve you."

Maeti gave Senwadjet a cold look, but as they turned to follow Antefaker, she took the opportunity to tickle Senwadjet's ribs. He leaped in surprise and was about to reciprocate when a threatening look from Nefrytatanen stopped him. He shrugged and followed peacefully, leaving the workers grinning at this prince and princess, who behaved like their own children.

"You're doing a fine job so far," Amenemhet told Antefaker as a servant filled his goblet. The wine had been stored deep in a cold spring, and moisture covered the goblet's surface. Amenemhet enjoyed the sensation, turning the goblet, making round wet marks with his finger tips in the even surface of the tiny beads. "I know it's far from easy to follow such odd measurements accurately on this scale," he said slowly.

"A fine degree of accuracy is naturally difficult working with great blocks of stone," Antefaker answered easily, his dark eyes warm with pride, "but the workers are willing and skillful. After your visit today, I know they'll be even more willing."

Nefrytatanen smiled faintly. "They found us made of flesh and blood and seemed surprised."

Antefaker scratched his closely shorn head. "They were a little uneasy when you arrived. Your graciousness and warmth not only overcame this but, I believe, struck deep into their emotions. To walk among them as easily as anyone, to so trust them, to ask questions and listen, to compliment and joke with them, and to even allow yourselves to grow dusty and moist with the sun's heat is something they're amazed at and will tell their families and friends about many times." Antefaker hesitated, then continued, "I mean this as no criticism of your parents—because I know they had no opportunity to do these things—but your being so accessible to the people wins more loyalty and love from them than, perhaps, any rulers have ever had."

Amenemhet's mind turned to the night before his wedding when he and his father, both unable to sleep, had sat at the foot of the thrones at Wast and talked intimately. "Shortly before my father died," Amenemhet said, "he told me of his dreams for the Two Lands, and the queen and I have tried to accomplish some of them. He was a wise man and, had he lived, would have acted as we do. I'm sure he would have gained love and loyalty to equal, if not surpass, what we have."

"I remember when your parents were poisoned. How shocked I was at that time! I'd always had a good opinion of them," Antefaker declared. "It was a disgusting, evil thing that priest did."

"I think we should return to the palace," Amenemhet said abruptly. He stood up, and Antefaker leaped to his feet, hoping he hadn't said something wrong. Amenemhet saw Antefaker's fear, and he smiled. "We have a number of other matters that need attending," he said. "We're satisfied with what you've accomplished so far. The queen has invited one or two of the crew leaders to the palace to study designs and decorations that will be reproduced here. When they have time to spare for this, release them for their visit."

"Yes, sire," Antefaker murmured, wishing he might be invited.

"Of course, you'll accompany them when they come to the palace," Amenemhet added tactfully.

"I would be honored," Antefaker said quickly, his smile radiant.

"You'll be welcome," Amenemhet replied and, with a glance at Nessumontu, signaled the end of the visit.

Hearing that the royal family was leaving, the workers put down their tools and stood on both sides of the road to obtain a good view of the royal visitors. As their rulers passed, they bowed low with respect, then rose slowly to stare at the diminishing figures. Remembering the stories they would have to tell their families that night, they smiled as they resumed their tasks.

Amenemhet looked at Nefrytatanen and smiled. "I didn't mind climbing around the stones and getting dirty as much as I minded trying to make polite conversation," he commented.

"The direct sun with a breeze is preferable to a tent where the air is still," she agreed. "But I'm certainly a mess." She turned to look over her shoulder at Senwadjet and Maeti riding behind them. Sighing at their appearance, she remarked, "I can't be worse than they are."

Amenemhet laughed aloud. "You're a considerable improvement. I think Maeti had better have Senet liberally cover her with oil after she's bathed—she's been burned."

"Perhaps oiling her won't be enough," Nefrytatanen said grimly. "I told her to be careful, but she wasn't. Now she'll itch and peel as she was warned, which will teach her more than warnings can." A vagrant breeze blew a strand of Nefrytatanen's hair across her face, scattering it gently, like a shining, sheer black veil over her skin. She shook her head to rid herself of it.

Watching her, Amenemhet observed, "For a dusty and disheveled woman, you don't look too bad." He moved his horse closer to take her hand as they rode.

Nefrytatanen looked at him out of the corner of her eye. "Your hair is standing up in little peaks and tangles," she said softly, "and you look most unlike a king."

"I really don't feel like a king," Amenemhet answered, "not at this moment, anyway." He breathed deeply of the clean air and stretched as the horse plodded docilely on without guidance. "I don't feel in the least bit noble, royal, or dignified," Amenemhet added as he yawned. When he looked at Nefrytatanen, his golden eyes glittered, denying his outwardly lazy mood. But he said nothing.

Seeing and hearing most of what had passed between his parents, Senwadjet thought of Ameni and his advice about observation. He chuckled to himself. He had always been far ahead of Ameni. He had always been most observant.

When Amenemhet closed the doors of their private chamber behind them, Nefrytatanen sighed. "The heat is excessive today." He turned to see her pulling off her bracelets and begin unfastening the clasp of her soiled robe.

"It's unpleasantly hot for people, but good for the crops," he commented, watching her struggle with the clasp.

"Perhaps the crops are happy, but I can hardly bear it," she muttered. She turned and saw his eyes gleaming with humor. "Why don't you help me?" she asked, impatient and perspiring with her efforts, "or call Dedjet?"

"I'll help you," he said softly. In a moment, he had undone the clasp. He began to slowly slip her robe from her shoulders.

Seeing Amenemhet's eyes and realizing his intent she exclaimed, "It's so hot for love! I'm disgustingly filthy!"

Amenemhet laughed. "You exaggerate, but I had it in mind to take a bath together—a very long and cooling bath."

Nefrytatanen smiled. "You've combined both our ideas into one."

"Does my part of the plan seem appealing to you?" he murmured kissing her bare shoulder.

"A bath first." She turned and looked at him from beneath her black lashes, "And love after."

Nefrytatanen removed Amenemhet's sash and loosened his robe. He stood motionless, his eyes becoming smoky topaz, still smiling slightly as she undressed him. He slipped her robe off, and it dropped to the floor with a whisper. Seeing the gold fires in his eyes growing brighter, she leaned her head against his chest.

"We've been married all these years and have made love countless times," Nefrytatanen said softly. "Our children are old enough to look at others with awakening desire." She looked up at Amenemhet. "Long ago did you unravel the last mystery of me, and I have no secrets left to intrigue you. Do you still find me so desirable?"

Amenemhet smiled and stroked her hair. "There's nothing about me you haven't learned. Do you still desire me?" He gave her no chance to answer, but took her in his arms and kissed her until he could feel her trembling. He stepped back a little. "There's the answer to both our questions," he whispered. She moved closer to him, again lifting her face to his, her eyes dark and glowing. Amenemhet looked at her steadily and murmured, "Didn't you want your bath first?"

"What bath?" Her voice was shaky.

"The one you need because you're so dirty," he said smiling.

She moved away and looked up at him. "You're right. A bath first," she replied.

Smiling, Amenemhet picked Nefrytatanen up. "Shall I throw you into the pool or on the bed?" he asked softly.

Nefrytatanen looked at his eyes and saw his feelings matched her own. She was about to answer when the door opened. Dedjet stood on the threshold looking at them with an open mouth.

Recovering herself, Dedjet said quickly, "A thousand pardons," and began to back away.

Amenemhet looked at Nefrytatanen and, still smiling said, "We're going to bathe, Dedjet. Will you bring towels and put them in the bathing chamber? Then leave us alone?"

"Yes, immediately," the maid answered and hurried out.

"I guess we must bathe," Amenemhet whispered, kissing Nefrytatanen's forehead.

"Yes," she sighed, "but we will be alone, and you did say a very long and cooling bath?"

He laughed at her expression and carried her through their private hall.

"Dedjet moves fast," he observed as they entered the room. "She's brought everything and disappeared already."

"She's a superior attendant," Nefrytatanen remarked as Amenemhet put her down. She remained close to him a moment, then moved closer. He stepped back a little to keep his balance.

"Are you still interested in bathing?" he asked, stopping his slow retreat.

"Yes, but I want one more kiss first," she whispered putting her arms around him. He kissed her lightly and quickly to tease her. "That," she said dropping her arms, "is a kiss for children or friends."

"You're a friend," Amenemhet said smiling.

"I'm a very good friend," Nefrytatanen replied slowly, "deserving a better kiss than that." She turned away with elaborate nonchalance adding, "But I believe I will bathe first." She walked to the edge of the pool and dove in, then swam quickly to its opposite side. She stood up and turned to face him. "If you wish to improve the quality of that kiss, I will permit it now," she said loftily.

Amenemhet dove, intending to follow her, but when he had surfaced, he found that she was swimming quickly away in another direction. He turned swiftly and, with a few powerful strokes, reached for and caught her ankle. He began to tow her backwards while she splashed and struggled to continue forward, her efforts weakened from laughter. Getting a mouthful of water, she began to cough, and immediately, he dropped her ankle and turned back to hold her head and shoulders above water, concerned until she caught her breath.

"Only a very good friend would risk his very life to save someone in these treacherous waters and currents," he teased when she was again standing steadily. She wiped the water from her eyes and stood blinking at him for a moment.

"You're a man of great courage," she said in exaggerated admiration. "I'm sure there are crocodiles, serpents, and many dreadful creatures in this water. You deserve a reward."

Glancing at the lotuses floating serenely on the perfumed water, Amenemhet said softly, "Yes, braving such dangers as this pool holds should be fittingly rewarded."

Nefrytatanen slid her arms around him, pressing herself close, caressing his lips with hers, sending tremors of warmth through him. She tangled her fingers in his hair, holding his head close, while she kissed his face all over.

Breathlessly he whispered, "This is some reward."

"Small enough for saving me from drowning," she murmured, continuing to kiss him.

"Haven't we bathed enough for the time being?" he asked, a little unsteadily. "Doesn't your narrow escape make you feel the need to rest on that couch awhile?"

"We've been in the water far too long," she whispered, letting her fingers slide from his hair down to his shoulders. She smiled into his eyes. "I do feel a little weak and would like to rest on the couch." Laying her face against his chest she added softly, "Too long a time in the water wrinkles the skin."

"I don't care for wrinkled skin," Amenemhet said. He grinned and lifted her out of the pool.

CHAPTER 10

"WHO'S COMING WITH US?" Amenemhet asked as he slipped a short cotton tunic over his head. He ran a hand through his black hair, hurriedly smoothing it.

"I told you yesterday," Nefrytatanen reminded him. She turned quickly to her maid. "Dedjet, see if Maeti and Senwadjet are nearly ready." She turned back to Amenemhet. "I thought it would be good to see Kheti and Neferset as long as they're at Ithtawe. We don't see them often since he's been so busy in his province. They're bringing Ameni, Bekhat, and little Nakht, of course."

"I thought this outing was to distract Nakht from his ambassadorial problems in Djemeh with King Zaretes, as well as from his personal problems with the lady Chamma," Amenemhet commented. "But it does seem a good way to visit with Kheti's family again, also." He paused, thinking, then remarked, "Do you know how long it's been since we saw Bekhat and little Nakht? I expect Bekhat will be quite a young lady and good company for Maeti, though she's three years younger."

"We might find Bekhat keeping company with Senwadjet," Nefrytatanen said, lifting an eyebrow, "from the direction his mind seems to be taking lately."

"Bekhat's still a child," Amenemhet mumbled.

Bekhat was three years younger than Senwadjet and Maeti, but Nefrytatanen wondered how childlike Bekhat was. Girls seemed to mature faster than boys, and three years might mean nothing. She decided to keep an eye on the two of them while they were in the forest. If Bekhat looked anything like Neferset, she was sure to catch Senwadjet's attention.

"Is Nessumontu coming, too?" Amenemhet asked.

"Can we go anywhere without him?" Nefrytatanen smiled.

"We could stay right here in our chambers," Amenemhet replied grinning, "but this is about the only place I can think of."

"It doesn't matter to Nessumontu how peaceful the land is," Nefrytatanen remarked. "Nessumontu is always watching, like a hunting hawk."

"He does his job well," Amenemhet said, tying a knot in his sash.

"Yes, and it's a comfort to have him to rely on, I admit, but it does seem like a lonely life for him, always watching someone else's family." Nefrytatanen turned. "Do I look all right? My bathing garment doesn't make the robe too bulky?"

"You look just bulky enough in all the right places," Amenemhet said smiling. He put his hands at her waist. "You feel good, too, as usual. Are you sure we really need to go?"

"You're teasing me," she replied. "You're acting as if you don't want to go, but you're really looking forward to it. Admit it."

"If I could be here with you unbothered by official matters all day, I'd be willing to stay." Amenemhet sighed. "But that's not likely to happen. Staying in the palace affords us little peace." He released her and stood back a little. "Tell me," he said, "can I look forward to that bathing dress becoming transparent when it gets wet?" His eyes were gleaming.

"Somewhat," Nefrytatanen admitted. She looked at him in pretended reproach. "If you wish to restrain Senwadjet awhile, you'd better restrain yourself in front of him. We need not hurry him in his education."

"If he's used us as an example—and I hope he has—his education began on the day he could first focus his eyes," Amenemhet replied.

"The prince and princess are ready," Dedjet announced, "and the others are waiting downstairs."

As Amenemhet and Nefrytatanen came down the steps and saw their smiling friends, they quickened their pace.

"I'm sorry we kept you waiting," Amenemhet said smoothly, "but Nefrytatanen dresses slowly." She looked at him meaningfully but said nothing.

Neferset embraced Amenemhet and Nefrytatanen in unrestrained joy, as Kheti and Nakht watched, smiling. "It's been too long since I've seen you," she said. "Kheti can come here on business, but I've had to stay at Orynx Province so long I decided I must visit you before I'm old and tottering."

"That would be far too long a time without seeing you," Amenemhet said warmly.

"Your manners are as charming as ever," Neferset replied, giving him one more squeeze. "But tell me, do you recognize our children? They seem to grow so fast I barely know them myself from day to day."

Amenemhet looked at Bekhat carefully while she was embracing Nefrytatanen. Bekhat wasn't like Neferset in coloring, but Neferset's silver hair was probably nowhere duplicated. Bekhat's hair was black, her eyes wide and dark grey like Kheti's. Although Bekhat was, like her mother, small in stature, Amenemhet noted that her figure was already almost Neferset's equal. When her small pointed face looked up at Amenemhet and her full little pink mouth brushed his cheek softly in greeting, Amenemhet began to wonder if he should keep an eye on Senwadjet, after all.

"You're a beautiful young lady," Amenemhet said softly. He smiled and turned to little Nakht, who also resembled Kheti. He said, "And you're at least a cubit taller since I last saw you."

"Surely you remember Senwadjet and Maeti," Nefrytatanen said, looking at Bekhat with slightly narrowed eyes.

"Not very well," little Nakht said bluntly. He grinned in apology. "I guess I was too small the last time I saw them."

"I wasn't too young," Bekhat said softly as she hugged Maeti. "I remember you both very well." Bekhat looked at Senwadjet and smiled, but she didn't touch him.

Senwadjet was looking at Bekhat with a very adult eye, Nefrytatanen observed, but she was surprised by his greeting.

"I remember you too, Bekhat," he said lightly, "for you always seemed like a sister to me." He rumpled little Nakht's hair playfully. "And who could forget a demon like you were, Nakht?"

"Let's be on our way," Amenemhet urged, "or we'll spend our whole day here reminiscing. The forest awaits us."

Amenemhet's private reserve was only a short walk from the palace gates. It contained a forest area carpeted with wild grass and flowers, and a pond fed by a natural spring. Along the Nile, papyrus grew freely. The stalks, reaching heights of ten to twelve feet, were capped with golden, umbrella-shaped flowers that swayed in the breezes from the north. The papyrus stalks sheltered a dense foliage at their base, which made a natural breeding place for game birds.

While the servants organized a camp, the party divided into smaller groups so they might move more quietly with their nets. If fortune were with them, they would end their day with a late supper of fresh baked birds.

Amenemhet and Nefrytatanen went into the papyrus alone, while Nessumontu promised to teach Senwadjet and Bekhat the finer points of trapping birds. Nakht took Ameni and his namesake, little Nakht, assuring them that they would catch more birds with him. Kheti and Neferset took Maeti, promising they would trap the most.

Each little group entered the papyrus from a different direction. They were as separated from the others as if they were alone in the world.

Nefrytatanen paused to look at the golden plants swaying over her head and to smell the warmth of the sun on the flowers, the green and moist earth. She touched a fat stalk, and a shower of pollen, like fine, golden powder, fell on her black hair.

Amenemhet smiled and brushed the dust from her, then took her hand and silently led her farther into the growth. They walked carefully, listening for the small sounds and movements indicating birds.

Amenemhet stopped walking. A sound came from a few steps ahead of them. He lifted his net, cautiously parting the foliage with his other hand. A small green snake escaped through the reeds, and Amenemhet relaxed and looked at Nefrytatanen, shrugging his shoulders. They moved carefully forward. An insect with iridescent wings hovered over Amenemhet's head, and Nefrytatanen waved it away.

With a soft whirring of its wings, an orange and yellow bird landed just above their heads on the swaying stem of one of the stalks. It began to sing. They stopped and listened to its song. It seemed the bird had come purposely to perform for them. Although it had a clear view of the hunters, the bird continued unafraid, its throat trembling with each note.

Amenemhet put down his net. "I have no heart to trap any birds now," he whispered. "Our little friend fills me with wonder and makes me thankful for life."

"I was thinking the same," Nefrytatanen agreed in a low voice. "Let the others find our supper. I prefer to sit in this golden place and look at the reeds arching over my head to the sky."

Amenemhet took Nefrytatanen's net and laid it with his on the marshy ground. Then he walked around the place, flattening the foliage, making a soft, dry carpet of the stems and a clear space large enough for them to sit down in comfort.

For a time they sat quietly, their knees drawn under their chins, looking at the changing sunlight and shadows on the moving plants, feeling the shady coolness of their golden roof, and listening to the bird. It continued to sing so exuberantly that it seemed its small body would burst with song.

After a time Amenemhet leaned toward Nefrytatanen and softly kissed the back of her neck. "What are you thinking of?" he asked.

"I'm thinking that if you continue kissing me this

way, I'll react in an unmistakable manner," she answered, her eyes still on the green shadows ahead.

"It's our little bird's singing that provokes me," he said. "It's the wind that brings the scent of your perfume my way, the feeling of your skin—like a flower petal warmed by the sun." He sighed and lay back in the leafy softness. "It's the feeling that life is good and beautiful, and I'm grateful for it, for this day, and for you." He took her hand and held it, saying nothing more, closing his eyes, drowsy and content. He heard her moving beside him and opened his eyes. She was lying on her side studying him thoughtfully. "Now, what are you thinking of?" he asked smiling.

"I'm wondering what the others will say when we return without birds—and with weeds and flowers all over us," she answered, smiling back. "They'll say we caught only each other in our nets."

Amenemhet laughed softly. "How dare they?" he asked. "We're their king and queen. Even if they think it, they'll say nothing. I expect they'll give us some strange looks, though."

"They'll think it, and they'll look," she murmured bending to brush his cheek with hers. "And what can we say? That we sat here because a bird sang so sweetly we could trap none?"

"We can say, if we wish to say anything, that we saw nothing but an insect that hovered over me, a small green snake, and a sweetly singing bird too small to catch," he whispered. "That's the truth."

Nefrytatanen turned to lay on her back, gazing at the sky smiling bright blue on them. Amenemhet sat up and looked at the blue reflected in her eyes. He leaned over and gently kissed her mouth. Her lips were cool and soft. He kissed her again, lingering until her mouth grew warm against his. Her hand crept up the arm he leaned on, reaching his shoulder and settling lightly around his back. He put his arms around her shoulders, cradling her head in his hands, continuing to kiss her, still softly and gently, but with a growing hunger.

She turned her face to the side for a moment to say, "If we keep kissing like this, they'll be right when they look at our empty nets with teasing in their eyes."

"How long will I need to kiss you this way before you're captured?" he whispered, brushing his lips to her temple.

"I'm caught in your net now," she murmured, her eyes closed as she turned her face again toward him.

Amenemhet laid his cheek against Nefrytatanen's, burying his face in her hair, whispering softly in her ear. When he parted the folds of her robe and untwined the cotton of her bathing dress, her arms reached around him, pulling him to her. The golden bird watched and continued singing.

When Amenemhet and Nefrytatanen returned to the grove where the others were gathered, they were met with the looks they had expected—although they had brushed the grass and pollen from their clothes and had smoothed their hair as best they could. Neither of them offered an explanation. They admired the catches of the others. Senwadjet, who had been careful to give them no suspicious glances, smiled to himself only after he had turned his back to them.

The birds were put in pouches, and a servant was sent back to the palace with them. There was time to swim in the pond, and they dove in enthusiastically. Their splashes made rainbows in the sunlight, and the shouts and screams of water fights rang brightly in the quiet day.

Maeti was the first to leave the water. Bekhat followed and joined her behind a bush, where Senet dried and dressed them.

The activity in the water soon stirred hunger pangs, and the rest of the group abandoned the pond to dry themselves and put on fresh garments.

When everyone had reclined in the shade and begun to eat, Nakht turned to Amenemhet.

"I've located the article you said you'd help me find for my friend in Djemeh," he said quietly.

Amenemhet looked up from his food and smiled. "Speak freely, Nakht," he said. "What did you find? I'll obtain it for you as I promised."

Nakht glanced at the others. They were listening. He felt self-conscious and answered hesitantly, "A necklace."

"What kind?" Amenemhet's tone was matter-of-fact.

"One made of gold by our own craftsmen. It's set with amethyst stones."

Amenemhet smiled. "If you think it will please the lady, get it and tell the maker to come to me for payment."

"That sounds like a gift to smooth Chamma's feathers," Nessumontu observed in a serious tone.

"Perhaps I can suggest something more to add to her gift," Nefrytatanen said slowly. "Nowhere in the world is perfume as skillfully made as in Tamera—as its cost and the demand for it plainly demonstrates. I'll send my own chemist to you and tell him to mix a perfume for Chamma. He'll ask questions about her, and when he knows what she's like, he'll make a scent to suit her alone. No one else will have it."

"That would be, indeed, a rare gift," Nakht said. "To have a perfume from your own chemist is a fine gift in itself, but to have the scent made to order should delight any woman." Nakht smiled as he considered the idea. He was sure of Chamma's reaction to such a gift. Slowly his smile faded, and he asked softly, "Speaking of ideas, have you had any about the treaty negotiations?"

Amenemhet shook his head. "Not yet, but I haven't had much time to give it thought."

"I'd like to see Zahi dealt with permanently," Kheti said suddenly.

"And I!" Senwadjet exclaimed. "The Hyskos have harassed us enough."

Amenemhet looked at the prince, surprised at this outburst. He wondered how much Senwadjet had thought about this. "And what of Djemeh?" he asked softly.

"Two can play their game," Senwadjet answered promptly. "Other lands have as much as Djemeh to offer us in trade. Why not let Djemeh know we don't need their goods for as dear a price as they demand? Why not also remind them of the craftiness of the Hyksos? Anyone who deals with them usually ends up poorer for it—or in chains."

"That isn't a bad idea," Nakht said slowly. "Until now I've talked softly to King Zaretes."

"Perhaps harder words would open his eyes to new wisdom," Senwadjet said fiercely.

Amenemhet was much interested in his son's attitude. Senwadjet had, evidently, been following state affairs closer than Amenemhet had thought he was.

"Or Djemeh might make a pact with Zahi out of

fear of us," Nefrytatanen pointed out. "We would have to be careful."

They fell silent for a while, knowing the truth of this.

Finally Senwadjet said, "I know you'll decide wisely when you've had time to consider all the details."

Amenemhet sighed. "A ruler must be wise all the time." He finished his wine and gave Yazid the goblet. "But on this day, I'll put aside these problems and rest. Perhaps we'll come to a decision after refreshing ourselves." He picked up a cushion and squeezed it experimentally, then put it behind Nefrytatanen, who sat with her back to the tree trunk. "I think I won't be long in sleeping," he said stretching. He smiled at Nefrytatanen. "Are you comfortable?" She nodded. "May I use your lap for my pillow?" She smiled warmly as he lay his head in her lap.

Nakht yawned. "That's an excellent decision. I haven't yet caught up on the sleep I missed during my journey."

There was little more conversation. One by one they adjusted pillows and settled themselves for a nap. It was customary to rest when the sun was highest, and it wasn't long before they all had closed their eyes.

The servants quietly gathered the remaining food and packed it in baskets. Then they, too, sat under the trees to nap lightly.

The bees hummed peacefully among the flowers, and the palm fronds swished softly in the light north breeze.

Senwadjet's golden eyes opened to the sound of Ahmes's flute. Senwadjet lay with his head on a pillow, listening, while the flute's notes floated on the breeze in a peaceful, wandering tune. Ahmes sat cross-legged, his back to Senwadjet, his curly black hair bent intently over his flute. Its melody drifted through the warm air.

Senwadjet wondered what would be decided for Djemeh. He realized Nefrytatanen's warning was valid, and he considered all the complicated twinings of diplomacy. He could think of no other suggestions. Amenemhet would find the solution, Senwadjet confidently decided. And he, Senwadjet, would learn from it. How could he ever replace his father? Would he ever be as wise? He had learned much by watching Amenemhet and Nefrytatanen at court. He had watched them see through clever lies and untwist emotional situations with such regard for the sensibilities of those involved that, more often than not, everyone went away satisfied. How would he ever do as well? How would he acquire the patience? He pondered these things for a while, awed by the responsibilities of the throne.

Senwadjet studied Nefrytatanen, admiring her beauty as she slept. She was, he thought, a woman any man would want to keep happy. Amenemhet and Nefrytatanen were always trying to find opportunities to be alone—but it was difficult for them. Senwadjet wondered if he might someday find a woman who would work such magic on him.

How could he ever achieve what they had? He felt acutely young and foolish so often. He was sure his own feet were much too small for Amenemhet's sandals.

The notes of Ahmes's flute faded softly. Senwadjet sighed. He would have to continue observing and learning what he could, and he decided to follow his parents' example now. They knew when to relax and forget their troubles. The forest sighed in the breeze, and Ahmes began another tune.

Senwadjet felt like walking alone in the forest and allowing the silence of the afternoon to enter his soul. He breathed deeply of the green-scented air. Life was good, Hyksos or no Hyksos.

He got up and walked soundlessly to the forest's edge. Ahmes didn't notice him, so lost in his music had the servant boy become. The melody trailed after Senwadjet, growing fainter with his steps, until it faded in the green shadows behind him.

Strolling among the spots of sun shining through the trees, Senwadjet listened to the wind softly rustling the leaves overhead. The ground was damp under his bare feet. His skin was cool in the shadows. The moment became one of profound pleasure, an interlude of feeling every sense at its height, a joining of his soul with nature in a celebration of life.

The colors and scents, the touch of the air on his skin, penetrated his being and gave him gladness. Senwadjet's young heart seemed to sing within him, and his step was light, quick, and graceful. It was in this heightened state of sensuality that he discovered Bekhat in the clearing.

She stood knee-deep in a small pond, holding her robe above the water with one hand, her other hand grasping a lotus in which she buried her nose.

Senwadjet stopped in the shadows of the trees. He gazed at her black hair shining in the sunlight, seeing her in a way he had never seen her before. His sharp eyes ran over the gentle curves of her body, and he was stimulated with a sudden rush of feeling warm and full, delighting and surprising him.

As though Bekhat sensed this intensity of perception, she glanced up. Her grey eyes were wide. For a moment she stood tense with surprise, poised as if to run.

"I'm sorry if I frightened you," Senwadjet said softly. He moved from the shadows into the warm sunlight. His voice was quiet, and she relaxed and smiled, then waded gracefully through the water to the shore, still holding the flower.

When Bekhat stood in front of him, Senwadjet suddenly realized how much smaller she was than he, and his awareness of her femininity grew stronger.

He said, "I would have called out, but when I came upon you standing in that pond, the picture was too charming to disturb."

Bekhat saw the look in Senwadjet's golden eyes and, alarmed by her answering instincts, dropped the hem of her robe hastily. At a loss for an answer, in a confusion of feelings, she held up the lotus.

"Its scent is sweet," she whispered.

Leaning closer to sniff the flower, Senwadjet was more aware of Bekhat's own clean, warm, sunny fragrance. He noticed that her hand trembled slightly, and he realized it was his nearness that made her tremble. Senwadjet looked into her face. Her eyes held a strange expression, both curious and afraid. How long her eyelashes are, he thought, and how sweet and soft looking her lips.

Bekhat stared into his golden eyes, mesmerized, unable to glance away, unable to move back, feeling drawn to him and somehow overpowered. But Senwadjet hadn't touched her. His face came slowly closer to hers, the intensity of those eyes capturing her. His lips touched hers in a kiss as warm as sunlight. Gently as the breeze from the north, he kissed her and slowly drew away, his eyes warm upon her.

Then he stepped back. Bekhat wanted him to come closer—and to kiss her again.

After a moment, he turned his eyes toward the path and said, "I think we've been away from the others for some time. By now they'll be wondering where we are."

In a sudden, unreasonable rush of anger, Bekhat turned to the path and began to walk quickly away.

"Why are you hurrying so?" he mumbled, striding swiftly behind her. Was she angry with him? Was it because he had kissed her? Why should she be angry about that? She had stood quietly waiting for his kiss and seemed to enjoy it as much as he had. Why was she rushing away? Senwadjet decided his mother might be right, after all, when she said girls were complicated.

He had kissed girls before. They hadn't acted this way. In fact, he thought, smiling, he had usually backed away first. They had been too aggressive. Bekhat's reaction began to irritate him, but his thoughts were interrupted by their arrival in the picnic area.

Everyone was awake, as Senwadjet had anticipated. Another kiss, he realized, and they might have been found.

No one said a word to Senwadjet or Bekhat, but they were both inspected. Kheti looked carefully at Bekhat, taking in at a glance her unsoiled robe and neatly arranged hair. Kheti also studied Senwadjet, who stared back without flinching.

When everyone had stopped staring, Amenemhet beckoned discreetly to Senwadjet. Senwadjet came closer, and Amenemhet turned his back to the others, walking a few steps toward the forest with his son.

"Where did you go with Bekhat?" Amenemhet asked softly.

"I went nowhere with her," Senwadjet answered in an equally quiet tone. "I awoke and felt like walking in the forest. I found her in a clearing, standing in a small pond. She had picked a lotus. She came out of the pond when she saw me, and we walked back together."

Amenemhet's golden eyes met his son's thoughtfully. "I see," he said. He made no further comments and asked no other questions, but started back to the group with Senwadjet a pace behind.

Ameni greeted Senwadjet with a teasing grin. "What were you doing in the forest with my sister?" he asked in mock suspicion.

"What would I do with a child?" Senwadjet replied lightly. He noted that Bekhat had heard his answer. Her face grew a little pink. Deliberately he added, "Bekhat is like a little sister to me. What would I do with her other than make sure she found her way back safely?"

Ameni seemed disappointed with Senwadjet's answer, but Bekhat's face had grown white. She turned to talk to Maeti, and they walked slowly away. With great satisfaction, Senwadjet observed Bekhat's reaction. Why he wanted to anger her wasn't clear to him, but his success at this made him feel better. He held his head a little higher.

Nefrytatanen had also listened to Senwadjet's remarks. She said nothing, but she guessed accurately what had happened by the pond. She smiled a little.

Maeti walked with Bekhat to a place a little away

from the others. Sitting down in the grass, Maeti picked a weed and began to play with it, turning it around between her fingers and tying little knots in its stem.

"What happened that you're angry with Senwadjet?" she finally asked. "Did he kiss you?"

Bekhat nodded in answer.

"You didn't want him to kiss you?"

Bekhat looked at Maeti, then at the grass, embarrassed.

"Then, why are you angry?" Maeti persisted. "If he kissed you and you wanted him to kiss you, why did that anger you? Did you dislike kissing him?"

Bekhat's eyes shot up, wide and grey like a cat's. "No!" she said quickly. Then she added more softly, "I liked it very much."

"Did he dislike it? Did you have harsh words?"

"Senwadjet liked it—or so it seemed." Bekhat looked at Maeti, her face slowly turning pink. "But he wanted to leave right away, and I really wanted to stay. It seemed as if he wanted to rid himself of me." Bekhat stared at Maeti. "I suppose that's why I was angry. I liked his kiss too well, and he said we must go because everyone would be looking for us."

"He was right," Maeti said, smiling faintly. "They were just mentioning your absence before you came. They would have gone in, in another moment. They would have found you."

Bekhat's face turned white. "Why did he speak of me—if he liked the kiss—as if I were his little sister?"

"Because the feelings aroused by your kiss confused him and your turning away and rushing off in anger made him think you were displeased by his kiss."

"But I wasn't," Bekhat said softly, an unfocused

look in her eyes. "I wasn't at all displeased. I wanted to stay there and kiss him many more times." She looked at Maeti, smiling a little. "It made me feel very strange and pleasant."

Maeti smiled and, dropping the weed, took Bekhat's hand in hers. "I wouldn't dwell too much on Senwadjet. His is, I suspect, the first kiss you've had." Bekhat nodded slowly in agreement, and Maeti continued, "Kisses may be enjoyable, but you must remember that others will kiss both of you." Maeti smiled wider. "Perhaps you'll like those other kisses better, or you may like them less. If—compared to those others— Senwadjet's kisses remain unsurpassed, then beware, Bekhat."

"Why?" Bekhat's eyes were wide.

"Because you may fall in love with him," Maeti answered promptly. "And I'm not sure he'll be free to love you in return. It will be some time, Bekhat, before Senwadjet will even begin to consider love with serious intentions. I would not have him break your heart—even though he meant no harm. He'll see many other girls come and go before he looks at any one seriously. You're a very pretty girl, and I like you very much, but he is the prince, Bekhat. Girls will be throwing themselves at his feet, and he'll take his time experimenting before he'll choose the one he wants forever."

"Does one always choose love?" Bekhat asked quickly. "I've heard it sometimes chooses you."

Maeti smiled, looking more than ever like Nefrytatanen. "I don't know, Bekhat. I've never even been kissed. Everyone is afraid to get that close to me. From what I've seen, though, it seems that sometimes one chooses, sometimes one is chosen and later convinced, and sometimes one makes sure one is chosen."

She got to her feet and playfully pulled Bekhat up with her. "In any case, bide your time and keep your head. Have patience and look at other boys, Bekhat. Senwadjet has, I think, discovered something exciting about himself today, and he'll want to learn more about it. Let him learn from other girls. If, someday, you're the chosen one, you may reap the rewards of what he's learned. Today Senwadjet wears a new look in his eyes."

"What look is that?" Bekhat inquired, wonderingly.

"A man's look," Maeti replied. "This will bring many more discoveries to him. You've made a discovery of your own, haven't you?"

"Yes," Bekhat said slowly. "Those feelings that threw me into such confusion are what a woman feels." She looked at Maeti, wonder on her face. "I'm no longer a child. I'm a woman," she whispered.

Maeti laughed. "So you are! Now that you know it, you may enjoy its rewards—but carefully, Bekhat, especially with Senwadjet."

They rejoined the others, and Nefrytatanen looked at Maeti's wistful expression and read her thoughts. She smiled and said, "Maeti, we're preparing to leave. Are you ready?"

Maeti shrugged her shoulders.

Nefrytatanen came closer and, putting an arm around Maeti's waist, softly said, "Your day will come, Maeti." Maeti looked up at her. "Yes, I know what's on your mind," Nefrytatanen murmured. "I was once an unkissed princess too, you know." She smiled at her daughter and added, "My day came." Giving Maeti a light hug, she resumed directing the servants.

By the time the group was ready to begin the short walk to the palace, the sinking sun had begun to tint the sky a soft gold.

Amenemhet delayed his steps, motioning to the others to go ahead on the path. When they had passed, he took Nefrytatanen's hand, and they walked more slowly behind the group.

"Let them get ahead of us," he said softly. "I'd like to share this walk with you alone." Nefrytatanen slowed her pace until the others were out of their view.

Expecting Amenemhet to mention Senwadjet's walk with Bekhat, Nefrytatanen was surprised that he remained silent, pacing slowly in the golden light, looking at the foliage and papyrus flowers. The day had taken on a new scent, and there was a coolness in the air. Amenemhet looked down at Nefrytatanen, smiled slightly, but said nothing. After a time, he stopped walking.

He put his arm around Nefrytatanen's waist and whispered in her ear, "Make no sound. Turn slowly to the right."

She turned cautiously, wondering. She looked into his eyes curiously. They were smiling, and with the slightest nod of his head, he indicated the horizon.

She saw nothing but waving, golden papyrus flowers, their green leaves and stalks.

"Watch," he whispered. He had a small pebble in his other hand. With a quick snap of his wrist, he sent the pebble skimming along the tops of the papyrus. A flock of birds began to rise from the concealing foliage. "Look at them," he said softly, wonder in his face.

Hundreds of white birds rose, the whirring of their

wings filling the air with a soft, rhythmic music. There seemed no end to them. Their feathers shimmered translucently, and the red of the sinking sun turned their wings to pale rose. They climbed higher, spiraling through the golden streaks of light, soaring in an endless column.

When the birds had circled and disappeared beyond the papyrus tops, Nefrytatanen turned to Amenemhet, wonder shining in her eyes. Wordlessly, he squeezed her waist again. Then he released her, took her hand, and they walked on.

At the foot of the palace steps, Nefrytatanen turned to Amenemhet and asked, "How did you know they were there?"

He smiled. "I don't know," he replied. "I couldn't see them, either. Perhaps when there is beauty to behold, an inner voice may whisper us to awareness."

They climbed the steps slowly, and she said softly, "Not every man knows these things, and rare is he who is sensitive to them." They continued up the stairs without speaking.

CHAPTER 11

NASSURTI STOOD QUIETLY outside the entrance to Gobryas's chamber. She was hoping to hear something of importance. When Ambassador Adadni came to visit her master, they were always plotting.

At this moment, they were silent. Idly, she stared at the colors and pattern of the nearby drapes. The materials of Tamera, more finely woven and brilliantly colored, made these look like rags. The Hyksos had no sense of line or color. Their cloth was confusing conglomerations of patterns and conflicting colors. Nassurti had come to violently hate all things of Zahi origin, however insignificant. When she thought of Tamera, she sighed and reminded herself that the Two Lands might as well be Tuat for all the hope she had of seeing her country again in her lifetime.

She heard Gobryas mutter, "Will they never stop their endless fanning? My neck is stiff with the wind they raise." Nassurti heard the familiar slap of the little whip he always carried and the squeals of the two slaves. She wished Gobryas's head might be separated from his stiff neck. He was in a vicious mood, and this foretold possible evil for her also.

Gobryas had ordered Nassurti to serve him, and she realized she dared delay no longer. Brushing a hand over her black hair, she stepped to the doorway.

Before entering the chamber, Nassurti bowed low, as Gobryas demanded, and remained bowed until he gave her permission to enter. Many beatings had forced her compliance in this and other humiliating matters.

Nassurti's back had begun to ache before Gobryas finally snapped, "Enter." She knew he deliberately waited a long time so as to cause her pain. She straightened, not allowing herself to flinch, and padded quietly to him. She didn't look at him, but kept her eyes down. He had also demanded this of her, but this was an easy task. She had no desire to look at him. Her face revealed her disgust, inevitably leading to another beating or other humiliations more loathesome. Nassurti could feel her flesh creep with Adadni's stare. Adadni desired her and had often offered Gobryas large sums for her purchase. Adadni was almost always smiling. He reminded Nassurti of a crocodile.

"You're a sneak," Gobryas snarled. "Why don't you make more noise when you walk?"

"Master, I will try," Nassurti said quietly. "What is it you wish?"

"Do you think, Adadni, if I sliced the largest toes off each her feet, she would make more noise walking?" Gobryas asked.

Nassurti's eyes shot up in alarm. Gobryas's hand was on his dagger. He laughed.

"Get us wine," he ordered.

Relieved, Nassurti turned to pour the wine. Adadni watched her.

"I ask again, my friend. If this slave is so troublesome, why not sell her to me?"

"She's worthless. I would be cheating you," Gobryas

replied. "When I decide to rid myself of her, it will be the dogs who will have her."

Adadni ran his hand over Nassurti's hips. She forced herself to remain motionless.

Adadni said, "Some slaves are good as maids, while some have other talents."

"She has none."

"I might teach her a few." Adadni's hand slid to Nassurti's buttock. She moved away to give Gobryas his goblet, then handed Adadni his. Adadni took the cup in one hand and placed his other hand on her breast. She stared at him, her black eyes shining with the fire of her anger. He removed his hand, and she stepped away.

"I have not dismissed you," Gobryas said softly.

"No, master. What else do you wish?" She stared at the floor, waiting.

"The ambassador will be my guest for tonight. You will await him in his room."

Nassurti stared at Gobryas. Was nothing beyond him? Gobryas turned to Adadni. "See what you can teach her," Gobryas said. "If you succeed, you can have her."

Nassurti wondered again if there was some way she might kill Gobryas.

"No," Adadni answered, surprising Nassurti. "I would have her in my own house," he continued. "One night will teach her nothing. I would expend my energies uselessly."

Nassurti breathed in relief.

Gobryas took her chin roughly in his hand. "You are worthless," he said quietly. "He doesn't want you even for one night. Off with you. Get out of my sight."

"Yes, master," Nassurti answered. Turning quickly,

she walked out of the room, breathing a prayer to Aset. Gobryas was bad enough, but to have him offer her to Adadni for a night and take her back the next was beyond disgust. Feeling like retching, she hurried to her quarters.

"Has King Shalmanesser agreed?" Adadni asked softly after Nassurti had left the room.

"Not yet." Gobryas stood up and paced a few steps. "He isn't eager to begin a war with Tamera. He's afraid."

"Nessumontu is a fine commander," Adadni reminded.

Gobryas laughed. "When King Zaretes joins us, we'll have Nessumontu's head as an ornament for the palace walls. Besides, Shalmanesser is greedy. He'll overcome his fear with the temptation of Tamera's riches. So will King Zaretes. Djemeh will join us. Astram, Zaretes's envoy, is on his way here now." Gobryas smiled evilly. "When the thing is over, Adadni, we'll have not only Tamera, but Djemeh, too, in our control."

"We must be careful when we talk to Astram," Adadni cautioned. "He's no fool."

"Astram will bring a story back to Djemeh that will make Zaretes beg to join us." Gobryas kicked a chair aside.

"You must convince King Shalmanesser first," Adadni said, "before Astram arrives."

"Not only will Shalmanesser be convinced by then, he will be anxious," Gobryas replied. "I'll have Amenemhet's head hanging next to Nessumontu's before this is done. I'll see all of Tamera bow as Nassurti bows."

Adadni left, wondering why Gobryas hated Tamera

so passionately. Surely a few embarrassing moments were not reason for such rage. Adadni shook his head. He sometimes wondered if Gobryas was a little mad.

"If that sorceress hadn't enticed Amenemhet to bed and marriage, Tamera would have fallen to us long ago!"

Nassurti dragged herself from the floor to stand unsteadily, her mouth bleeding, staring at Gobryas, who continued, "All your people are as worthless as you!" His slap sent Nassurti spinning to crash against the wall. She leaned dizzily against it a moment, trying to catch her breath.

"Why are you people so unbending in your pride?" he demanded. "You're a slave, but you won't allow yourself to cry even when I beat you."

Nassurti gathered together the tatters of her robe and stood quietly, obediently staring at her feet, although her back was very straight. She was again promising herself to kill him one day.

"Go!" he commanded. "Get your ugly, slanted eyes from my sight." Gobryas couldn't understand Nassurti's composure. He wondered why she wouldn't ask for mercy like the other slaves. Even now she walked as if she were Nefrytatanen in the throne room. Although her clothes were in shreds and her walk unsteady, her grace was still apparent.

"When I have Amenemhet's head and his son's head, when his daughter kneels before me—then Nefrytatanen will beg for mercy," Gobryas called loudly. He saw no reaction from Nassurti, and he kicked the door shut after her.

Remembering Nefrytatanen's cold sapphire eyes, Gobryas smiled grimly. She would beg when his sword was at Maeti's throat. Then—he would slash it. He muttered an extensive variety of curses on Tamera and its royal family.

After King Shalmanesser had been seated, Gobryas sat down. He said nothing for a moment, but Adadni saw his smug look and was confident Gobryas had a fine plan in mind.

Shifting his considerable bulk to a more comfortable position, King Shalmanesser looked expectantly at Gobryas. When Gobryas said nothing, the king muttered irritably, "Will I have to sit here staring at you all day before you speak?"

Gobryas was undisturbed. Shalmanesser always spoke harshly when he wished to hide his anxiety. Gobryas smiled. "I asked Sargon to attend this meeting because the military commander has a part in this plan."

"Which is?" Sargon stared at Gobryas, his black eyes reduced to a glitter under his bushy eyebrows.

"The wealth of Tamera is worth a little time in which to consider plans carefully," Adadni remarked.

"For the cost of a little traveling and Adadni's smooth tongue, we can have not only Tamera, but Djemeh as well." Gobryas enjoyed the looks they gave him. "I propose we convince Djemeh to make an agreement with us promising to share Tamera's treasures equally. Have our army attack Ithtawe from the east and have Djemeh, at the same time, attack from the west. I go one step further: we will obtain yet one more ally to attack from the north, so we'll surround Ithtawe. When Ithtawe falls, all Tamera falls with it." He sat back, awaiting their responses.

"Who would be this third ally?" Shalmanesser stared at the table before him. "Why would they bother?"

Gobryas smiled. "We'll make sure Djemeh's army bears the greatest burden of battle. When we've won, they'll be too weak to resist us. We'll pay Djemeh nothing and take them instead. Then we can afford paying a third ally. I look to Troy."

"Troy! They've never been our friends."

"They've never been our enemies," Gobryas said quickly. "Also, there's a special aspect of this that's to our advantage."

"And what is that?" Shalmanesser was skeptical.

"Acetes is Troy's chief counsel, and King Melanpus leans heavily on his advice. If we convince Acetes to raise his voice in our favor and we offer King Melanpus sufficient reward for his trouble, we'll have their help."

"Why should Acetes speak for us?" Sargon grumbled.

"Because he's still mad for Nefrytatanen. From the first time he laid eyes on her, he's wanted her. He's never married because he's never forgotten her. We can promise Nefrytatanen as his personal reward." Gobryas smiled with triumph. "All we need do is get Acetes to help us. We'll pay the Trojans and have both Tamera and Djemeh in our hands."

"Magnificent results for so small an effort," Adadni breathed.

"I have heard you mention repeatedly your own plans for Queen Nefrytatanen," Sargon commented drily. "Do you really intend to hand her to Acetes?"

"I wondered why you were always so interested in Tamera," Adadni remarked sarcastically, "and now I have my answer."

"Gold is my first interest. Tamera is filled with

treasures." Gobryas directed this to Shalmanesser. "True, I have a personal score to settle with Amenemhet," he added softly, "and it would please me greatly to see his blood drench the ground. Queen Nefrytatanen is an enemy from long ago when she was ruler of Tamehu. I would like very much to see her in chains. Senwadjet must be killed because I think the young hawk would be no easier to deal with than his father is. He would not bend his neck until we took it off. With Princess Maeti as our hostage and with no one to defend them, Nefrytatanen will be my slave."

"What of the bargain with Acetes?" Adadni asked.

"During war, many people are killed in the confusion," Sargon said. He sighed heavily. "Who will say who killed whom?" He looked at Gobryas, wondering if that man kept a bargain with anyone.

"That was exactly my idea." Gobryas smiled. "We can make sure Acetes has no breath with which to complain."

"In return for obtaining both Tamera and Djemeh, we pay only Troy for their help." Shalmanesser considered this. "It's worth the effort," he concluded. "Let us see Astram's reaction when he hears our offer to Djemeh. Adadni, that will be your task. Convince him that we're sure of Troy's help and that the three countries can conquer Tamera together."

"We can't fail," Gobryas said, his eyes gleaming.

"Tamera's army is strong," remarked Sargon, "but it can't fight us all."

When the ambassador from Djemeh entered the room, his blue eyes and sun-bleached hair were a startling contrast to the dark complexions and black hair of the Hyksos. Astram was tanned to a deep bronze color that resembled a Tameran's tan. Nassurti felt a pang of homesickness as she looked at him.

Astram greeted King Shalmanesser respectfully, his slender frame making the king appear even more mountainous. Astram was carefully polite to Ambassador Adadni, smiled coolly at Prime Minister Gobryas, and met Commander Sargon's gaze levelly.

Nassurti found herself wondering if Astram would be taken in by their story. She had thought Astram was an enemy, of the same cloth as the Hyksos. But she now realized he might be only a statesman doing his job. Had she misjudged him?

As Nassurti served them wine, Astram's were the only eyes that met hers without leering. And, to her amazement, he thanked her. The others thanked slaves for nothing. She withdrew to stand quietly in a corner and await further orders. Nassurti knew Gobryas had demanded her presence at this meeting so she could watch his triumph and hear for herself how they would draw Astram and Djemeh into their evil scheme against Tamera. It was one more way for Gobryas to make her suffer. It was one more way for him to take revenge on Tamera. To Gobryas, she represented Tamera. Although his cruelty to all his slaves was appalling, he took special pains to torture her in any way possible.

Adadni spoke persuasively for the Hyksos plan while Gobryas watched with glittering eyes and Shalmanesser looked properly sincere. Adadni was at his best, his manner respectful and polite. He did his utmost to convince Astram of the benefits Djemeh would gain if they agreed to join the invasion of Tamera. Sargon sat quietly.

Astram listened silently, his face betraying nothing of his inner thoughts. When Adadni had finished outlining his plot, Astram sat playing thoughtfully with the rim of his goblet, saying nothing for a long time.

Shalmanesser was beginning to worry. Even Adadni, so supremely confident of his ability, became uneasy in this silence. Gobyras ordered Nassurti to pour more wine. As she refilled Astram's cup, she looked again into his eyes. She couldn't read them. Would he be fooled?

Astram rose from his chair and strolled to a window opening. At last he spoke. "You will strike Tamera from the east, Troy will strike from the north, and Djemeh will attack from the west." He paused, his back toward them. "We will divide Tamera three ways—equally?"

"That's our plan," Adadni said quickly.

"It wasn't Djemeh's intention to engage in war," Astram said quietly. "We've been interested in trade treaties."

"Why bother with treaties when we can have Tamera?" Gobryas asked.

"I haven't the authority to make such a decision. I must bring your proposal to King Zaretes," Astram said. "I can only give him my recommendation."

"And what will that be?" Gobryas asked bluntly.

Adadni looked at Gobryas, warning him with his expression. "We're a little anxious to know if we can rely on your recommendations. There's much preparation ahead," Adadni said quickly.

"Troy is still unsettled," Astram reminded. "Are you so sure Acetes will urge King Melanpus to join these plans?"

"We're certain of it," Adadni answered. "Acetes has

always been an ambitious man." They had decided not to mention their idea of using Nefrytatanen as a personal reward. Astram might have distaste for the bribe.

Astram was again silent. He thought about Acetes. Unknown to the Hyksos, Acetes was Astram's personal friend. Acetes had been ambitious at one time, but he was content with his present place, and he was already rich enough to live as well as he wished. But Acetes had seemed bored lately, Astram reminded himself. Perhaps Acetes would agree to this venture out of boredom? No. Acetes wasn't a soldier and had never been particularly interested in military matters. Astram decided the Hyksos must be either entirely ignorant about Acetes, or they had some offer to present to Acetes that they didn't wish to tell him about. . . . An idea came to him, a sudden flare. Nefrytatanen! She was all Acetes lacked, and Astram knew Acetes wanted her.

Astram turned back to them and smiled. His smile was a mask that didn't reach his eyes. He strolled back to the table, sat down, and picked up his goblet. "As I said," he began, "I have no authority to say yes or no, but I'll tell my king your plans. I think he might agree to your bargain." Astram had decided he would urge his king to come nowhere near these treacherous men.

Gobryas smiled with triumph, and Adadni settled back in his chair. Sargon stared at Astram without blinking, and King Shalmanesser smiled widely.

"That is good news," Gobryas said eagerly.

Nassurti's heart sank in despair. Were Astram and his king fools enough to believe they would benefit from a Hyksos alliance? She shivered at the thought of Ithtawe being attacked from three directions. When Tamera was drenched in blood, when Djemeh was weakened from the struggle, then the Hyksos would have both lands under their control. They would suck both countries dry and make slaves of the people. How could Astram believe them?

Nassurti shuddered. If only she could tell Astram what they were plotting. It would cost her her life to do so, but what did that matter?

She planned what she would do. Silently, she prayed for strength and wisdom and for her soul's quick admittance to Tuat.

As Nassurti padded forward, she observed that Sargon's wine had begun to affect him, and she was thankful. If his reactions were slowed even slightly, she might succeed. Moving quietly around the table, she poured wine for each of the group. Sargon was the last she approached. As she refilled his goblet, she purposely caught the lip of the container against the cup, upsetting it into Sargon's lap. The wine ran down the outside of his leg—the opposite leg from where his sword rested.

Sargon quickly leaned over to blot and brush away the wine, cursing Nassurti's carelessness. Pretending to bend over to help, she then swiftly tore his sword from its scabbard and stepped with her back to the wall.

The unexpectedness of her move paralyzed them all for a moment. Then Sargon rose quickly, cursing, and moved toward her. She slashed and tore his cape, the tip of the sword drawing a neat red line across his chest. He looked down at it in surprise. The line became less neat, and he backed away, staring at the widening red. The wound was bloody, but not deep.

Nassurti regretted this. She wished she had struck at his throat.

King Shalmanesser was rooted to his chair. Adadni stepped a pace or two back. Gobryas came a few steps toward her. But at the look on her face, he stopped, staring at her in hatred and frustrated fury. Astram had risen, upsetting his chair, but he moved neither closer nor farther from her. He watched her intently.

"Come no closer, Gobryas," Nassurti warned. "I have more than enough reason to be joyful at your death, and I'll use this sword more wisely on you than I did on Sargon."

"She's gone mad!" Shalmanesser breathed.

"If I've gone mad, it's Gobryas who drove me to it. Hear me, Astram, for I know more of their ways than you do. They plan to share nothing with Djemeh, but will take Djemeh along with Tamera. You'll lose if you join the Hyksos."

Astram said nothing, but watched her carefully.

She turned to Gobryas. "Come, Gobryas," Nassurti invited softly. "You wished to make me beg for mercy from you? Come and take the blade from me. Kill me. My life isn't worth living as I've had to live it in your house.

"Astram, does Djemeh have slavery? Do your people treat slaves as Gobryas does? I could tell you stories to give you nightmares all your life." She paused to take a breath.

"Come and take me, Gobryas. Show them that one Tameran slave cannot frighten you." She laughed harshly. "Come, so I can avenge what you've done to me. Let me show them how well you die."

"Astram, I beg you, don't advise your king to listen

to these wicked plans. They'll drench your land in blood. Djemeh will see no treasures from Tamera's looting. The Two Lands will never fall. But if Tamera could fall, you'd give your people nothing but Hyksos ropes around their necks."

"You can't stand there forever," Adadni said softly. "Put down that sword and this moment of madness might be forgiven." He glanced meaningfully at Astram. "She's been behaving strangely lately, and I fear she's lost her reason."

"I reason clearly," Nassurti said quickly. "If I put down this sword, I'll die one second after. I know I cannot stand here forever, but this is the first moment I have stood straight and with honor since the Hyksos demons dragged me from my home. I know I'll die for this, so what will I lose if I take all of you with me?

"Come closer, Gobryas," she whispered, "for I wish to take you first. Come, Gobryas, your eyes look willing, but your coward's feet stand still. See him, Astram? See this man who offers you a bargain he would never keep if he could? Notice how bravely a man of Zahi faces a woman of Tamera, and learn from your observation."

Nassurti didn't see Sargon moving very slowly toward her. Her attention was on Astram, begging him to believe her.

"Nassurti, put down the sword," Adadni urged softly. "We'll have a physician attend you. Perhaps you have a fever."

"No physician from your miserable land can quench the fever I have or heal what Gobryas has done to me," she spat.

"Perhaps a holy man might calm you, child,"

Adadni whispered. "I'll call a priest." Adadni took one step and stopped.

"You'll call no one," Nassurti said sharply. "No priest from your filthy temples will purify my soul or give me peace from the memories of what Gobryas has done to me.

"Come, Gobryas," she coaxed. "Show us your courage. What is a slave girl to you? It's not fitting that you shrink from a slave. Surely your eye alone is enough to rout me?"

"Gobryas will sell you to me," Adadni soothed. "I'll treat you gently. Put down that sword and listen to wisdom."

"Hear your lies?" She glanced at Astram. "He knows nothing but lies. The lies that slide from his oily tongue are convincingly told because he's so used to telling them. Adadni has, I'm certain, never spoken the truth in his life. Beware of them all, Astram. See a physician, indeed! I know what I'll see if I'm given time to see anyone. They have a torturer who will be my physician and priest. Or, perhaps, once I'm in chains, Gobryas will tend me himself."

She looked at Gobryas and smiled bitterly. "Yes, I can see it in his eyes. He'll gladly attend me. Astram, look at him! See the evil so plain on his face and make Djemeh's plans accordingly."

"I command you to put down that sword." King Shalmanesser finally found his voice. "How dare you hold a sword on me?"

"You command it!" Nassurti sneered. "At last you have a tongue. Your throat is no longer paralyzed with fear. You command it." She mocked his tone. "I recognize no command of yours. You're my jailer, not my king. Gladly would I obey King Amenemhet and

Queen Nefrytatanen if they requested I push this blade into my *own* breast. You command me? I spit on your command, you tyrant.

"Astram, this person who calls himself a king is leader of a gang of murderers. Even as they killed my family before my eyes, they will not hesitate to take Djemeh."

Astram was looking slowly from face to face, saying nothing. This girl was either mad or more courageous than any he had seen. Her black eyes burned with a hatred so intense that Astram could feel it as a tangible thing. He wondered what they would do. They couldn't allow her to continue saying these things in front of him, whether the charges were true or the product of a twisted mind.

Adadni looked at Astram apologetically. "You can see the girl is mad. She thinks she's from Tamera, and she isn't. She's the child of a criminal taken into bondage," he said.

"You lie! You lie!" Nassurti screamed. "I won't let you steal even my identity from me. I am of the Two Lands! This is all I can be proud of." Nassurti shivered. "If I had one drop of Hyksos blood in these veins, I would drain them to purify myself."

Sargon leaped from a low angle, striking her hips with his shoulder, grasping the arm that held the sword. Nassurti's eyes, wide but unsurprised, looked at Astram as she fell. Gobryas not Sargon, dragged Nassurti to her feet. Sargon was bleeding profusely now from his wound and had grown very pale. Adadni raced to the door, returning with two guards who grasped Nassurti's arms and began dragging her toward the door.

"Astram," she cried, "see where they take me and

know I speak the truth." She panted and struggled as the soldiers pulled her. "The divine beings of Tamera will curse you and all your people, Shalmanesser," she called. "When King Amenemhet's army has beaten you, Queen Nefrytatanen's magic will follow you to the afterlife." The door closed upon her voice.

Astram stood motionless, stunned. Did they take her to a torturer? He watched Sargon as he crept toward a couch, holding his bloody robe tightly against his wound.

Gobryas turned to Astram. "I must get Sargon to a bed and the physician to him." He shook his head. "You will excuse us."

"Of course," Astram replied, wondering where Gobryas would go while Sargon was being attended. Would he be the girl's torturer?

After Gobryas and Sargon had left, Adadni took Astram's arm and led him to a chair. "Sit down and have some wine," he soothed. "This has been a terrifying experience. How sad that a young and beautiful girl should be mad, is it not?" Adadni shook his head sympathetically.

Astram sank into the chair and accepted the goblet given him. Was Nassurti mad? One thing Astram knew was that Adadni had lied about her being from Zahi. She was not. She was from Tamera as surely as he was from Djemeh. No Hyksos woman had eyes like Nassurti's. No Hyksos was ever born who looked like a Tameran.

Nassurti lay sprawled on the floor of the cell into which she had been thrown. She was stunned by the magnitude of what she had done. Slowly she smiled, remembering Gobryas's face. At last Gobryas had heard her say what she had wanted to say so many times. If only Astram would believe her and convince his king not to join the plot! It would be worth the price she was going to pay.

Nassurti dragged herself from the floor, and finding nowhere else to sit, she brushed a spider web from a corner and sat on the rough stones again, her back against the wall. How her head pounded! She leaned forward to rest her forehead against her bent knees. This pain would be nothing to what she faced. How long would it be before her torturers came, she wondered. How long would it take to die? Did she dare hope her life would be ended cleanly by an arrow? However death would come, Nassurti decided, now was the time to prepare for it.

"Now you regret your deed, Nassurti?" The voice of Gobryas cut through her thoughts. She heard the jailer removing the bolt and ice ran through her veins. "Beg forgiveness, slave." Gobryas stepped inside. "Perhaps, if your pleading is sufficiently humble and convincing, I might have mercy on you and kill you quickly."

Nassurti got slowly to her feet. She stood straight and looked defiantly into Gobryas's eyes. "I weep because I'll never see my home in Tamera," she said calmly. "I weep because I didn't kill you. Beg?" She smiled. "Dishonor myself by pleading to continue this disgusting life? Give me to your torturer or your dogs and expect no cries of mercy from me. Beg *you*?" Her eyes were black fire. "I beg only that Sutekh takes your soul one day soon and gives it to the demons of Apep."

Gobryas grew livid with fury. "Take her to the room of torture," he commanded, "before I lose my temper and kill her here, depriving myself of the pleasure of her punishment."

The jailer took Nassurti's arm to drag her from the cell. To his surprise, she didn't scream or struggle as other prisoners always did. She smiled coldly.

"I will go on my own feet." Nassurti's voice was firm and clear. "Take careful note, Gobryas, of how I meet my end. Think on it when you face Tamera's army." She followed the jailer calmly.

A chill crept over Gobryas. What kind of people were these? This one silly peasant girl defied him even now. What did the people of the Two Lands think they were? Gods and goddesses? Invincible?

Nassurti must be mad, Gobryas decided. He smiled. Mad or sane, Nassurti would be glad enough to die when he was ready to let her. He watched her walking ahead, straight and calm. He would see how calm she remained! She was made of flesh and bone like anyone else, her nerves were as sensitive to pain, and her blood would run as redly on the floor as anyone's. He would see how proud and calm she remained when he started on her!

The jailer snapped chains on her wrists and ankles, and Gobryas was perplexed by the serene expression on Nassurti's face.

She wasn't aware when Gobryas began his tortures because she had turned her mind to her memories and was again a child walking beneath Tamera's blue skies toward the temple. She entered the shadowy coolness where the statue of Aset smiled down on her. She brought an offering of flowers to her goddess and tiptoed over the shining granite floor toward the smiling golden statue to lay her handful of wild flowers at the feet of Aset. The sun streamed through the high slitted windows, making rainbows on the floor. The smell of incense lingered richly in the air.

The first pain Nassurti felt was insidiously subtle, sliding like a serpent through the grass toward her. She clenched her teeth and turned her mind to the temple at home, to peace and protection. She willed her mind to Tamera. She forced herself to think of home, the papyrus along the river, the lotuses floating in the pond, the ibises wading in the water near the shore. The pain became a crocodile rising from the mud. She thought of the stars, the soothing blackness of the night skies, the shadow of an obelisk.

Anguish dragged her to the present. O Father Tem, O One Alone, Unknowable One, give me strength, she prayed silently. She clenched her teeth. Give me the strength to make no outcry.

It was forever, she thought. It would never end. When would she die? How long must it take to die? Would she approach Asar the way she looked now? She would be clothed with blood and smell of this evil place when she went to Tuat. How long would it take for her body to give up her soul? O Aset, she silently cried, I can bear it no longer!

Although her teeth remained clenched, Nassurti couldn't stop the betraying moan that escaped her lips. It had come from too deep within her. She opened her eyes and could see nothing. Did blood fill her vision or was she blinded? In the blackness before her, she saw sparkles of light. Her face was growing cold. She knew she would shortly faint again. Someone slapped her face—she heard the sound of the slap—but that meager sting was beyond her shocked nerves. Dimly she heard Gobryas complain of blood that had splashed his robe.

"She's fainted again," the jailer said. "Shall I pour water on her?"

"No," Gobryas answered. "I have grown weary. Lock her in the cell. I'll return when I'm rested. Then I'll enjoy her slow death more." His voice receded. "See that you keep the rats from her."

Astram sat in his room wondering if beneath these floors in the dungeons there was a room for torture where the girl lay in agony. Adadni had lied about her being insane. She had seemed sane enough—but angry and desperate.

Astram didn't like Gobryas at all and never had. He was sure that Gobryas was capable of any evil. Astram thought about Nassurti. She had looked into his eyes when she had poured his wine. Her gaze had been intelligent. Her look had carefully appraised him. Had she planned this from the beginning?

Astram stood up and walked to the window. If that poor girl had deliberately waited for the chance to get Sargon's sword, she had known what retaliation she faced. Astram whistled softly.

Since Gobryas had left with Sargon to get the commander's wound attended, Astram had seen nothing of the prime minister. Was he downstairs in the torture room applying pain in layer after layer to the girl? Where was Gobryas, if not there? Astram paced the floor. He resolved to find out. He couldn't allow her to be treated cruelly.

But Astram had to remain above suspicion. He couldn't allow himself to be caught spying on the dungeons and meddling in Zahi's business. He was an ambassador.

But Astram was a man before he was anything else.

He put a dagger in his belt and took off his boots, replacing them with the soft slippers he wore for comfort. They were silent enough for spying.

He hesitated. What would he do if he did find her? He threw a dark-colored cape over his shoulders and picked up the small bag in which he carried his gold. Glancing around the room, he tried to decide what else he would take with him if he must flee. He took his sword and threw his cloak over the cape to hide the weapon. He wouldn't be able to take more. His clothes and other personal possessions must remain behind.

Astram put his ear to the door and heard nothing. Slowly he opened it a crack and peered into the hall. No one was in sight. He stepped back into his room and arranged the bolt to fall into place behind him. It would indicate to servants or other visitors that he was asleep for the night. He didn't know how he would manage to get back into his room if he did not find the girl. But he was fairly convinced the girl had spoken truthfully. He must save her and return to Djemeh. Above all else, he must tell King Zaretes of the plot. Tamera lay between Zahi and Djemeh. If he could get to Tamera's border, he would be safe. It was far enough, but possible.

The hall was still empty. He stepped out quickly and closed the door, hearing the bolt fall into place. It was the sound of commitment. Now it would be almost impossible to go back. Astram sighed. He was an ambassador, a peacemaker, but it was a good thing he had also learned how to use a weapon.

Silently he crept down the hall to the slaves' stairway at the back of the palace. He held his breath, praying to various gods and goddesses.

Astram made his way out of the palace to the stables. He crept up behind a stable boy and knocked him unconscious with a rock, taking care not to harm the boy seriously. Then, he got his own horse and another one ready for escape, hiding them carefully.

A heavy door stood in a shadowy place a little below the level of the ground. If there were a dungeon or a torture chamber, this door was probably the entrance. It swung open easily. He hesitated, suspicious, then reasoned that prison doors were made to keep people in—not out.

Beyond the doorway was a narrow, winding staircase enclosed on both sides by grim stone walls lit at intervals with torches. It certainly looked like a dungeon. He began to creep slowly down the stairs wondering why there were no guards.

At the foot of the stairway, there was another closed door and probably a sentry. There was no way to get through the door by stealth, so he knocked on it loudly, hoping Gobryas wasn't there.

The door opened a little, and Astram could glimpse the uniform of a guard.

"Who's there?" the guard demanded.

"Astram, ambassador of Djemeh," he answered firmly. "Prime Minister Gobryas told me to come here." He felt fear prickle his scalp and hoped he would think of something to say to Gobryas if he were present.

"He isn't here," the guard replied.

Astram disregarded the temptation to breathe a sigh of relief and said sharply, "He doesn't have to be here. He told me I could talk to that slave girl who was brought here today. This is the place, isn't it? I haven't made a mistake?"

"This is the place," the guard answered, recognizing the ambassador and wondering why he should wish to speak with the girl. "Why do you wish to talk to her?" He was curious.

"That's none of your affair, guard," Astram said brusquely. "I'm here to speak to her. That's all you need to know. Stand aside."

The guard was too dull-witted to question a superior and didn't have the nerve to say any more. He opened the door and stepped aside.

"Where is she?" Astram demanded.

"Third cell on the left," the guard muttered.

"Well, show me!" Astram ordered. "Do you know how to open the bolt, or will I have to search for someone else?"

"I can open it," the guard answered quickly. These brusque orders were unmistakably from someone used to giving orders and expecting obedience. The guard was used to taking orders. He said no more, but led Astram to the cell door, took off the bolt, and swung the door open.

"Bring the torch," Astram snapped. "I have no wish to trip and fall in this filthy place."

The guard turned, and Astram struck him with the weighted handle of his dagger. The guard crashed to the floor.

Astram got the torch and brought it back to the cell, marveling at the evil of the place.

He saw Nassurti in the corner on the floor and hurried to her, hoping he wasn't too late. As he lifted her head, she moaned a little. Her eyes opened and struggled to focus. By all the deities of every land, he thought, what had they done to her?

Nassurti recognized Astram's light hair first. Her

eyes slowly cleared, and she saw his face. She stared in amazement.

"Make no sound," Astram said. "I'm getting you out of here." Gently he pulled Nassurti to her feet. "Can you stand alone?" he whispered.

She stared at him in disbelief. Her ankles were numb and her knees were like water. He was holding her up now as she leaned against him. She laid her face helplessly on his chest and began to cry.

"Please don't make noise," he begged. "I know it's been terrible, but you must find the strength to be silent. I'll have to carry you to the horses." She stopped her tears, but her shoulders still trembled. He picked her up. "We can talk of this later," he whispered, "when we're safely away from here." She put her arms around his shoulders and was silent.

Nassurti wished she could walk so that she might, at least, help Astram a little. She was thankful she wasn't taller and heavier. He was very gentle, avoiding places where she might bump the walls, aware that even the slightest bump would mean agony. By the time he had struggled up the stairs, he was panting.

Outside, Astram leaned against the door, closing it softly behind him. Fresh air revived Nassurti's spirit, and she took great, deep breaths of it. Each breath was painful, but the sweet smell of freedom was wonderful. He hurried her to the bushes where he had hidden the horses.

"Can you manage to stay on a horse?" Astram whispered.

"I'll do it somehow," Nassurti answered. She shivered slightly, and Astram took off his cloak, wrapping it around her and placing the hood over her head.

"Thank you," she whispered. Only now did she realize her robe had been torn from her, and she was naked. She blushed, then felt foolish.

"It is I who thank you," Astram murmured. He stood next to her horse a moment. "We'll go west to Tamera. When we cross the border, I'll be able to travel safely to Djemeh."

"Tamera." Nassurti said the name softly. "I thought I'd never see it again."

"You will," Astram whispered and smiled. There was a whirring sound, then a soft thud. A strange expression came over Astram's face. "West," he said aloud. "Tamera."

Astram sank slowly from Nassurti's sight, and she painfully leaned over to see him collapse on the ground, the feathered shaft of an arrow protruding from his back.

"O Asar," she moaned, as shouts filled the air. Now they would come after her. She would be delivered again to Gobryas. "No," she whispered, then raised her voice to repeat defiantly, "No!"

Tamera was the last word Astram had spoken. Nassurti drew her horse around sharply and dug her heels into its ribs. The horse reared once in objection, then raced forward. Nassurti held on tightly. Each leap sent fresh pain through her, but she must endure it. Astram had given his life. She would get to Tamera.

Gobryas and Sargon dragged the guard through the doorway.

"What will we do now?" Sargon asked. "I've just killed Ambassador Astram!"

"We'll send Adadni to Djemeh," Gobryas answered quickly. "Just get that girl. Get her!"

251

Sargon raised the alarm immediately. The tone in Gobryas's voice told Sargon that he should have also killed Nassurti. Sargon muttered a curse. How could anyone have shot another arrow so quickly? He marveled that he had managed to hit Astram.

When Gobryas ran into the palace, he sent the first servant he saw racing for Adadni. Moments later Adadni came rushing down the steps, grasping a robe around his shoulders.

"What happened?" Adadni called.

"Astram helped the girl escape," Gobryas answered. "Sargon's going after her, but the ambassador is dead."

Adadni stared at Gobryas, his thoughts racing. "I'll go to Djemeh," he said. "I'll tell King Zaretes that Astram died in a hunting accident. I'll persuade that fool Zaretes that Astram was agreeable to our bargain. I'd better prepare now in case that girl escapes."

"She can't get away," Gobryas said. "She's in no condition to ride that hard. She's lucky if she stays on that horse for ten minutes."

"She'd better not get away," Adadni said firmly, "but I can't take the chance. Tell King Shalmanesser what happened."

"Why me?" Gobryas didn't wish to tell the king this story.

"Because it's your fault," Adadni snapped. "If you'd killed her instead of playing with her, this wouldn't have happened." Adadni glared at Gobryas. "I don't have the time." He turned and ran back up the stairs, muttering.

Amenemhet crossed the courtyard slowly. Nefrytatanen hadn't yet returned from the temple, and he never went to bed until she did. He walked on, hoping she would come back soon. Ahmes padded quietly behind him.

Amenemhet passed a large bush and hearing a rustle, quickly stepped away.

"Something is in there," Amenemhet said softly, "perhaps a serpent." Ahmes ran to the wall and took down a torch, returning as Amenemhet drew his sword.

A figure stepped hesitantly from the shadows. Amenemhet couldn't see the face under the hood, but upon seeing him the small figure prostrated itself on the ground.

"Bring that light closer, Ahmes," Amenemhet said quietly, "so I may see who this is."

The body at Amenemhet's feet wore a tattered and filthy cloak smeared with stains suggesting blood. Some intuition warned him that this was an object of pity, not scorn.

He said gently, "Who are you? Rise and show your face."

The figure trembled slightly, and a muffled voice answered, "Sire, I'm ashamed that you see me. I had thought to speak to a servant, surely not you."

Amenemhet was perplexed. The voice sounded feminine. He reached down to gingerly touch the ragged shoulder. "Rise," he commanded. "I won't speak to you while you're prostrated. Stand up," he coaxed. "Address me as a man, not groveling like a beaten animal."

"Sire, I cannot stand up," came the answering whisper.

Amenemhet grasped the chin of the bowed head and raised Nassurti's mutilated face. At the sight of her, he gasped, and then, unconcerned with the encrusted blood and filth, he reached down to pick up her slight body.

He turned to Ahmes. "Get Horemheb," he snapped. Ahmes was off at a run.

Inside the palace, Amenemhet lay Nassurti on the first couch he found, and she turned her face from him, hiding herself.

"Young woman," he said softly, "whoever has done this is to blame, not you. Tell me how this happened and to whom the shame belongs so this evil may be punished." Very gently he turned her toward him. "Speak, little one," he urged, "if you have the strength." He marveled at the damage done her. He could barely see her eyes. They were concealed under swollen lids.

"I've come a long way to find you—from Zahi," Nassurti whispered. "I am of your people, but a slave of Gobryas." She shivered and flinched. A wound across her lips opened and bled with her words. "If you would send me back to him, grant me the mercy of a dagger so I may end this misery. I have heard you're just with your people. Would you show mercy to the property of a Hyksos?"

"I'll give you no dagger," Amenemhet said sternly, "nor will you be returned to him or any other. My physician is coming to attend you. I would hear your story now, if you have the strength to tell it. If you would wait until you've rested, I'll also wait. But I will hear the details of this matter."

His eyes were triangles of burning gold, and Nassurti was afraid, despite his reassuring words. She stared at him silently.

"You need not fear me or anyone here," Amenemhet said firmly. "You're safe. I can see you're too weak to relate what happened. You can tell me when you're stronger."

Amenemhet moved as if to turn away, and Nassurti reached out in desperation to grasp his hand and hold him there. It had been a long time since any kindness had been shown her.

Amenemhet settled on the edge of the couch, saying nothing. He could see wounds all over her. What kind of man could do such a thing?

"I must tell you while I have strength," Nassurti whispered.

"You'll be stronger later," he assured her. "My own physician will attend you." He looked up as Horemheb entered. Horemheb rushed to the couch and stared at Nassurti in silent dismay.

"I must speak now," she said hoarsely.

"You'll speak later," Horemheb said firmly, "not now. You'll sleep while I treat you." He mixed a cup of liquid quickly, in a jerky motion because he was so angry. He held up her head and put the cup to her lips. "This will not harm you," he said gently, "but you'll sleep and feel no pain while I attend to you."

Nassurti swallowed the liquid obediently, and he laid her head down. Her eyes fluttered, and in moments she was asleep. Horemheb looked at Amenemhet angrily.

"I'm afraid to move her from this couch," he said. "I fear she has many broken bones. To move her may be to crush them all the more."

Amenemhet turned to Ahmes, who was watching silently, his great black eyes wide with horror. "Find someone to carry this girl and the couch to a room where Horemheb can work on her," Amenemhet said quietly. "When you've sent someone here, go for whatever else Horemheb needs."

He looked at the physician. "Bandages, something to splint her fractures? What else?"

"Just have her brought to my quarters carefully," Horemheb said. "I have what I need there, although perhaps more bandages will be necessary. Also hot water in great quantities. She's filthy, and I must cleanse her before I can do anything."

Ahmes looked at Amenemhet, who nooded his approval. Then Ahmes raced out.

Horemheb stood up, and his disgust was obvious. "Whoever did this work deserves to have his skin peeled from him in small strips."

Amenemhet was startled to hear these words. Horemheb was always a peaceful man, a man of infinite gentleness and patience.

"I have seen wounds of many kinds," Horemheb said. "I have attended soldiers after battle. I have treated burns, extensive burns. But, by Heru, I cannot see how any man could deliberately inflict such suffering on a helpless girl."

"Gobryas did this," Amenemhet said softly, remembering how Gobryas had looked at Nefrytatanen. If ever Nefrytatanen fell into Gobryas's hands, what might he do to her?

Horemheb turned toward the door. "I'll take care of the girl," he promised.

Amenemhet paced the room. When would Nefrytatanen get back? He heard the palace doors open and close, and he hurried to the hall door.

Opening the door, he saw Nefrytatanen dismiss her guards, then turn for Dedjet to remove her cloak.

Seeing Amenemhet's expression, Nefrytatanen quickly asked, "What's happened? What's wrong?"

Amenemhet took Nefrytatanen's arm and led her toward the staircase. "We have a visitor," he said.

Nefrytatanen stopped with one foot on the step. "Who?" she asked, baffled.

"I don't know her name yet. She came just a short time ago." Amenemhet started up the stairs. "She's been tortured, and Horemheb gave her a drug."

Nefrytatanen stopped and stared at Amenemhet. "Did she say anything at all?"

"Only that she's a slave of Gobryas and that he did this to her. She was terrified she might be sent back and begged me for a dagger first." Amenemhet's eyes reflected what he had seen.

Nefrytatanen was speechless for a moment. She resumed climbing the steps. Finally she asked quietly, "Did Horemheb say anything about whether she'll be able to answer questions?"

"He said maybe tomorrow—if she lives that long." Amenemhet looked at Nefrytatanen. "I don't know if she will," he said. "Horemheb couldn't tell the extent of her injuries. She may have looked worse than she was." Amenemhet took Nefrytatanen's hand tightly in his and added, "I'm glad you're home safely."

CHAPTER 12

Amenemhet sat with Nefrytatanen beside the fountain. The morning still retained the night's coolness, and the wind from the north was gentle.

Amenemhet held Nefrytatanen's hand tightly and looked at her so steadily she began to feel uncomfortable. His eyes held an expression she didn't understand.

She reached to touch her fingers to his lips and asked, "What are you thinking of, beloved, that you stare at me so strangely?"

"How beautiful you are," Amenemhet murmured. He smiled, but the smile was unconvincing.

"There's more in your eyes," she said softly.

"Yes," he admitted, glancing away. "I think of that slave girl and what Gobryas did to her. I saw some of her wounds, and they were terrible. If she lives, she'll be disfigured."

"There's still more than that on your mind."

"Yes." He was hesitant to tell her more, but the sapphire eyes on him couldn't be resisted. "I think of Gobryas, of his hatred for us and how he looked at you." His golden eyes turned from her so she wouldn't see his pain. "I think of what he'd do to you if he could."

Nefrytatanen put her arms around Amenemhet and rested her head on his shoulder. "He'll never touch me," she said. "He wouldn't get past you even if he had the chance to try."

"Not as long as I'm alive," Amenemhet said grimly.

"What a dreary conversation!" Senwadjet interrupted. "I creep up silently, seeing you embracing, expecting to hear words of love and learn about the spells you cast to enchant each other. But instead I hear of death." He added, "If anyone needs protection—though I'm not as skilled as you, father—my sword is ready." Senwadjet dropped to the grass at their feet, looking up at them speculatively. "It's that girl's coming that brings such thoughts, I suspect. But other ideas have occurred to me."

"What ideas?" Amenemhet asked softly.

"I think that girl knows something exceedingly important to force herself to travel all the way here in her condition. I think we should find out who else knows she's here and make sure they keep silent—at least until we find out what she came to tell us."

Nefrytatanen smiled proudly.

Amenemhet said softly, "You are sometimes wise, Senwadjet." He looked at Nefrytatanen. "Do you think he may become a proper king one day?"

"There is some hope," she answered lightly.

Senwadjet smiled widely. "I've tried to learn something from you," he said. He got to his feet and brushed the grass from his tunic.

Amenemhet stood up and faced him. "Then, give orders to have this done. It was your idea, and you'll be responsible for its satisfactory results."

Senwadjet stared at him. Although he had given many orders in the past, this was of a different level.

"Try your wings, my son," Amenemhet said softly. "See how it feels to be Heru."

"I will try," Senwadjet whispered in awe.

Nefrytatanen stood up and took Senwadjet's hand. "To be Tamera's ruler, Senwadjet, is to be divine. You cannot merely try."

"I know," Senwadjet replied. He squeezed her hand and walked away, his head very high.

"He will do," Amenemhet commented, watching Senwadjet's retreating figure. "He'll manage very well someday, I think." He put his arm around Nefrytatanen's waist, and they started toward the door. "We should see if Horemheb has any news for us," he said.

"How old is this girl, would you say?" Nefrytatanen asked.

Amenemhet stopped walking and turned to her. "I cannot say." He shook his head sadly. "I really couldn't tell by looking at her. I would guess she's older than Senwadjet and not as old as we are."

"That leaves a fifteen-year margin!" Nefrytatanen was shocked.

"That's how badly she was mutilated."

They walked slowly into the palace. Once inside, Nefrytatanen sat on a couch staring at her hands. Amenemhet saw a tear splash on her fingers and sat down next to her, putting his arm around her shoulder.

"The sight of her is what made me think grim thoughts," he said softly, "but Gobryas will never touch you or Maeti or even put one foot in this palace again—unless he's in chains."

Yazid entered the room, followed by Nessumontu. "Horemheb instructed me to tell you the girl is awake now and can speak."

"Good." Amenemhet stood up. "Thank you, Yazid. Nessumontu, I'm glad you're here because I have a feeling what she says will be of interest to you."

Nessumontu couldn't imagine what an escaped slave

might say to interest him, but he nodded and followed them. He had heard nothing about her aside from the news that she was in the palace.

As they entered the bright and airy room, Horem-heb said softly, "She'll survive. I'm sure now. She's weak, and weak she'll remain for some time. Please try not to tire her out too much or excite her. She needs peace and quiet badly."

"Will her injuries have any permanent effect?" Amenemhet whispered.

Horemheb looked angrily over his shoulder at the bed by the window, then turned to them and answered softly, "Her bones and flesh will heal in time, but I don't know what wounds will remain in her mind. She seems stable enough, though she moaned about all kinds of frightening things in her sleep. One thing I do know is she'll be scarred. After she has healed sufficiently to see how bad the scars are, perhaps I can still do something to minimize them. I can't be certain."

They received this news with disgust. Nessumontu looked as if he would say something. But when he saw the small bandage-covered face turn in their direction, he closed his mouth. They crossed the room quietly. Nefrytatanen sat on a chair by the bed. Amenemhet and Nessumontu remained standing next to her, and Horemheb hovered discreetly in the background. He wished to be sure his patient was not over-taxed.

"You're from Tamera, I understand," Nefrytatanen began gently. "How did you fall into the hands of the Hyksos?"

Nassurti's voice was muffled by her bandages. "My name is Nassurti. I was taken from the north before your marriage joined the Two Lands. I was a child when the Hyksos came." She was having some difficulty speaking with the many stitches in her face. "My family was killed—all of them, I think—and our home was burned. I was sold into the household of a Hyksos family where I did menial jobs. When I grew older, I was allowed to attend the lady of the house. It was an unfortunate promotion. When Gobryas visited the family and saw me, he offered so high a price the lady couldn't resist. In Gobryas's house I was treated differently. He always seemed to hate Tamera passionately and saw in me a way to vent his rage. He amused himself with me. He wished to break my spirit, but I somehow found the strength to remain unbroken."

The low voice revealed the emotions Nassurti's bandage-masked face could not.

"When Gobryas revealed his plan to attack Tamera, I was present. I knew he deliberately had me serve him so I could hear how he planned to bring you to your knees. It was too much. I laughed at him in front of Astram, the ambassador from Djemeh and in front of Sargon, his own army commander—and even King Shalmanesser. I said Tamera's army would beat them all. I said Gobryas was evil, a fool, and a coward."

"How did you manage to say all this?" Nessumontu asked in bewilderment.

"I had stolen Commander Sargon's sword and stood with my back to the wall." Nessumontu whistled softly in amazement. "I wanted Gobryas to try to take it from me," Nassurti said grimly. "I tried to coax him to do it." She stopped a moment, then continued. "I think I was insane with anger. I warned Astram not to agree to their plan. Gobryas intended to cheat Astram. They had me dragged away for exposing their plot."

"You weren't insane," Amenemhet said quietly. "You were very courageous."

"I paid for it," Nassurti said, sighing. "When Gobryas tired of torturing me, he ordered me set aside so he could rest and enjoy killing me later. Something I had said made Astram wonder if I spoke the truth. I had told him what I expected Gobryas to do with me, and Astram somehow got into the dungeons and helped me escape. He wanted to get away and warn his king of their plans, but he was killed by an arrow. I don't know how I managed to get here. I think I was only half conscious most of the time."

"If you're tired," Amenemhet said, "we'll wait to hear the rest of your story. But if you have the strength, relate what you can remember of their plot. We would act as quickly as possible."

"I'll tell you now." Nassurti was determined. She was weary, but she would chance waiting no longer, for she still wasn't convinced she would live. "I came to warn you if you would listen."

"We're listening," Nefrytatanen said grimly.

"I don't know why Gobryas hates Tamera so much," Nassurti said, "but he's greedy, too. So is King Shalmanesser, and he listens when Gobryas tells of Tamera's riches. They want Djemeh's help, and Djemeh might agree. Their plan is to have the army of Djemeh launch an invasion from the west and the Hyksos from the east at the same time. They plan to attack Ithtawe itself, believing that if this fortress falls, the rest of the land will be easily won. Then, Zahi would take over Djemeh, too, when that army was weakened from fighting you.

Nassurti paused to catch her breath and Nessumontu muttered an angry oath. Horemheb came closer, but Nassurti began to speak quickly.

"They would like to interest another country in sailing up the Nile to attack from the north. They have made no agreement with anyone yet—but they talked about Troy."

Amenemhet looked at Nefrytatanen and tried to control his anger. "You know why they chose Troy," he said. She looked thoughtful, but said nothing.

"Why?" Nessumontu asked.

"Because Acetes is now chief counsel to King Melanpus, and Acetes could, they hope, be bribed by offering Nefrytatanen as his prize," Amenemhet said. Nessumontu stared at him, but made no comment.

"What Gobryas doesn't know about Acetes," Nefrytatanen said calmly, "is that Acetes wouldn't want me as a prisoner. When Acetes visited Tamera, he and I spoke as friends. He respects me. I believe he's an honorable man and would advise his king against this venture. But if Troy said no, the Hyksos would look for another ally."

"I have an idea," Nessumontu offered slowly, "although maybe you won't like its implications." He looked at Amenemhet warily.

"Tell us," Amenemhet said, "and we'll decide if we like it or not." He shook his head. "We must do something. I'm sure King Shalmanesser will send Adadni to Djemeh to offer some lie about Astram. If their plans are carried out, I don't know that we could resist their combined forces."

"We might find an ally in Troy ourselves, if the queen pleaded our cause with Acetes." Nessumontu fell silent, not knowing what to say next, embarrassed.

"It might succeed," Nefrytatanen said quickly.

"I won't have you endangered by such a journey," Amenemhet said firmly. "I won't have you bargain with Acetes by using yourself as bait."

"I, tease Acetes? No!" Nefrytatanen exclaimed. "Once he offered friendship. We could offer payment for their trouble. Troy's king is as likely as any other to accept Tamera's gold."

Amenemhet was silent. A plan was beginning to form in his mind. Although he didn't like it, he knew Nefrytatanen and Nessumontu were right. Finally he said, "If we asked Troy to pretend to fall in with the Hyksos plan, to launch their ships and sail here but at the last minute refuse to fight—if we paid them well for this deception—" He looked at Nessumontu thoughtfully. "If we send Nakht to Djemeh, supposedly to continue negotiations, and he spreads the rumor that Astram was killed purposely, then we might make King Zaretes hold off. If he's really hesitant now, that might stop him."

"If Nakht also spread a rumor or two that we're well prepared to beat the Hyksos yet still interested in a treaty with Djemeh, that could help our cause as well," Nessumontu suggested.

"Yes," Nefrytatanen said slowly. "If King Zaretes thought he could make a treaty with us, it might make the difference." She looked at Amenemhet. "I would sail to Troy and ask Acetes to intercede with King Melanpus in our favor."

"I still don't like to see you go," Amenemhet said.

"Nakht would be in Djemeh to see that these stories are spread properly," she reasoned. "Acetes would listen to me. He surely will be more disposed toward me than toward you, and one of us must stay here.

No one with less authority can persuade them in so delicate a situation."

"I have no doubt Acetes would be disposed to listen to you," Amenemhet's voice held sarcasm, "but what more would he be inclined to do?"

"No more," she said quietly. "I can manage Acetes— one way or another. Have Necho command the ship, arm it well, and I'll be safely back in Tamera before the Hyksos even begin to march."

Nassurti whispered, "It sounds like a good plan to me, if I may comment."

"You have, I think, done enough to deserve an opinion on this," Nessumontu said softly. He looked at Amenemhet, waiting for a decision.

Amenemhet sighed and turned to Nefrytatanen. "When you said you can manage Acetes one way or another, did you mean what I thought?"

"If necessary," she said quickly. "I can take what I need."

Amenemhet turned to Nessumontu. "Have a messenger dispatched to Acetes immediately, saying only that Queen Nefrytatanen is coming to speak with him. Get our ship ready to sail." He put his hand on Nessumontu's shoulder. "Make sure the ship is heavily armed and well manned. Send Necho to me."

Nessumontu nodded. He glanced once more at Nassurti and, hesitating a moment, bent over her slightly. He could see only her dark eyes looking at him through the bandages. He said softly, "You will get well. Believe this. You've come so far. Even if Horemheb had doubts, I wouldn't believe them. You have too much courage." He smiled. "I would tell your story later to my men to inspire them." Nessumontu turned and left the room, and the others stared at him in surprise.

Amenemhet turned to Nassurti. "We will leave you now so you may rest. I fear we've overtired you. Nessumontu is right, Nassurti. When you're well, look forward to being rewarded for what you've done. We cannot compensate you for your suffering, but we'll do what it's possible to do."

The black eyes staring at him from the bandages were luminous with tears. Finally she said brokenly, "Being home is enough reward. I've dreamed of returning to Tamera ever since I was carried away."

"That's enough," Horemheb said sternly. "You must rest if you want to get on your feet soon."

"I will walk?" Nassurti asked quietly.

"You will certainly walk, unless you grow too lazy," Horemheb said.

"I wasn't sure," Nassurti said in wonder.

At this, Nefrytatanen quickly turned and left the room. Amenemhet followed her into the hall and saw that she was weeping. He put his arm around her waist, his own vision blurring.

"I've seen few men or women with such courage," he said, "very few."

Nefrytatanen lifted her face to look at him. "I can't even begin to imagine what Gobryas did to her." Amenemhet wiped her tears gently, but his face was grim.

"I can," he said quietly.

News of the additional fortifications at Ithtawe spread rapidly throughout Tamera, and to reassure the frightened peasants, the nobles were ordered to return to their provinces. Messengers were sent speeding into the night with orders to take no action against Djemeh's army unless defense was necessary. Amenemhet hoped King Zaretes would advance cautiously, if at all.

Any raids from Zahi, he ordered, were to be dealt with swiftly. The necessary outposts were being reinforced, and Nessumontu was soon engaged in fulltime war preparations. Amenemhet was too occupied with military matters to do much else, so the task of holding public audience fell on Nefrytatanen.

Senwadjet followed Amenemhet and Nessumontu everywhere, learning about military preparations, so Maeti was left mostly alone. However, Ithtawe was gradually being filled with soldiers from distant garrisons, and since many of these men were young and some were very attractive, Maeti found her time pleasantly filled.

One particularly hot day Sitah, Nessumontu's aide, paused while passing through the palace garden. Taking off his headpiece, he stood for a moment in the shade of an acacia tree, his black hair ruffled by the northern breeze. The cool scent of the trees and shrubs greatly tempted him to delay his errand, and he gave in to temptation, settling himself in the grass. He closed his eyes, feeling the breeze cool his skin, and without realizing it, he slipped into dreaming.

Sitah became aware of a tickling sensation and awoke, startled. Princess Maeti knelt at his side. She was gently drawing a blade of grass across his nose. He had slumped to a reclining position and was horrified at having her find him napping. He sat up quickly, ready to apologize.

"Your tunic is wrinkled," Maeti commented, "and your hair is messed." While Sitah hurried to repair his condition and recover some semblance of dignity, she said, "If you're an example of Ithtawe's defense, I think I'll learn to defend myself."

"I'm sorry—" Sitah began, more than a little unnerved.

Suddenly Maeti smiled widely. "I'm only teasing you," she said. "It's pleasant to meet someone who isn't rushing somewhere, for a change." Her eyes began to sparkle, and she added, "I've never been alone with a soldier in my garden before. I find it an interesting experience."

Sitah quickly glanced around. "No one is with you? No servants? No guard?"

"I've managed to elude them all for a time," Maeti replied. "What is your name?"

"Sitah," he answered slowly, uncertain how to address the princess when she was not behaving like a princess.

"You're Nessumontu's aide, then," Maeti said slowly. "I assume you do more than sleep."

Sitah smiled faintly, not knowing what to say.

Maeti decided he had a nice smile. She stood up, and as Sitah got to his feet, she studied him more carefully. He was well put together on all accounts, and his black eyes held an intriguing expression.

"Let us sit for a moment by the lotus pond," she suggested.

Sitah's heart leaped. "Will no one object?" he asked cautiously.

"Who would dare?" She flashed him a mischievous glance that made his heart skip a beat. "Even Nessumontu is unlikely to interfere when the princess has invited you to stay."

When Maeti sat on the grass by the lotus pond, Sitah remained standing, one foot resting on a stone. For a time they said nothing, and she continued to look at him appraisingly. Her gaze was unnervingly direct, and he finally decided to look honestly at her.

She resembled Queen Nefrytatanen, he observed, but she had an impishness the queen had not—or hadn't shown in his presence. Her skin was pale gold and her full lips the color of a dusty rose. A smile hovered on her lips.

Maeti said, "Now that we've inspected each other, do you find my appearance as pleasing as I find yours?"

Sitah grew warm and turned his eyes to the water. "You are beautiful," he said simply.

Staring straight ahead, Maeti said, "Is that really your opinion, or do you think you must say so?"

"You are." His eyes turned toward her a moment, then shifted back to the water. "Would it be improper or disagreeable to you if we became better acquainted?" he asked slowly, still looking at the water, almost afraid to breathe.

"No," Maeti answered promptly. "It could become most agreeable to me, I think. You're from a noble family, and my parents shouldn't object to our friendship."

Still facing the pond, Sitah looked at Maeti from the corner of his eye. Although she faced straight ahead, he saw that her eye, too, turned toward him. At their discovery, they laughed, and he came to sit beside her.

"Sitah," Maeti murmured, wonderfully aware of his nearness, "would you like to join us for the evening meal?"

"It would be an honor and a pleasure to be in your company," he said softly.

Her eyes met his and didn't turn away. It was he who finally glanced away. Seeing Nessumontu watching them from across the garden, Sitah stood up quickly and said, "If I have your permission, I should go."

Maeti laughed lightly and got up. "You needn't ask permission. I can see he's waiting for you. I'll expect you tonight."

Maeti turned and walked toward the palace door. Her robe clung softly to her young curves, and Sitah watched her all the way. She reached the entrance and turned to wave at him, and he raised his hand, smiling in return. His heart felt very light.

Nessumontu looked at Sitah curiously as he approached. "I've been searching for you," he said.

"I met Princess Maeti, and she stopped to talk. I'm sorry," Sitah said.

"She's friendlier than you would have expected?" Nessumontu's slanted eyes were intent on Sitah.

"Yes. I was surprised," Sitah answered. "She even asked me to have the evening meal here tonight."

They stepped out of the garden, and Nessumontu waited while Sitah closed the door. Then Nessumontu put his hand on Sitah's arm.

"Although I have a high opinion of you, Sitah," he said softly, "I would have you know the princess means much to me." Sitah stared at him in surprise. Nessumontu shook his head slowly. "Not that way, Sitah—she's far too young. But she's like a sister to me. Do not hurt her. Not only is Maeti our princess, she is unlike any other girl."

Sitah's black eyes flared with anger. "Whether she's a princess or a peasant, whatever she means to you, I can easily see for myself she's not like any other girl."

Sitah remembered his place and added, "If I'm wrong to speak this way to you, I must yet say this man to man, Nessumontu. Princess Maeti spoke to me first and was friendly. I find her beautiful and charming. And I will have the meal, as I promised, with them."

Nessumontu smiled slightly. He liked Sitah's spirit. "Of course you'll be there tonight, as I will. Unknown to Maeti, King Amenemhet has invited us. Nakht leaves for Djemeh tomorrow, and he'll also be there. You'll hear some interesting conversation and should be somewhat distracted from Maeti's charms."

Sitah was carefully groomed, each hair neatly in place and his uniform spotless. He and Nessumontu were greeted by Amenemhet and Senwadjet, who had appraising looks for Sitah. Nakht came soon afterwards, and in a short time Nefrytatanen and Maeti joined the group. On seeing them, Sitah caught his breath.

The queen wore a rich robe of purple and Maeti one of blue that matched her eyes. Both wore simple gold diadems. Sitah was further reminded that Maeti was no ordinary girl, for she wore the royal cobra on her head. Her walk was straight, her manner dignified, and her smile subdued. But her eyes were still dancing as she greeted him politely.

When Sitah looked into the eyes of the queen, he saw they also sparkled, but they had another cast. They made him uneasy.

"I have seen you before," Nefrytatanen said softly, "but I've never met you. Nessumontu, where do you hide your young officers when they're not on duty?"

"They are always on duty," Nessumontu answered quietly.

"Surely not at our table," Nefrytatanen said, "unless, of course, some emergency arises?" She looked at Nessumontu meaningfully.

Sitah decided she was much like her daughter after all, even to the impishness.

Restraining an impulse to smile, Amenemhet took Nefrytatanen's arm. As they led the party to the table, he leaned to whisper in her ear, "Go no further than that, beloved. Your point has been made, and Sitah must not think himself above Nessumontu."

"Of course not," she agreed, "but Maeti likes him, and I think I like him, also. We must not have Nessumontu watch Maeti so closely that all young men are frightened away."

"I think this one is not so easily frightened," Amenemhet said, "and if Senwadjet is .somewhat young for these matters, Maeti is, too."

"I agree," Nefrytatanen said softly, "but they should have friends."

"Yes," Amenemhet whispered when they were seated, "but Sitah is no child. He's four years older than Maeti."

Nefrytatanen said no more, signaling for the meal to begin. Servants began to carry in the food, and a young girl seated herself on a pillow on the floor and began playing a lute.

Sitah spoke only when directly addressed, but he found it difficult to concentrate on his food or even this minimum of conversation. He found himself having to deliberately avoid looking Maeti's way too often. Maeti, aware of each glance, looked at him not at all. She ate quietly, a faint smile always on her lips. Although Amenemhet seemed relaxed, he also was reserved. The others were cordial and conversed informally with the royal family, but the meal slowly became an ordeal for Sitah. He was glad when it was finally over and Nefrytatanen signaled for the dishes to be carried away and fresh wine brought.

A dancer replaced the lute player. Sitah's black eyes were on the entertainer, but his mind was again on that afternoon when he and Maeti had been alone and free to speak their minds. As great an honor as it was to sit at the royal table, Sitah found himself preferring the garden.

When the dancer was finished, Amenemhet commended the girl on her grace and dismissed her. Then he stood up. "Before we begin to speak of certain important matters, we should go to another room," he said: "Only Yazid and Dedjet will serve us there, and we can be comfortable and still talk freely."

Sitah was curious. What was it they planned to discuss? Evidently he was to be included in the conversation. Glancing over those present, he decided it must concern the latest Hyksos trouble. He was proud to be present at so solemn a meeting, but he wished the evening had more pleasantry to offer.

Sitah stood up with the others. Amenemhet and Nefrytatanen took the lead, and the rest of the group followed. Maeti walked with Senwadjet, Nakht with Nessumontu. Sitah walked alone.

In a circular room looking out onto the darkened garden, they reclined on green couches piled luxuriously with cushions. Sitah gazed at the carvings of the pale green walls for some time before he realized the walls were carved from stone panels. He had thought his father's house in Uto Province richly appointed, but the palace was far more luxurious.

After they had been served wine and small honey cakes and fruit, Amenemhet questioned Nakht once again as to how he had decided to carry out his mission. Nakht made it clear he intended doing this with great caution. To keep secret his real reason for visiting Djemeh, he would pretend to negotiate a trade treaty and would also court Chamma.

When Nefrytatanen began to discuss her trip to Troy, Sitah listened with real interest. This had been kept absolutely secret. This was the first time he had heard exactly what she planned to accomplish. She spoke frankly of seeking the personal assistance of Acetes in intervening with King Melanpus, and Sitah wondered what she planned to do if Acetes would not help. Sitah couldn't resist asking her.

Nefrytatanen smiled at Sitah's question, hesitant to say more, and looked to Amenemhet for advice. Amenemhet shook his head, almost imperceptibly, and Nefrytatanen turned to Sitah, still smiling.

"I would like to answer you in detail, Sitah," she said, "but I hesitate because this involves something unusual and rather too personal to discuss casually. We have a plan, but I can explain it to no one."

Sitah wondered what this plan involved. It seemed very peculiar, but he couldn't believe the queen intended offering herself to the Trojan. Sitah's onyx eyes grew blacker at the thought, but he said nothing more.

Amenemhet saw Sitah's expression and knew what he was thinking. It was too embarrassing to allow Sitah to think such a bargain could be considered.

Amenemhet turned to Nefrytatanen. "Tell him, beloved," Amenemhet said. "We cannot have him think such things as are going through his mind now."

Nefrytatanen looked thoughtful. When those glowing eyes turned on Sitah, he felt like shivering. "I am a winged priestess, Sitah," she said finally. "Although it has been some time since I've needed to turn to magic to obtain what was necessary, this is what I plan to use should Acetes prove uncooperative. It's a drastic method, and I'll use it only if absolutely necessary."

Sitah stared at Nefrytatanen, then at Amenemhet, unable to comment. Nefrytatanen smiled, and Sitah realized now why her eyes had seemed so strange to him. His mouth parted a bit in wonder.

"Yes, Sitah," Nefrytatanen sighed. "If necessary, I'll make Acetes do what I wish by taking his will from him. I can't tell you how—I can tell no one those details."

Sitah looked at Maeti, studying her eyes, wondering. Did the daughter know magic, too?

"No, not yet," came Nefrytatanen's answer. He started. "I don't always read minds and didn't have to read yours. Your question was clearly written on your face."

While Sitah was absorbing this news, Nakht suddenly got up from his place and put his goblet on a table.

"I must leave early," Nakht said. "If you don't mind, I'll go now so I can get some sleep."

"We wish you success, Nakht." Nefrytatanen took his hand. She added under her breath, "And I mean success in *all* you wish to accomplish." He smiled and thanked her.

"We also should be leaving," Nessumontu said. "We can walk with you part of the way."

Sitah stood up, disappointed. It had been pleasant to think of Maeti for one afternoon. He would have no chance for more, since he must leave with Nessumontu.

Sitah thanked them all with formal courtesy. He

felt strange when Nefrytatanen gave him her hand
and looked into his eyes, but she seemed merely
amused at his discomfort. Saying goodbye to Amenemhet and Senwadjet was an easy enough matter—they
were very friendly. Sitah took Maeti's hand and
thanked her warmly for inviting him. She smiled, looking into his eyes, and pressed a bit of papyrus into
his palm. Sitah took it carefully, as discreetly as she
had given it, and held tightly to it until he was out
of the palace.

In the courtyard Sitah carefully put the papyrus in
his tunic to save for a private moment. He listened
only partly to Nakht's and Nessumontu's conversation.
He was wondering what the papyrus contained.

When Sitah was alone in his room, he fastened the
door securely. Then he lit his lamp and took out the
precious scrap, unrolling it with great care.

It contained only a short message: "I walk in the
garden, when I can, at the same hour every afternoon."

Sitah was almost delirious with joy. Maeti knew he
was at Nessumontu's side almost constantly, but she
let him know where she would be when he was able
to get away.

When Sitah went to bed, he couldn't sleep for planning ways to escape Nessumontu. He had placed the
note inside a small pendant given him by his mother
which no one would ever touch. He decided he would
wear it always now.

Sitah fell asleep smiling.

Nefrytatanen stood before the mirror inspecting her
white and red robe, the golden symbols she carried,
and the double crown she wore. She suddenly saw a
similar image behind hers. Turning, she faced
Amenemhet dressed in his court robe and crown,

carrying his scepters, wearing even his hated beard. She stared in surprise.

"I felt we should appear together," Amenemhet said quietly. "Nessumontu can manage alone for today." Nefrytatanen said nothing, but she smiled at his thoughtfulness. "Perhaps we'll have a short session, and I won't have to endure this beard too long," he added.

"It's been busier than ever lately," Nefrytatanen said. "People have many complaints because of the military movements. Land has been trampled, and animals have wandered away. I've wondered if we could at least tell them something of what we're doing, give them some explanation."

"I'd like to tell them everything," Amenemhet replied, "but you know we can't. We'll have to wait until the last possible moment."

She took his arm. "You're right, I know. I'm glad you'll be with me today."

Amenemhet squeezed Nefrytatanen's arm. "I've missed being with you. Also, I would much rather sit in the throne room looking at you than stand in the dust watching a squad of sweating soldiers." He grinned.

Nefrytatanen laughed lightly, and they went to the throne room in good spirits. Pausing outside the door, they carefully checked each other to make sure nothing had been forgotten.

As Amenemhet impulsively bent to kiss Nefrytatanen's cheek, the doors opened. His kiss was witnessed by the waiting crowd. When the king and queen walked past the throng to their thrones, the people's faces were lit with warmth.

After seating themselves, Amenemhet whispered, "Where are Senwadjet and Maeti?"

"Senwadjet's with Nessumontu, as usual," Nefrytatanen answered. "I'm surprised at Maeti's absence, though. She's often come to the audience since you haven't been coming."

Seeing Amenemhet's signal, Meri stepped toward the crowd to call for the first petitioner. One man came forward hesitantly. At the foot of the dais, he bowed low.

"You may rise," Amenemhet directed. "Tell us your complaint."

The man straightened slowly. When he spoke, he chose his words with great care. "Your Majesties, day after day you have listened to our petitions. Today we have already spoken among ourselves, and we have resolved our problems. We don't know exactly what's happening lately in the Two Lands, but we all know it's important. The garrisons are heavily manned and soldiers practice daily. Her Highness—for the first time in many years—plans to leave Ithtawe to take a long journey. We know there are greater problems than ours."

The man paused, his eyes steady before their amazed faces. "We only wish to tell you that, whatever is coming, we will be prepared for it. We've had many years of peace without hunger—because of you. We've enjoyed health and prosperity. As the great prophet foretold, we who live in your time rejoice. The troubles gathering over Tamera we willingly bear. You won't have to drag us to your side at sword's point. We trust your wisdom and ask no questions."

Amenemhet and Nefrytatanen were speechless. They rose together and stared at him and into the faces of the crowd. He was speaking the truth. The others were with him.

The man smiled. "You're surprised," he said. "We wish Queen Nefrytatanen a successful journey, fair winds, and a swift return. While she's gone, sire, you will be occupied with many things. Therefore, we'll solve our own troubles by ourselves or wait until this larger trouble is over."

Amenemhet and Nefrytatanen stood dazed. The man bowed deeply and melted back into the crowd.

After taking a moment to recover from his own surprise, Meri stepped forward to ask if anyone else wished to speak. Senwadjet and Maeti stepped through the main doors and walked down the aisle. They bowed low before the thrones. The room was silent.

"May we rise?" Senwadjet finally asked his father, who was staring at them.

Amenemhet found his voice. "Of course. Why did you come this way to us?"

"Does not your law say anyone may approach you today?" Maeti asked.

Still staring at them, Amenemhet asked, "But why here? In this fashion?"

"Senwadjet and I have a problem," Maeti murmured.

"Which is?" Nefrytatanen asked, a little suspicious. If they were playing a prank, this was no time for it.

"We have grown up," Senwadjet said solemnly, "mostly, anyway. But our parents are still unaware of this."

Amenemhet and Nefrytatanen exchanged looks of amazement.

"We have attended court regularly," Senwadjet said calmly. "We have learned much regarding Tamera, its people and politics. I have learned about military matters from Nessumontu. We have listened with you to the problems of the people and have learned from your decisions. We realize we still have much to learn, but when we heard what was said just now, we realized it would be unfair to the people if their cases were delayed." Senwadjet paused to take a deep breath, then continued. "We ask that we might be permitted to hold court in your place. We could ask for help from Meri or Ankhneferu or you, father, if we felt we couldn't solve something."

Surprised and pleased, Amenemhet said nothing. For a time the crowd also was silent. Then it began to buzz with excited whispers. Finally the man who had previously spoken approached the dais once again.

Again he bowed low, and Amenemhet quickly gestured for him to speak. "It would be agreeable to the people to have Prince Senwadjet and Princess Maeti do this," the man said clearly. "If we may express an opinion, we welcome their offer." He bowed and again backed into the edge of the crowd.

Amenemhet looked at Senwadjet and smiled. "You'd have to wear this prickly beard," he whispered.

Senwadjet shrugged his shoulders as if in resignation. "Seeing as how I cannot yet produce my own fine bushy beard, I suppose yours will have to suffice."

Laughing aloud, Nefrytatanen gave Meri a signal. He rapped the metal tip of his staff on a golden hawk emblem inlaid in the floor. It rang, indicating a royal decision had been made. The people were silent, waiting.

Amenemhet and Nefrytatanen took Senwadjet and Maeti by their hands, inviting them to step up to the dais before the thrones.

"You were crowned in Tamera as infants," Amenemhet said clearly, "and while the queen is away and I am occupied with other matters, each ten days you will wear these crowns and robes and hold court in our place." He took off his double crown and placed it on Senwadjet's head. Nefrytatanen removed her crown and put it on Maeti's brow.

Nefrytatanen and Amenemhet glowed with pride.

Nefrytatanen stood gazing sadly at the garden. She remembered vividly when she had stood in this same place before they had begun the journey to Atalan, before Senwadjet and Maeti had been born. Amenemhet had then lain poisoned and helpless, and she had wept bitterly that morning.

Now Nefrytatanen would leave Tamera again, this time for Troy, but this time alone. She was homesick already.

"I sent Dedjet and Yazid away for a time," Amenemhet said behind her. Nefrytatanen turned to him. His eyes held clouds that matched her own. He put his arms around her lightly. "When we go to the moorings, we'll say goodbye and embrace as calmly as possible, for many will be watching. Here in the privacy of our chamber, I wish to say our real goodbye, the one I'll remember when we're apart."

Nefrytatanen leaned her head against Amenemhet's shoulder, her eyes filling with tears, and tried to swallow so she might speak.

Amenemhet held Nefrytatanen closer and whispered into her hair, "I'll miss you more than I can say, my beloved. All the years we've never been separated makes this moment that much harder to bear." He released her, putting his hands around her head, lifting her face to his. "Already your eyes shine with unshed tears," he whispered. He smiled. "They are permitted to fall now so there will be fewer of them later."

Nefrytatanen stared at Amenemhet. The stubborn tears had their way and ran down her cheeks.

"Whatever problems Acetes may give you," Amenemhet said softly, "remember this. If Tamera must fight the Hyksos, Djemeh, Troy, and all the world— we are ready. If your situation needs magic, use it with wisdom. If it seems you fail, come home. Return to me safely. Risk nothing." His smile faded. "Don't worry about my behavior. Lonely will I be, and lonely will I remain." The smile returned faintly. "This place will be empty without your presence, but there will be no one else for me." He added lightly, "I trust you will feel the same."

"Oh, beloved," Nefrytatanen managed to whisper brokenly, "who could ever replace you?"

Amenemhet put his arms tightly around Nefrytatanen. Her face pressed against his neck as she clung to him. His eyes, too, were glistening. He prayed she would be safe.

"Do you think," Amenemhet said, softly tilting her face to his, "that we might manage a kiss or two before you leave?"

Nefrytatanen stared up into his golden eyes and saw the pain they held, the fear. Her reply was in her lips. She poured out answers to the questions he couldn't bring himself to ask.

"I love you," Nefrytatanen whispered fiercely. "I love you and never would I ask for more." Trembling, she kissed Amenemhet again and again, and he held her as tightly as he dared.

Yazid opened the door quietly and, seeing them, knew they would never hear his voice. He closed the door carefully, then turned to Dedjet. "Don't disturb them while they say goodbye," he said softly. "Let the world wait until they return to it."

Dedjet nodded in understanding, and they remained by the door, making sure no one else interrupted.

CHAPTER 13

NEFRYTATANEN STEPPED from the ship's gangplank, and Acetes immediately came forward to greet her. As she watched him approach, she noted he was as trim as when she had seen him last. He walked with his head high, his dark blond hair softly curling. He looked dignified, but his blue eyes were as warm on her as when she had seen him the first time.

She was aware her appearance seemed alien to these people in their gracefully draped robes and ringleted hair. She lifted her head high, knowing the Trojans would be curious at her straight black hair and almond-shaped eyes. Her soft cotton sheath and her jewelry would seem strange to them. She smiled slightly. They would see Tamera in her, and she resolved they would see Tamera at its proudest.

"Time has been generous to you, Nefrytatanen," Acetes said in the language of Tamera. "It has diminished nothing of your beauty, but has given you even more."

"Neither have the years been unkind to you," she answered in the Trojan tongue, "for you look the same as when I saw you last."

"You've learned my language." He smiled. "You speak it well, and your accent gives it a charming lilt." He took her hand and, lowering his voice, spoke

284

again in Tamera's words, "I never forgot you and have thought of you more often than you can know."

Intending to have the crowd understand her, Nefrytatanen replied clearly in his language, "It warms my heart to know a friend has not forgotten me." A murmur went through the throng. Nefrytatanen knew they were curious about Tamera's queen. They were disappointed in their hopes for an exciting scandal. She continued, "You've advanced your position with great success, and I congratulate you. You have been in good health, Acetes? And your family?"

"I'm well enough, but have no family. I never married." Acetes spoke in his language and sighed softly. He would have to play this game for a while until they were alone. Later he might discreetly discover if her voyage was only for political reasons. "You'll stay at my house, of course."

"Do you have space for all my guards and servants?" Nefrytatanen asked, suppressing a smile. She knew Acetes had room, but she meant to assure him she wasn't going to be alone with him.

"Yes, places for them and those who manned your ship, also."

"They'll stay with the ship," she said. "It needs some small repairs and must be resupplied for the return voyage. You won't need to make a place for them."

"I'm amazed you didn't bring your children this time," Acetes said softly.

Nefrytatanen smiled and answered, "They're at an age to make unreliable chaperones. They might, perhaps, cast their own eyes in the wrong directions."

Acetes smiled to himself, then asked in the Trojan

tongue, "They are, I gather, healthy? And King Amenemhet?"

"Senwadjet is almost as tall as his father and looks very much like him. Maeti is well and resembles me." Nefrytatanen paused, then added meaningfully, "Amenemhet is most vigorously healthy."

Acetes ignored this and commented, "If Maeti has your beauty, it was wise of you to leave her at home. I see many warm eyes on you now."

"As you look at me?" Nefrytatanen lifted an eyebrow as she returned to her own language.

Acetes laughed softly. "Yes, exactly." He paused a moment, then remarked, "Switching back and forth from your language to mine must be most confusing to those who can hear us."

"They may blame it on my ignorance of your tongue," she said.

"I don't know if they'll do that since what you do speak is fluent enough," he observed.

They reached a covered litter. She looked at it suspiciously as he pulled the curtain aside. He smiled. "I'll ride on my horse, not in there with you. That would surely cause a scandal."

"I'm grateful for your thoughtfulness in preserving my good reputation," she replied coolly as he helped her inside.

"I hope you'll be comfortable," Acetes said, then let the curtain fall into place.

Nefrytatanen settled back on the sumptuous cushions and took a deep breath. If there was anything she detested more than a conveyance of this type, she couldn't think what it was. She wished Acetes had given her a horse.

She sighed. It was as Amenemhet had predicted,

but perhaps not as bad as she had feared. Acetes was certainly still interested in her. But maybe he would have enough sense to be discreet once he realized she wouldn't return his overtures.

Thinking of Amenemhet, Nefrytatanen suddenly ached with longing. She felt sharply her strangeness in this land. She felt, too, a certain helplessness. Nefrytatanen sat up straighter and reminded herself that she was a queen on a legitimate mission in a civilized and friendly country. She would act with dignity and be gracious, then leave this place, her purpose accomplished. Surely King Melanpus would agree to her bargain. Tamera's gold was welcome in any land, and Amenemhet had suggested a generous sum to offer in payment for Troy's part in this scheme. If King Melanpus didn't agree, she had brought the articles she would need to gain Troy's cooperation through magic. She would also use them, if necessary, to cool Acetes's ardor. All would be well.

Acetes led Nefrytatanen into a sitting room that was cool, airy, and spacious. The room was decorated with graceful elegance in a sophisticated harmony of white and soft grey. The furnishings were simple and clean of line.

"Would you like to go to your room immediately and rest, or stay and tell me why you are here?" Acetes asked. He added quickly, "I couldn't be sure of your arrival time. Otherwise, a bath would be waiting for you now. It will take a few minutes, so if you wish, you can sit here."

"Gladly will I sit on a chair that doesn't move," Nefrytatanen replied. "After traveling on a ship, then in a swaying covered litter, I'm still finding my balance."

Acetes smiled. "Rest on this couch and speak or not, as you wish."

"My feet are unsteady, but my mind is not." Gratefully, Nefrytatanen reclined on the couch. "I've come to ask you to plead our case with your king."

"I'll do that without knowing what it is," Acetes said promptly.

Nefrytatanen allowed herself a small smile. "You have never forgotten the skills of diplomacy."

"For you," Acetes quietly replied, "I'd plead anything with anybody."

"You have lost none of your charm," Nefrytatanen said slowly. "But what I have come to talk about is most serious. We've been trying to negotiate a trade treaty with Djemeh, but they've held us off. They're being plied with an offer from Zahi to join in an invasion of Tamera."

"Can Tamera repulse such an invasion?" he asked, alarmed.

"Perhaps, but we've learned the Hyksos look for another ally as well, one that could sail up the Nile to attack from the north. Troy is first in their minds."

Acetes stared at her. "What makes them think we'd be interested? We don't wish to join Zahi in any venture and surely not in war on Tamera!"

"I'd thought not," Nefrytatanen said. "We're sure they'll approach you, offering to divide the spoils. They will, no doubt, approach you personally, asking you to influence King Melanpus. They'll probably use me as bait to interest you."

"You certainly come to the point," Acetes commented. "They think I'd accept such a bargain?"

"The Hyksos ruler thinks everyone acts as they do—take what you want however you can." Nefrytatanen looked at Acetes. "Without Troy helping us, Tamera's chance of winning grows considerably slimmer. If we did win, it would be at a high cost to life and property. We already have dispatched our ambassador to Djemeh, again to try bargaining with them as if we knew nothing of this plot. Our ambassador has directions to spread certain rumors to make the still hesitating Zaretes even more cautious.

"Acetes, the Hyksos won't be stopped except by force. Gobryas has Shalmanesser's ear, and he'll start a war not only from greed, but from hate of us. I ask you to stand behind me when I tell King Melanpus Tamera's plan."

"Which is?" Acetes stood up to look out a window opening as he thought about this news. His own emotions were a turmoil.

"We want you to pretend to strike a bargain with Zahi." He turned quickly to look at her as she continued, "Sail up the Nile as they wish, but don't fight. The army of Djemeh may very well back out even at the last minute and the Hyksos would stand alone against us. Then we will win. We'd pay Troy in gold for all your trouble, but no Trojan blood would be spilled. And fewer of my people will die." She finished softly, "It may mean Tamera's very survival."

"I don't know that King Melanpus and Queen Pythia will agree to your plan, but I'll try to convince them." Acetes's face was grim. "I'm sure they wouldn't join Zahi."

"If they refuse the Hyksos offer, Gobryas will think of another king to bargain with—perhaps one who will accept."

"I'll do my best," Acetes promised. He came closer and bent to peer at her. "You're tired," he said. "Bathe and rest. We can discuss this later at dinner. I'll send a message to the palace asking for an audience for you."

Nefrytatanen rose wearily from the couch. "I am tired," she admitted. "I'm grateful for your help."

"I promised it long ago," Acetes said softly. He led her to the door, where one of his servants and Dedjet waited in the hall. Before Nefrytatanen left, she turned to Acetes and smiled.

"It's good to see you again," she said.

Acetes smiled warmly. "The pleasure is mine, I assure you."

It was going to be a delicate business, Nefrytatanen decided, as she followed Dedjet to her room. It was clear Acetes would speak sincerely in her favor. But it was also plain he hadn't given up hope of winning her.

Nefrytatanen felt a pang of sympathy for Acetes. He had no family and lived only with servants in this great house. After all his efforts and his many successes, his personal life was lonely. Was no woman of Troy attractive and charming enough to win him? She hoped he didn't wait for her. How sad it was, she thought, if he believed she would leave Amenemhet.

After dinner, Acetes's servants disappeared. Dedjet hovered circumspectly near, having been instructed not to leave unless instructed to do so by Nefrytatanen herself.

Acetes, looking at Nefrytatanen over the rim of his goblet, was smiling slightly. "Your handmaiden might be better occupied preparing your chamber for the night rather than standing around here. One word will bring whatever you desire," he said softly.

"Will a word bring me a servant I trust more than Dedjet to keep safe my reputation?" Nefrytatanen asked pointedly.

"Reputations are not so easily marred in Troy." Acetes put down his goblet. "Dedjet isn't needed to guard you—you're quite safe with me."

Acetes made Nefrytatanen feel foolishly overvigilant, which was exactly how he wished her to feel. She knew this, but courtesy gave her no choice. "You may go, Dedjet," she said.

Dedjet left obediently. Acetes sat silently looking at Nefrytatanen. His eyes told her plainly his desire hadn't diminished, but had increased with time.

"King Melanpus and Queen Pythia will receive you tomorrow morning," Acetes said quietly. "They already know I stand as your friend, although I haven't told them why you came." He stood up and walked behind the wide, backless couch on which Nefrytatanen sat. "I would tell you my opinion of them, but perhaps it's best to form your own. They will be in a receptive mood, for I have praised you highly, and they usually hear my advice."

"They should feel able to trust you," she remarked.

"One thing I would tell you is King Melanpus has an eye for beauty. The queen is aware of it. If you can manage to charm the king and still gain her trust, your success is assured—with my interceding in your behalf."

"And the price for your help, Acetes?" she asked softly.

"There is no price." From the sound of his voice, she could tell he stood directly behind her. "I told you long ago I was your friend, and I'm glad to confirm my words with action." He sat next to her on the bench and looked into her eyes. He was so close she could feel the warmth of his body.

"I have come prepared to pay for any help in gold," Nefrytatanen offered.

"I need no more gold," Acetes said.

"I offer nothing else." Nefrytatanen looked steadily into his eyes.

"I know." Acetes touched her hair lightly. "Be not so alert for a wrong move from me, Nefrytatanen." He smiled tolerantly. "You really have remarkable eyes. I feel as if I could fall right into them and disappear. You're one of the few truly beautiful women I've ever seen."

He sighed and stood up, moving away from the bench. "Please be comfortable. I'm not a man to force my attentions on a woman. That I admire you isn't news. That I desire you is not a surprise, either."

Acetes turned to look at Nefrytatanen again. His head was high. He would not give up easily. "Nefrytatanen," he said softly, "I would also have you desire me. I said I have no need for gold. I need only one thing. I lack only you.

"Beautiful Nefrytatanen," he sighed, "I would offer you riches, but you have them. I would offer you all I own and will ever possess. I would offer myself, my faithfulness—a thing for which I'm not famous." He smiled a little. "I'll try, while you're here, to win you, but it must be that you come willingly to me. You're the kind of woman who would never submit to the will of another. I would have you want me, be eager for me, come to me happily. You may rest easy in your chambers here, for you're as safe as in your own palace."

Nefrytatanen stood up and walked slowly to the door where Acetes now waited. He looked at her for a long moment.

"Have I mentioned that the grace of your movements has always charmed me?" Acetes asked softly. "Have I said the way you walk lights fires in my soul?"

"No," she whispered. "You have not."

"It is the truth," he said quietly. "It seems a shame the world holds only one Nefrytatanen. That identical flowers should bloom in extravagant profusion while you are unique seems unfair indeed." He leaned forward, brushing her cheek with his lips. "Sleep well," he said and, turning, walked quickly away.

Nefrytatanen spent most of the night alternately tossing in bed and pacing the floor. When she awoke, the sunlight had almost lost its morning faintness.

Horrified, she leaped from bed calling, "Dedjet! Dedjet! Where are you?"

Nefrytatanen was searching for something to wear when she heard a soft tap on the door. She cried impatiently, "Come in! Come in! Why didn't you call me? I must be late already!"

"You aren't late. The meeting time was changed." Nefrytatanen froze at the voice, then turned slowly to see Acetes leaning in the doorway, his blue eyes examining her. "Do you always sleep unclothed?" he asked softly.

Nefrytatanen stared at him. She had forgotten her nakedness. She quickly wrapped the nearest length of cloth around her. "Yes," she answered coolly. "We always sleep unclothed. It's more comfortable. What are you doing here? Where is Dedjet?"

Acetes still watched Nefrytatanen. "Dedjet is on an errand. I did knock—if you remember. You did tell me to come in."

"I thought you were Dedjet," she said faintly.

"Well, I'm not," he replied, smiling. "I received a message that some business necessitated changing the meeting time. King Melanpus and Queen Pythia sent apologies and asked if you would have the evening meal with them. I replied for you, if you don't mind. I thought you might as well sleep late, so I gave orders not to disturb you."

"Thank you for your thoughtfulness." Nefrytatanen clung to her wrapping with as much dignity as possible. Acetes remained unmoving. "Now, will you leave me so I can dress?" Nefrytatanen asked.

Acetes nodded, still smiling. "Of course," he replied. "I suggest you dress comfortably. We'll have a quiet day." He was in no hurry to leave. "You are quite a sight standing in the sunshine," he commented, trying to delay his departure. "I wonder why the women of Troy hide their bodies from the sun. It has made you so beautifully golden."

"Acetes," Nefrytatanen said again, "please leave me."

"If you insist." He began to turn as if to go, then changed his mind and stopped. "But if you're so casual about nakedness in Tamera, I don't know why it should bother you here."

"One should observe the customs of the land one visits—out of courtesy," she answered sarcastically.

Acetes smiled. "I must see what I can do to change some of Troy's customs as soon as possible."

"Please go!" Nefrytatanen burst out in exasperation.

"I might as well," he said glancing over his shoulder. "Dedjet is coming, anyway. Join me in the garden later. Come dressed according to Tamera's or Troy's custom—the former preferred." He left laughing.

Later Nefrytatanen joined Acetes. He never mentioned the morning's incident, but escorted her around his house and property. She asked about seeing the city, but he said it was possible only if she was willing to ride in a covered litter with a guard.

"Why?" she asked in surprise. "I could see nothing then."

"It's the only way a proper lady travels in Troy," Acetes answered. "Only slaves and women of pleasure move freely in the streets."

Nefrytatanen stared at him but said no more, reminding herself that she was a guest in his land and had no right to criticize the customs, especially when she had come to ask a favor.

Nefrytatanen dressed carefully for the evening. After one attempt at a Trojan hairstyle, Dedjet gave up. Nefrytatanen's hair remained adamantly straight, so she wore it loose with a simple golden coronet. Her robe was of a sheer woven turquoise material, and her delicate gold necklace and bracelets were of a lotus and papyrus design set with turquoise scarabs.

When Acetes saw her, he said softly, "The sight of you will make King Melanpus agree to anything, but Queen Pythia is another matter."

Nefrytatanen smiled up at him. "Stay with me and guide me, Acetes. I'll try my best."

As Acetes had predicted, King Melanpus looked at Nefrytatanen with obvious appreciation. His blue grey eyes traveled her entire height slowly, stopping at intervals. Although he was younger than Nefrytatanen had anticipated, he had a jaded look in his eyes that made him seem older. Queen Pythia was gracious, but her green eyes were cool on Nefrytatanen. Her elaborate robe was the color of a ripe apricot, and her cinnamon curls were arranged in a formal, artificial manner.

Melanpus was in favor of many congenial goblets of wine before dinner, but Nefrytatanen noticed Pythia drank little and guided the conversation to business. Nefrytatanen was more than willing to follow her lead. She responded frankly, from time to time laughing at the king's jokes and accepting his compliments with a polite smile.

The meal was a private feast in Nefrytatanen's honor. Servants silently saw to their every need, and the dishes were numerous. Slaves waved lavish feather fans over the royal party as they dined, and a girl provided quiet entertainment, singing softly and accompanying herself on a lyre.

Melanpus asked Nefrytatanen questions about Tamera, continuously keeping her aware of his admiration. Pythia asked questions about Zahi's scheme. Without hesitating, Nefrytatanen continued to give Pythia the facts.

"How did you learn of this plot?" Pythia asked.

"A girl from Tamera, taken as a slave by the Hyksos, heard all of it. Ambassador Astram was killed before her eyes when he tried to help her escape. She returned to Tamera almost dead." Nefrytatanen's eyes flashed with anger as she remembered it. "Gobryas had tortured her. When I left Ithtawe, she was yet unable to get out of bed and may never do so." Nefrytatanen was grim as she thought of Nassurti's bandage-swathed face. "She'll be disfigured for life, or so our physician thinks."

Pythia looked sympathetic. "It's that bad?"

"She was wrapped with bandages from head to toe. Only her eyes and mouth were uncovered." Nefrytatanen shivered slightly and said, "Amenemhet may know what was done to her, but I cannot guess, nor do I wish to try." As Melanpus shook his head, Nefrytatanen continued, "Amenemhet knows our own fates would be worse, should Gobryas get his hands on us. That's why my ship is so heavily guarded."

Melanpus stared at her. "They would attack your ship even before they notified you of an official war?"

"Amenemhet won't rest until I'm home," Nefrytatanen said quietly, her eyes bleak.

By the time the conversation had progressed to the gold Tamera offered Troy, the meal was over. Expecting to get into even deeper negotiations, Nefrytatanen was surprised by the sudden entrance of a group of dancing girls. Although dancing was common enough entertainment in Tamera, these dancers' movements were startlingly provocative. They shocked her. Nefrytatanen took in at a glance the purpose of several young and attractive women who stood off to one side of the room as if waiting to approach the royal party. Nefrytatanen's mouth dropped open in amazement.

Pythia stood up at her place. "Shall we leave now, Queen Nefrytatanen?" she asked. Pythia's eyes were as cold as her tone.

Nefrytatanen grew hot with anger, and she turned to look at Acetes for advice. His eyes told her to go quietly with Pythia. She wondered how Pythia could accept such a thing. She wasn't only the queen but Melanpus's wife as well. How could she leave her hubsand in the company of these women? Nefrytatanen hesitated a moment. Then, controlling her anger, she followed Pythia without a word.

King Melanpus hadn't missed the look in Nefrytatanen's eyes. He decided that she was exceptionally beautiful when her eyes flashed that way. Melanpus turned to Acetes. "This isn't done in Tamera?"

Acetes smiled slightly and shook his head. "It is not done in Tamera. If it were, she wouldn't permit it in the palace."

Melanpus chuckled at this. "What could she do to prevent it?"

Acetes looked at the approaching girls thoughtfully and murmured, "Quite a lot, I'd think."

In Pythia's sitting room, Pythia asked, "You don't leave your men after the evening meal in Tamera?"

Although Nefrytatanen had by this time suppressed her anger, she couldn't help giving Pythia a look of disapproval. "When our men are to be entertained in that fashion, we do it ourselves. We aren't so tolerant of professional women of pleasure. We have a different view of lovemaking. Few men in Tamera have the need of professional services, which is one reason why so few women follow that trade. In Tamera, such women are mostly foreigners." Her eyes blazed as she gathered momentum. "If such a thing occurred to Amenemhet, I swear I wouldn't walk away quietly! How do you endure such a thing in your home?"

"I have no choice." Pythia stared into space as she answered. Then her green eyes turned to meet Nefrytatanen's as if a new thought had occurred to her. "Do women have such influence in your land?"

Nefrytatanen replied firmly, "From what I've seen here, slaves in Tamera have more influence than you do. We don't have to stay in special areas of our houses, and we walk on the street when and where we wish—without escort if we choose. We have as much freedom as men."

"How have you managed to win this?" Pythia's eyes were wide.

"It has always been this way," Nefrytatanen said softly. "Our men as well as our women are content with this. In the Two Lands, slaves are thought of as human beings. How can free women settle for less?"

"But how do you manage the slaves, then?"

"As people," Nefrytatanen replied. "Some slaves in Tamera are criminals who are being punished by paying for their crimes as free servants. Some are captured in war, because we don't believe in the slaughter of prisoners. There are those who, because of misfortune, sell themselves into service for a certain length of time. Slaves in Tamera have some rights, and if these are violated, they have recourse in court. When slaves marry and have children, their children are free. It seems to me women in Troy are less than slaves in Tamera."

"You have some interesting ideas," Pythia observed.

Nefrytatanen said, "They aren't merely ideas, but our laws. They've worked well for centuries. The laws apply to everyone—men and women, free or enslaved."

"And the women are considered no less feminine?" Pythia asked thoughtfully.

"Our men seem well satisfied. When a man of my land wins the heart of a woman, he knows she has given it freely, and the joining is that much sweeter for them both." Nefrytatanen smiled faintly. "We're women who enjoy being female because our men are surely male."

"I have heard the blood of your people runs warmly enough," Pythia murmured.

"It does," Nefrytatanen replied. "No one in Tamera is confused regarding that matter."

By the time a servant came to tell Nefrytatanen that Acetes was ready to leave, Nefrytatanen and Pythia had almost come to an agreement on the amount Tamera would pay Troy for its help.

Nefrytatanen said nothing to Acetes on the way to his house regarding either her talk with Pythia or the circumstances leading to it. Instead, she thought of Pythia and wondered how Melanpus could consider his wife intelligent enough to discuss treaties, yet treat her as if she were mindless in other matters.

At Nefrytatanen's door, Acetes hesitated a moment as if he wanted to say something. But he only bid her fair dreams and walked away.

Nefrytatanen was so pensive while Dedjet prepared her for bed that Dedjet finally asked, "Didn't the meeting go well, my lady?"

Nefrytatanen sighed. "The business I came to discuss went very well. But it would have been even better if Melanpus would give more attention to his wife and less to other women."

"My lady!" Dedjet was shocked. "Did he offend you in some way?"

"He offended me—and I think Pythia has been offended for some time—by sending us away after the meal; then he and Acetes were entertained by women I'd never permit in Ithtawe." When Nefrytatanen saw Dedjet's eyes, she warned, "Not a word of this, Dedjet, not to anyone."

"My lady, I speak to no one of any confidential thing you say."

"I know, Dedjet," Nefrytatanen said softly. "I wish I could do something to help Pythia. She must truly love Melanpus to put up with such nonsense in her own house."

"Sometimes," Dedjet offered, "a lady allows such things because of her own attitude. Is Pythia uninterested in lovemaking and so considers it a burden?"

"I think not."

"Is she ugly? Does she have no charm or intelligence?"

"Pythia is far from ugly," Nefrytatanen said thoughtfully, "and she has sufficient intelligence to discuss the treaty with me. She is rather reserved, and I think it's possible that her resentment of what Melanpus does may somewhat cool her charm."

"Perhaps if she were warmer, her husband would also be warmer."

"You may have a point, Dedjet," Nefrytatanen murmured as she got into bed. "If Melanpus and Pythia had fewer problems between them, it would make my way easier."

When Nefrytatanen came downstairs for the morning meal, she was told Acetes had already left the house on business. She suspected he didn't want to see her because he knew she disapproved of last night's entertainment.

A messenger came from the palace with a note. Thinking it might be from Pythia, Nefrytatanen opened it eagerly, then turned her back to the messenger so he couldn't report her expression. It was from Melanpus, a discreetly worded note. He wanted to know

when he might meet her again—and he meant alone.
She closed the scroll and laid it on the writing desk,
then wrote her answer. Her tone was one of innocent
friendliness, as if she hadn't understood his real meaning, telling him she would be happy to meet with King
Melanpus and Queen Pythia at any time they chose.
With cool satisfaction, she gave this response to the
messenger. Melanpus wouldn't mistake her meaning.

When Nefrytatanen returned to her room, she stood
staring out the window opening for a time, wondering
how Trojan women could endure staying meekly in
their quarters all day and night. It would bore her
to distraction.

To a light tap on the door, Nefrytatanen called permission to enter. She did not turn from the window
opening.

"Queen Pythia," Dedjet said softly.

Nefrytatanen took a second to compose herself, then
turned a serene face to Pythia. She dared not reveal
a hint of the message Melanpus had just sent. She
knew this queen was the real strength of the throne.
Pythia must be well aware of all her husband's frailties.

Pythia's face was as serene as Nefrytatanen's. Nefrytatanen smiled and invited Pythia to recline on one of
the couches. Pythia sat in a chair, her eyes revealing
suspicion. Nefrytatanen asked Dedjet to pour wine for
them, then sat facing Pythia.

"Queen Nefrytatanen," Pythia began softly, "I hope
I haven't imposed by coming without warning you."

"No," Nefrytatanen replied, accepting the goblet
Dedjet offered. "You're welcome. Please, let us drop
our titles when we address each other." Nefrytatanen
smiled in open friendliness. "My name is mouthful

enough. I'm afraid there's no way to shorten it. We aren't in the custom of using diminutives."

"It is difficult for my tongue, trained as it is only in my own language," Pythia admitted.

"It's a melodious and expressive language," Nefrytatanen replied, "although I had some trouble learning it."

"It seems to be easy for you. I couldn't learn yours, I'm sure."

"You could learn it. You're too modest."

"Do you often travel from Tamera?" Pythia asked. She seemed not to know how to react to Nefrytatanen's compliment.

"This is the first time I've been away from Tamera alone," Nefrytatanen said. "Before, I always felt it was best to stay home and keep a close eye on two lively children."

Pythia smiled a moment. Then her smile faded. "I have no children," she said. "I have given the crown no heir."

"You're young," Nefrytatanen said easily, learning a great deal from Pythia's expression. "You'll have children yet."

"I doubt it." Pythia's eyes were truly grieved.

"Perhaps you could come to Tamera and consult my own physician," Nefrytatanen suggested. "If you have a problem, maybe he can help you."

"Do you think so?" Pythia's eyes were suddenly alive with hope, and Nefrytatanen felt compassion for her.

"I can't promise it," she answered bluntly. "But Horemheb is certainly knowledgeable. If anyone can help you, he can." Nefrytatanen had doubts that this was where the problem lay.

"If I don't have a child soon, I think Melanpus

might seek another wife and set me aside," Pythia suddenly confided.

"If Horemheb examined him, he might learn the fault is his, not yours," Nefrytatanen suggested. She saw surprise in Pythia's face. This possibility hadn't occurred to her. Nefrytatanen sat quietly until Pythia looked at her again.

"Nefrytatanen, you are a most beautiful woman. If you stay in Troy any length of time, many nobles will surely notice you. Would they tempt you?" Pythia asked.

Nefrytatanen looked shocked, although she wasn't. She knew Pythia wasn't concerned with nobles, but with Melanpus. "To risk the loss of Amenemhet's love for a short adventure?" Nefrytatanen looked steadily at Pythia a moment, then said quietly, "I would be a fool."

Pythia sipped her wine, thinking. Finally she commented, "He must be quite a man to have you speak so of him."

Nefrytatanen's eyes glowed. "I would ask for nothing more than him."

Pythia smiled and said softly, "Tell me of him."

Nefrytatanen hesitated, thinking of Amenemhet and the night before she had left Ithtawe. Her eyes told Pythia much. "I don't know where to begin," she whispered.

"How does he look? Make a picture of him for me," Pythia urged.

"He is taller than I by this much." Nefrytatanen gestured with a hand. "He hasn't grown soft or fat with time." As she thought of Amenemhet, Nefrytatanen was unaware of her growing smile. "His hair is dark, not black but nearly so, very luxurious and cut to jaw length. His skin is deep bronze from the sun, and his eyes are a golden color."

"Gold eyes? I've never heard of such a thing."

"They are different," Nefrytatanen said softly. "Our son also has them." Nefrytatanen thought about Amenemhet's eyes, and Pythia saw in her expression the effect such eyes might have on a woman. Then Nefrytatanen took a deep breath and continued, "His brow is wide and clear, his nose straight and well formed, his chin firm." She hesitated again. "His mouth is—" She smiled, "It's just right," she finished.

Pythia laughed easily and asked, "And his character? What is he like?"

"He has intelligence and humor," Nefrytatanen said quietly. "There are times when he's so playful it's difficult to realize he is a king, but his royalty is beyond question. He has great dignity. Amenemhet has the confidence to be gentle and the strength to be merciful. He has known pain and sorrow, but he stands unbowed." She smiled to herself. "He has great pride, yet he isn't inaccessible. His attitude isn't one that makes people fearful—unless they have reason to fear him. He commands respect."

"I think you must have to chase away women with regularity," Pythia remarked drily.

"They look, it's true—and some have tried." Nefrytatanen's eyes began to gleam with the light of remembered battle. "But he loves me as I love him. He's faithful to me."

"How can you speak with such confidence?" Pythia watched her intently.

"I keep him too occupied with me," Nefrytatanen said bluntly. "My arms are always open to him, and I show him my enthusiasm in many small gestures."

"Ah," Pythia sighed, "but what if he doesn't respond?"

"I make sure he does!" Nefrytatanen exclaimed.

"I speak frankly, Nefrytatanen, for I think you're a friend," Pythia said. "I admit I haven't been so successful with Melanpus."

"Perfumes and beautiful garments aren't always enough," Nefrytatanen said quietly. "There are other ways, sometimes unexpected and surprising, that are more successful."

"What secrets do you speak of?" Pythia leaned closer.

Nefrytatanen laughed. "I learned once to dance like a sand dweller. I do it for him sometimes when we're alone. This may seem like an unlikely thing for a queen to do, but it usually is most effective. For me, it's enjoyable and good exercise." Pythia's eyes widened, but she said nothing, and Nefrytatanen went on. "An impulsive walk one night in the moonlit private garden became so memorable an event that I've made certain to repeat it from time to time, making only enough noise when I leave our chambers to awaken him." Nefrytatanen paused, looking thoughtfully at Pythia, then suddenly asked, "Have you ever made love in a sunlit glade on a very private picnic?" Pythia's startled look was answer enough. Nefrytatanen continued softly. "With the birds supplying music, and the fragrance of trees and flowers, it surely can be worth a grass-stained robe and tumbled hair."

A new light had begun to glow in Pythia's eyes, and she smiled. "Nefrytatanen," she said, "you're a queen in public and a harem girl in private!"

Nefrytatanen readily nodded. "Our marriage contract allows Amenemhet a harem. My behavior keeps him from wanting one."

"Your marriage contract allows him a harem?"

"Our marriage was arranged for political reasons, and the contract was written before we'd met." Nefrytatanen smiled at her memories. "We were fortunate to find love."

Pythia stood up, and Nefrytatanen followed her to the door.

"Thank you for these ideas," Pythia said. "I'll go home and think all this over."

Nefrytatanen looked at her slyly. "Think about it if you will, but not to excess. Too much thinking sometimes makes one hesitant."

Pythia laughed lightly in understanding and left.

Nefrytatanen wondered if Pythia would actually follow her suggestions. She wondered if it would matter. She thought again of Amenemhet, missing him more than she dared dwell upon. Nefrytatanen lay back on the cushions of the bed thinking of how he would welcome her, planning what she would wear for the moment when he saw her. Thinking again of Amenemhet's eyes, she forgot Melanpus, Pythia, and Acetes. She resolved to end this business quickly so she could go home.

Pythia's usually neat curls became disordered as she shook her head and forcefully stamped her foot. "I will not have you staring at her in such a fashion!" she cried. "I will not endure it. You insult not only me, but also Nefrytatanen with your leering."

Melanpus stared at Pythia in surprise. She defended a woman she considered to be her rival?

"Nefrytatanen is a lady of high character," Pythia

scolded. "Her devotion to her husband is well known. If anyone could have won her from Amenemhet, Acetes would have done it long ago. He failed. You will behave in the manner she deserves and show respect!"

Melanpus's mouth had fallen open. Finally he closed it and found his voice. "I admire her beauty, but I have no intention of laying one finger on her. I have great respect for her."

"That's what you say now," Pythia said more calmly. "Just be sure you don't change your mind." She turned away and began to unfasten the clips of her robe. She was thinking that Amenemhet must surely be some man to hold a woman of Nefrytatanen's beauty and wit. Pythia wondered how he looked in person, and she decided she would like to meet him one day. To win against Acetes with his many charms was no small thing.

"Melanpus," Pythia said sweetly, "do you think we might someday travel to Tamera? It sounds like an interesting and beautiful place."

Melanpus looked at her in bewilderment. Pythia had never shown interest in traveling. What had happened to her today? he wondered. "Yes," he answered, wanting to please her, "we might do that sometime."

Pythia nodded, saying nothing. She was remembering the things Nefrytatanen had told her and her eyes grew soft in anticipation.

"Melanpus," Pythia murmured.

At her tone, Melanpus was again startled. He turned to see his usually sedate wife drawing a nearly transparent gown over her head, unconcerned that her curls now tumbled richly down. His mouth fell open.

"Melanpus, why don't we dismiss the servants and bathe alone tonight?" Pythia asked this in a velvety soft tone Melanpus couldn't believe. She added, "Together?"

He stared at her in amazement. She put a finger gently against his mouth, as if he would refuse her, and lightly brushed his shoulder with her lips. Her green eyes became even greener. Smiling, she took his hand and led him dazed and unprotesting to the bath chamber.

"Leave us—all of you—until we call!" Melanpus said sternly to the waiting servants. With curious looks, they obeyed.

Pythia dropped her gown on the tiles and stepped daintily into the water. "Shall I help you wash?" she offered, her eyes slowly rising to meet his.

Melanpus stared at her but quickly recovered himself and removed his robe. "Only if I may help you," he said, smiling cautiously.

"As I'd hoped," she murmured and waited for him to come to her.

Melanpus and Pythia had their evening meal in their private chambers, and no dancing girls were called. Pythia made sure Melanpus didn't dream of them, either. She allowed him little slumber.

Nefrytatanen sat on a bench under an umbrella-shaped tree. The garden seemed abandoned by even the caretakers. She fanned herself slowly. Lost in thought she didn't notice Acetes approaching until he spoke.

"Are you thinking of home?" he asked quietly.

"I was, in a way," she answered smiling. "I was comparing some of our habits and customs with yours.

309

I was wondering why no one here ever sits in the grass." She shifted her position uncomfortably. "It's more inviting than this hard bench."

Acetes laughed. "I don't know, but I think you're right." He took her hands and gently pulled her to her feet. "Don't feel restrained by our habits. Let's sit in that quiet place by the bushes." He had chosen a place Nefrytatanen had already eyed, and she went willingly with him.

It was only after they were settled that Nefrytatanen realized how secluded the spot actually was. Acetes sat down close to her, and she wished she had remained on the bench.

"You wear the same scent as you did the first time I saw you," Acetes said softly. "It's most alluring and suits you."

"It's my own invention," Nefrytatanen said distantly. "Amenemhet is pleased with it."

"I'm sure he's more than pleased with it." Acetes smiled and added, "As I am."

"Thank you." Her tone was purposely formal and cool.

Acetes decided to try a different approach. "Is it true," he said in a conversational tone, "that you dabble in magic?"

"I dabble in nothing." Nefrytatanen's eyes leveled their gaze at him, and the expression in their sapphire depths was his answer.

Although this knowledge startled Acetes, it didn't frighten him. Instead, it added an intriguing new aspect to her fascination. Acetes leaned closer. "What is magic, then," he murmured, "if it isn't your eyes and your hair, your fragrance and the curve of your lips?"

His arms slid around her and pressed her close, and his mouth was soft and warm against hers.

Nefrytatanen had kissed no one save Amenemhet for many years, and her response was automatic for an instant. But the fire Amenemhet aroused in her was absent. She submitted quietly to Acetes's kiss. Finally he drew his lips away. His eyes stared into hers for a long time. Then he released her and sat quietly. When he looked at her again, his eyes were sad.

"I'm sorry," Acetes whispered. "Although that kiss aroused me greatly, I can see it was nothing to you." Getting slowly to his feet, he added, "Perhaps it's just as well I kissed you, after all. My hope of winning you can now be stilled. I can tell that Amenemhet has your heart, and you will never love me or any other." He helped her to her feet. "You need not worry about this happening again. Curse me if you wish," he said wryly, "but I'm already cursed by loving you."

"I curse no one," Nefrytatanen said quietly.

In silence, they walked to the door, where she stopped him. "Acetes," she said gently, "perhaps, now that you've realized I can't return your love, you'll be able to love someone else."

He looked at her intently, almost angrily, but his voice was soft. "Once a man has fallen in love with a goddess, how could he be content with a mere woman?" Then he turned quickly and left her.

Nefrytatanen dined alone again that evening because Acetes had left the house without a word. She was a little relieved by his absence, but she wondered where he had gone.

Nefrytatanen was awakened at a late hour by the sound of Acetes's slamming the entrance door. She could tell from his sharp, loud commands to the servants that he had been drinking and was angry. She heard him come quietly up the stairs and walk through the hall, then pause at her door. When the door began to open, she closed her eyes to slits, watching from beneath her lashes, feigning sleep, wondering what he would do.

Acetes took several cautious steps into the room, walking very quietly for one who should—Nefrytatanen thought—be unsteady on his feet. He hesitated a moment, then came closer to stand next to the bed and stare down at her. She was glad she had some covers over her and made a supreme effort to breathe evenly, as if in deep slumber. She was terrified.

It seemed he stared at her for hours before he finally turned and went silently out, closing the door softly behind him. Nefrytatanen breathed a deep sigh of relief. She slept lightly during the rest of the night. She was afraid he might return.

Early the next morning, Acetes was called to the palace. When he returned, he sent a servant for Nefrytatanen. She joined him, a cautious look on her face.

Acetes's eyes were red from lack of sleep, and he spoke quietly, avoiding looking directly at her. "This morning King Melanpus and Queen Pythia directed me to tell you they agree to your request. They will accept the sum you discussed with the queen. Let me know when you wish to sail so I can tell them. They would like to meet you at the moorings and say goodbye."

Nefrytatanen couldn't hide the look of joy that lit her eyes. She had accomplished her mission despite everything—and she could go home. When she

When the ambassador from Zahi entered the room where Acetes awaited him, Acetes wore a calm face. But he was wondering what Adadni would say about Nefrytatanen's ship. What would he answer?

After exchanging the necessary formal greetings, Acetes invited Adadni to be comfortable. A servant poured wine for them, and Acetes watched it stream into the goblet. The turmoil of his emotions at Nefrytatanen's departure was mixed with his confusion about how to handle the ambassador's inconvenient arrival.

"I saw a ship from Tamera sailing from the harbor," Adadni said immediately. His narrowed eyes watched Acetes intently. Acetes hated him even more.

"It just left," was all Acetes could manage and retain any fragment of his outward poise.

"It carried the personal insignia of the royal family," Adadni prodded further.

Acetes sipped his wine, feeling the cool liquid ease his parched throat. When he met Adadni's eyes, it was without flinching. "Queen Nefrytatanen came to buy a treaty with their gold," he said.

"Tamera has great quantities of gold—and other treasures." Adadni drank several swallows of wine, then added slyly, "And a beautiful queen."

"She is that," Acetes said sadly. He had finally decided how to handle the situation.

"Was a bargain struck?"

"Not yet." Acetes allowed a small sigh to escape him.

"Perhaps we can make an even better offer to Troy." Now Adadni was allowing a secretive tone into the conversation. Acetes knew which direction Adadni was taking and would help him along his evil way.

315

"What sort of offer?" Acetes asked with deliberate caution.

"Troy, Djemeh, and Zahi might divide Tamera's gold three ways," Adadni said flatly. After a moment he added, "And all the other treasures Tamera holds." He smiled. "Nefrytatanen would be a lovely prize."

"Would we divide her three ways, also?" Acetes allowed his anger to show.

"No," Adadni replied. "Neither I nor our friends from Djemeh have an interest in her, but perhaps you, particularly, would enjoy such a personal reward? Have the years faded her beauty?"

"They've added to it." Acetes sighed again. His face was open for Adadni to read, but it was deliberately so.

"I can tell by your expression you find her alluring."

Acetes looked at Adadni intently for a moment. Then he leaned forward in his chair. Now was the moment he would draw Adadni in completely. "The turn of her eye is beauty," Acetes said. "Her smile is enchantment. The most beautiful of goddesses must wring her hands in envy of Nefrytatanen."

Adadni's eyes glittered. Now he was sure he had Acetes. "How would you like to have Nefrytatanen in your arms, in your bed—yours?"

"To think of it makes my head reel." Such thoughts did make Acetes's mind whirl, and he let this show on his face.

Adadni said quietly, "Acetes, you know how you can accomplish this."

Acetes sat back, as if considering the matter. "It's a serious thing. I must think about it."

"Think about it! From the way you speak of Nefrytatanen, you're sick with love of her! Would you leave this woman you love and desire to another man?"

"Amenemhet is her husband—also the king of a country with a powerful army," Acetes said grimly.

"Their army wouldn't have a chance against our three lands combined," Adadni said. "You would do your king a service by persuading him to join us. You would have Nefrytatanen for yourself, day and night, as long as you wish. Think of that." Adadni stood up. "I must leave you now. Perhaps we can speak of this again tomorrow morning before I have my audience with King Melanpus and Queen Pythia."

"Yes," agreed Acetes, rising to walk with him to the door. "Come before the audience. I'll go with you to the palace."

When Adadni had left his house, Acetes threw his goblet on the floor, taking satisfaction in the shattering noise. How he would like to agree to Adadni's bargain—but he couldn't. He hated Adadni for presenting such a tempting scheme.

If there were a battle at Ithtawe—and Acetes was sure there would be—he couldn't help but hope Amenemhet would be killed. It was the only honorable way Acetes could win Nefrytatanen. Acetes was disgusted with himself. Still, he wished Amenemhet a courageous and honorable death—so he could have Nefrytatanen.

Acetes sat at his writing table and wrote a message for Melanpus and Pythia, sealing it immediately. He could have no servant write it for him or read it on the way because it recounted his discussion with Adadni. Melanpus and Pythia must know before meeting the ambassador what had happened here, and be forewarned so they would act appropriately.

After Acetes had dispatched a trusted messenger, he went into his garden to sit in the same place where he had kissed Nefrytatanen. He looked into the sky at the sun, squinting, then turned to the grass beside him. That was about where she had sat, he decided.

Acetes muttered, "Damn Amenemhet! Die in this battle!"

Acetes would give up his place in Troy. He would give up his home. He wouldn't interfere with her ruling Tamera. He would help her when she needed his help. He would become friends with Senwadjet— the boy would need a man for a friend. It would be easy to love Maeti, if she were like Nefrytatanen.

"Amenemhet," Acetes whispered, "you have had Nefrytatanen for these past years. That much time is enough. Die, Amenemhet. Why can't I have her awhile?" He was ashamed, but he could not help himself.

He saw one of the gardeners clipping a nearby bush and hailed the man. Acetes said softly, "Never change this little place—not a shrub. I want to keep it exactly like this, always."

CHAPTER 14

NEFRYTATANEN WALKED SOFTLY through the darkness, hurrying as much as possible without making noise. She heard a sound and stopped. Did he still follow her? She listened carefully, but there was nothing. She could see only blackness, and she was terrified. She might blindly step into a hole or stumble across a rock and reveal her presence. Almost afraid to breathe, she peered into the impenetrable blackness. But it was impossible to see anything.

There was another soft sound, then silence. He was waiting for her to move again. How could he know she had stopped? He couldn't see her. She was sure she had made no noise. The air was still. Perhaps her perfume left a revealing trail? She began to run, desperately trying to see the ground she ran over. Her streaming hair blended into the blackness behind her as she fled. Did the very air tell him her direction?

She had to stop running because she was beginning to breathe too fast. In another moment she would start to pant, and he would surely hear that in this stillness. Why was there no wind, not even the slightest breeze?

The low shrubs served only as obstacles on which her robe caught and tangled. Already her legs were scratched and bleeding. The wounds burned. It was peculiar the way they burned. She didn't know what kind of plants grew in this place—could they be poisonous?

She wished she knew where she was. Where was Ithtawe? How far? She had lost her sense of direction completely. Some small creature moved the leaves ahead, and she shivered. Was it a serpent?

From behind her came the sound of a footstep, distinctive, nearer than the last. Serpent or not, she began to run again. He was much closer now. What would she do when dawn came? He would see her clearly.

Nefrytatanen prayed silently to Aset. She had never been so afraid before. She could see Nassurti's eyes revealing the horrors Gobryas had in mind for her. Necho was dead, Dedjet was dead—all of them! The ship was gone. Everything was gone—except Gobryas. He followed silently, relentlessly, until Nefrytatanen thought she would fall from exhaustion.

The snapping of a small twig nearby made her start. Was it some wild creature or was Gobryas that close? How could the night be so black? There was no moon. There were no stars. There was only Gobryas stalking her.

Nefrytatanen suddenly felt before her a wall of stone. For a moment she was terrified that she was trapped. Then she realized she was at the base of a cliff. Brushing one hand lightly over the stone, she followed the cliff's wall, dislodging small pebbles that made alarmingly clear sounds in the stillness. She ran, feeling under her feet a slight rise in the ground that edged the solid rock. She was beginning to pant again. She stopped running and leaned against the cliff to rest a moment. Her fingers touched an opening. It was a cave. She turned and felt around the opening eagerly. It was just large enough for her to slip through. Perhaps she could hide here.

Inside the cave, Nefrytatanen sank down upon the soft sand to rest. At her waist she had her small bag. She needed it now, but dare she make a small fire? Perhaps she could manage just enough of a flame to cast a mere pinch of her powder. She would beg Aset for help. Surely the goddess would answer her!

A pale, sickly flame flared briefly, then glowed. It wasn't much of a fire, but it was the best Nefrytatanen could manage. Cautiously Nefrytatanen took a pinch of her powder and sprinkled it on the fire, expecting a few sparks and only the faintest scent. A thick shower of sparks shot into the air, horrifying her. The perfume that was hers alone drenched the cave and swept into the night. Nefrytatanen spoke the words quickly, the secret words and names known only to a winged priestess. She said them as loudly as she dared. Then she realized Gobryas must be able to see the sparks and smell the scent outside. She repeated the words loudly, commanding the forces to obey. What did it matter if Gobryas heard? Aset would save her. Sekhmet would come and strike down this evil Hyksos.

Gobryas laughed. Nefrytatanen leaped up and saw him looking at her through the cave's opening.

"O Aset, Mistress of Magic, I beg your help! Save me from this evil man! O Sekhmet, Lady of Flame, destroyer of evil, stop this Hyksos murderer!" Nefrytatanen cried aloud the secret names and words, but there was no answer, and she felt fear run coldly through her. Aset had always answered. Why didn't Aset answer now?

The blue air rippled slightly. Hope rose in Nefrytatanen's soul. From the shadows of the scented haze came the sound of laughter—such exquisite, beautiful laughter—surely the laughter from the throat of a divine being.

"Aset, it's you! You've come to me at last!" Nefrytatanen cried. The laughter continued, but it mocked her. Nefrytatanen stared. How could it be?

"Your goddess won't save you," Gobryas said coldly. "She's turned from you. Now, Nefrytatanen, I need not wage war on Tamera to bring Amenemhet to his knees. I need only send word to him that I have you. He'll do whatever I ask."

Nefrytatanen backed farther into the cave, her terror rising. Her back touched stone. She was trapped.

Gobryas moved slowly toward her. "Before we leave this place," he said softly, "I'll know all that Amenemhet has known of you."

"You cannot," she whispered. "He has known love."

Gobryas smiled. "He has his kind of love and I mine. I'll know what it is to possess a sorceress whose powers are gone." He stepped on the pitifully small fire she had made, grinding out its last traces with his boot.

"Later," Gobryas whispered, "you'll find what I did to Nassurti was nothing compared with what I'll do to you." His face was close to Nefrytatanen's. She felt his breath on her cheek. "Before I ruin your beauty forever, I will enjoy you many times."

Gobryas's face came toward Nefrytatanen's until, for the first time in her life, Nefrytatanen screamed. Again and again she screamed. The cave rang with the sound.

Amenemhet sat up in bed with a jerk, his ears filled with screaming. His heart pounded. He was drenched with sweat and shivering with fear. He stared into the darkness, his eyes finally focusing on the room. He could still hear the screams.

The soft draperies moved with the night breeze, and the scent of the garden floated through the doorway. Amenemhet put his hand to his forehead, dazed. It had been a nightmare, he realized. His heart continued to pound, and he was cold with fear. He took a deep, shuddering breath. It was difficult to shake off the horror.

Amenemhet swung his legs off the bed. The linens were tumbled on the floor. He stood up weakly, still trembling, trying to relieve the nightmare's hold on him. He took the edge of the light cover and, giving it a slight shake, let it fall smoothly over the bed. He stared at her empty place, and grief washed over him.

He poured water into a goblet and drank a few swallows, then pressed the cool metal of the container against his forehead. The throbbing began to ease. Nefrytatanen must be on her way home by now, he reminded himself. He sat on the edge of the bed and thought of her on the ship. He wondered if she would be thinking of home, or peacefully sleeping—confident each breeze brought her closer to him.

Amenemhet stood up and, sighing, walked slowly to the door. The breeze would cleanse him of this clinging fear. He stepped out upon the stones of the terrace and leaned against the top of the low wall bordering the terrace edge. He felt as weak as if he were just recovering from a long illness. He breathed deeply of the cool air, wondering how long it would take for the horror to dissipate.

After a time, Amenemhet went back to bed. He shut his eyes, determined to sleep. He thought of tomorrow, when Nassurti would take her first steps. Amenemhet planned to be present to give her encouragement. It would bring her little cheer if he came to her with tired, haunted eyes. But again he could see the vision of Gobryas holding Nefrytatanen against the cave wall. He opened his eyes quickly, shuddered, and turned on his other side. The cover was tangled, and he kicked it off. He closed his eyes and saw Nefrytatanen staring at Gobryas in horror. He opened his eyes and groaned.

Dawn had begun to light the sky before Amenemhet's exhaustion won the struggle against fear, and he fell asleep at last.

Amenemhet stood leaning wearily against the wall while he watched Horemheb gently guiding Nassurti's feet to the floor. Nessumontu had also come to give Nassurti encouragement, and he stood near the bed ready to catch her if she wavered.

Although many of Nassurti's bandages had been removed, her face was still covered. Her dark eyes glanced self-consciously at Amenemhet.

"Don't be worried," Nessumontu said. "Try to stand up. If you start to fall, I'll catch you. I won't let you be hurt." He took a step closer.

Amenemhet smiled. "Go ahead, Nassurti," he said encouragingly. "Don't mind my dreary look. I didn't sleep well last night. I'm as anxious as Horemheb to see you well again."

Nassurti looked at Nessumontu a little shyly. "I would feel better," she whispered, "if you would hold my hands." She reached out to him, and he took her hands in his without hesitation.

"Come, Nassurti," Nessumontu urged, "just put your weight on your feet a moment. I won't let you fall."

She stood up cautiously, wavering a little. It was obvious she was dizzy for a moment. Recovering herself, she looked up at him.

Horemheb watched closely. "Try taking a step or two if you can," he suggested.

Nessumontu took one pace backwards, still holding Nassurti's hands. "Come on," he whispered. "One step." She took a shaky step and looked up at him. "Another?" he asked, moving back again. She took another step. Then she tried again without further urging. After the fifth step, she leaned against Nessumontu's chest. He could feel her tremble from weakness. "Enough?" he whispered.

"I think so," she said, her cheek against his shoulder. She was panting slightly.

"I think so, too," Horemheb said, coming forward. "Later you can get up again, but I don't want you to get strained."

Nessumontu picked up Nassurti and in a few strides reached the bed. He gently placed her on it. Amenemhet came closer, smiling. Looking into his eyes, Nassurti wondered why he was so sad.

"You did very well," Amenemhet said. "I expect it won't be very long before you'll be walking easily."

"I'll do my best," Nassurti murmured, "but I think it will take some time."

"We'll see how you progress," Horemheb said. "The most difficult part is over. To get out of bed and try to stand is the most frightening. You feel as if nothing will work, and you'll collapse into a heap. You did very well."

Nassurti's eyes had been on Nessumontu all the while they spoke. "I don't think I would have done it if you hadn't been here," she said. Noting Nessumontu's self-conscious expression, she added, "I felt safe with you holding my hands."

"Horemheb could have held you the same as I," Nessumontu replied. "It was you who did the walking. If you continue like this, I think you'll be walking alone by the time the queen returns. She'll be very pleased to see that."

"Yes," Amenemhet said quietly, "she will be pleased to see your improvement."

Horemheb saw the pained look in Amenemhet's eyes as he spoke of Nefrytatanen, and he wondered about it. Pulling the covers around Nassurti, he said, "It shouldn't be very long before she arrives, so you'd better rest and get the strength to try again."

"How soon?" Nassurti asked. Her black eyes glowed with anticipation.

Horemheb laughed softly. "After the evening meal, you can try to get to that chair and sit for a short time."

"I will do it," she said firmly. She looked at Nessumontu. "Will you come and help me?"

"I'm sure I can find the time for that pleasant task." He smiled. "Take a nap now, and I'll return later."

Nassurti laid back and closed her eyes. Then she opened them again. "Thank you both for coming," she said softly.

Horemheb walked with Amenemhet and Nessumontu into the corridor. He closed the door behind them. "Now we know at least that she'll walk again," Horemheb said quietly, "but I don't know how she'll feel when I take those bandages off and she sees for the first time how she looks." He sighed. "It's a shame. I think she was beautiful before this happened."

Remembering his dream, Amenemhet felt a stab of

renewed pain. He put it from his mind and turned to Horemheb. "We'll both be back later to see that Nassurti gets to that chair."

When Amenemhet went to bed that night, he was very satisfied with the day's events. He and Nessumontu had progressed far in fortifying Ithtawe, and after the pleasure of seeing Nassurti reach the chair with Nessumontu's help, Amenemhet felt especially content. As he closed his eyes, he decided that the dream's last traces had disappeared. He was confident he would sleep well and be refreshed by morning.

Amenemhet was mistaken. He lived through the identical dream, watching Nefrytatanen creep through the night in terror of Gobryas. Again he saw her crawl into the cave and light her fire only to hear the laughter of the goddess who turned from her pleas. Again he watched Gobryas capture Nefrytatanen in his arms and hold her to bring his mouth to hers, while her widened eyes glowed blue in terror.

Amenemhet awoke with his head throbbing and sat on the edge of the bed telling himself repeatedly it was only a nightmare born of loneliness. Once again he went out onto the terrace and waited until he stopped trembling. He returned to bed and lay awake throughout the night, afraid to sleep, wondering if the dream were a prophecy.

Kheti noticed the shadows around Amenemhet's eyes. "Are you not well?" he asked in concern.

"I'm well," Amenemhet answered. "I've had some trouble sleeping lately."

Kheti smiled wryly. "It's a large and empty bed when you're its only occupant."

"Yes, it is," Amenemhet agreed, unsmiling. As they

entered the room where Amenemhet set his seal, he asked, "What brings you to Ithtawe?"

"I have a favor to ask."

Amenemhet stopped inside the doorway. "Speak and it's yours," he said immediately.

"I'd like to bring Neferset and the children to Ithtawe if we have a war," Kheti said softly. "Although I'm sure Ithtawe is the first place the Hyksos will attack, I think it's the safest."

Amenemhet nodded. "Send them here, Kheti, while it's still safe to travel." He looked at Kheti as if a sudden thought had occurred to him. "Has Neferset had any of her prophetic dreams lately?" he asked.

"No." Kheti shook his head emphatically. "Why do you ask?"

Amenemhet hesitated a moment, then answered. "I wondered if she's had a dream that urges you to bring them here."

"I just decided it would be safest," Kheti replied. "If she'd had any distressing dreams, I'd surely know it. I'm a light sleeper, and we sleep very close."

Amenemhet seemed relieved at his words, but he said no more. Kheti wondered if he had heard bad news from Nakht.

"Has Nakht returned?"

"No, and I've heard nothing." Amenemhet sat on one of the couches. "Word should come soon."

Kheti began to understand what brought so dark a mood to Amenemhet. He laid his hand on Amenemhet's arm sympathetically. "She'll return soon," Kheti said softly. The gold eyes confirmed his suspicions. "She will come back," Kheti assured him again.

Amenemhet nodded, and they began to speak of other matters.

* * *

Nakht impatiently paced the floor, waiting for Chamma. He was aware of her scent before he heard her step, and he turned quickly to face her as she came through the door.

Chamma paused in the doorway. She smiled. Her gown was a new one, made of several sheer layers of silk, each layer a different color—violet, rose, and pale orange. They blended and changed with her movements. She wore the necklace Nakht had given her, and the perfume as well. The scent suited Chamma as no other could, warm and tangy. Her hair was arranged in the fashion of Tamera. Seeing the way he looked at her, she smiled and turned slowly for inspection.

"Are you pleased?" Chamma asked. As she came toward him, she added, "You are most pleased. I can see it in your eyes." She put her arms around Nakht and kissed him lightly.

As she stepped away, Nakht smiled and said, "Now I can see your body. It isn't hidden by the gown."

Chamma laughed softly. "But you've already seen it with no gown, and you know how I feel as well." She turned to her maid and waved her away. "Don't return until I call," she instructed. When the woman had left, Chamma closed the doors and turned to Nakht. "Recline," she murmured, "and I'll serve you myself."

Chamma poured wine as Nakht made himself comfortable. She sat at his side and leaned over to kiss him lingeringly before giving him the goblet. Taking a sip of her own wine, she looked at him with sadness in her dark eyes.

"Nakht," she said softly, "I know why you provoked our quarrel. I also know why you came back."

He stared into his goblet, not wanting to reveal his face.

She went on, "It wasn't for me, but I am happy you returned." She was silent a moment, gazing across the room beyond him. "You wished to have an excuse to leave quickly because you learned Djemeh was secretly negotiating with Zahi. Now you've returned to spread rumors while pretending to continue negotiating a treaty." Her black eyes returned to him. "You've completed your task and have laid your trap for the Hyksos.

"I know Astram had no hunting accident. I guessed it from the first. I knew him too well to believe Adadni's lies. Astram was a good hunter, and he was a careful man in every way. I've said nothing to anyone else of these things. And no one has discussed these matters with me. These are my own conclusions."

Chamma put down her goblet and took Nakht's. Then she leaned over him, pressing her body close, kissing him softly for a long time. When she drew away, she sighed. "I know much more beside what I've just told you. When King Zaretes saw that you desired me, he commanded I spy for him to find out what I could from you, to use my body to gain your trust and coax you to speak of secret matters. I had no choice. He commanded me. His commands are always obeyed."

Nakht grasped her shoulders tightly, incredulous. Chamma, whom he had come to love, a spy? He stared at her. "No," he whispered, sitting up. "No—not you."

"Yes, Nakht, me," she said clearly. "It hasn't come

330

to much so far. You've said little that I could disclose to them, and I've only told them enough to keep them satisfied. I've even lied to them to keep them from being suspicious. They insisted I dress as you'd like me best. But I chose this dress and did my hair as a woman from your land, to please you, not them. They want to know what plans you take home with you tomorrow. But all I want is to beg you to stay." Her eyes pleaded with him. "Stay here with me, Nakht."

So stunned was Nakht that, for a moment, he couldn't speak. He recalled their intimacy, and his heart filled with grief. Then anger flooded through him. Zaretes had used her for political reasons. Zaretes had spoiled what they had made together. Nakht tightened his grip on her arms.

"Chamma," he said softly, "there are two things you've forgotten."

"You're causing me pain," she whispered. He ignored this, and Chamma saw great anger in his face.

"There's a saying about my people," he said. "No child born of Tamera's blood ever leaves its borders forever by choice. It's true we think a life lived elsewhere isn't worth living. I am of Tamera, and I couldn't live in another land happily. The other thing you forgot is that I'm loyal to my king and queen. Chamma," he said softly, "I must ask you to drink a drug I'll mix for you."

Chamma's eyes widened. She had revealed herself as a spy, and now she was sure he couldn't let her live.

"It isn't poison," Nakht said quickly. "I don't want to harm you. It will put you in a deep sleep for several days. When you awaken to tell them the story of this night, I'll be far away." He smiled unhappily.

331

"How can I be sure it isn't poison?" she asked quietly.

"You have my word," he answered. "If I wanted to kill you, I'd take my dagger and do it quickly, laying your body in some dark corner of the city where these incidents are common. Do you think I could do that to you? Drink the drug and sleep for a few days," he urged.

He pulled her close to him. "I love you, Chamma. If you had loved me, I would have taken you to my house as my wife." He looked into her eyes and smiled sadly. "Would you kiss me once before you drink this? It will be the last embrace we can share."

"Gladly will I kiss you," she whispered, her black eyes shimmering with tears, "although I fear it's the last kiss I'll give anyone. I didn't do as I was commanded. When I awaken from your drug, I'll tell them nothing of your plans, and they'll know I fooled them all along. They'll kill me." She stared at him and said softly, "What I felt for you was truth."

Without looking at her, Nakht poured a powder into Chamma's goblet and waited for it to dissolve. Silently, he handed her the goblet. She took it and drank without hesitation.

"I love you, Nakht," Chamma murmured. "Take that truth home with you." Her eyes began to close, and he caught her before she fell. Holding her in his arms, he stood gazing down at her.

Chamma had trusted him. Had the powder been poison, she would have drunk it all the same. She needn't have told him of the plot, if she hadn't loved him. But she did love him.

If he left her here, she wouldn't tell Zaretes what she knew. They would have her killed. What could he do? In a moment, he had made his decision. He could not leave her to face death.

Nakht laid Chamma on the bed and spread his cloak over her. He looked out the windows. No one stood in the street. He came back and wrapped her in the cloak, then picked her up. He stepped carefully through the window opening—thankful it went almost to the floor—and crept through the empty streets, keeping near the buildings where it was darkest.

Nakht planned to send Captain Tati to his quarters in town to gather his belongings. He would leave a message for King Zaretes that he sailed tonight because of coming bad weather. He planned to go back to Chamma's room quietly. He would play the part of the angry lover once again, but he would be alone in her room when he did so.

When he left, he would tell the serving woman that Chamma was furious. The maid wouldn't be anxious to enter. If the woman didn't enter Chamma's room until morning, Chamma's absence could be attributed to anything. He would rumple the bed as if she had slept there and perhaps smash a vase or two to demonstrate a fight.

"Aset," Nakht muttered, "keep our secret."

Senet entered the royal bedchamber, and finding Yazid dusting, she said, "Since the queen has left, many things seem to be neglected."

Yazid looked at her questioningly and answered, "The king is too occupied with battle plans, and the prince and princess with their problems to notice the palace housekeeping. Also," Yazid continued, "the king is very worried about the queen's continued absence. Have you noticed how silent he's become?"

"Yes, and I don't like it," Senet said. "If this trip takes much longer, he'll be sick before she arrives." Senet looked at Yazid carefully. "Do you think something's wrong?"

"No, no," he answered promptly. "She'll return."

To hide her fear, she remarked, "I don't care to see her welcomed by an unkempt palace."

"Unkempt?" Yazid looked startled.

"When I walked through the hall just now," Senet said sharply, "I felt sand grains beneath my feet." She looked at Yazid's dusty sleeve meaningfully. "Someone has been lax."

"There has been much wind lately," Yazid replied, "and it must be difficult to remove it all."

"There has always been both sand and wind," Senet observed sarcastically, "but the sand hasn't been allowed to gather in small heaps in the corners. The halls of the palace are not desert tents and the royal table is not a picnic lunch." Senet paused as if to turn away, then added, "Next we'll find insects in the cabinets and spiders merrily spinning webs in the throne room." She stared at Yazid reproachfully. "I wouldn't wish to be responsible for what happens if the queen returns to find a creature of many legs in her bed."

"Nor I!" Yazid exclaimed. "I'll speak to the housekeeping staff myself. Such things can't be tolerated. I have no wish to find insects in unexpected places, either!" Yazid turned and marched out, resolving to settle this matter immediately. He had a strong aversion to bugs. It would be a disgrace for Nefrytatanen to return and find the palace uncared for.

Yazid shook his head. There were so many things to worry about. It was becoming difficult to choose which problem to occupy himself with first. Sand in the halls seemed the least of evils to him, but the Hyksos did not dwell in Ithtawe yet. Until they did, the palace would be well cared for. "What am I thinking?" he muttered. "They won't take Ithtawe—not while one stone stands in its place or one Tameran is left alive."

Amenemhet sat in the forest glade beside the lotus pool, the trees sighing softly in the breeze, the light making golden patterns on the grass. The sweet scent of lotus blossoms mingled with his memory of Nefrytatanen's perfume. He lay back on the grass, feeling its soft touch and thinking of Nefrytatanen's lips. The wind in the palm trees sang softly. He could feel her lips move over his face.

Amenemhet opened his eyes, and Nefrytatanen was there, looking at him, her face radiant with love. Her fingers touched his temples, moving to his hair, tangling themselves in it as she loved to do. As she leaned close to him, her breasts brushed his chest. He lifted his arms, drawing her closer to him, feeling the curve of her back, sliding his hands to her waist. He held her closer, kissing her, drawing life from her lips.

"I have been a dead thing without you," Amenemhet whispered. "I have been like a tomb." Nefrytatanen kissed his words away. "Why did you stay so long from me?" he asked. "I've worked all hours of the night to avoid that lonely bed, trying to put this aching from me, trying to distract myself. But I couldn't do it. There was no help for me."

Nefrytatanen drew away, saying nothing. She sat beside him, not touching him.

"Why do you say nothing?" He was confused. A cold streak of fear ran through Amenemhet at Nefrytatanen's look. She stared straight ahead at something behind him, her eyes filled with terror. "What is it, my beloved?" he asked, alarm rising in his heart. "Why are you afraid?" Amenemhet sat up quickly, turning. Gobryas stood staring at them, grinning.

"What are you doing here?" Amenemhet demanded. "Guards!" he shouted, leaping to his feet. He pulled Nefrytatanen from the grass and pushed her behind him. He had no weapon, but his own body stood between Gobryas and Nefrytatanen. "Guards! Guards!" he cried.

"There are none to answer you," Gobryas said quietly, "except for my own." At his gesture, four Hyksos soldiers came from behind the shrubbery. Amenemhet backed away, forcing Nefrytatanen to move with him.

The guards leaped at Amenemhet and tore Nefrytatanen from him. Amenemhet's arms became leaden. His feet would not move.

He could do nothing. They dragged him into a building he had never seen there before.

The building was like a tomb, dusty and dark, quiet but for the sound of his panicked breathing. The torchlight crawled in patterns like fingers on the stone walls. There were no window openings, and once the door had been closed, Amenemhet couldn't see where it had been. The soldiers dragged him to a wall where they snapped metal shackles to his wrists and ankles. The shackles were attached to chains buried deep in the stone. He was helpless.

Where was Nessumontu? Where were the palace guards? What was this place he hadn't seen before? Gobryas watched Amenemhet, a sneer playing over his face, and Amenemhet's eyes flashed gold fire as he saw the guards chaining the unresisting Nefrytatanen to a stone table a short distance from him. She turned her face to Amenemhet, looking at him with sorrow.

"What have you done to her?" Amenemhet cried. "Have you given her some drug? How did you get inside the palace walls without raising the alarm?"

"She called upon Aset," Gobryas said softly, "and her goddess—all your gods and goddesses—turned away and laughed. I decided to save this moment for your viewing. It wasn't easy to wait. I was much tempted by her beauty, but I decided my revenge would be more pleasant for my patience. It will be more satisfying to have you witness this. Afterwards I'll kill you."

Amenemhet stared, horrified. "You're mad! Senwadjet will call the guards. Nessumontu will stop your escape."

"While you slept in the garden, I took the palace by stealth," Gobryas said smugly. "Even now the prince is bound and waiting to be brought here."

Amenemhet thought of Senwadjet and of Maeti, and he was filled with despair. "Nefrytatanen will kill herself and Maeti too, before she'll allow you to touch her," Amenemhet whispered. Again he struggled against his chains, and their metallic clanking was the only sound in the place.

"She'll do nothing. I'll kill her when I grow tired of her. I'll do with her just as I'd planned to do with Nassurti, but this will be slower." Gobryas moved to stand just outside Amenemhet's reach. "Stop struggling with those chains," he advised. "They'll hold an elephant. Quiet yourself and watch." Gobryas turned away and went to Nefrytatanen, whose face had been turned toward them through all this. She had listened silently, her eyes dull with pain.

"Beloved!" Amenemhet cried. "Call for Issella! Your own mother's spirit won't turn away. Ask her for help. Ask for death for us!"

Nefrytatanen gave no answer. Tears rolled from her eyes to the table, making dark spots on the stone.

Amenemhet's eyes were glowing triangles of fury. "Gobryas," he said softly, "I curse you myself. By Heru who gives me my crown and by Wadjet who guards it, by Sekhmet who holds the fire of vengeance and by Sutekh who is the lust for blood, by all the ancient forces of Tamera, I curse you and all who follow you—here and reaching into eternity."

"Curse all you wish," Gobryas said. He turned to Nefrytatanen and tore her robe with the point of his dagger. "But notice they ignore you." He drew his cloak to one side to free his hands.

Nefrytatanen ignored Gobryas and continued to stare at Amenemhet, her tears silently falling.

"Watch me, mighty king," Gobryas said softly. "Watch my pleasure with her."

Amenemhet smothered a groan as he struggled uselessly with his chains. He stopped struggling a moment and said in a very low tone, "Gobryas, I'll come from my tomb for you. Even my death won't stop my revenge." Seeing Nefrytatanen watching him, the tears running down her face, Amenemhet cried, "My beloved, do something. Do something! Beloved! Beloved!"

Yazid shook Amenemhet and slapped his face sharply.

"Sire, forgive me for striking you," he begged, backing away slowly. "You were screaming in your sleep, thrashing around in a nightmare. I couldn't awaken you."

Amenemhet sat up slowly, shivering, cold. Gradually he began to realize it had been another dream. His face was still wet with tears. Speechless, his head throbbing, he stared at Yazid. When he tried to stand, he nearly fell, so weak and shaking were his legs.

"Sire, don't stand," Yazid begged. "I'll bring Horemheb for you. Stay there, please."

Amenemhet sank to the edge of the bed again, his face in his hands. Yazid ran out. Amenemhet felt faint and lifted his face to take great gulps of air. He sat shivering in the dark until Horemheb burst into the room.

After one glance at Amenemhet, Horemheb wrapped a blanket loosely around him. "Yazid!" Horemheb snapped. "Light all the lamps so he knows where he is." He sat next to Amenemhet on the bed. "Lie down and tell me what dream brought you to this state," he urged. "The telling of it will release some of the fear."

Amenemhet looked at Horemheb with anguish. Gathering the blanket around him, still shaking, he stood up and paced for a moment in silence. "I cannot bring myself to repeat it," Amenemhet said. "It hasn't been the first nightmare I've had."

"I knew something was wrong. You've looked tired and pale," Horemheb said quietly. "The dreams are about the queen?"

Amenemhet nodded, then turned to the physician.

"I dream over and over that Gobryas has her. This was the worst yet. I'm afraid that, like Neferset, I dream prophecy. I'm not usually given to dreaming." He sat beside Horemheb, again putting his head in his hands. "I can't understand why she hasn't returned."

"It has seemed long to you," Horemheb said softly, "but it isn't overlong for such a journey." He stood up and walked to the terrace, staring into the night. Then he turned and regarded Amenemhet silently for a moment. "I have no medicine to cure this malady," he said. "I have only a sleeping potion to offer."

"I prefer not to sleep at all," Amenemhet said softly.

"You cannot do that," the physician answered. "I think Ankhneferu could be of help. He might stop these dreams and still your fears. I think you're afraid because of the terror when the queen was kidnapped. I think that still lays deep inside your mind. You've never been separated from her since, and this trip has aroused your old fears. I do not think this is prophecy."

"Perhaps you're right." Amenemhet sighed wearily, beginning to feel calmer. "But when I think of what Gobryas did to Nassurti, I cannot help myself." Amenemhet's shadowed eyes were filled with despair, as did his voice. He shook his head, feeling the icy shiver of returning terror. "I won't rest until she returns safely," he said.

Horemheb said softly, "Let the past be dead. Troy isn't our enemy, and Acetes is the queen's friend. The ship is swift and well armed. Necho is too good a sailor and his devotion to you and the queen too deep for him to let her fall into enemy hands. Did he not take you to Atalan and back when he was little more than a boy?"

"I know, I know," Amenemhet said. "I've reminded myself of these things many times."

"The ship she took on your wedding night was only lightly guarded, and everyone was in a mood of celebration," Horemheb recalled. "No one had reason to think such a thing would happen. The ship she now sails in is well prepared. And the chance of an attack is very remote."

"I know, Horemheb." Amenemhet looked at Horemheb with bleak eyes. "But I cannot rest until she's here again. Only when she's in my arms will I know the certainty of her safety." Amenemhet looked away. "I can't help myself, Horemheb. The pain is too great."

Horemheb laid a sympathetic hand on Amenemhet's shoulder. "I think tomorrow you should go to Ankhneferu and talk to him. Tonight I'll give you something to bring deep sleep. If I could somehow hasten the queen's return, I would do it, but nothing more than giving you dreamless sleep is in my power. Go to Ankhneferu tomorrow. This obsession and the resulting lack of sleep could influence your judgment—and the land needs you terribly now."

Amenemhet looked at him angrily. "Sometimes I tire of this crown," he snapped. "I wish I could be a farmer in the field. At least he can sleep in peace, without fear for himself or his family."

Horemheb stared at him, shocked. It had never occurred to Horemheb that a king might wish to renounce his crown. His king and queen were his patients, and he knew well enough they were made of flesh and blood like himself. But he had never forgotten their royalty. He said softly, "The farmers and all the people of the Two Lands are safe because you've made them safe."

Amenemhet said nothing. He drank the potion Horemheb mixed for him, then lay on the bed once again. He still dreaded sleeping. He breathed a silent prayer for Nefrytatanen.

Horemheb left, quietly closing the door. Yazid was careful to keep the door to his adjoining room open.

Amenemhet paid no attention to either of them. He couldn't still his fears. He could not endure such terror again. He could not.

In the morning as Amenemhet walked slowly downstairs for the meal he knew he couldn't eat, word came that a ship had been sighted. He lifted his head quickly. He was afraid to hope. He hurried out of the palace, his guards running to keep pace with him.

Amenemhet reached the moorings and peered into the distance. He saw a red and white sail, and his heart leaped. It was their ship, he realized incredulously, staring with blurred eyes. Only their own personal ship carried those markings. He stared, unmoving, as it drew closer.

At last, Amenemhet breathed a sigh of relief. Nefrytatanen stood near the rail, her bright blue veil floating in the northern breeze like a greeting. She waved and moved nearer the rail.

As soon as the vessel was moored and the ramp laid in place, Nefrytatanen ran down the gangplank, the blue veil a streamer behind her, and plummeted into Amenemhet's arms. They clung to each other, oblivious of the sailors and bystanders smiling at them. Finally Nefrytatanen loosened her grip and stepped back to smile happily up at Amenemhet.

"If we continue in this fashion," she said, laughing, "there will be a scandal."

Amenemhet smiled faintly. He couldn't laugh. His fear was still too near him. He absorbed the sight of her, alive and smiling.

Nefrytatanen's smile faded. "What is wrong, beloved?" she asked in alarm.

"Now that you're here," he said softly, putting his arm tightly around her waist, "nothing is wrong that cannot be put right again." He bent and kissed her cheek, inhaling her perfume, silently thanking all the divine beings for her safety. He whispered, "Beloved, I cannot tell you how glad I am you're home again. I think I'll spend tonight on my knees in the temple, out of gratitude."

"Spend tomorrow in the temple, if you will," Nefrytatanen whispered. "I prefer you spend tonight with me. If you wish to give thanks for my return, demonstrate your gratitude with our own joy." She smiled. "The divine beings know of your heart's gladness—and mine."

Senwadjet and Maeti, arriving with enthusiastic affection, distracted Nefrytatanen from Amenemhet's strange expression.

Senwadjet was the first of them all to remember her mission. "Tell us, mother," he asked quietly, "how did it go?"

Nefrytatanen turned to him. How like Amenemhet he looked! She remembered the doubts she had had from time to time, and she realized that what she had thought were hints of frivolity had been the natural instincts of a healthy, high-spirited youth. She could see clearly his intelligence and courage, and she smiled proudly at him.

"You're the first to ask," Nefrytatanen observed. "It speaks well for Tamera's future under your rule."

Senwadjet's sunny smile was Nefrytatanen's reward. Even Amenemhet's expression brightened.

Nefrytatanen said, "All the plans have been laid exactly in accordance with what we wished. Although Troy wasn't hesitant to accept our gold, they asked for less than we had been prepared to offer. I, of course, didn't argue."

"Mother," Maeti ventured, a shy look on her face, "how did you deal with Acetes?"

"Surely you don't think I became part of the bargain!" Nefrytatanen laughed softly. "Once again, Acetes and I parted as friends. Even King Melanpus is now very favorably disposed toward Tamera."

Amenemhet looked hard at her. "You have another admirer to add to your growing list?"

"Two. Queen Pythia and I also parted on the best of terms." Nefrytatanen's eyes sparkled.

"How did you manage it?" Maeti looked at her with awe.

"Perhaps Nakht might learn from your diplomacy," Amenemhet remarked drily.

Nefrytatanen turned to Maeti. "My daughter, you and I will speak of this in more detail later—in privacy."

Amenemhet understood Nefrytatanen's purpose and demanded in mock jealousy, "Why not now?"

"There are many things a mother should teach her daughter," said Nefrytatanen coolly. She squeezed Amenemhet's hand. "It's important that Maeti learn how to handle delicate situations. It's my duty to teach her these things. Men need not know each detail of feminine behavior."

Maeti's face showed the eagerness with which she would add to her knowledge of delicate situations.

"What has happened while I've been gone?" Nefrytatanen turned a serious face to Amenemhet.

Looking into her upturned eyes, Amenemhet answered softly, "A number of things. I think you and I should go into our chambers and discuss them in privacy."

"I think that would be most wise," Nefrytatanen whispered. She smiled knowingly.

Amenemhet took Nefrytatanen's hand and led her upstairs, looking all the while into her eyes.

Yazid, standing at the base of the stairs with Horemheb, watched them go. He turned to the physician and said quietly, "He won't need Ankhneferu now. He'll have no more nightmares." Horemheb nodded solemnly in agreement. "In fact," Yazid said, "he'll probably have little time for dreaming tonight."

Horemheb smiled. "Whatever sleep he gets will be sufficient."

CHAPTER 15

STRIDING SILENTLY through the dark garden, Nessumontu smiled at himself. He was commander of the whole army, but he still inspected the palace grounds at night. He would never be anything other than a soldier, he reflected. His own nature was predatory! Why else would he creep around in the dark, eyes and ears alert, rather than sleep? His laugh was as soundless as his steps. Like a nocturnal hunting animal, he traveled in a calculated but undiscernible pattern, covering the grounds efficiently and thoroughly.

He stopped, like a wolf scenting prey. Eyes as keen in the dark as in daylight, he scanned every shadow, moving not a muscle.

Under a sycamore's low-hanging branches, he saw someone sitting huddled on the grass in a posture of abject misery. He walked openly toward the figure, forgetting that his steps were as silent as before.

When he spoke, the figure leaped in fright. Eyes stared up at him from a face shining with tears. Then the figure quickly turned away.

"Nassurti!" Nessumontu exclaimed. "What are you doing here?" He crouched beside her. "Why are you weeping?" he asked softly. She gave no answer, but he saw a droplet fall on her shoulder. With a gentle fingertip, he wiped the tears. "Nassurti, surely you

346

aren't sorry you came here? Did you leave someone you love in Zahi?"

Nassurti shook her head vigorously, still keeping her face turned aside. With his fingers under her chin, Nessumontu tried to turn her face toward him, but her neck was rigid. She would not move.

"Look at me," he coaxed, "for I feel as if I speak to a statue. But statues don't weep. What's wrong? Are you in pain? Do you still suffer from your injuries? If so, you must tell Horemheb. Don't be afraid of going to him whenever you need him."

"I'm not afraid," she whispered.

"If your injuries don't pain you, why do you sit alone in the night?" Nessumontu sat down in the grass beside her.

"The injuries that give me pain cannot be healed by Horemheb," Nassurti murmured, tears running more freely down her cheeks.

"Perhaps to speak of them would ease your pain," Nessumontu said softly. "To speak to someone you can trust—perhaps the queen?"

"No!" she exclaimed. "She's been too kind. I cannot further burden her with my troubles when she has so many more important things to think about."

"Burden me, then," Nessumontu offered. "I know how to keep silent." He waited a moment, but got no reply. "Come, Nassurti, you can trust me. You can't sit weeping in the garden every night."

Nessumontu's voice seemed so sympathetic that Nassurti was much tempted. But what would he know about such matters? He would probably think her foolishly vain. Yet, he seemed concerned.

As if he read her mind, Nessumontu said, "Look at

me, Nassurti. See if I'm unsympathetic." He tried
again to turn her face, but she wouldn't allow it.

Her voice was caught on the sharp edge of a tear.
"Have you not noticed how I've kept to my room?"
Her words were bitter, as if they dragged themselves
out of her. "I can't turn my face to you now that my
bandages are gone. I wish no one to see my ugliness."

Nessumontu was silent. He didn't know what to say.
Finally he ventured, "Perhaps it's only in your own
eyes that you're so disfigured. If someone else had the
chance to look at you and give you an opinion, it
might not be as bad as you think. I would tell you
frankly. Perhaps Horemheb can do something for the
scars. Have you asked him? Have you seen him recently?"

"I haven't seen Horemheb for days. I've avoided
everyone."

"Then how do you know you look so terrible? How
do you know Horemheb can't help you?"

"I know what I see in the mirror!" Nassurti flashed
back. "How could he do anything with what I see?"

"You see the worst because it's your face. What
someone else sees might be different. I'm not a physician so I don't know what Horemheb can do for you,
although I've seen him do much for soldiers scarred
in battle. I know he's the finest physician in the land.
You're being stubborn," Nessumontu said firmly. "Let
me look at you—even in this faint light—and tell you
what I see. Do you want to hide for the rest of your
life?"

Nassurti was silent, still turned away from him,
head drooping. Finally she said, "All right, Nessumontu, I'll let you look at me if you promise to tell
no one else what a horror I am."

"I'm unlikely to go around proclaiming your ugliness," he said drily. "In Tamera, if you remember the teachings of your childhood, we place great value on keeping promises. I'll tell you the truth, and I'll speak to no one else of this. I promise. Turn your face to me," he said gently. "Don't be afraid."

Very slowly Nassurti turned toward him. Nessumontu knew she didn't realize how sharp his eyes were in the dark. She thought the shadows softened her features, but he could see them plainly. He studied her carefully for some time, deliberately keeping his own expression unchanged, all the while feeling pity for her.

Finally Nessumontu said quietly, "I see a brow, smooth and clear and well shaped. Your eyes are somewhat swollen from weeping, but they're wide and almond shaped. You have beautful eyes, Nassurti, black as the sky is now." He smiled faintly. "Your nose was broken and has healed crooked. It's not too bad. I've seen worse that Horemheb has rebroken and set straight again. In fact, I've seen people born with worse noses. Your face is delicate, the shape of a heart, and this loveliness hasn't been changed. Your mouth is full, but not too wide. You have a small scar or two on your chin and brow, but they are, I think, likely to fade in time."

"And the other scar?" Nassurti's voice was harsh. "You've avoided mention of that. Tell me how delicate and beautiful that scar is that twists my lips on one side and pulls the corner of my eye crooked."

"I was coming to that," Nessumontu said calmly. "That scar won't fade. However, I think it might be hidden with cosmetics. As far as its effect on your eye and the corner of your mouth is concerned, it would seem to me it is the skin pulling together that has caused this. It wouldn't surprise me if Horemheb could ease the tightness of the skin and let your mouth and eye resume their normal shape. Go to him and ask about these things. See if he can fix the scar and reshape your nose. If it can be done, only the line of the scar itself will show. And cosmetics would lighten it. The women of Tamera know much about cosmetics. Perhaps the queen or Dedjet could advise you. Would you remain hidden and throw away a normal life?"

"If all this can be done, I could face sunlight again. How I have longed to feel it on my face once more!" Nassurti's eyes began to fill with hope, but when she smiled, her mouth was lopsided. Nessumontu didn't allow himself to react to this, but she was aware of it. She stopped smiling and looked down again.

"And I, being repaired and well schooled in the art of cosmetics, could fool a man in the light of day. But should I fall in love and want to marry, what would my husband say on our wedding night, when my face is cleansed of cosmetics and this scar shows clearly?" Nassurti's tone was sarcastic, but it didn't fool Nessumontu.

"If I were that man," Nessumontu said slowly, "I wouldn't be examining your scar on our wedding night. There would be many other, more interesting, things to do." He smiled, a gleam in his eyes.

Nassurti stared at Nessumontu in surprise. He could look at her in her present state and say such a thing? He looked at her as if she might be desirable, after all.

"You are most desirable," Nessumontu said, again reading her mind. "I don't give compliments I don't mean. My friends consider me particularly tactless."

Suddenly Nassurti laughed. "In fact, Nessumontu," she said, "I've heard it said you're most brutally honest in your opinions—when they can be wrenched from you at all—for you are generally known not to be talkative."

Nessumontu raised his eyebrows. "And what else have you learned of me, little sister?" he asked.

She stared at him again. To be treated as an equal was delightful and to be called "little sister" like any woman was amazing. She looked away a little nervously now. She was beginning to feel very attracted to Nessumontu.

She said softly, "Your reputation for the conquest of ladies is almost the equal of your military accomplishments."

Embarrassed, Nessumontu said, "Reputations of that kind are mostly rumors and usually less than half true."

"I doubt your reputation as a soldier is a rumor, or you wouldn't be commander of the army," Nassurti retorted. "As for the other, perhaps you're too modest?"

Nessumontu frowned slightly. He had no wish to discuss his romantic life with this girl. After an awkward silence, he said, "I think we'd better go back to the palace. It's very late." He stood up and helped her to her feet.

Neither spoke again until they reached the door to her room. Then Nessumontu paused and whispered, "Nassurti, visit Horemheb tomorrow and ask his advice. I'd like to know what he says."

She looked at him in renewed amazement, and her heart skipped a beat.

He added, "When you know me better, you may be

better able to judge the truth of my reputation. Good night, little one."

Nessumontu turned quickly and left Nassurti standing in her doorway, her eyes shining with hope, her scarred smile warm and glowing.

After a long session in court, Nefrytatanen removed Amenemhet's beard gently. He winced, then sighed with relief.

"How did you enjoy wearing this thing?" Amenemhet teased Senwadjet.

Senwadjet touched his chin in sympathy. "The wearing of it wasn't so bad," he said. "I was too interested in hearing the cases to pay much attention. But when Maeti removed it"—he rolled his eyes toward the ceiling—"what hairs I'd managed to grow on my chin were ruined!"

Maeti laughed. "There weren't enough to make a commotion over as you did."

Nefrytatanen turned to Maeti and asked sweetly, "Did you enjoy the weight of the double crown?"

Maeti stopped laughing. "My head aches to remember it," she said, "and my neck is pressed shorter."

A servant approached them in the private corridor and bowed. "Ambassador Nakht has returned from Djemeh," he announced.

Amenemhet looked at Nefrytatanen meaningfully. "Now we'll see if his mission was as successful as yours." He handed Yazid his crown and scepters.

Nefrytatanen quickly gave Dedjet her own scepters and crown, and when the servants had left with their precious burdens, the royal family was joined by Nessumontu. They went together to see Nakht.

Nakht came toward them smiling widely.

"Welcome home, Nakht," Amenemhet said. "How did it go?"

"Very well. In fact, it was much better than I'd anticipated."

"You do look pleased with yourself," Nefrytatanen observed.

"I patiently negotiated for the trade treaty until my face turned blue," Nakht said. "Meanwhile, I spread the rumors as planned. I'm sure more than one eyebrow was raised in doubt about Zahi's motives. And something more happened that may cause Zaretes some concern."

"And what was that?" Amenemhet asked.

"I brought someone back with me I'd like to present to you," Nakht answered, his smile growing.

"Who is it?" Nefrytatanen's curiosity was too great to be contained.

"A spy from Djemeh," Nakht replied.

They looked at each other in surprise.

"A spy!" Nessumontu exclaimed. "What spy?"

"This spy was commanded to befriend me and obtain information," Nakht said softly. "But she only pretended to spy to satisfy Zaretes. She confessed this to me on the night before I was supposed to leave.

"She was willing to face death rather than betray me. I couldn't leave her behind, so I made it look as if we'd had another violent quarrel and I'd left her. Then I sent word to Zaretes that I was sailing that night rather than the next morning because we expected bad weather at sea. Her absence wouldn't have been discovered until after we had sailed. In any case, Zaretes couldn't be sure she'd gone with me. What he's thinking now, I can only guess. But I'm sure he isn't happy."

Joyce Verrette

"It sounds as if you allowed for all possibilities," Nessumontu remarked. "This spy wears perfume made especially for her in Tamera?"

Nakht gave Nessumontu a smug look. He went out to the garden, and returned accompanied by a woman with long black hair and great black eyes. She knelt before Amenemhet and Nefrytatanen.

"May I present Lady Chamma, lately of Djemeh," Nakht said softly, "who will shortly become my wife."

Amenemhet looked with surprise at Chamma, whose eyes remained on the floor as she knelt. "Rise, Lady Chamma," he said. "Welcome to Tamera and congratulations on your personal conquest." When Chamma's eyes lifted in surprise, he was smiling. "Nakht's surely one of our most elusive men," he said. "Tamera's women have pursued him unsuccessfully for some time."

Nefrytatanen took Chamma's hand and she rose. "It's clear that Chamma's beauty and courage are far above average," Nefrytatanen said, smiling at Chamma. "It's no wonder you've captured Nakht. May you find your new life in Tamera a happy one."

"You're very gracious," Chamma replied softly.

"I never thought Nakht would get married," Nessumontu said, "but now that I see you, I can understand his change of heart. I wish you happiness."

"We would have a great celebration for your wedding, but if you plan it soon, an elaborate party is impossible," Amenemhet warned.

"We plan on it very soon," Nakht said quickly.

"Then we'll have a small party," Nefrytatanen said. "Surely Nakht has friends who will wish to share your happiness."

"Nakht has friends, all right." Nessumontu's eyes

354

glittered. "But they won't all be willing to share his joy. They had plans of their own for him."

Amenemhet smiled. "We won't invite those," he said.

Chamma looked at Nakht and remarked, "It would seem I've won a prize."

Nakht launched a frown at Nessumontu. "He's envious."

"I admit it," Nessumontu said softly, "for Chamma could turn even my head."

"Those words should be carved in granite, covered with gold, and placed on display," Nakht declared. "The day any lady turns Nessumontu's head sufficiently that he thinks of marriage, I'll faint with the shock."

Chamma looked Nessumontu over with deliberate care and smiled. "I can easily see why the commander can afford to be choosy," she observed.

The wedding celebration was held the night after Kheti had arrived with Neferset and his family.

Upon seeing Bekhat come down the stairs in a pale lavender pleated sheath, wearing jewelry and eye paint, Senwadjet stopped and stared in surprise. He was sorry he had teased her at the hunting party about her being his little sister. Seeing her dressed for the evening, he found himself feeling as unlike a brother as possible.

Bekhat nodded politely to Senwadjet as she went by, but said nothing. It would take some effort to change her coolness, Senwadjet decided, but it would be worth the trouble. Smoothing his hair one last time, Senwadjet took a deep breath and put a calm look on his face. Then he followed the scent of Bekhat's perfume, which he already recognized.

Bekhat stood with her back toward Senwadjet, conversing with Maeti and Nessumontu. Senwadjet approached. Maeti, seeing the look on her brother's face, called out to him as though he had been passing by without intending to stop. Senwadjet silently blessed her.

"Senwadjet, come see how beautiful Bekhat is!" Maeti called.

Nessumontu glanced at Senwadjet and smiled knowingly. "No," Nessumontu said, teasing, "Stay away, Senwadjet. I want no competition."

Senwadjet looked at Bekhat with obvious admiration. "You'll have competition from every man in the kingdom," he said smiling.

Bekhat glanced coolly at Senwadjet, then turned to Nessumontu. "Surely no one can compete with you," she said in a purring tone that made Nessumontu's eyes widen.

Maeti couldn't help but admire Bekhat's poise. Yet she felt sorry for Senwadjet, who stared speechlessly at Bekhat. Maeti took Nessumontu's arm.

"Stay away from him, Bekhat," Maeti said, trying to discreetly tug Nessumontu away. "Nessumontu has promised he's mine alone."

"It's said Nessumontu makes no promises to any lady," Bekhat returned, still speaking in a tone that made Senwadjet's spine tingle. "You can't steal him from me."

Nessumontu had begun to wish he had stayed home. When he saw Sitah standing a short distance away, he called, "Sitah, come here and meet two charming young women." Nessumontu knew very well that Maeti and Sitah had already met.

Seeing who Nessumontu indicated, Sitah's black

eyes lit up. He came promptly. "I've already met Princess Maeti," he said, smoothly giving Maeti a look that made her feel strangely uneasy.

"Bekhat, this is Sitah, my aide," Nessumontu said, stepping back a little and hoping to escape quickly. "Sitah, Bekhat is Lord Kheti's daughter."

"I'm happy to meet you, Bekhat," Sitah said politely.

When Bekhat turned to Nessumontu, he had smoothly disappeared. She turned back to Sitah, intending to use him as her target.

"Come, Sitah," Maeti said quickly. "I'd like to have you meet Nakht's new wife." She took his arm and began to lead him away, intending to drag him, if necessary. Sitah, she decided, was going to spend some time with her, not be used by Bekhat to make Senwadjet jealous. Maeti said, "Chamma is very beautiful and, I understand, was a spy. Doesn't that sound fascinating?"

Sitah went willingly with Maeti, having neither spies nor anyone else in mind but the princess herself. When they were a safe distance from Bekhat, he stopped walking. "I will not go to meet Chamma again," he said firmly. "I have spoken to her and Nakht already, and as charming as she is, she's a married lady now. Besides, this room is getting too crowded for me." He looked down at Maeti, his black eyes glowing. "Would you like to walk in the garden?" he invited.

Maeti felt as if her jewelry might melt from his look. She smiled in agreement, letting Sitah lead her to the doors, her knees weak and her heart unsteady.

"I apologize for kissing you at the hunting party," Senwadjet told Bekhat quietly. "It was rude of me."

"Do you apologize because you think it was rude or because you wish you hadn't?" Bekhat asked tartly.

Senwadjet's gold eyes began to look disturbed. "I apologized because you appeared angry with me then and still seem so. I didn't think I was rude. I enjoyed it very much. It seemed as if you enjoyed it, too, at the time. You certainly didn't push me away. I don't know why you were suddenly so offended, but you ran off as if you wished yourself devoured by crocodiles rather than see me again." He was tired of all this nonsense, and he asked, "Why are you angry with me? I want to know the truth."

Bekhat stared at him. "Is that a royal command?" she asked coldly.

"No." Senwadjet regained his composure. "I would just like to know. I've thought of it many times, and I don't understand." The anger had left his eyes and was being slowly replaced by the golden glow Bekhat had seen just before he had kissed her. She felt her coolness melting. "Why are you angry?" he asked quietly.

Bekhat looked away, suddenly unsure of herself. "That day," she began hesitantly, "I enjoyed your kiss very much." She blushed furiously. She hadn't meant to blurt that out.

Senwadjet held back his smile, knowing he had won this struggle.

"I was angry because"—Bekhat searched for a word then sighed—"because it seemed to affect you so little. You said immediately that we must leave."

"We did have to leave," Senwadjet said softly. "They would have come searching for us." He took her hand. "It wasn't that I wanted to go, for I did not."

"Neither did I," Bekhat admitted. She looked up at

Senwadjet, resigned to her fate, continuing her confession, unable to stop. "I didn't want to leave at all. I wanted to stay and kiss you more and more. That's why I was angry. Then you teased me and treated me as if I were a child, and it made me angrier. When I found out we were going to this party and I knew you'd be here, I decided to behave as if it never mattered at all." Bekhat dropped her eyes in embarrassment. "I shouldn't say such things. I should be more discreet." She looked at him helplessly. "I'll be a hopeless failure in the art of courtship, I think," she finished.

"Not if you continue to kiss the way you did at the pond," Senwadjet said softly. He smiled. "Surely not if you continue to grow more beautiful each time I see you."

Bekhat blushed hotly again, not knowing what to say. Senwadjet took his hand out of hers and put his arm around her waist.

"Now that we understand each other," he said softly, "may I get you a goblet of something cool to drink? We can begin all over and forget everything that has already passed—except that kiss." He gave her a slight squeeze, and her eyes looked up in surprise, wide and grey as they had been at the pond. "I don't want to forget the kiss," he said, "and I hope to repeat it as soon as possible."

Senwadjet smiled at Bekhat, and she sighed. "I am undone," she confessed. "I wanted to be sophisticated and composed so you would turn green with jealousy, and I am undone."

"I like you the way you are," he murmured, releasing her. "Stay here, and I'll get you a drink."

Bekhat had decided she wouldn't move even if the combined armies of Djemeh, Zahi, and Troy attacked the palace in that instant. She sank onto a couch and stared at Senwadjet's back as he moved across the room. Girls would be throwing themselves at his feet— she recalled Maeti's warning. Maeti had been right. But it was not only because Senwadjet was the prince. She might have to wait awhile, but Bekhat resolved she would win Senwadjet, however long it took. She considered her motives and decided she would marry him. She would be sure the marriage contract allowed no harem. Somehow, she would manage all this.

When Senwadjet returned with the wine, Bekhat smiled sweetly up at him and thanked him, dropping her eyes modestly, fully knowing how long her eyelashes were when they spread against her cheeks.

Maeti looked at Sitah calmly, her eyes glowing in the moonlight. Would he never get on with it, she wondered. She deliberately offered him a kiss, but he didn't seem to know what to do about it. After an appropriate amount of time, she smiled at him. "I think we'd better go back," she said regretfully. "Although the garden is pleasant in the moonlight, the setting is too secluded. Someone will come looking for us. Will you help me up?" She put out her hand.

Sitah's heart sank. He'd lost his chance—or had he? He took both of her hands and pulled her to her feet, not releasing her until she leaned gently against him. His heart pounded as he stared into the eyes looking up at him. When he cautiously slid his arms around her, she didn't seem alarmed. He bent to kiss her gently, in experiment.

At the first soft touch of Maeti's lips, Sitah felt warmly pleasant. He felt her arms slide slowly around him, and taking this as a sign of encouragement, he held her tighter, continuing to kiss her softly but with considerably more feeling. She did not back away, and he was amazed. She pressed even closer. His heart beat faster. The grasp of her arms around him had become unshyly tight. Their lips met again, this time not so softly and not hesitantly at all. They clung together until they were breathless. Then she drew away.

Maeti was smiling when she looked at Sitah. "You're the first man I've ever kissed," she said. "I'm glad it was you, for I like the way you do it."

"I would never guess you'd kissed no one before," Sitah murmured into her hair, not wanting to let her go. "It takes some practice to cause such feelings."

"I wouldn't mind practicing." She smiled wider and stepped away. "But I think we'd best go back now." She took his hand and turned toward the path. "Perhaps some afternoon we can continue the lessons," she suggested.

"Gladly, as soon as possible," he agreed. "But wouldn't someone come upon us in the daytime?"

"Not if we're careful to choose the right place," she answered, smiling, "and I think I can find the right place."

As Maeti and Sitah entered the palace, Amenemhet grinned at Nefrytatanen, who had just finished commenting on the attention Senwadjet was giving Bekhat. He said, "Look at your daughter and Sitah." Nefrytatanen appraised the situation quickly. "What do you see written on her face?" Amenemhet asked.

Nefrytatanen sighed. "I am resigned. Such expressions don't come from childish instincts." She looked up at him and smiled. "It looks as if we're embarking on an entirely new set of problems with them."

* * *

Nassurti had sent Nessumontu a message: her new bandages would be removed today. She asked that he come and tell her what he thought of the results.

Nessumontu nodded to the servant who admitted him, then followed the servant upstairs to Nassurti's chambers.

He had many misgivings. As much as he hoped Nassurti's face was healed, he wished he didn't have to be the one to tell her how it looked. He scolded himself silently for having allowed himself to get in this position. He was deeply touched that she trusted him so much. At the same time, he felt protective toward her, and he didn't want to be the one to tell her the operation had resulted in failure. He didn't want to even see if this had happened. But he knew that she would want the truth. He admired her courage, and he dreaded seeing her.

The servant left Nessumontu at Nassurti's door. He stood a moment, then tapped softly. She called and, sighing, he pushed the door open.

Nassurti was alone, sitting by the window opening, her back to him. She dared sit with the sun streaming full on her face? He hoped her display of courage wouldn't end in disappointment. At the sound of the door, she stood, but she didn't turn around. Hesitant to approach her, he paused. Still she didn't turn. Her soft green robe clung slightly, and he could see the curves of her body through the fragile cloth.

"Will you come no closer, Nessumontu?" Nassurti's voice was soft. "You told me to have courage, and I am trying. The waiting makes it more difficult. You told me you'd be truthful, and I'm depending on you.

If I can stand in the sun waiting for the truth, would you make me wait even longer? Come and look at me." She added very softly, "Please?"

Nessumontu's heart turned over. For the first time in his life, he wanted to flee. But he moved forward.

He could see she was trembling slightly and trying very hard to hide it. He put a hand on her arm. He opened his mouth to ask her to turn around, but he had no chance to speak.

Nassurti whirled and faced him.

Nessumontu's eyes went wide with surprise—and joy. Nassurti's happiness was an explosion that seemed to spill from her with each breath. She laughed easily, assured that her smile was even.

Nessumontu stared at Nassurti. She was too beautiful. He could not find the words to tell her. The radiance of her eyes, the joy in her smile, the beauty of every line and curve of her face shone so brightly that the single scar was diminished to nothing. Large black eyes, luminous in the sun, twinkled up at him. Her skin was soft olive, smooth and clean as a flower petal. The black silk of her hair flowed to her shoulder and down her smooth throat to the silk of her robe.

"I have not looked at myself, Nessumontu," she said. "I didn't put on cosmetics or let anyone else apply them. Aside from Horemheb, whom I begged to reveal nothing to me, you're the first to see how I look. I am seeing myself for the first time in your eyes. I'm filled with joy at what I see."

Nessumontu gently put his hands on Nassurti's shoulders, wanting to embrace her. She looked up at him with softer eyes than he had ever known. No one had ever looked at him in quite that way.

Nessumontu decided he had better step away now,

while he was able. He should go from Nassurti and never see her again. He would be safe if he left now. But the idea caused such a wrenching pain he almost couldn't bear it. If he turned from her now, he might as well draw his sword and run it into her breast. He shuddered.

Nassurti watched Nessumontu's eyes, reading every thought that passed behind them. She waited for his decision. If he walked away, she might as well die where she stood. She would have no reason to live. Her own will would demand release from this body, demand the end of her breath. If he walked away. . . .

Nessumontu stepped backward. He took several more paces from Nassurti, and she swayed toward him like a flower toward the sun, without knowing she did so.

"Please—"

She didn't know she had said it. The word hung in the air between them, waiting in the silence.

Nessumontu moved one slow step toward her. A few more steps, long strides, and she opened her arms. He went into them, holding her close. She blinked in wonder, unable to believe such joy. Then she abruptly drew away from him.

"Nessumontu," Nassurti whispered, "there are other scars my robe conceals."

"As a soldier, I've collected a few myself." Nessumontu's smile held no humor, but slowly, warmth grew in his eyes. "Shall we compare our scars one day soon?"

Nassurti began to smile, but the smile faded suddenly. "There is more you should know." Her head dropped, and she whispered in embarrassment, "As a slave, I had to do many things I had no wish to do, ugly things—."

Nessumontu took her face in both hands, tilting it to his. "Nassurti," he said, "don't wound yourself with memories. I am no virgin, either."

Nassurti stared at him, and her embarrassment faded into relief. He asked no questions, nor would he ever ask.

Nessumontu brought his mouth to hers, sliding his arms around her, pulling her close to him, demonstrating with his kiss exactly how experienced he was. When their lips finally parted, she was trembling— and for the first time the trembling was not from fear.

"None of the past matters," he whispered into her hair, "and your kiss would erase it from my mind if it did."

"That's the first kiss I have ever given," she said softly. "The rest were taken from me."

A new look had crept into Nessumontu's eyes, a look Nassurti hadn't seen before. Nessumontu was, after all, much more than a hunter.

CHAPTER 16

MAETI HAD FOUND a quiet place near the garden wall, as she had promised, and her first meeting with Sitah had been a delightful confusion of laughter and kisses. He knew to what degree he could go before he became too serious—and he never forgot who Maeti was. The intervals between embraces had been filled with quiet conversation. The second meeting found Maeti learning for herself when to stop, and Sitah obeyed without argument. Each time they separated, they either talked to distract themselves or drifted into the silence of private dreaming. On the third occasion, while they had been talking quietly, a gardener had come upon them. Excusing himself, he had left hurriedly. But feeling uncomfortable, they had stayed no longer.

During their fourth meeting, Sitah and Maeti kissed and held each other close until they finally moved shakily apart by mutual agreement, and lay on their backs in the grass, staring up at the sky, not touching.

"Maeti," Sitah said after a time, "I am in a peculiar position."

"Why?" Maeti brushed her hair aside and turned her head to look at him.

"Being Nessumontu's aide is a favored position, but seeing you could endanger it," he said quietly. "If you weren't the princess, I might go on with these meetings and see where they would lead. But I have to remember you're the daughter of my king and queen."

Maeti thought about this for a while. Continuing their friendship depended on what Sitah had in mind. She decided to ask him. "Sitah, are you meeting me because you like me for myself or because my position makes it interesting to associate with me? Is it ambition that brings you to me?" she asked bluntly.

Sitah looked startled, but he answered promptly, "At first, you were a pretty girl in the garden who beguiled me with her charm. I wanted to know you better. At the party when I saw you dressed for the evening, you were so beautiful I didn't know what to do. Your kiss was sweet and innocent and exciting.

"During these meetings your kisses have grown sweeter and more exciting, although perhaps less innocent. If you were anyone else, I would want to continue seeing you—but I would want to do so openly."

"Sitah," Maeti said softly, "we don't have to be secret. We can keep company."

"Your family wouldn't object?" His black eyes turned to her.

"No," she answered. "Even if I were going to inherit the crown, I wouldn't be expected to remain unmarried forever. Who but a man from an old and honorable noble family would be more eligible? For me to choose eventually, I must become acquainted with such men."

"But I thought you would marry into a royal family."

"Who?" Maeti smiled. "With the Two Lands united, there's only one ruling family. Do you think I would marry into the family of another land? My parents, I think, would prefer my marriage to someone here."

Sitah considered this information a moment, then said, "What if we saw each other for a time, then decided to end it. Or what if we had a quarrel?"

"Do you think my father would have your head hacked off?" she asked, smiling.

"He could." Sitah smiled without humor.

"If he did that, he'd quickly reduce the number of my suitors by scaring them away before they even approached me." Maeti chuckled.

"What shall I do, then?" Sitah was curious. "Should I ask your parents if we could become better acquainted?"

"Yes." Maeti was serious, her smile fading. "That much should be done. You might have Nessumontu come with you to lend support." She could see the idea made Sitah uneasy, and she added, "You'd say you and I would like to know each other better and ask if father and mother have any objection to this."

Sitah looked at her, thinking of how uncomfortable he would feel. Slowly he asked, "What if they have objections?"

"Then we couldn't see each other again," Maeti replied. "But why should they? Have you kept a tarnished reputation secret from me?"

He shook his head. "My reputation with women is hard to find—it's that small. Nessumontu keeps me too busy."

"You learned to kiss somewhere," Maeti teased.

Sitah looked at her and smiled. He said, "It didn't take *you* long to learn." Abruptly, his head went up and he listened. "Someone is coming," he murmured.

Maeti could hear nothing. Just then, Nessumontu

came around the bushes. Sitah leaped to his feet, but Maeti stayed where she was and wondered why Nessumontu walked in on them as if he had known exactly where they were.

"Forgive my interruption, Princess Maeti," Nessumontu said, ignoring her glare, "but I need my aide." His eyes swept over them with approval.

"You knew we were here," Maeti said softly.

"Yes, I knew," Nessumontu replied.

"How?"

"Your father told me," Nessumontu answered calmly. Sitah and Maeti exchanged startled glances. Nessumontu explained, "He has noticed your disappearance each afternoon, and it wasn't difficult to find your whereabouts. He's fairly well acquainted with the layout of his own garden," Nessumontu said drily.

He turned to Sitah. "We've received a report that the Hyksos have crossed our eastern border and are advancing in this direction. The army of Djemeh has also begun to move. We expect the Hyksos forces to arrive tomorrow morning and Djemeh's by tomorrow night. The Trojan ships have been sighted approaching the mouth of the river, and I think they'll arrive about the same time as the troops from Djemeh."

Sitah looked at Maeti questioningly, and she motioned him to leave. She watched him follow Nessumontu out of sight, and then she ran through the garden into the palace. No one asked her questions or teased her about where she had been. There was no time for levity. Everyone was hurrying with last-minute preparations for the siege.

The evening meal was a silent one. The royal family went to bed early, to sleep while they could.

* * *

Dawn found Amenemhet, Senwadjet, Nessumontu, and Sitah dressed for battle, walking along the parapet looking for a sign of the Hyksos forces.

"Evidently we still have some time," Amenemhet remarked. "They're nowhere in sight."

"It's an indication of their ability," Nessumontu commented, "that they're late for their own invasion."

Amenemhet smiled. Noting Senwadjet's grim expression, he put his arm around Senwadjet's shoulders. "If they fight like they march, I predict an early victory for us."

"I hope Zaretes has sense enough to stay out of it," Nessumontu said softly. "The reports so far show they've marched rather carefully and avoided open conflicts along the way."

"I wonder what they think," mused Sitah, "when they pass villages who ignore them."

"If I were commander of their army," Nessumontu said, "it would make me suspect a trap. At the least, villagers flee. At the most, they do what they can to harass invaders."

"We might as well have our morning meal," Amenemhet said. "Join us. We have to wait until the sentries sound the alarm, and we might as well be comfortable while we're able. We've done everything possible to prepare for them."

Senwadjet noted Amenemhet's calmness. It reassured him.

Nefrytatanen sat at the table with Neferset, Maeti, and Bekhat. Their faces were tight with tension.

"They aren't even in sight," Amenemhet announced, removing his war crown. He sat.

Nefrytatanen shrugged as if unconcerned, but it was a show. She remembered too well what battles were like, and whether this one began now or later mattered little.

Nassurti came in quietly. She dreaded the arrival of Gobryas and was terrified for Nessumontu. But she smiled and greeted everyone, then sat next to Nessumontu. His eyes lit at the sight of her.

While Amenemhet was eating, a soldier entered. In the sudden silence, as he bowed, his sword rattled ominously. He gave the anticipated report—the Hyksos army had appeared on the horizon coming from Eastern Lance Province.

Amenemhet put down the remains of the cake and stood up. He said nothing as he put on his war crown. Ignoring the others, he embraced Maeti, who looked at him fearfully.

Then Amenemhet kissed Nefrytatanen and said quietly, "Keep them inside the palace and stay away from the window openings." He kissed her again, adding quickly, "Stay here with them." He left immediately, giving her no chance to question or argue.

Nefrytatanen watched the others say goodbye and was thankful none of the women wept. When Senwadjet came to her, his golden eyes were dark with fear. But he kissed and embraced her, saying nothing.

When the men had gone, the women sat for a time in silence. Finally Nefrytatanen signaled the servants to clear the table. When they had left, she stood up. "If you want to cry, as I do," she said clearly, "now is the time to do it and have it over." A tear ran down one cheek. She added, "We'll have no other time for weeping until this is over. Let us hope we won't need to weep then." She turned quickly and left the room.

* * *

Although prime ministers seldom went on military expeditions, Gobryas wouldn't have missed the attack on Ithtawe for any amount of gold. He was riding next to Commander Sargon as they came over the last hill and saw Ithtawe's great walls in the distance. Sargon called the march to a halt.

"I don't like the situation at all," said Sargon as he looked around uneasily.

"Why?" Gobryas asked.

"They act as if they've had weeks to prepare for us."

"Of course they've had some advance warning," Gobryas said impatiently. "You can't move an army through a foreign country without news getting to its king."

Sargon gave him a dark look. "I know well enough how armies move and news is passed." He took off his helmet and wiped his brow. "Look at how that place is locked up. Notice the silence." He looked at Gobryas with worry. "We've been ignored in most of the villages we've passed through. And now Ithtawe stands locked and barred without the usual signs of last-minute refugees seeking shelter, as would be normal if we had surprised them." He gave Gobryas a grim look. "Are you sure that slave girl couldn't have managed to get here?"

"How?" Gobryas sneered. "She was half dead when she escaped. Alone and without gold, not even knowing where to go, how could she get all the way here? She lies somewhere as food for jackals."

"I don't know how she'd get here, because I'm certain you did a fine job on her before she left." Sargon didn't approve of the way Gobryas treated his slaves, although he was less than gentle with his own.

He spat and turned to his men. Before he gave his orders, he said to Gobryas, "These people of Tamera are peculiar. It wouldn't surprise me if she got here like a pigeon, on instinct."

"Nonsense," Gobryas answered.

Sargon ignored him and roared orders to his captains. Then, still shaking his head, he turned to face Ithtawe, while the army began to move into attack formation.

"I tell you, Gobryas," Sargon said once more, "they knew we were coming. If we're marching into a trap because of your fooling around with slave girls, you'll answer for it. I don't like risking my men, much less risking my own neck."

"And how would I answer to you for it?" Gobryas sneered. "Don't think you'll frighten me with empty threats. Will you bring charges against me?"

"When you're in the middle of battle, especially if the men have to flee in retreat, there's considerable confusion. Who knows? Perhaps I wouldn't have to bring formal charges," Sargon said.

Gobryas stared at him, shocked. He was angry, but he suddenly was also afraid.

Amenemhet stood on the parapet overlooking the plain and the slowly advancing Hyksos. But he wasn't watching them. He knew what formation they would be taking, and he was more interested in Senwadjet's reaction. Observing the prince from the corner of his eye, Amenemhet could tell that Senwadjet was very apprehensive about this, his first, battle. Although Senwadjet stood looking out over the invading army, his apparent calm didn't fool Amenemhet. He felt sympathy for his son, who didn't know what to expect and couldn't be sure of himself.

Amenemhet vividly remembered his own first combat experience. Even now, he didn't really feel much better. They all were afraid, even if no one admitted to it.

Unexpectedly Senwadjet turned to Amenemhet. "Father," he said softly, "I'm afraid."

"Anyone who isn't is a fool." Amenemhet met his son's eyes.

"Then, you're also afraid?" Senwadjet's voice was very low.

"Yes," Amenemhet answered without hesitation. "The difference between us is that I've faced it before and survived. I didn't run. It's a small comfort." He smiled at Senwadjet. "You won't dishonor me."

Senwadjet still stared at him, and Amenemhet added softly, "You're unsure of yourself at this moment, as I was unsure of myself at my first battle. But I know you well." Amenemhet looked out over the plain again. "When the time comes, you'll do what you must. I only hope you won't be foolish."

"What do you mean?" Senwadjet was curious.

"Whether or not you survive a battle depends often on keeping one small part of your mind free from your immediate concerns to watch yourself unemotionally—even if you're engaged in hand-to-hand combat."

"Watch me in what way?"

"In every other way except with what occupies you." Amenemhet turned to Senwadjet. "It's difficult to explain. Having this small part of your attention free is like having an extra eye. It tells you when to step back for no immediately apparent reason. It tells you when to duck, when not to go forward, when to rush forward. It's the difference that can mean life or death to you."

Glancing again at the plain below, Amenemhet saw that the Hyksos had their ramming device ready. The foot soldiers were about to begin their assault. He heard the roar of a burning missile, launched from a catapult, and he turned to see flames blooming from the roof of a house. "Here they come," he said quietly.

Officers shouted orders, and men stood ready at the walls, fitting arrows to their long bows. Between the archers stood others, prepared to assist when and if the Hyksos managed to get ladders against the walls.

Signals were called, and the powerful bows were drawn back. The Hyksos continued marching forward. The bows were stayed for a moment to let the troops come nearer. Then the arrows whistled softly in their deadly flight.

Senwadjet shivered as men fell. Again and again, the archers replaced arrows in their bows and sent them shimmering into the morning light.

Senwadjet was startled when one of the first returning arrows struck the stones beside him, shattering its shaft, falling at his feet in a tangled mess of splinters and feathers. He put up his shield and got ready for the others he knew would follow.

A man Senwadjet recognized fell almost at his feet, brightly colored feathers arranged at a small, red hole in his throat. In that moment, Senwadjet felt the whole awful reality of war. Sadly he turned to take the archer's place until a replacement came.

The Hyksos advanced steadily, stepping over their dead and wounded as they went, knowing they must get to the walls as quickly as possible. Holding up shields that shone dully in the sun, they deflected many arrows. But too many of the missiles fell to avoid them all.

Sargon roared an order to move faster, and the soldiers obeyed, many of them falling on the way. By the time they reached the walls, their numbers were greatly reduced. But Senwadjet was comforted little as he watched the first ladder go up and heard the first crash of the ram against the gates. The men at the ramming device immediately found themselves under so heavy a hail of arrows they fled for cover, afraid to try again.

Amenemhet put his foot against a ladder and kicked it aside before anyone could get on it. Then he faced a Hyksos soldier whose ladder had lasted long enough for his climb.

Glancing around him, the soldier realized both that he was the only Hyksos soldier on Ithtawe's parapet and that he faced Tamera's king. Amenemhet saw the man's surprise and gave him no chance to recover his wits.

As Amenemhet withdrew his sword, he saw Senwadjet glance at him, then at the bloody sword, then turn to release another arrow.

Commander Tharma rode beside King Zaretes, who was silent. "We've had an unusually peaceful reception," Tharma said cautiously.

"I don't like it at all," Zaretes mumbled. He looked around nervously.

"I think we have two choices," Tharma said suddenly. The king looked at him in surprise. "We can withdraw, as we came, harming no one—or we can chance riding into a trap."

Zaretes's eyes widened at this blunt summary of what he himself had been thinking.

"I think King Amenemhet has deliberately given us this choice," Tharma continued. "The villagers should either have run or fought, but they have stood quietly to the side and watched us pass."

"Let us proceed as far as Ithtawe," Zaretes said stubbornly. "Let us see, at least, how Zahi's army fares."

"I hope we don't get entangled with this battle before we have a chance to see which way it goes," Tharma said flatly.

"I've heard enough!" Zaretes snapped. "Keep silent with your doubts."

Tharma shut his mouth, though he had been ready to say more. Riding through such a densely populated area as they had would normally have brought some reaction from the people. He was convinced the rumors were true: King Amenemhet had given Djemeh its choice, to fight and die with Zahi or to withdraw and sign a treaty as soon as possible, as if they had never considered joining Zahi.

When Tharma saw Ithtawe ahead, he knew immediately what answer *he* would have given. He looked at Zaretes, who nodded. Tharma ordered a halt, and they sent a man up a tree to study the battle.

"Djemeh's army is standing at the edge of the oasis!" Sitah told Nessumontu excitedly.

"Excellent," Nessumontu replied, signaling for a replacement for the man who had fallen next to him. "Let us hope they continue standing at the oasis."

An archer, glancing up as he took a fresh arrow, suddenly called out, "Trojan ships are in the river, very near the last bend!" An arrow struck him with a soft sound, and his dark eyes were filled with disbelief as he fell.

Moments later, the Hyksos discovered the appearance of the Trojan ships, and a great roar rose from their ranks.

Senwadjet watched them slowly retreat from the walls and looked questioningly at Amenemhet.

"They fall back, thinking the Trojans will attack and give them time to rest and tend their wounds," Amenemhet said softly. He watched the Hyksos, whose retreat became steadily more accelerated.

"They're bleeding badly." Nessumontu's voice came from behind them.

Amenemhet turned, a thoughtful look in his eyes. "What do you say, Nessumontu, to letting them get into bunches just beyond the range of our arrows, to await Trojan help?" He was talking slowly, as if the plan were forming in his mind as he spoke. "Then we could attack them with chariots." His eyes turned to meet Nessumontu's.

"Where they expect Trojan reinforcements, they'll find Tameran lances?" Nessumontu smiled, and his eyes gleamed. "I think that's a fine plan."

"Do it," Amenemhet said. "Use just one wave of chariots. Have them return immediately."

"No second tries?" Nessumontu asked.

"No second tries." Amenemhet put his sword away. "It's too risky, and we could lose too many. Strike fast and get back fast."

Nessumontu turned to give the orders. He watched the Hyksos, as Amenemhet had predicted, drawing into groups just beyond the range of Tamera's arrows.

While they were still having some confusion, Nessumontu gave the order.

Amenemhet stood next to Nessumontu at the top of the wall, watching as the gates suddenly opened and the chariots roared through, pulled by the fastest horses available.

The Hyksos were shocked when the wave of riders raced toward them. When the chariots were near enough, the riders launched their lances at the Hyksos soldiers nearest them. Before the Hyksos could recover from their surprise, the chariots had made a wide turn and raced away. The Hyksos, still dazed by the attack, watched the chariots disappear.

Finally realizing they wouldn't return, they looked for help from the Trojan ships. Having dropped anchor, they floated calmly in the middle of the Nile.

Sargon turned disgustedly to Gobryas. "What are your friends from Troy waiting for?" he demanded. "Do they expect Tamera's soldiers to swim to them?"

Gobryas stared at the ships. He could say nothing.

"'Offer Acetes Queen Nefrytatanen, and offer King Melanpus gold,'" Sargon muttered, "'and they'll help us.'" Giving Gobryas a murderous look, he uttered a string of curses in a variety of languages. He turned to see how many men he had left, trying desperately to think of some plan.

Commander Tharma looked hard at the ships, then turned to King Zaretes in disgust. "Well, it seems they'll receive no help from Troy," he said. "Do you wish to give Zahi assistance?" He was quiet a moment as he watched the wave of chariots, then added sarcastically, "It looks like they need some assistance."

King Zaretes turned and mounted his horse again.

"Let Sargon lead his men to death at Ithtawe," he muttered. "I want no part of this comedy." He shook his head, thinking of the gold and treasures in Ithtawe he would never see.

Relieved, Tharma turned to his men and ordered them to prepare to march. He glanced at Zaretes and wondered what the king would say when Tamera's ambassador next approached him with a treaty. What kind of bargain could Zaretes possibly ask for now? Djemeh would be fortunate if Amenemhet sent an ambassador at all. Tharma wondered if it would be Nessumontu and the army that would come to negotiate—with a ramming device.

Acetes stood at the ship's rail silently watching the battle. He wondered where Nefrytatanen was and if she was safe. He thought of Amenemhet and wondered if he had been wounded or killed. His glance turned to the ship's crew. They crowded by the rail placing bets among themselves. The odds shifted further and further in Ithtawe's favor, and when they saw the chariots attack the Hyksos and return swiftly to Ithtawe, the betting changed to how soon the Hyksos would flee.

Acetes saw the forces from Djemeh standing in the distance and wondered if Amenemhet's plan would work. Zaretes seemed undecided.

"They're fools to have stayed this long," Commander Berasus said, moving to stand beside Acetes.

"When this is over," Ambassador Abaris remarked with a faint smile, "I'd like to attend the negotiations for a trade treaty between Tamera and Djemeh just to see what Zaretes can think of to offer."

Acetes sighed and said nothing. It seemed as if

380

Amenemhet would triumph in every way, if he had survived. And Acetes was sure he would come through without a scratch. Acetes glanced up and saw Djemeh's army preparing to leave. He turned away.

"I'm going to have a goblet of wine," he said to the ambassador. "Will you join me?"

"Yes," Abaris answered, "I don't enjoy this next part of a battle. It's too messy. Are you coming, Berasus?"

The Trojan commander smiled. "No, thank you," he replied. "I'm learning some new strategies today, and I don't wish to miss a lesson." He turned to the rail to watch and muttered, "I only hope Tamera continues on friendly terms with Troy."

"We haven't done too badly," Nessumontu commented, watching the chariots return. "I think I see our newly loyal friends from Djemeh getting ready to leave."

Amenemhet smiled. "I believe I'll go with Nakht to negotiate our treaty with them. I think it will be too interesting an experience to miss." He turned to Senwadjet. "Would you like to come with us?"

"I certainly would!" Senwadjet exclaimed, then looked puzzled. "What do you think King Zaretes can offer us?"

"A great quantity of wine and food, women and other forms of hospitality—to begin with," Nessumontu commented. He laughed quietly.

"Don't celebrate too soon," Amenemhet warned, watching the movements of the Hyksos troops. "I think they're going to attack again."

Nessumontu scanned the scene slowly, turning at last to Amenemhet. "Sargon must be mad," he said softly. "He has only half his men left, and they must be greatly discouraged by now."

"Either Sargon is mad or dead, and Gobryas is giving the orders," Amenemhet said grimly.

"Then Gobryas is mad," Nessumontu concluded. He thought of Nassurti and turned to Amenemhet, his slanted eyes glittering with an orange light. "I would like to lead an attack on them, but we would be foolish to leave these walls now. I hope they do attack. I want to kill Gobryas."

"We won't open the gates, but you may be able to get your wish," Amenemhet replied. "They're coming again."

"Archers!" Nessumontu shouted. "Ready!"

The Hyksos came as before, holding their shields almost over their heads against the arrows which flew at them in a dense rain. Once again, ladders landed against Ithtawe's walls and fell quickly backwards, carrying their luckless climbers with them. The soldiers were unenthusiastic in their climbing and quickly became more discouraged when hot oil was poured over them. Their screams faded as the other soldiers around the base of the wall fell back, leaving their comrades to moan and writhe on the ground. The few men who had gotten up the wall were trapped.

Senwadjet found himself facing one of these desperate men. He had drawn his sword but seemed undecided as to whether he should fight. Senwadjet could hear others surrendering and wondered if this one would. Poising himself to fight, he watched the soldier closely.

The man made his decision and suddenly lunged at Senwadjet. Senwadjet struck the blow aside, surprised at the ease of it. It seemed no more difficult than practice.

Senwadjet remembered Amenemhet's telling him to keep one part of his attention free, and he suddenly realized that the soldier thought he could kill him easily. The Hyksos' eyes said that Senwadjet was too young to vanquish a battle-hardened soldier. Senwadjet's eyes narrowed, shining with a new light.

Now it was Senwadjet's sword that led the attack. He no longer waited for his enemy to move, but slashed and thrust rapidly, his brain calculating, measuring, anticipating, his body obediently following its commands.

Senwadjet's attack was so unexpected and so ferocious that the soldier was startled into merely defending himself. The look in Senwadjet's golden eyes sent a chill through the soldier, and he hesitated an instant. In that instant, Senwadjet's sword found its place. The soldier fell.

Senwadjet stared for a moment at the body, amazed at what he had done. Then he straighted himself and looked with outward calm over the parapet, still marveling at what he had just accomplished, his heart still pounding.

Amenemhet had seen the Hyksos soldier and had watched the fight, wanting to help Senwadjet but allowing him to stand alone. When Amenemhet saw the soldier fall and Senwadjet turn coolly to look over the wall, he breathed a sigh of relief and wiped his forehead. Catching Nessumontu's glance, Amenemhet smiled. Nessumontu nodded his head in admiration.

Those Hyksos soldiers who could still move retreated without waiting for the order. They ran from Ithtawe, not even bothering to use their shields.

Nessumontu looked at Amenemhet for orders, and Amenemhet said, "Let them go. They're so decimated it will be a long time before they'll be able to look at any land with greedy eyes."

Nessumontu gave the signal halting the archers.

Amenemhet put his arm around his son's shoulders. Senwadjet smiled up at him. They went down the steps together.

Gobryas watched the fleeing soldiers bitterly. "What kind of army have you trained?" he snarled over his shoulder at Sargon. "What kind of commander are you? When we're home, you'll answer for this pitiful rout." He turned to glare at Sargon and stared, instead, at the sword he faced.

"Instead of dishonor on your return," Commander Sargon said quietly, "it will be told you died in battle. Consider this a favor."

Gobryas started to lift his shield, but he wasn't fast enough. Sargon drove his heavy sword through Gobryas's body.

Sargon withdrew the sword and watched Gobryas fall. "May the jackals of Tamera enjoy you," he said as Gobryas lay staring blankly at him. Then Sargon mounted his horse and rode after his retreating men.

Amenemhet and Senwadjet walked silently among the wounded and dying, looking at the clean-robed physicians, who contrasted sharply with the grimy, bloodstained men they attended. Amenemhet and Senwadjet passed Nessumontu, who was staying behind to give directions for putting out fires and clearing the debris. Sitah, who had remained at Nessumontu's side, was helping with the cleaning up.

The gates to the palace courtyard stood open, and Amenemhet, his arm still around Senwadjet's shoulders, walked slowly through them. The courtyard, untouched by the battle, was a haven from the sight of destruction.

Nefrytatanen stepped cautiously out of the palace doors, looking at them across the distance. Then she ran to throw her arms around them simultaneously, saying nothing, her relief too great for words. Maeti was the next to run across the pavement to them. Others followed at discreet intervals with compliments and questions.

When Nessumontu appeared at the courtyard threshold, Nassurti stood like a statue watching him walk toward her, staring at the red stain on the side of his tunic. When Nessumontu stopped in front of her, she wordlessly looked up at his face, then down at the red blotch.

Nessumontu smiled. "A lance came too close and brushed me in passing. It will make another small scar for you to study." He put his arms around her, and she leaned against his chest. "I don't know about Gobryas," he said. "If he's one of the dead or wounded, we'll find him."

Suddenly Nessumontu glanced up at Senwadjet, and his eyes gleamed with their old wolfish look. "You did well on that Hyksos soldier, with your sword," he called. "What you lacked in elegance of style, you made up for in ferocity."

Senwadjet smiled sheepishly, recalling all the rules he had broken as he slashed and hacked at the Hyksos soldier.

Amenemhet laughed. "I think your enthusiasm frightened him so much he was unable to defend himself. I've never seen you move so fast in so many directions at once."

Senwadjet said nothing to this joking praise because he had noticed Bekhat's eyes widen in awe, and he strolled in her direction.

"Beloved," Amenemhet whispered to Nefrytatanen, "you should have seen him. Never did he flinch. As frightened as I know he was, he stood fast. You would have been impressed."

"I am," Nefrytatanen replied, looking up at Amenemhet's glowing eyes. "I've always been impressed with the results of everything you've done."

Amenemhet smiled and put his arm around her waist.

Acetes entered the courtyard and saw Amenemhet and Nefrytatanen standing together, gazing into each other's faces. Amenemhet's war crown dangled from his hand, and his tunic was bloodstained and torn. A pang went through Acetes when he noticed that Nefrytatanen was standing as close to Amenemhet as she could manage, hip to hip, leg to leg. Acetes paused a moment to compose his face, then continued toward them.

When Amenemhet glanced up, Acetes saw that his eyes were filled with the glow of Nefrytatanen. Nefrytatanen turned slowly toward him. When Acetes saw the radiance of Amenemhet reflected on her face, his heart sank.

"My compliments, King Amenemhet," Acetes said. "Commander Berasus was greatly impressed with the battle, as we all were. I am glad you are safe."

"Welcome to Ithtawe," Amenemhet answered. "Your timing was perfect."

Acetes smiled. "Yours was better."

386

Nefrytatanen perceived the awareness between them and said lightly, "Acetes, you and your men must take part in the celebration we'll have as soon as the wreckage is cleared. The whole city will be a party."

"Thank you," Acetes said carefully, watching Amenemhet with a wary expression. "We accept the invitation gladly."

Neferset had been standing a short distance from Amenemhet and Nefrytatanen. She realized with growing interest that this Trojan was in love with Nefrytatanen. She smiled to herself. She didn't think it was harmful to Amenemhet to know this. If ever another woman came upon the scene, Neferset decided, it might lessen Amenemhet's struggle with temptation to remember Acetes.

By the time Kheti arrived at Ithtawe, less than two days later, the fortress-city was a festival. Celebrants spilled out of each house into the streets, mingling until they were joined into one great party. Kheti grinned at the happy faces but continued hurrying through the crowds toward the palace. He was anxious to see if his family were unharmed, and he was thinking that they would have been safer at home. None of the invaders had come near his province.

When Kheti came through the palace gates, he saw Bekhat standing with a tall, young soldier in the garden. He was startled when he recognized the soldier as Senwadjet. Kheti paused, wondering whether to approach them. Bekhat was very much engrossed with the prince. Kheti smiled and went on.

Acetes had no heart to enjoy himself. Each time he saw Nefrytatanen, she was with Amenemhet. Acetes could hardly contain his feelings. The looks she gave Amenemhet tore Acetes with jealousy and guilt at the same time. Yet Acetes couldn't hate Amenemhet. On the contrary, Acetes had to admit he admired him. And this was doubly galling.

Acetes wanted to go home as soon as possible, but whenever he saw Berasus and Abaris, they were enjoying themselves immensely.

Finally Acetes's patience was at an end, and he managed to drag Abaris from the arms of a pretty girl and talk to him. Abaris's face fell, but he went to find Berasus.

Three days later Acetes had the ships ready to sail. It had taken only one day to prepare the vessels, but it had taken two days to locate the crew and get them into condition to do their jobs.

Acetes was standing at the moorings watching the last of his men board the ships. He turned and saw Amenemhet and Nefrytatanen approaching. Resolving to face this last meeting with dignity, he smiled. Before Acetes could say anything, Amenemhet excused himself and walked away a few paces to talk to Nessumontu.

Standing alone with Nefrytatanen, Acetes looked at her longingly for a moment. "I doubt I'll come back," Acetes told her softly. "I'll probably have no official reason to do so, and my good sense advises me against it." She said nothing. Finally Acetes could bear it no longer and whispered, "Nefrytatanen, surely you know I'll never forget you. Once again I extend my invitation. If ever you need me, come to me."

"Thank you, Acetes," she said softly. She glanced away as Amenemhet returned.

Amenemhet turned to Acetes. "Acetes, have a safe

journey home," he said. "We appreciate your help. Perhaps we can reciprocate someday."

Acetes managed to smile and thank Amenemhet, then turned to Nefrytatanen. "Before I forget it," he said, "I have a personal message for you from Queen Pythia."

"What is it?" Nefrytatanen looked surprised.

"She said to tell you they will visit Tamera, but the trip will have to be delayed for a time. She has good reason to think she will have a child," he finished.

"Tell her I'm filled with delight at this news," Nefrytatanen exclaimed. "Give King Melanpus our congratulations. And tell Queen Pythia that when they do come to Tamera, we may have even more ideas to exchange." Acetes looked a little confused at this, and Nefrytatanen added, "Tell her exactly what I said. She'll understand."

"Thank King Melanpus for his help," Amenemhet said. A strange look came into his eyes, and he added, "Tell him we would welcome their visit."

Acetes waited a moment, expecting Amenemhet's invitation to be extended to him, but Amenemhet said nothing more. Finally Acetes said slowly, "My ship is ready, it seems."

"Have a safe journey," Amenemhet said, stepping back a little.

"Thank you," Acetes replied, a little coolly. He turned to go up the ramp.

"Farewell," Acetes called from the rail.

As the lines were cast off, Amenemhet said under his breath, "Farewell—and goodbye, Acetes."

Nefrytatanen glanced at Amenemhet, surprised at his tone of voice. He put his arm around her waist and unsmilingly waved to Acetes as the ship began to move into the current. Acetes returned the wave with equal solemnity.

"Did you and Acetes have unpleasant words?" Nefrytatanen asked.

"No," Amenemhet replied. "Why do you ask?"

"You weren't very friendly," she answered.

Amenemhet faced her a moment, then said quietly, "That's because we aren't friends." Then he took her arm and turned toward the palace, saying nothing more.

CHAPTER 17

FROM HIS BALCONY, King Zaretes silently watched the double column of soldiers approaching his city. The red and white uniforms made a bright splash of color against the grey walls, and the sun glanced off their polished weapons, almost blinding him with the glare. Even from this distance, he could recognize King Amenemhet and Prince Senwadjet at the front of the column. The familiar figure of Nakht made him frown. The crowds lining the streets were silent, and the smell of fear hung over them.

Zaretes's face was creased with many frown lines as he turned to his prime minister. "Pazalam, get those crowds to act alive," he ordered. "I don't care how you do it—but do it."

"Perhaps that task would be better left to me," Commander Tharma offered.

"Then, *you* do it," the king said loudly.

Tharma left immediately, relieved to escape Zaretes.

"We cannot have everyone looking terrified," Zaretes muttered, going back to his balcony. "We must appear confident and welcome them warmly."

Pazalam wondered what they could pretend to feel confident about, but he wisely said nothing.

The king went on, "We must treat them as friends.

If we behave as if they came to conquer us, they may think us so easy they'll try it."

Pazalam thought that the soldiers King Amenemhet had brought were probably enough to do it. The battle at Ithtawe had already become almost a legend, and Djemeh's army was terrified of Tamera's army. If one believed the stories that were circulating in the city, Tamera's army was invincible.

As the gates to the city opened, Zaretes heard the crowds begin to cheer in welcome. He was relieved that Tharma's men had reached them just in time. He turned to Pazalam. "Have you made sure of their quarters? Has the best wine been brought?" Pazalam nodded. Zaretes shook a jeweled finger at him. "What about the women, the dancers?"

Pazalam sighed. "We have dragged the best from every corner of the land. I, myself, have chosen them. If they aren't satisfied with these, they'll be satisfied with nothing."

"If they aren't satisfied with our hospitality," Zaretes said coldly, "they may be satisfied with our blood! What kind of women did you find for the king and ambassador? By the gods, do you have one for the prince? We didn't expect him, too!"

"There are so many women here, they can each choose a harem." Pazalam's patience was worn to nothing. They had discussed these matters many times. "It's said that King Amenemhet isn't interested in any woman but his queen. As for the prince, I can't anticipate what he'll do. Ambassador Nakht, as you know, has been inclined to choose for himself."

"I can't believe King Amenemhet has no interest in other women," Zaretes mumbled. "Every man takes other women. His queen is a woman like any other."

"Not quite," Pazalam remarked. At Zaretes's look, he added quickly, "You've heard she has magical power."

"There's no such thing," Zaretes said. "That's only a story, a story like all the others they spread, that their king is a god and immortal. What is that god's name?"

"Asar." Pazalam answered wearily. "They think their king is Asar returned from the dead and their queen is Aset, or some such nonsense. Anyway, if King Amenemhet declines a female companion, I don't think we should press the matter."

"Do you suppose we should obtain a boy for him?" Zaretes scratched his chin thoughtfully.

"Never!" Pazalam exclaimed. "Don't even hint at such a thing!" Pazalam looked at Zaretes with more humility and explained, "Sire, such activities are expressly forbidden by their beliefs. Amenemhet would be insulted if you offered that."

Zaretes was deeply puzzled. "What do these people enjoy?" he asked.

"I don't think they'll be in a mood for any kind of amusement on this visit," Pazalam observed. He was thinking they would probably be sufficiently entertained by the comedy of negotiating. He hoped Zaretes would let him do the talking, although he still didn't know what he could say.

Amenemhet looked at the crowds lining the street and saw the fear behind their smiles. He turned to Nakht and observed, "They're being forced to pretend gladness at our visit."

"It's as Nessumontu said." Nakht smiled humorlessly. "They'll pour much wine, offer all sorts of dishes, and present us with many women." His smile faded, and he looked dismal. "The wine is inferior, and the food is made from Tehuti knows what. As for the women, Chamma is a rare exception in this land."

Amenemhet laughed softly. "Do you have any other advice?"

"Yes," Nakht said seriously. "Drink the wine and not the water, or you'll be sick for six decans. Eat lightly and only what you recognize. As for the women, that's your decision. The best I can say is they will have been given baths. I think I finally convinced them, from my own habits, that we bathe daily and are offended by stale body odors."

Amenemhet stared at him. "Are these people civilized?"

"Barely," Nakht said drearily. "Staying in this place to negotiate treaties was never one of my favorite occupations."

"Senwadjet!" Amenemhet turned to him. "You heard Nakht?" Senwadjet nodded. "You will have the wisdom to follow his advice?" Senwadjet nodded again. "Senwadjet," Amenemhet said slowly, "I haven't frowned on your interest in the opposite sex in Tamera, but I suggest you restrain yourself here."

Senwadjet smiled faintly. "Looking at the women in the crowd, I can't say any of them arouses the faintest interest in me."

"There will be some improvement in quality at the palace," Nakht said, then added, "not much, but some improvement."

"How can you tell with the kind of garments they all wear?" Senwadjet asked.

"They'll wear considerably less in the palace," Nakht said softly.

"And if we refuse them altogether?" Amenemhet asked.

Nakht cleared his throat, looking embarrassed. "We have already discussed some of their less appetizing habits—" he began. He hesitated, not knowing quite how to say what he had in mind. He decided to just say it quickly. "It's entirely possible they'll offer us boys."

"By Asar!" Amenemhet glared at him. "Do I resemble one of those?"

Senwadjet stared at Nakht, not knowing what to say.

"No, you certainly do not," Nakht stated firmly. "Do I?"

"Of course not." Amenemhet shook his head. "Did they make such an offer to you? Yes, they did. I can see that in your face."

He looked at Senwadjet meaningfully. "I never thought I'd have to tell you such a thing, my son. But, apparently, I must warn you not only about local women, but about men as well."

Having recovered a little from his surprise, Senwadjet answered quickly, "I will defend myself from such an experience, if need be."

"I didn't mean to imply you'd be interested or willing," Amenemhet said dryly. He turned to Nakht. "Let us have these negotiations over with as quickly as possible. Already, I wish to go home."

Thinking of Bekhat, Senwadjet said, "So do I." He fell into daydreaming of Bekhat.

As they entered the hall, they were greeted by a group of palace guards who fell in with their own guards. They were escorted to the throne room. Amenemhet was unimpressed. He greeted King Zaretes in a reserved manner, giving him a cold look, which made Zaretes nervous. When Nakht presented Senwadjet, Zaretes found the young prince equally cool.

Abruptly, Amenemhet asked to be shown to their quarters, saying they would like to rest awhile, emphasizing they would also like to bathe. Zaretes immediately summoned servants and gave them instructions to see to their visitors. Amenemhet looked suspiciously at the male servants and dismissed all of them, explaining they had brought their own servants. Zaretes said nothing. As they were about to leave, Amenemhet paused and turned again to Zaretes.

"We will begin negotiations after the evening meal?" Amenemhet asked pointedly. Without waiting for a reply, he turned and left.

Amenemhet pretended to watch the dancers, hoping to discourage the girls who swarmed around him. In truth, he thought them all boring. He smiled, wondering what Zaretes would think of Tamera's dancers.

The girl dancing closest to Amenemhet thought he smiled at her, and she broke from the group to place herself directly in front of him. Amenemhet stared beyond her, and she moved to block his view. For lack of anything else to do, he found himself counting the beaded rows in her vibrating girdle.

When the dance was over, the girl, who thought she had won Amenemhet's favor, dropped into his lap. As Amenemhet stared at her in surprise, she slid her hand around his neck and began to play with his hair. Amenemhet was too surprised to move, and his stillness encouraged her.

Recovering himself, Amenemhet whispered, "In Tamera, to touch me without permission can mean death. Did you know that?" He smiled humorlessly while she looked as if she didn't believe it. Softly he added, "Find another nest, little bird, or I'll dump you ignominiously on the floor."

The dancer stared at Amenemhet a moment; then, affronted, she got up and left.

Amenemhet turned to Nakht, giving him a piercing look, signaling that he wanted to begin negotiations. Nakht was relieved to leave the girls and go to Pazalam with instructions. Pazalam went to Zaretes, who whispered quickly to him, then returned to Nakht.

"King Zaretes doesn't feel well and would rather negotiate tomorrow," Nakht said softly to Amenemhet.

Amenemhet gave him a look of disgust. "I don't feel well myself. I feel as if I'm going to suffocate from lack of breathing space. I have a pain in my head. I'd like a goblet of clean, fresh water instead of this noxious liquid they call wine." Impatiently, he motioned the girls away and whispered to Nakht. "Is there no way I can be rid of these females without being offered others?"

Nakht smiled in understanding. "You can say you'd like to go to bed and emphasize your desire to sleep."

Amenemhet's face was grim. "They'd probably send me a boy." He looked exasperated. "Is there no way we can push him to negotiate?"

"None that I can think of unless we simply behave like conquerors and scare him." Nakht shrugged. "Why not?"

Amenemhet ran a hand through his hair. "I want to leave tomorrow. I will not spend another day here. Give Pazalam this message—I want to draw the treaty before this night is over." As he spoke, Amenemhet gave Zaretes a long, cold stare.

Nakht found it unnecessary to relay the message. Zaretes's health suddenly improved.

After three hours of polite haggling in a hot and airless room, Amenemhet's patience had declined to its lowest controllable level. He was tired and thoroughly disgusted. Each time he thought he and Zaretes had made an agreement, Zaretes asked for some new condition.

The latest problem Zaretes had thought of was Djemeh's fear of Zahi. Amenemhet had been shocked at Zaretes's effrontery at even mentioning it. But he kept silent, his face expressionless.

Zaretes finally ended his long and tiring explanation of Djemeh's helplessness. A servant moved among them pouring more tepid wine. Amenemhet resolved he would waste no more time with this farce. He turned his goblet upside down with a sharp sound, then looked calmly at Zaretes with an expression that made Zaretes very uncomfortable.

Amenemhet rested his chin in his hands. "I can see you're really interested in protection, not gold," he said slowly. "You're afraid Zahi's revenge will follow a treaty between Djemeh and Tamera, and you'll need the extra gold you mentioned to strengthen your army and your fortifications?"

"Yes," King Zaretes replied, worrying at Amenemhet's tone. "As you can see, we have but a small army and could never withstand an invasion from Zahi."

"The Hyksos army seems somewhat weak these days," Amenemhet said sarcastically. He took his sword from its scabbard and laid it across his lap.

Zaretes fell silent. He looked at the sword and vividly remembered the flight of the Hyksos from

Ithtawe. Surely Amenemhet wouldn't become violent right here in the meeting room?

Amenemhet smiled coldly at Zaretes. Senwadjet found himself struggling not to laugh.

"I'll do even better than merely give you gold, for you're not only our friends, as you've already proved," Amenemhet said smoothly, "but it's to Tamera's own interest to protect its western border. I'll send a garrison of Commander Nessumontu's best men to this city to protect you. If an emergency occurs, I'll even send reinforcements. Is that not better than gold?" Amenemhet's eyes met Zaretes's in an unrelenting stare. "Is that not a generous offer? It saves you considerable bother recruiting and training more soldiers. You know how excellent Tamera's army is. Does not the idea of my soldiers right here beside you in this very city ease your mind?" Amenemhet's lips were curved in a smile, but the golden eyes were cold.

Commander Tharma's muscles tensed. He could do nothing. Several of Tharma's soldiers had taken a step closer behind him. After a moment, Tharma relaxed. Having Nessumontu's men here might really be an improvement, he decided.

Pazalam clenched his jaw in frustration. He had known Amenemhet had lost patience. Amenemhet had gone far out of his way to behave with honor and allow Zaretes to retain his dignity. Zaretes had thrown honor aside, haggling like a street merchant. Pazalam hung his head, ashamed.

Not waiting for Zaretes to answer, Amenemhet nodded for the treaty. He had brought Lakma, his own scribe, to the negotiations. Lakma had been recording the agreement as Amenemhet spoke. Lakma gave Amenemhet the papyrus, and Amenemhet read silently. The wax was melted and poured, and Amenemhet pressed his signet ring in it. As the treaty was carried to Zaretes, Amenemhet lifted his sword in both hands, turning it slowly. It flashed in the flickering light.

Nakht sat back in his chair, relaxing at last. A faint smile hovered over Senwadjet's lips.

Zaretes numbly put his seal on the papyrus without looking at it. At Amenemhet's gesture, Lakma took the treaty away.

"We'll take it to Ithtawe for safekeeping, but my scribe will make a copy for you in your language," Amenemhet said, putting his sword back in its scabbard. He yawned, then stood up and stretched. "I think we've done enough business today," he said softly. "I think we deserve some sleep."

Nakht and Senwadjet stood up and followed Amenemhet out the door. Amenemhet's personal guards also marched out, ignoring Zaretes's soldiers.

Amenemhet pressed the bed, a disgusted expression on his face. "It's too soft," he grumbled, "but I'm tired. Are the guards posted?"

"Yes." Nakht yawned. "Not that there's a threat. Zaretes was so paralyzed with fear he's probably afraid to leave the meeting room."

"This is a strange situation," Senwadjet remarked. He turned slowly as Ahmes undressed him. "We're in Zaretes's palace in Zaretes's city, and his whole army is at hand. We have only those we brought with us. But *he's* afraid of *us*." Senwadjet looked at Amenemhet. "We should be the ones who are afraid to sleep tonight."

"My only fear concerns his sending those women in," Nakht said solemnly.

Amenemhet and Senwadjet laughed.

"What were you doing with that dancer in your lap?" Nakht asked Amenemhet.

"How can you ask so foolish a question?" Amenemhet looked amazed. "Have you not eyes to see how much more alluring she was then Nefrytatanen?"

Nakht laughed in reply.

Amenemhet lay down with great caution and sank deep into the soft mattress. He turned, trying to find a less uncomfortable position.

"I have one more bit of advice on how to survive in Djemeh," Nakht said smiling. He was pulling the linens off his bed.

"What is it?" Amenemhet turned again, getting his feet tangled in the covers. Irritated, he sat up to straighten them.

"Sleep on the floor," Nakht said smugly. "Every bone and muscle in my body will ache by morning if I sleep in that accursed bed," he added.

Amenemhet and Senwadjet looked at each other in surprise, then laughed, and decided to take Nakht's advice.

As Senwadjet spread his blanket on the floor next to Amenemhet, he said, "Even if those women were irresistible, can you imagine making love in that bed? Whoever was on the bottom would smother."

Amenemhet sighed. "There's a way to manage everything, if one must."

Senwadjet was confused for a moment. Then he smiled in understanding as Yazid put out the lamps.

Amenemhet stretched luxuriously in the morning sun, glad to be home again in his own clean and comfortable bed with Nefrytatanen beside him. It was

401

the first night's sleep he had enjoyed since leaving for Djemeh.

Being close to Ithtawe at sunset the evening before, they hadn't made camp, but had continued riding into the night and had arrived long after everyone was sleeping. Amenemhet smiled, remembering how he had crept silently into bed, not disturbing Nefrytatanen in her sleep. She would be surprised when she awakened to find him home.

Amenemhet turned slowly to look at Nefrytatanen's profile. He raised himself on an elbow and leaned to brush his lips softly against her cheek. Her eyes opened, and she turned to look at him in surprise.

"Did you think a stranger was here?" Amenemhet whispered.

"No." Nefrytatanen smiled. "I know your touch too well. I was dreaming and awoke to find the dream reality." She put her arm around him. "I missed you," she whispered. "How did it go?"

"As Nessumontu predicted, we were given much wine and food, offered women—" he began.

"What women?" she asked, her eyes suddenly wide.

"Beautiful, voluptuous creatures," he murmured, "dripping with exotic perfumes, very eager to serve us in every possible way."

Nefrytatanen sat up stiffly. "And how well did they serve you?" Her eyes narrowed as she waited for his answer.

Amenemhet laughed. "The truth is the wine was terrible, the food indescribable, and the women—" he shrugged.

"And the women?" she urged.

"They were eager, all right," he said, smiling, "but there was nothing tempting about them. I was look-

402

ing at you just before you awoke, thinking that comparison was ridiculous." He put his hand on her shoulder and pulled her gently back to the bed before continuing, "Zaretes was so uncooperative I had to frighten him so we might get to bed before dawn. I saved us some gold in the process, because in the end, I generously gave him a garrison of our soldiers to protect Djemeh."

Nefrytatanen smiled at the idea. "You must tell me the details of this," she said.

"I will," Amenemhet whispered, "eventually." He leaned over her. "I've been gone for some time," he said, smiling faintly, "and if you expect me to resist women who throw themselves my way, you must make sure to keep me contented." He played with a strand of her hair.

Looking into his eyes, Nefrytatanen murmured, "What can they do that I cannot? If you've learned something of interest, you must teach it to me." She put her hands behind his head and slowly pulled his face to hers. "Can anyone kiss you better than I?" Nefrytatanen demonstrated her skill until Amenemhet's arms clasped her tightly to him. She turned her face away, smiling, letting her hands slide slowly down his back to his hips. "Tell me, beloved, what would you have me do next?" she asked softly. "If I would keep you contented, you must say what would please you." She turned her face to his again and looked up into his eyes, waiting.

He leaned closer. Between gentle nibbles on her ear, he told her.

The sun was considerably higher when Nefrytatanen called Dedjet to dress her. Amenemhet went onto the terrace while he waited for her, and he saw Senwadjet in the garden below, sitting on the grass with Bekhat.

Amenemhet could understand now why Bekhat had asked to remain at Ithtawe until Kheti returned from his current trip. Senwadjet had her in his arms, kissing her with an expertise that raised Amenemhet's eyebrows. Senwadjet was making an effort to take at least one step beyond kissing. It wasn't until Bekhat pushed Senwadjet away that Amenemhet realized he had been holding his own breath.

When Amenemhet saw Senwadjet and Bekhat leave the place to walk into the open garden, he went back inside where Nefrytatanen stood alone waiting for him.

"I think it's time for Senwadjet to leave Ankhneferu's instructions and go to Anu to continue his education," Amenemhet said thoughtfully.

Nefrytatanen looked surprised. "I didn't know you planned to send him there," she said. "When did you decide this?"

"Just now," Amenemhet answered. He looked at her, smiling slightly. "Did you know he meets Bekhat? I surmise—from what I've just witnessed—that they've met often."

Nefrytatanen's expression revealed her confusion.

"I saw them in the garden, in a place where they couldn't be seen by anyone passing by."

Nefrytatanen's eyes widened.

"It's Bekhat's hand that restrains them, and I would judge that her hand is growing somewhat weak."

"What were they doing?" Nefrytatanen asked quietly.

"No more than kissing and embracing with enthusiasm," Amenemhet replied, "but he's making a definite effort to do more." Amenemhet shook his head, still smiling. "Senwadjet would seem to have a technique that will eventually win his cause."

"He follows in your footsteps," Nefrytatanen remarked. She looked perplexed. "It seems wise to allow him to continue his education in Anu. Didn't you go there?"

Amenemhet nodded and sighed. "Yes. I did learn quite a bit, too."

"Studying what?" she asked pointedly.

"Many things," he replied. "Despite those, I found some time to prepare myself for the throne." Amenemhet's gleaming eyes met hers.

Nefrytatanen put her arms around him and laughed. "Beloved, what will I do with you?"

"I thought I explained that just a short time ago." He kissed her lightly. "Come," he said suddenly, taking her hand and leading her to the door. "Before we go downstairs, I have a surprise for you."

"What is it?" Nefrytatanen asked, as he led her down the hall.

"I've managed to persuade Iuti to do something I've had in mind for some time," Amenemhet said walking fast.

"The sculptor?" Nefrytatanen was breathless struggling to match his pace.

"Yes," Amenemhet answered. He opened a door.

The room had been cleared of furniture. In the middle of the floor stood two large blocks of green stone. Iuti turned quickly from his examination of the stones and prepared to kneel.

"Don't bother," Amenemhet said. He led Nefrytatanen to the two stones. They were about the same size and shape. "Can you see one of these stones carved into a sphinx wearing my face?" he asked.

Nefrytatanen nodded, looking closely at the stone. "It should be a fine statue," she commented, running a finger over the stone's cool surface.

"The other will also be made into a sphinx, but it will have your face." Amenemhet watched Nefrytatanen's expression change from serious interest to surprise and delight. "If as you've said, the knowledge is lost in the future that you are queen and not merely my consort, then here in stone will be proof that you and I ruled together."

Before she could speak he said, "Come. Sit here by the light and let Iuti look at you." When he had placed her by the window opening, he turned to the sculptor and asked, "What do you think, Iuti? Will she make a good sphinx?"

"Yes," Iuti said readily. "Queen Nefrytatanen's face will be most beautiful as a sphinx. If you agree, I would like to inlay the eyes. Blue stones, like the ones in your pendants, would be striking."

"That's a fine idea," Amenemhet agreed. "I'll make sure the stones are located. It may take some time because they're very rare."

Nefrytatanen interrupted, "If my statue's eyes are to match my own, so must stones the same gold as your eyes be found."

"There are such stones from the very Far East," Iuti said slowly. "They would be most appropriate and, again, costly. These stones are called 'eyes of the sun.'"

Amenemhet said, "I'll have the matter investigated."

"Tell me," Nefrytatanen said thoughtfully, "Iuti,

must I have so grim an expression as I have seen other statues wearing? I don't want to look as if my heart is made of stone, but I would wish to have dignity. What do you think, beloved? What expression should be recorded on this sphinx to best reveal myself?"

Amenemhet looked at her a moment, then smiled. "Form your lips as if you're going to kiss me," he said. "It will be most characteristic of you and surely won't make a grim statue." His eyes gleamed with humor.

Going along with the joke, Nefrytatanen complied, holding back laughter.

"Now smile—just a little—so your lips curve up at their corners," Amenemhet prompted.

Nefrytatanen tried and succeeded for a moment, until the scene struck her as too comical. The smile escaped her control, and she laughed. Amenemhet and Iuti joined her.

Finally Amenemhet's smile replaced his laughter, and he took Nefrytatanen's hand, saying quietly, "For a moment, Iuti, it was perfect. Carve the statue with that expression, half kiss and half smile. All the world will know that Tamera had at least one queen not made of stone."

Nefrytatanen smiled and, squeezing Amenemhet's hand, whispered, "As long as you know it, beloved, that is all that matters."

Key to Pronunciations
and Meanings

Because the Egyptian names in this novel are authentic, the following explanation will aid the reader's understanding and enjoyment.

Absee (Ahb-see)—A servant
Ahmes (Ah-mes)—Senwadjet's personal attendant
Ameni (Ah-men-ee)—Kheti's oldest son
Amenemhet (Ah-me-nem-het)—King of Tamera
Ankhneferu (Ahnk-nef-er-oo)—Tamera's high priest
Anpu (Ahn-poo)—Divine being who was patron of medicine and science and guardian of the dead, more commonly known as Anubis
Antefaker (An-teh-fah-ker)—Supervisor of King Amenemhet's pyramid complex
Asar (Ah-sar)—Divine being symbolizing man immortal, more commonly known as Osiris
Aset (Ah-set)—Divine being symbolizing women, patroness of magic, more commonly known as Isis
Bast (Bahst)—Divine being symbolizing prophecy
Bekhat (Bek-hat)—Kheti and Neferset's daughter
Dedjet (Deh-djet)—Nefrytatanen's personal attendant
Djanah (Dj-ah-nah)—A temple singer
Hat-Hor (Haht-hor)—Divine being symbolizing love, music, and dancing and protector of infants

Heru (Her-oo)—Divine being symbolizing the living king or Asar reincarnated, more commonly known as Horus

Horemheb (Hor-em-heb)—The royal physician

Ineni (Ee-nen-ee)—A servant

Ithtawe (It-tah-wee)—Palace-fortress built by King Amenemhet as capitol of Tamera

Iuti (Ee-oo-tee)—The royal sculptor

Kheti (Ket-ee)—Governor of Orynx Province

Maeti (Mah-ee-tee)—Princess of Tamera

Meri (Meh-ree)—Prime minister of Tamera

Montu (Mont-oo)—Divine being representing war

Nakht (Nah-kt)—Ambassador of Tamera; also name of Kheti and Neferset's youngest son

Nassurti (Nah-ser-tee)—Egyptian girl who was Gobryas's slave

Necho (Nek-oh)—Captain of Queen Nefrytatanen's ship

Neferset (Nef-er-set)—Kheti's wife, Sarenput's sister

Nefrytatanen (Nef-ree-tah-tah-nen)—Queen of Tamera

Nessumontu (Nes-oo-mon-too)—Commander of Tamera's military forces

Noph (Nohf)—City in northern kingdom later called Memphis

Ra (Rah)—Divine being symbolizing the sun, life and well-being, also known as Amen-Ra

Rahmzi (Rahm-zee)—An officer in Tamera's army

Senbi (Sen-bee)—Tamera's next ranking priest after Ankhneferu

Senwadjet (Sen-wah-djet)—Prince of Tamera

Sekhmet (Sek-met)—Divine being symbolizing justice

Sitah (Sit-ah)—Lord Semerkhet's son, Nessumontu's aide

Semerkhet (Sem-er-khet)—Governor of Uto Province

Senet (Sen-et)—A servant

Sutekh (Soo-tek)—Divine being symbolizing violence

Tamera (Tah-mer-ah)—Egypt

Tehuti (Teh-oo-tee)—Divine being symbolizing wisdom, more commonly known as Thoth

Tem (Tem)—The Creator, the Universal Intelligence, the Source of Life, also called Ptah

Tuat (Too-aht)—Heaven

Wast (Wahst)—City in southern kingdom later called Thebes